ALSO BY D.E. IRELAND

Wouldn't It Be Deadly
Move Your Blooming Corpse
Get Me to the Grave On Time

I could have read all night! A delicious homage... terrifically clever and authentically charming.

Join Eliza and Higgins in this delightful romp through early 20th century London and at a country house party as they try to find a killer.

Pull out the stopper! D.E. Ireland once again uncorks a charming and high-spirited mystery. An enjoyable and amusing read!

I love these characters and enjoy the imaginative way the authors take them on this little journey to the countryside. There is never a dull moment when Eliza Dolittle is around.

— DOLLYCAS REVIEWS

I never knew when I picked up the first book in this series what a grand time I was in for. Now four books in, and I can't get enough! Eliza Doolittle and Henry Higgins take readers on their most exciting adventure to date.

— LISA K'S BOOK REVIEWS

The unique combination of a serious look into early 1900s London coupled with the unexpected and lighthearted laugh-out-loud moments... You never know what to expect next.

— ELEANOR CAWOOD JONES, DERRINGER AWARD WINNER

WITH A LITTLE BIT OF BLOOD

D.E. IRELAND

GRAINGER
PRESS

ACKNOWLEDGMENTS

Our thanks to many research books on English country houses, including *The English Country House Party* by Phyllida Barstow, and *Big Shots: Edwardian Shooting Parties* by Jonathan G. Ruffer.

DEDICATION

To our brilliant and supportive daughters

"What Englishman will give his mind to politics as long as he can afford to keep a motorcar?"
—George Bernard Shaw

CHAPTER 1

*L*ondon, September 1913

AT THE SOUND OF A DEAFENING CRASH, ELIZA DOOLITTLE JUMPED to her feet. Shouts rang out, followed by the raised voice of the housekeeper.

"Is something wrong, Mrs. Pearce?" Eliza asked. But she heard only the tinkling of broken glass in response. Had a gang of hooligans pushed their way through the front door of 27-A Wimpole Street? She scanned the drawing room for a weapon. Two decades in London's East End slums had taught her to be prepared.

"What's happening, Miss Doolittle?" her elocution student asked.

"I'm not certain," Eliza told Miss Nash as she grabbed a brass poker from the fireplace. Thankfully, Professor Higgins did not have pupils scheduled this morning. Otherwise, he would be teaching in the drawing room, while she gave instruction in a parlor down the hall. And her usual "classroom" contained neither a fireplace nor a heavy metal poker to protect herself with.

"Can we lock ourselves in?" Nineteen-year-old Loretta Nash looked nervous.

"Unfortunately, no." Eliza frowned at the oak pocket doors which lacked a keyhole. "But if anyone bursts in, Miss Nash, get behind me."

Eliza had no sooner spoken when those pocket doors banged open. With a dismayed cry, Miss Nash scurried behind her. Ready to wield the poker like a cricket bat, Eliza raised the weapon, then stopped. "What are you doing here?" she asked the intruder.

Her stepmother, Rose Cleary Doolittle, stood in the open doorway. She put her hands on her hips. "Looking for that rude professor you're living with. Don't think for a minute I come to see you. I don't enjoy having to put up with your snobbish ways."

"Any more than I enjoy spending time in your company." Eliza felt a twinge of regret that she wouldn't be able to brain Rose with the poker.

"Shut yer mouth, girl. I'm your mother and deserve respect."

Eliza tapped the hearthrug with the tip of the poker. "My mum died when I was two. You're merely the latest woman playing house with my father."

"I'm his wife, proper and legal. And don't you forget it."

"I only wish I could," she muttered.

Alfred Doolittle had lived with a number of common-law wives since the death of Eliza's mother, all of them ill tempered and foul mouthed. One of his former "wives" was currently serving time in Holloway Prison for theft and larceny. Eliza viewed it as bad luck that Rose happened to be living with Alfred when he experienced a financial windfall. Not surprisingly, Alfred felt his new status demanded a move to a proper middle class neighborhood. He also decided to make his personal life more respectable by marrying the woman who had illicitly shared his bed for three years. Eliza blamed Professor Higgins. He was the one who had convinced an American millionaire to hire her garrulous father to lecture for the Moral Reform League. Alfred was so successful as a lecturer that he toured six times a year, for which he received an annuity of three thousand pounds. In fact, his rise out of poverty this past year had been as rapid as her own.

"What's the reason for this visit?" Eliza returned the poker to the fireplace rack. "And where is Mrs. Pearce? I heard her voice, along with all that banging and glass breaking. If you've upset her, I'll kick your blooming arse all the way back to Pimlico."

"I ain't done a thing to the housekeeper. She's busy with your dad. He's a handful, let me tell you." Rose threw herself onto a nearby chair, her silk taffeta skirt ballooning around her.

At forty, Rose was too old to wear a pink ruffled dress, especially one covered in enormous cabbage roses. Even worse, the color clashed with her brassy red hair and heavily rouged cheeks, as did the purple ostrich feather bobbing from her hat.

"That man will be the death of me," Rose complained. "Soon as he makes his way in here, I'm telling that bossy housekeeper to get me something to drink."

"And why is Mrs. Pearce busy with my father? Is he drunk?"

Pulling out a handkerchief from her drawstring bag, Rose mopped her damp forehead. "Listen to you. Talkin' about your own flesh and blood as if he was some street beggar you buy oranges from. Oh, wait. That's what's you did, hawking fruit and flowers to the toffs, like one of them barefoot children on Dorset Street."

"It was honest work. And I never begged, no thanks to you. I've made my own way in the world since you told Dad to throw me out of the house three years ago."

"Count yerself lucky. If you'd been my daughter, I would have kicked you out the moment you turned fourteen."

Miss Nash cleared her throat. "Should I leave, Miss Doolittle?"

Eliza had forgotten about her pupil. Then again, Rose Doolittle always proved an unwelcome distraction. "We only have five minutes left in today's lesson, so we'll end it now. But you're doing well. Another two or three lessons, and my instruction will be complete."

With a proud smile, Miss Nash gathered up her pocketbook and gloves. "I practice my vocal exercises every night. The other ladies in the boardinghouse often help me, too."

"Whatcha want to talk different for?" Rose asked. "You got a fine way of speaking."

Miss Nash turned to Rose with an earnest expression. "I've been working at a laundry house since I came to London. But now I have a chance to be hired as a perfume counter sales girl at Selfridges. Only I'm from Birmingham and need to lose my Brummie accent first."

"You don't owe my stepmother an explanation," Eliza said. "Besides, she is incapable of understanding why a woman might want to improve herself."

Rose shook her finger at Miss Nash. "You might want to take lessons from someone else. Eliza comes from the East End, not Mayfair. She barged in here a year ago last summer to ask for lessons from Professor Higgins. Before you know it, she's acting like Queen Victoria. Even fooled people into thinking she was a duchess. Maybe that's because she spends all her money on clothes. Like some chorus girl trying to impress the stage door Johnnies."

A glass bowl filled with chocolates sat on the piano. Eliza considered throwing the bowl and its contents at Rose. "A chorus girl couldn't afford my wardrobe. However, I can."

She glanced down at her silk taupe dress from the House of

Paquin, which appeared last month on the cover of *Vogue*. But it wasn't only her voice lessons that paid the hefty dress bill. Along with her father, Eliza was co-owner of an Irish racehorse called the Donegal Dancer; her share of a recent winning purse had been most impressive.

"Miss Doolittle should be proud she worked her way out of the East End to a place such as this." Miss Nash gestured at the elegant book-lined room that served as Higgins's laboratory. "Besides, everyone in London knows she was once a flower seller. And that after learning how to speak and dress properly, she fooled the upper crust at an Embassy Ball. That's why so many of us want to take lessons from her. She's famous." Her round cheeks flushed pink. "And not just for becoming a lady. Miss Doolittle and Professor Higgins are also famous for catching criminals. If I were her stepmother, I'd be proud of her."

Rose looked as if she'd swallowed a bad oyster. "You're as cracked as she is."

"Where are ya, Rose?" a voice bellowed. "You left me out here to fend for meself!"

Eliza rushed out into the hall and gasped at the sight of her bruised and bandaged father. With an arm draped over Mrs. Pearce's shoulders, he brandished a cane in one hand.

"Crikey! What happened?"

"About time you come to greet me, Lizzie. Thought the Colonel taught you manners."

Eliza helped Mrs. Pearce walk him into the drawing room. "Did you try to ride the Donegal Dancer again? The jockeys told you to stop doing that."

"Weren't no horse I fell from, girl. Horses love me, specially my Dancer."

"I can tell you what doesn't love him," Rose said as they entered. "That bloody car he bought this summer. Your father drives like the Mr. Toad character in a book I been reading to my nephew. Soon as Alfie gets behind the wheel, he turns balmy on the crumpet."

Eliza eased her dad onto a leather covered chair. She was more shocked by the thought of Rose reading a book than the sight of her father's bruised face and limp. "Was there an accident with the motorcar?"

"The fool nearly got himself killed." Rose banged her hand on the chair's arm. "Can we get something to drink? Your housekeeper's here now, and it's only polite to offer your guests something. Gin, maybe."

"A pot of tea, please," Eliza told Mrs. Pearce. "And thank you for assisting my father."

"I had all the housemaids helping me, especially after he knocked over two side tables and a floor lamp with his cane. The girls are busy cleaning up the mess. But I'll put a kettle on for everyone." Mrs. Pearce took a deep breath. "The staff, too."

The housekeeper nearly ran out of the parlor. Miss Nash followed close behind.

Now that she was alone with Alfred and Rose, Eliza examined her father's injuries: nose swollen to twice its normal size, two black eyes, a bruised forehead, and his right foot swaddled in a mountain of bandages. He winced when she gently probed his shoulder.

Eliza sat back on her heels. "It was a mistake to buy that roadster. For one thing, it cost too much. I'm sure the people at the auction cheated you."

"They did not. It was only seven hundred pounds. And worth every penny."

"It's not worth your life. You drive as if you're the only motorist on the road."

Alfred grunted. "A pity I'm not."

"Last week he knocked the grocer clean off his feet," Rose announced. "Plowed right into him and his turnip crates."

"Blimey, is the grocer all right?"

"He will be when his hip heals. We had to give him fifty quid not to report it to the police." Rose sighed loudly. "The greedy sod was lucky Alfie didn't finish him off. But he did run over the grocer's cat."

"You killed a cat?" Eliza cried.

"Not on purpose."

"It ain't the first animal he's run over," Rose added. "Not by a long shot."

"How terrible! Dad, you're a danger to everyone when you're behind the wheel."

"Blame the people who don't get out of my way," Alfred protested. "The animals, too."

Rose snorted. "That ain't the end of it. Two days after Alfie killed the grocer's cat, he crashes into a milk wagon. Milk and broken glass everywhere. The milkman got his kneecap broke. This time your father got hurt, too. Serves him right, I say."

"You are never driving again." Eliza used her sternest voice. "Take the bus or the underground. Hire a cab. But your driving days are over, do you hear?"

His lower lip stuck out in a stubborn pout when Rose said, "Exactly what I told him."

Eliza got to her feet. "At least the car is gone. After crashing into a milk wagon, it has to be useless. Good riddance."

Alfred chuckled.

"What's so funny?" Eliza asked.

Rose shook her head. "The car looks good as new. No more than a few scratches on it. The blasted thing was speeding along like the Donegal Dancer on the way over here."

"*You* drove the car to Wimpole Street?" Eliza asked her stepmother in chagrin.

"Don't be daft. Your dad drove."

"How? He could barely walk from the front door to the parlor."

"I still got the use of my arms," Alfred said. "And I used my left foot to drive. Rose put her own foot on the pedal whenever I got a sudden pain in my leg."

Eliza's outraged response was halted by a familiar voice from the hallway. "What the devil is going on here? Who broke my lamp?"

"Thank heaven the Professor is home." Eliza stomped over to the piano bench, eager to let someone else deal with her father and Rose.

"Good. That's why we came." Rose gave Alfred a knowing glance.

Higgins seemed more energetic than usual when he strode into the room. And he didn't look surprised to see Rose and Alfred. Although his expression soon turned to concern.

"I had no idea your injuries were this severe." Higgins scrutinized Alfred as intently as a flower fancier examining a hothouse orchid. "You resemble boxer Matt Wells after his last championship match."

"I told you on the telephone that I'd gotten banged up," Alfred said.

Eliza's temper flared. "You knew my dad was in an accident and didn't tell me?"

He nodded. "Rose called three days ago, right after it happened. They didn't want me to inform you of anything. At least not for awhile."

"Knew you'd make a proper fuss," Alfred told her. "And I had to rest. Didn't need you coming over to try and force oatmeal down my throat instead of gin."

"Hold on," Eliza said. "You were injured in a motorcar accident only the Professor knew about. Now you show up here, still not recovered. Why?"

"Alfie wanted to drive the car one last time," Rose said. "For old time's sake."

"I don't understand."

Alfred and Rose turned their attention to Higgins, who appeared sheepish. "I bought your father's roadster," he said. Her mouth fell open.

"I can see from your inability to speak that I've taken you by surprise," he went on. "But when we visited Banfield Manor for Clara's wedding, I had a marvelous time larking about in Lord Ashmore's Stutz Bearcat. Well, now I can go anywhere I like without having to bother with trains or the underground. I feel as free to wander as Odysseus." He gave her a pleased smile. "And you father sold it to me for a most reasonable price."

"It's a dirt cheap price," Rose broke in. "Only I'm so determined to take the car away from him that I'm almost ready to give it away for free." She paused. "Almost."

"Breaks my heart it does, selling my beautiful blue darling," Alfred lamented. "Been drowning my sorrows since the accident just thinking about it. But Rose won't give me a moment's peace till I hand it over to someone else. May as well be a bloke I know." His face creased into a wide smile. "This way the Governor here can take me for a spin once in awhile."

"If I ever hear you let Alfie get behind the wheel, Professor, you'll be as dead as the grocer's cat," Rose warned him.

"This is absurd." Eliza finally found her voice. "You can't buy the roadster."

"I transferred the funds to his bank this morning," Higgins said. "That's where I was."

Eliza narrowed her eyes at him. "Does Colonel Pickering know about this?"

"Not yet." Higgins busied himself with the lamp chimney on a nearby table.

She knew Higgins cared about few people's opinions other than his own, except for Colonel Pickering. "This explains why Dad delivered your car while the Colonel is at a doctor's appointment. You know what he'll think of your decision."

"All I've done is buy a roadster. You're behaving as if I did something ridiculous, like adopt a giraffe." He chuckled. "Or a peacock."

"Don't bring Percy into this." She wouldn't hear a word against her gloriously feathered pet. A thank you gift from Lord Ashmore, the peacock had been part of the household for nearly two weeks. Although thrilled with her bird, Eliza knew no one else at Wimpole Street shared her affection for him.

Rose glanced over her shoulder. "Hope that fancy bird ain't gonna to sneak up on me like he did last time I was here. Scared ten years off me, he did."

"I don't understand why you're opposed to my ownership of a motorcar." Higgins grew serious. "Not so long ago, you wanted to buy one. What changed your mind?"

"You know perfectly well what changed my mind. It was that terrible accident at your niece's wedding. I may never feel safe riding in a car again." She glanced at her injured father. "What's done is done. But I have an awful feeling Dad's car is bad luck."

"Nonsense," Higgins said. "Your father is simply a dreadful motorist. Sorry, Alfred."

Her father's expression turned rueful. "Where's that tea we was promised? A cuppa will make all of us feel better."

But it would take more than a pot of Earl Grey to make Eliza feel better about Higgins's purchase of the blue roadster. The car might not be bad luck, but she knew trouble when it appeared. And trouble now sat parked outside their house.

CHAPTER 2

*T*he last time Higgins felt this thrilled, he'd just met an ancient fellow from Wexford who spoke Yola, a nearly extinct Anglo-Saxon dialect. But as one of the most celebrated phoneticians in Europe, Higgins had grown accustomed to discovering linguistic marvels. Driving his very own Hudson 'Mile-a-Minute' roadster at sixty miles an hour was a brand new experience. And a damned exciting one, too.

However, his passenger seemed to disagree. Jack Shaw clutched his hat so tightly in his lap, the brim was crushed.

"Relax, Jack. You're a Scotland Yard detective inspector," Higgins said. "You've chased down killers in the worst parts of London. No reason to be unnerved by a simple Sunday drive."

"I feel as if we're chasing criminals right now. Or being chased by them." Jack Shaw looked behind him. His eyes seemed especially large behind the driving goggles Higgins had lent him. Because the car had neither windows nor a roof, both men wore goggles, as well as linen topcoats to keep their suits dust-free. "But all I see are terrified pedestrians. By the way, you scared the life out of that hansom carriage horse."

"I saw the people in that carriage, dressed in their Sunday finest. Off to church, no doubt. They'd get there a lot faster in a motorcar."

"We should go to church at the end of this drive to give thanks for having survived it. Assuming we do." Jack raised his voice to be heard over the wind whipping past them.

"I thought you'd enjoy seeing London from a high speed roadster."

"I might if we went a bit slower. Are we in Putney yet?"

"Almost." Higgins squeezed the car horn, causing a passing cyclist to topple off his bike in fright. "We're about to cross the river. Hold on."

Jack covered his eyes as Higgins barreled onto the granite and stone bridge. Luckily, Sunday morning traffic was light. Still, enough vehicles made their way across Putney Bridge that he had to swerve among them as if he were maneuvering through an obstacle course.

Honking his horn again, Higgins prepared to pick up speed once they'd crossed the Thames. Because he'd driven this route for the past eight days, he knew exactly where to go in Putney to enjoy the least amount of traffic.

"Marvelous motoring weather, isn't it? Always had a fondness for September." Higgins sped past a truck filled with crates, barely avoiding the vehicle's rear fender.

"You drive like a maniac. I don't blame my cousin for refusing to get in the car."

"Perverse female. She won't walk within ten feet of it."

"Smart girl. See here, Professor. I'm grateful you offered to take me for a little drive, but whenever you want to head for home will be fine with me."

Higgins frowned. He wasn't trying to frighten Jack. He enjoyed the fellow's company, along with Sybil, his charming suffragette wife. Since the Nepommuck murder case this past spring, the two men had often been thrown together. At first their association was purely professional, but Higgins soon took a strong liking to the shrewd and personable detective. And it pleased Eliza that he got along so well with her cousin. Higgins hoped Jack would have fun on their motoring excursion. If not, he feared all his drives in the roadster would be solitary.

Like Eliza, Colonel Pickering also refused to drive with him. A traditional fellow, Pickering mourned the disappearance of horse-drawn rigs and hackneys from London's streets. And he'd been quite vocal against motorcars after learning of Alfred Doolittle's mishaps.

Higgins had finally persuaded Mrs. Pearce to let him drive her to the Covent Garden flower market to purchase blooms for the weekly household arrangements. But she became upset when he scraped the side of an excursion steam bus. With a shriek heard all the way to Dover, she jumped out at the next cross street and walked all the way back to Wimpole Street, leaving Higgins to transport the chrysanthemums and asters.

He'd assumed the Scotland Yard detective was made of sterner stuff, only Jack didn't appear to be enjoying the experience. "Stop looking so troubled," Higgins said. "I'm taking us to a residential area in Putney. Sleepy little neighborhood surrounded by a park. Barely any traffic, even on a weekday. And I should know. I've been driving this route every morning since I bought the car. The other motorists out here seem far too cautious, however. Don't know why they bother to purchase a motorcar if they only want to plod along like a dray horse."

"A wish to stay alive, perhaps?"

"At least one fellow enjoys speed. This past week, a motorist in a black car tried to outrace me once I reached Putney. But he couldn't even get close. Hah! What fun."

"Let's hope he doesn't show up this morning," Jack said. "I'd hate for our Sunday drive to turn into the Tourist Trophy race."

"You're as bad as Eliza. Motoring is marvelous. I don't have to grumble at the inattention of a cab driver, or get my feet stepped on at Piccadilly tube station."

"But how will you eavesdrop on a stranger's speech patterns if you're in this roadster?"

"I can go anywhere I like for my research now. Why buy a train ticket when I can drive myself to Northumberland or Cornwall? All I need is petrol. The tank holds thirty gallons."

"It is a fine looking machine, I'll grant you that." Jack ran his hand over the dashboard.

"The car's American. Manufactured in Detroit, Michigan. This is the Hudson 1912 model, designed for racing. Four-cylinder engine, Prest-O-Lite tank, luggage carrier, demountable rims, lamps, and an extra tank in the back for ten gallons of oil. Also the fenders can be removed to attain optimal speed."

"This speed seems optimal enough. How much did you pay Alfred for the car?"

"A fair price, considering it wasn't new when he bought it. Alfred got it at an auction. Someone neglected to claim their motorcar after the ship carrying it docked in Southampton."

"I don't like the sound of that," Jack said after a long pause. "Most suspicious."

"You work for Scotland Yard. Everything seems suspicious to you."

"But why wouldn't the owner claim his car? Unless he met with foul play during the ocean crossing. Did the same number of passengers depart the ship as embarked on the voyage?"

"I have no idea. It went unclaimed for the requisite amount of time, was put up for auction at a dockside warehouse, and legally purchased by Alfred Doolittle. Who sold it to me."

"Perhaps the motorcar was stolen and the thief feared being caught," Jack said.

"Perhaps you worry too much."

"These steamship auctions sound like an easy way to smuggle things into the country."

"Stop being a policeman for a moment." Higgins cast an admiring gaze over the blue leather seats. "Did I tell you the car is capable of speeds up to a hundred miles an hour?"

"We're going fast enough. Remember what happened to Alfred."

"Alfred never paid attention to the road. But I do. I know every crack in the pavement and every bush concealing the next turn." Higgins honked once more. "After my first night of ownership, I rented a garage in a former mews close to Wimpole Street. They keep it locked, too. I can't have anyone stealing my motorcar."

"You'll be hiring bodyguards to watch over it next."

"Not a bad idea." Higgins had now arrived at a sedate area of Putney with no vehicles in sight. Up ahead, he caught his first sight of a row of plane trees leading to Wandsworth Park. The morning sun broke through the clouds, turning the trees aflame in their autumnal colors of gold and amber. "Right after this turn is a lovely view of—"

But the only thing that came into view was an unhitched wagon in the middle of the road. Jack yelled as Higgins tried to swerve out of the way. But he was going too fast. There was no time to brake. The awful sound of metal smashing against the wagon filled the air, along with the shouts of Higgins and Jack. Suddenly, everything turned upside-down and Higgins's arm burned like it was on fire.

After the car came to a standstill, Higgins found himself on top of Jack, who moaned. It took him a stunned moment to realize the car was on its side, one of the tires still spinning. "Are you hurt, Jack?" Higgins tried to move, but the pain in his arm almost made him black out.

"It's my leg." Jack said with a gasp. "I think it's broken."

Higgins looked for any signs of blood. "Don't worry. Someone is sure to come along and rescue us. And if I had the use of my arm, I'd thrash the fool who left that wagon in the road." He bit back a cry of pain. "Of course, Eliza won't blame the wagon for this mess. The silly girl will say it was the car bringing bad luck again."

"Bad luck, my arse," Jack grunted. "We crashed because of your bloody bad driving."

CHAPTER 3

The front bell jangled again. Eliza prayed one of the overworked maids answered it this time. She was busy taking a tray with fresh tea into the laboratory, the latest in a long line of demands made by the injured Professor Higgins. Twenty minutes ago, he'd insisted she open the mail for him, then sent her off to find his pouch of tobacco. And this was the fourth cup of Earl Grey she'd brought him this morning.

Eliza tried to mask her irritation when she entered the room.

"It's about time you showed up with my tea," Higgins snapped at her. Ensconced in his favorite armchair, he struggled to hold the newspaper.

She muttered under her breath.

"Who the devil is ringing the bell? If it's another visitor come to gawk at me in my dressing gown, send them away." He cursed when the newspaper slid to the carpet. "How can I read if I'm unable to hold the pages with both hands? Blast this sling."

"I say, old chap, it's not that difficult." Colonel Pickering rose from his chair by the writing desk. He fetched the pages and propped them against a pillow on Higgins's lap.

Higgins grumbled his thanks.

Eliza was grateful for Colonel Pickering's calming presence. Even though he wouldn't admit it, so was Higgins. How fortunate that Pickering left India last year for the express purpose of meeting Higgins; ironically the Professor had wanted to make the acquaintance of Colonel Pickering as well. Both men met each other the same night she first encountered Higgins while selling violets at Covent Garden. A momentous evening for all three of them. Higgins had invited Pickering to live at Wimpole Street, and both men agreed to teach Eliza how to speak and act like a lady. All for the purpose of a scholarly wager, however. But it paid off handsomely, especially when the Colonel took her under his wing during Higgins's mind-grueling speech lessons. The older gentleman was now more like a father to her than Alfred Doolittle.

"The gardener promised to nail together a stand to make it easier to hold the newspaper for you. Just be patient." Eliza set down the tray on the table beside him.

"Well, how long does it take to hammer a few pieces of wood together?"

"I've asked him twice, but he tends the gardens of three houses on Wimpole Street. He has other responsibilities."

"He's a lazy wretch." Higgins reached for the teacup with his right hand.

"If I was handy with a hammer and nails, I'd do it," Pickering said. "But I'm only a scholar of Sanskrit, not a carpenter. No use to anyone except other language scholars."

Eliza gazed with fondness at the older gentleman. "You're of far more use than that. What if you helped Professor Higgins add a few pages to his Universal Alphabet? An updated edition perhaps."

"Silly tomfoolery," Higgins cut her off. "My book's perfect as is."

"A lot more perfect than your behavior," she shot back. Eliza counted to ten. "Professor, we've all tried suggesting things to take your mind off that broken arm."

"I don't need suggestions which waste my time. I've already wasted plenty!"

"So have we all, you old billy goat. For nearly a fortnight, everyone in the household has been run ragged trying to keep up with your requests. Cook threatens to quit if you ask her to make porridge again at three o'clock in the morning."

"By George, I cannot ask for a simple bowl of porridge? I am paying the bloody woman to cook!" Higgins flung the pillow and newspaper to the floor. "Mrs. Lowell is not here as my damned barber." He launched into a full-blown tantrum.

Eliza stopped her ears. Even Colonel Pickering looked annoyed; he rarely reacted to Higgins, given his easy-going nature and their friendship.

When she judged they'd heard enough, she grabbed the newspaper from the floor, rolled it up, and smacked Higgins in the back of the head with it.

"Ow!" Higgins sent her a shocked look. "What the devil are you doing?"

"Putting an end to your caterwauling. I've never heard anyone complain so much in my life. You have a broken arm, not cholera."

"Eliza's right," Pickering added. "I've been in hospital with grievously wounded soldiers who bore up better than you. It is rather alarming."

"The least you could have is have a little sympathy," Higgins whined. "I've never had a broken limb before. And don't forget about the bruises on my body."

Eliza and Pickering exchanged remorseful looks. They both had seen the large purple bruises on his back and arms when trying to help Mrs. Pearce change his shirt. No doubt he felt discomfort each time he changed position, and Eliza did sympathize. But two weeks of walking on eggshells around Higgins had taken its toll. No one in Britain could be a worse patient—except for her cousin Jack.

"He does need a distraction," Pickering said to her. "Perhaps it's time for him to resume his lessons."

She bit her lip. Even in the best of times, Higgins had little patience with his phonetics pupils. If one of them displeased him now, she feared for their safety. "I don't know. Can we trust you not to throttle a student if they get a vowel sound wrong?"

"I'll throttle you if I have to sit here another day with nothing to do but wrestle the newspaper." Higgins nodded at the telephone. "Ring up whoever we cancelled for Monday. I want to expend my energy on a barbarous accent. Bring me a student!"

"Like the Christians into the lion den." Pickering retreated to his writing desk.

"Let me think on this. I need to pick a student with the easiest temper." Eliza sighed. "And the ability to run fast."

"Speaking of speed, have you spoken to the Scotland Yard garage about my roadster? Ring up Detective Ramsey. The repairs should be completed soon."

"What does it matter when they're done? You're just going to sell it." Eliza narrowed her eyes at him. "Unless you're balmy enough to want to drive it again."

"Of course I plan to drive it. Granted, I was a bit reckless that morning—"

"A bit? A bit! More like bloody mad, racing about at top speed," Eliza retorted. "You're lucky you didn't kill my cousin Jack outright."

"Hmph."

"Here you go, sir," Mrs. Pearce said, bustling past her. "This should ease you a bit." She set a tray on his lap with his favorite treat, a quivering blancmange. "I've taken a treacle pudding to Detective Shaw. The poor dear, with his leg plastered to the hip. He's so uncomfortable."

"Yes, yes. However, Jack isn't the only one who's uncomfortable, you know."

Trying to ignore his grumbling, Eliza turned her attention to the papers scattered on top of the filing cabinet. Hadn't she predicted the roadster would continue to bring bad luck? And that was before she realized Higgins drove even worse than her dad. She felt far more sympathy for Jack, his reluctant passenger in the car. And now look at her poor cousin. Because he couldn't climb stairs, Jack's broken leg and collarbone had confined him to the parlor where she normally taught her students.

She missed giving lessons, too. Being taught how to speak correctly had transformed her life. It gave her pleasure to do the same for others. But with her teaching space turned over to Jack —and Higgins's incessant demands—she had no opportunity to work. Accustomed to the intense rigors of police work, Jack was even more frustrated with his idle status than Higgins and Eliza. Thank heaven it was Sybil, Jack's wife, who was responsible for his care.

As though she knew Eliza had been thinking about her, Sybil hurried into the room. She wore a frustrated expression familiar to Eliza. "Is the *Times* here? Jack's read through every paper this morning, including *The Police Gazette* and *The Suffragist*. If I can't find more reading material to distract him, he'll start describing the Professor's driving skills. I can't listen to that litany of woe again." She glanced at Higgins. "Sorry."

Higgins frowned. "I expect he'll be wheeled in here soon, so I can receive my daily dose of guilt."

"I'm afraid that's true." Sybil tucked in her white blouse, then straightened the belt on her teal blue skirt. "I've finished shaving him. His fractured collarbone doesn't allow much freedom of movement."

"Sybil, you know how damnably sorry I am," Higgins began.

She waved him away. "The accident wasn't your fault."

"That's not what Eliza thinks."

Eliza looked up from the filing cabinet. "You *were* driving too fast."

"The fault lies in whoever left the wagon in the road." Sybil spotted the rolled up *Times* on the piano. "And I'm grateful you offered Jack and me a home while he recovers. Our new lodgings won't be vacant for another week, and our old flat is on the fourth floor. Without a lift, I don't know how we would have gotten Jack up there. We owe you our thanks, Professor."

"I'm only glad the gentlemen's bathroom is on the first floor here."

"Amen to that," Sybil said with a laugh.

A loud shriek resounded through the house, followed by two trilling calls.

"Oh no! That peacock is probably after Jack's scones again. He snatches it right out of his hand."

"Percy may take it right from his mouth." Eliza chuckled. "I've seen him do it. He's fond of scones and cake."

"Get this bird off my lap!" Jack yelled from down the hall.

Eliza and Sybil ran out of the room. By the time they reached the parlor where Jack's bedroom had been set up, Percy had gotten his scone. The bird swept past the two women as they arrived. He left a line of crumbs in his path.

Jack looked like he wanted to bolt out of his wheeled chair and pursue the thief. "By heaven, that peacock is nimbler than the Artful Dodger."

"Percy does love his cake," Eliza said as she looked closely at her cousin. His skin appeared pasty and his thick black hair needed a trim, but thankfully Sybil had removed two days' growth of stubble on his jowls. A light blanket covered his plastered leg. "Did you sleep well?"

"Not a whit," he growled. "How can I sleep with my shoulder on fire?"

"If you'd take your medicine, you'd sleep like a proverbial babe," Sybil reminded him.

"Gives me headaches! I won't."

A shame the Shaw marriage was being tested so early. Indeed, their wedding day had been disrupted when someone shot at the bridal party. Jack had been lucky to survive the attack. This was followed two months later by the motorcar crash. Fortunately, both Jack and Sybil were level-headed, mature people who deeply cared for one another. Still, it was more than most newlywed couples weathered.

"How about some treacle pudding?" Eliza picked up the bowl from the tray Mrs. Pearce had delivered earlier. "Remember how Aunt Marie used to nip a bottle of treacle from Mr. Ardle's shop when we all lived on Chancery Lane? She never did get caught. Auntie was even quicker then Percy."

Sybil kissed Jack's brow. "Have a bite while I read to you about the arrest of those bank robbers on Fleet Street. That will cheer you up."

He dutifully spooned up some of the treat as she opened the *Times*. "Any word on the accident?" Jack asked. "Has a witness come forward about that wagon?"

"I'm afraid not. Now enjoy your pudding." Eliza collected an armful of towels and linen and shut the door, giving them privacy.

Eliza considered Jack's question. No one had any idea why an abandoned wagon had been left in the middle of the road that day. Seemed most irresponsible. It might have proved deadly had another car been speeding along behind them. Instead, a brougham filled with churchgoers came upon the accident from the opposite direction. They were the ones who brought help, and comforted Jack and Higgins as they lay injured. Eliza got the family's address from the police and sent them an enormous basket of flowers from Covent Garden. At Christmas she'd have a fruitcake delivered to the family as well.

However, no one had come forward with information. This didn't surprise the police. Being a Sunday morning, dutiful Christians were at church; less dutiful ones were still asleep or enjoying a late breakfast. Even on a weekday, that road saw little traffic. And the trees from Wandsworth Park largely hid the road from view.

Eliza had no time to worry about it. What she did worry about was Higgins's intention to drive again. Wasn't one brush with disaster enough? After the accident, the unlucky car had been towed to the Scotland Yard garage. Jack insisted their mechanics were among the best in London. He included in that group his younger partner, Detective Colin Ramsey, who came from a family of mechanics. Eliza hoped Ramsey declared the car unfit to drive again. Perhaps she could bribe him. If not, she wondered how difficult it would be to set a motorcar on fire.

CHAPTER 4

*C*olonel Pickering stopped Eliza in the hallway later that day. "Another tantrum is about to ensue," he told her. "Higgins can't find the buttonhook. His arm is itching inside the plaster."

"I've no idea where it is. And don't ask the servants." She sent him a warning look. "They're itching as well. But to leave."

With a resigned expressions, Pickering returned to the drawing room. Eliza did not follow him. She had just spoken with Cook about dinner, and for one brief wonderful moment, she had nothing to do.

If only she dared leave the house. Eliza missed her weekly trips to the cinema and the shops on Oxford Street. And it had been almost two weeks since she visited the stables where her racehorse was kept. Instead, her only excursions had been to the local chemist for pain medication and liniment. Dismal.

Things had to improve soon. Eliza regretted inviting her cousin to recover at Wimpole Street, even though she welcomed Sybil's company. Caring for two short-tempered men plagued by boredom had grown wearisome. Maybe she could snatch a few minutes of peace on the front steps or take a stroll down the street. It was warm enough that she needn't retrieve a jacket.

On the way out, she passed the hall table where the morning post had been placed. She'd already given today's mail to Higgins, but a fancy envelope sat propped against a yellow vase. Eliza picked it up, admiring once more the gold-embellished, black inked letters swirled over the vellum. Clara had sent this invitation to her two days ago. If only she could attend the week-long house party. *Lord and Lady Ashmore cordially invite you to Banfield Manor on Monday, the thirteenth of October. . .* Eliza sighed.

With a grateful smile, Eliza stepped onto the small front porch. She welcomed the sun on her face and the sound of motorcars driving up Wimpole Street. Because the house felt stuffy, she left the door open to let in some fresh air. Also she could hear if Higgins began to harass the servants. Eliza glanced down at the vellum card.

"Reading the party invitation again?" Colonel Pickering stood behind her in the open entrance. "You really should attend, Eliza. It will do you good."

"I thought you were looking for the button hook."

"Higgins has the entire staff searching for it. They've begun to turn over cushions and look under the carpet." He raised an eyebrow at her. "And don't change the subject."

"I'd love to go to the house party. The invitation says there will even be a fox hunt. And a hunt ball! But I can't."

"Why ever not? Clara's your friend and it's the first house party she will give as the new baroness. You ought to attend."

"And leave poor Mrs. Pearce and Sybil with two irascible monsters?" Eliza shook her head sadly. "I couldn't."

"Eliza, you need a holiday. After all, I can escape to my club. You've worked harder than anyone here since the accident. Take the time for a bit of fun and relaxation. You're twenty, not sixty. I insist you get away."

How tempting. She'd enjoyed her last visit to Banfield Manor for Clara's wedding. Except for that part where a murderer attacked her. But the beautiful mansion was filled with artwork and servants and the most comfortable bed she had ever slept in. Also her sweetheart, Freddy Eynsford-Hill, was already there. Indeed, he'd been spending all his time at Banfield Manor since Clara and Richard returned from their honeymoon. Eliza thought he enjoyed his younger sister's new elevated status even more than Clara did.

"Higgins will be out of that plaster cast in no time," Colonel Pickering went on. "Despite his complaints, the injury is not serious. And Jack has a wife to tend to him."

"But the Professor will be in an even worse mood if I leave." She brightened at a sudden thought. "What if he comes, too? Both our names are on the invitation. And I could bring Percy with us. I'm sure he'd love to see his peacock friends again."

Pickering looked doubtful. "Higgins has never seemed overly fond of Clara and Freddy."

"Banfield Manor is so huge, he never has to set eyes on them."

A black motorcar drove past, diverting Eliza's attention. She strained to see inside the closed car, but the driver remained hidden behind goggles and a cap covering their hair.

"Is something wrong, Eliza?" Pickering asked.

The motorcar disappeared around the next corner. "The black car that just went by. I swear, the same one has driven up and down Wimpole Street every day for a week. Several times a day, too. It always goes slow, as though the driver is looking for something. Once I saw it parked down the street with the driver in it." Eliza shivered. "I can't help feeling he's watching this house."

His expression turned wary. "That's disquieting."

"I hope it isn't a criminal with a grudge against Scotland Yard. Or against one particular Scotland Yard detective. Think of all the nasty people Jack has helped put away. What if one of them wants revenge? Or one of their dangerous cronies do?"

"You should tell Jack."

Eliza shook her head. "My cousin has broken bones to deal with, and Sybil has to deal with Jack. My worries about a black car will make things worse. Besides, I have no proof of anything. It could be a jealous husband spying on his wife."

"But if you think this person is watching this house. . ."

She thought about the garage at Scotland Yard and the men repairing Higgins's car. "The Professor asked me to ring Detective Ramsey. What if I invite him to Sunday dinner tomorrow? I'll find a moment alone to mention the black car to him."

"Higgins should like that. He'll have a chance to talk about his roadster."

"And Jack will be happy to see him, too." Eliza didn't mention that Ramsey's presence would also please her. Even though she and Freddy were a couple, Eliza was not immune to the appeal of another young man. A bit of flirting might lighten her mood.

"Where is that button hook?" Higgins shouted from inside. "If I can't get at this scratch, I shall rip this cast off with my teeth! Just see if I don't!"

"Oh my," Pickering said. "I'm afraid he may actually do that."

"Damnation!" Higgins yelled, followed by the sound of a loud crash. "Bloody hell!"

Pickering left to assess the damage.

With a last look at the sun-filled street, Eliza slowly shut the door. House parties, fox hunts, and mysterious black cars had to wait. For now, attention must be paid to Higgins's latest temper tantrum. But things needed to change soon. Or else Eliza would lose her patience—and her sanity.

HIGGINS BANGED HIS KNEE ON THE BEDPOST AND CURSED. Blasted dressing gown. Why couldn't he tie a simple knot one-handed? Bad enough he'd lost to Jack at chess this afternoon. Yesterday, actually. In the moonlight, he noted the bedside alarm clock. Nearly three. It maddened him to be up so early in the morning. But he'd been too restless to sleep long. He blamed his sore body and his idle days.

If he didn't resume teaching soon, Higgins feared he might alienate everyone in the household, including Pickering. Mrs. Pearce had warned him they might even lose staff if he didn't "put a lid on the boiling pot." That was the last thing he wanted, but idleness and pain kept him in a foul mood.

His arm beneath the plaster cast began to itch again. And that miserable button hook remained missing. He wouldn't be surprised if Eliza's bloody peacock had made off with it. Higgins's itchy skin soured his mood even more. Only tea would help.

The small lamp left on in the stairwell helped Higgins make his way to the ground floor. He snuck past the closed door to the parlor, careful not to wake Jack and Sybil. The sound of Jack's snores mingled with the usual creaks and noises from the house. Outside, Higgins heard the clopping hooves from a hansom cab horse, and then a motorcar drive past. Big Ben's three chimes reminded him of the lateness of the hour.

He entered the kitchen and switched on the light. Thankfully, no one had been alerted to his presence, especially that peacock. Percy often slept in the small back garden, but he'd been known to spend the night somewhere in the house depending on his mood. Higgins did wonder where Percy was at the moment.

As usual, the door to the back garden had been left slightly ajar, which meant Percy was probably outside. Eliza insisted on this in case Percy wanted to come in. This decision appalled

Cook and Mrs. Pearce, who warned that any number of mice could now make their way into the house as well.

"I don't care about mice," Higgins muttered, "but the door stays closed come winter. I'm not paying for extra coal just so that infernal bird can traipse about at will."

He fiddled with the cook stove until a flame appeared, then filled the kettle. Higgins fetched a teacup and tea tin. Once his brew had steeped, he carried his cup upstairs.

After settling into his bedside armchair, he sipped with a sigh. The glow of a nearby lamp illuminated the book he managed to prop open. Before too long, Higgins dozed off, his tea forgotten on the table beside him.

An ungodly shriek woke him. He sat bolt upright.

A series of piercing shrieks rang out from downstairs. What the devil was the matter with that bird? Had Percy become injured? Confused, Higgins looked about his bedroom. Maybe he was dreaming all this.

Footsteps ran past his door, accompanied by shouts. He lurched to his feet as Eliza burst into the room.

"Professor, we have to get out!"

"Get out? What are you talking about?"

Pickering stuck his head in "The kitchen is on fire! I'm going to make certain all the servants leave the house. Hurry, both of you!"

Eliza shoved Higgins into the hallway and down the stairs. Not only did he smell smoke, his eyes began to water. Percy strutted near the front door. His shrieks and cries grew even louder, no doubt prodded by the loud bells now clanging in the street.

Mrs. Pearce took Higgins by his uninjured arm and ushered him outside. Eliza and Sybil, supporting Jack between them, were a few steps behind. The fire brigade rushed past, and thick smoke poured out of the kitchen door to choke them all. A fireman helped them outside and across the street to safety. Eliza and Sybil coughed, trying to clear their lungs.

"Where's Percy!" Eliza cried suddenly. "Why didn't he follow us? After he made sure we all left, I bet he went to the back garden. I must get him. He saved our lives!" She sprinted across the street, then around the ironwork fence to the side gate.

"Eliza, come back!" Higgins ran after her. Flames and black smoke billowed from the ground floor windows. He watched Eliza race to the garden's corner and gather the peacock into her arms. She then ran lopsided, the bird's feathers trailing her, to the gate. Higgins pulled her to safety, cursing under his breath.

Tears filled Eliza's eyes. "He's done it once again. Saved my life. Saved all our lives, he did! If he hadn't made so much noise, we would have slept while the fire burned the house down around us. What a good bird. Yes, you are, you precious darling."

Higgins wondered again if this was all a dream. If so, it was a bloody loud one.

Residents of the neighborhood, along with their servants, now watched the brigade's efforts to put out the fire. Maids in caps and dressing gowns gossiped with footmen, despite one wearing only his nightshirt; Mrs. Pearce wagged tongues with the housekeeper next door.

Dressed in a flannel robe, Jack leaned on his crutches, his plastered leg propped on the curb. A shocked Sybil stood beside him, watching the flames. Higgins and Eliza joined Colonel Pickering, who seemed the calmest of anyone. Meanwhile, Percy stretched his neck over Eliza's shoulder and crowed in the chill night air.

"Don't worry," she reassured them. "Percy isn't hurt."

"What a relief," Higgins said, although no one seemed to catch his sarcasm. "Does anyone know how the fire started?"

"Mrs. Pearce might know." Pickering turned up the collar of his dressing gown.

"Mrs. Pearce!" Higgins bellowed.

His housekeeper appeared, folding her arms over the blanket she'd draped around herself. "No need to worry, sir. All the staff have been accounted for."

"Have you heard how the fire started?" he asked.

"I believe it started on the cook stove, although I can't imagine why the gas flame was on. I check the controls before going to bed. And none of the servants would have a reason to need the stove after that."

"I made a cup of tea," Higgins admitted. "But I turned off the gas afterward."

The maids exchanged skeptical looks with Mrs. Pearce. Had he actually checked the stove's controls before returning to his bedroom?

"I know I turned it off," he said, although his voice sounded uncertain.

"The kitchen is gutted," Mrs. Pearce said with a sigh. "We'll not be able to cook or make a cup of tea for a long while. I'll have to call the workmen first thing."

"Of course." Higgins felt guiltier by the minute. Was the fire his fault?

When the fire brigade allowed them back inside, everyone gathered in Higgins's laboratory. The smell of smoke hung everywhere. They all started coughing until the sound filled the room. Ash and sooty flakes coated the furniture and walls.

"After this has been cleaned up, I'm giving the staff an extended holiday," he said. "Paid, of course. I understand you must find somewhere to stay in the meantime."

"That would indeed be generous, sir," Mrs. Pearce said, her voice hoarse.

Pickering nodded. "I'll stay at my club. In fact, I'll go upstairs now to pack."

"We'll move in with my parents at their house in Kingston-upon-Thames," Sybil said as she slowly helped Jack walk out of the room. "They initially offered us one of their bedrooms, but Jack would have had to climb stairs. Given these new circumstances, I'm sure they'll agree to set up a bed in the downstairs parlor. We'll make do."

"We all will," Eliza said. "And I have the perfect place for us to go, Professor."

Higgins sighed. "If the perfect place includes either the Savoy or my mother's flat, you should know Percy will be denied entrance."

"No need for either," she said, sounding gleeful. "Wait here."

She set Percy down on the ash and soot trampled carpet, then rushed upstairs. The servants left to begin the clean up. The leader of the fire brigade took Higgins aside to inform him that repairs might take anywhere from one to six weeks. Percy shrieked.

Eliza reappeared and waved the fancy house party invitation at him. "We can go to Banfield Manor," she announced. "Tons of servants to wait on you hand and foot. Percy can visit the other peacocks. And there will be all sorts of guests to entertain you. Shooting, too, and a fox hunt. Although your broken arm will make that difficult."

"Impossible is more like it." Try as he might, Higgins couldn't deny the logic of such a visit at this time. "The house party isn't even a week long. What will we do the rest of the time while the kitchen is being repaired?"

"I'm sure Clara and Richard will let us stay as long as we like." Eliza looked down at Percy, who had settled at her feet. "And it's Percy first home. He'll be so happy to be back."

Higgins preferred an extended stay at the Savoy Hotel, but even he couldn't justify the expense compared to a free invitation to a country house party. He had no choice but to resign himself to spending far too much time with Clara and Freddy

Eynsford Hill. He prayed the other guests had more sense than those two.

"Bring your fanciest clothes," Eliza said. "There's a hunt ball, too."

Percy let out another mournful shriek. Higgins wished he could do the same.

CHAPTER 5

y the time the gables of Banfield Manor came into view, even Higgins was sick of riding in a motorcar. While the train trip from Charing Cross to the Gravesend station had been brief and uneventful, the drive from the station to the manor house proved unpleasant. His arm hurt like the devil as they jostled over the uneven country roads. The trip also took longer than planned, what with the train porters having to load and unload Eliza's trunks, followed by the chauffeurs doing the same. The exasperating girl had packed almost her whole wardrobe.

Percy's presence made things even more complicated. Thankfully, Lord Ashmore had the foresight to have two cars waiting at the train station: one for Higgins and Eliza, the other for Eliza's luggage and the peacock.

Mindful of his injured arm, Higgins cautiously stepped out of the car. At least his recovery would take place under an impressive roof.

Higgins's admiring gaze swept over the rose red brick of the mansion before him. It was an excellent example of Jacobean architecture, built during the reign of the first King James. Two projecting wings flanked the front entrance—forming a U-shape—while curved gables, chimneys, and towers capped the expansive roof. The imposing grandeur of the house verged on intimidating, but Banfield Manor had the good fortune to be surrounded by more than a hundred acres of gardens and parkland. And the famous Rose Maze was regarded as one of the most intricate mazes in Britain, which Higgins and Eliza learned to their chagrin last month.

Of course, his injury prevented Higgins from doing little more than hiking about the grounds or reading in the study. He'd been informed the house party included a massacre of small animals, ending with the mayhem of a fox hunt. His broken arm gave him an excuse to abstain. Unlike other men of his class, Higgins had no stomach for blood sports.

"I wonder if Percy will remember Banfield Manor was once his home." Eliza watched the chauffeur remove the crate containing the restless bird.

"I daresay he will. Percy's only lived at Wimpole Street for a month."

The peacock darted out of the crate when the latch was lifted. His long turquoise feathers swept after him. Percy strutted over the clipped grass before stopping to emit a series of calls. Identical calls echoed from behind a privet hedge.

"Look!" Eliza pointed as a trio of peacocks hurried into view, all three of them making their way to see Percy. The air rang with their shrieks and caws. Higgins judged it a most harmonious reunion, albeit a trifle loud.

Eliza sighed as Percy set off across the lawn with the other birds. "Percy has missed his peacock mates. Maybe I shouldn't have accepted him as a gift. I feel bad now."

At the moment, Higgins felt a damned sight worse than she did, wincing as he re-adjusted his sling. He couldn't wait to be shown to their rooms. Although Higgins disparaged naps and the lazy fools who took them, he wouldn't mind lying down for an hour. Maybe two. He envied Colonel Pickering, now comfortably situated at his London club, where he was no doubt being waited on by a silent manservant while he studied the latest Sanskrit monographs. Speaking of being waited on, why was no one here to greet them? He eyed the closed front door, the family crest of the Ashmores carved above it. Where were their hosts?

The great oak door opened just then, and a slender blonde in an azure blue dress appeared. "Eliza, you're finally here!"

Eliza ran to meet Clara, who was followed by a line of servants. The uniformed men and women positioned themselves to one side of the steps leading to the entrance. Higgins took special note of the tall, willowy man with an imperious profile who watched over the scene like a general surveying his troops. The butler, no doubt. Although it was customary to have servants line up for the more illustrious guests, two phonetics instructors hardly qualified for such a reception. The newly married baroness had a lot to learn about running a great household.

Higgins didn't hold it against the girl. Yes, he regarded the former Clara Eynsford Hill as a ninny, but she was just shy of her nineteenth birthday. In addition, she'd been raised in a family whose diminished finances barely allowed them to cling to their genteel pretensions. Now Clara found herself the wife of the most powerful baron in England. It would take the girl months to understand what this new position required of her. Maybe years. She should count herself lucky her groom was a sensible young man, ten years her senior.

That young man now emerged from the house, giving Higgins a cordial wave.

"How splendid to have you join us," Ashmore said to him.

"But your injury is unfortunate. I should have given you more motoring lessons when you were here last month."

Higgins liked the young baron, an agreeable fellow without airs. As a third son, Richard Ashmore had not expected to inherit the title and all that went with it. Therefore he had made his own way in the world; first at university, then as a captain of the King's Hussars. But his two older brothers—useless wastrels from all accounts—died at an early age, leaving Richard the sole heir upon his father's death a year ago. Inexplicably, he had fallen in love with the empty-headed Clara. Such a decision proved Richard Ashmore was not entirely sensible. A pretty face, trim figure, and golden hair had won out over all logic and reason.

"I have only my love of speed to blame for the accident, Lord Ashmore," Higgins said.

"Please call me Richard. I dislike such formality."

While Higgins admired his lack of pretension, he suspected being called "Lord" still made the former Army captain uncomfortable. "Only if you call me Henry."

"Agreed." He frowned at Higgins's left arm in a sling. "A shame you won't be able to hunt. We'll be shooting hares tomorrow in the south forest, and grouse later in the week. You won't be able to take part in the fox hunt either. Hopefully, the ladies will provide sufficient entertainment. One of our guests is the spiritualist Madame Evangeline. We met her at in Paris while on honeymoon. She comes highly recommended by Sir Arthur Conan Doyle. Despite that, my sister is not pleased we extended the invitation without seeking her approval."

Clara broke off her giggling conversation with Eliza. "I don't know why we have to ask permission of your sister. This is our house party. Not hers."

"And neither of us has the faintest idea how to properly throw one, darling. We're lucky she and the count haven't returned to Austria yet." Richard turned to Higgins and Eliza.

"The Ashmores hold a series of house parties every autumn at Banfield Manor. Mother expects that tradition to continue." He frowned. "Even if she refuses to attend any herself."

Higgins and Eliza exchanged knowing looks. His mother had obviously not recovered from Richard's whirlwind marriage to a young girl of little breeding and even less wealth.

"His sister orders me about as if I were a child," Clara said with a pout. "And her husband is even worse. I have to address them as Count and Countess, even when no one else is around. But they call me Clara, never Lady Ashmore. I find that dreadfully rude."

Richard shrugged. "My sister *is* being difficult, but she has rarely been anything else."

"Fortunately, she had no objection to including you and the Professor on the guest list." Clara linked elbows with Eliza.

"The two of you have been in all the papers of late because of your sleuthing," Richard added with a laugh. "That means you're in fashion this season. Don't be surprised to receive more invites to country house parties."

Higgins shuddered. "And no one should be surprised when we turn them down."

"Speak for yourself," Eliza said.

"All I care about is that you're at *our* house party," Clara said. "You and Madame Evangeline. She's quite the exotic. I hope she gives us a demonstration of table tipping."

Higgins grimaced. "Good grief."

"What's table tipping?" Eliza asked.

"It's a way to talk with the dead. Won't it be fun seeing what the ghosts say to us?"

Eliza's eyes widened. "You shouldn't fool with such things, Clara. My Uncle Liam once owned a goat that was possessed by the spirit of his late wife. Scared him something awful. He ended by drinking himself into the grave."

"I'd hardly blame the goat," Higgins said. "Drunkards and Doolittles are synonymous."

Eliza shot him a warning look. "Say that again and I may injure your other arm."

"Stop it," Clara said. "Both of you need to be on your best behavior. We have famous and important people coming to our house party."

"Are they all as august as the woman who tips tables with ghosts?" Higgins asked.

"Oh, I don't care about this ghost lady. Where's Freddy?" Eliza scanned the front lawn. The chauffeurs had finished unloading the luggage, prompting the butler to bark quiet orders at the footmen. "I haven't heard from him in days."

Higgins noticed the Ashmore couple exchanging furtive glances. "He's off with the horses somewhere," Clara said hurriedly. "Freddy is nervous about the upcoming fox hut. He's been taking riding lessons all week."

"I never knew Freddy cared a fig about horses. All he ever talks about are motorcars and his rowing club." Eliza winked at Richard. "In fact, I expected to see him driving about in your Stutz Bearcat. He fell in love with it the last time he was here, just like the Professor did."

Clara sniffed. "Freddy falls in love far too often, if you ask me."

Eliza looked confused. "Why do you say that?"

The butler cleared his throat. "Sir Anthony has arrived, my lord."

A car appeared in the distance. The grounds of Banfield Manor were extensive and the gravel drive to the front door of the manor house exceedingly long. It would be several minutes before this latest guest reached them.

Richard smoothed down his jacket. "Thank you, Baxter."

Clara fussed with her hair and repinned a stray blond curl. "Do I look all right?"

"Ravishing," he reassured her, but the young baron also sounded anxious.

Higgins had little interest in this latest guest, even if he did have a 'sir' in front of his name. Titles didn't impress him, and Eliza treated everyone with the same breezy insolence. Although Higgins wouldn't be surprised if he knew the man making his way toward them in a black Rolls Royce. His older brother William was a member of Parliament, predicted by some to be Prime Minister one day. The Higgins family might not be aristocrats, but they weren't without influence. And their acquaintances and friends reached even to Buckingham Palace.

"How fortuitous our arrival coincided with your next guest," Higgins remarked. "It's one less time the servants have to parade out here to welcome us."

"Don't be silly, Professor." Clara threw him an exasperated look. "We knew Sir Anthony was due to arrive at this time. That's why I instructed the servants to give him a proper greeting. You and Eliza aren't important enough to take them away from their work."

"Clara, all our guests are important," Richard gently chided her.

She lifted her chin in defiance. "Some of them are more important and you know it."

A middle-aged couple appeared on the steps of Banfield Manor. He'd been introduced to the Count and Countess von Weisinger, otherwise known as Clara's insufferable in-laws, at the Ashmore wedding last month. Higgins tried to recall the count's first name. Franz? Albrecht? No, Rudolf. As for Richard's sister's name, he hadn't a clue. All he remembered were her prominent profile and overbite, along with a haughtiness that could probably make the Kaiser quail. She turned that expression in his direction.

"Professor Higgins, Miss Doolittle," she intoned in a loud voice, making no effort to move toward them. Count Rudolf gave Higgins a brief nod. The couple returned their attention to the Rolls Royce. Clearly, its occupants were far more important than he and Eliza.

A rumbling suddenly met their ears. As the buzzing grew louder, everyone's attention shifted to the blue sky overhead. A white aeroplane came into view. Higgins swept off his hat and shaded his eyes to get a better look. Two red circles were painted on the wings' undersides.

Clara clapped her hands. "Oh my, look! Philippe's arriving as well. This is too thrilling."

"Jolly good show he's putting on." Richard seemed as excited as his bride as the plane circled overheard. "He told me he planned to land right on our front lawn, and by heaven he is."

"How loverly," Eliza said. "I've never seen an aeroplane in person. Now one is going to set down right in front of us."

"Let's hope he lands a bit farther away from the house." Higgins watched as the plane made its descent, propeller spinning. "If he comes too close, he may hit the topiaries. Or us."

"Have no fear. I believe Philippe Corbet could land his aircraft in the confined space of a Wimbledon tennis court. That's how skilled he is," Richard said. The plane smoothly touched down, well clear of the trees in the surrounding parkland.

"Philippe Corbet?" Eliza repeated. "I saw him in one of the newsreels at the cinema. He won some sort of award."

"Indeed he has." Higgins had only a passing interest in aviation, but even he had heard of the dashing Frenchman who broke three speed records and won the Matheson Cup in America.

Eliza nudged Higgins. "He looked handsome in the newsreel. Lots of dark wavy hair and a corking smile. A lady wouldn't mind flying about the clouds with that gentleman."

"Control yourself, Eliza, or else Monsieur Corbet may fly right off again."

"I've quite an interest in flying myself." Richard waved at the man now climbing out of the aircraft. "Philippe flew here in a Bleriot XI. Good news for us. That's a tandem two-seater touring model, often used for training. He may take us up for a spin. A splendid aeroplane, too. Named after Louis Bleriot, who flew an earlier model of the aircraft across the English Channel in 1909. The flight took only thirty-six minutes. And in bad weather."

Higgins nodded. "Ah yes. The first man to fly across the Channel. I remember *The Daily News* headline: 'Britain is no longer an island.' I saw the aircraft after it was put on display at Selfridges that summer."

"You'd love her, Henry. It's built for speed *and* endurance. A military version of the Bleriot XI can be broken down and then reassembled in twenty-five minutes."

Higgins caught movement out of the corner of his eye. Everyone was so intent on watching the plane, no one had noticed the Rolls Royce now rolling to a stop a few yards from the front steps of the house. He leaned toward Richard. "Sir Anthony is here."

Both Clara and Richard turned to the car with anxious expressions. Higgins hoped the new arrival wasn't some dreary MP from Croydon South or Tewkesbury.

Count Rudolf and his wife walked past. Neither spared a glance at Higgins and Eliza.

"May I ask who this Sir Anthony is?" Higgins said in a stage whisper.

"Sir Anthony Dennison," Richard replied.

He whistled. "Philippe Corbet *and* Sir Anthony. Shall we also expect a visit from the First Lord of the Admiralty? Or is Mr. Churchill not a fan of table tipping?"

But the Ashmore couple had joined their in-laws, preparing to greet the latest arrival.

Eliza tore her attention from the French aviator, who strode across the wide lawn toward them. "Who's Sir Anthony Dennison? I've never heard of him."

"Sir Anthony is an explorer, knighted fifteen years ago by Queen Victoria. The chap's written a number of books, the latest recently published to great acclaim. This looks to be more entertaining than I expected. The tales Sir Anthony must have." Higgins hadn't felt this intrigued about something unrelated to phonetics—or murder—in a long time. "During a 1906 expedition, Sir Anthony got lost and disappeared while mapping the Amazon. He was presumed dead for two years until he finally turned up in a native village in the rain forest."

Eliza smirked. "Doesn't seem much of a mapmaker if he got lost for two years."

"I don't know why I bother to converse with you at all."

"Because everyone else bores you silly after ten minutes." Eliza tried to peek over the shoulders of the footmen and chauffeurs for a glimpse of Sir Anthony. "There's a woman with him. A redhead. And it looks like her walking suit comes from the House of Worth."

"I fail to see why anyone gives a damn about overpriced textiles."

"Only someone with the fashion sense of a chimney sweep would say that."

Richard beckoned them. "Let me introduce you both to Sir Anthony and his wife."

Higgins's indifference to social niceties faded. If he and Sir Anthony hit it off, the next few days might revolve around scholarly discussion, not grouse and gunfire. When he approached the couple, he immediately recognized the explorer's weathered visage from newspaper articles. Short and stocky, Sir Anthony boasted a luxuriant mustache and beard—equal parts gray and light auburn—which contrasted with his shiny bald head.

"Pleased to meet the accomplished Sir Anthony Dennison." Higgins extended his hand.

"I am equally pleased to meet the acclaimed author of *The Universal Alphabet*." Sir Anthony gave his hand a hearty shake, then shifted his attention to Eliza. "And who is this delightful young lady?"

He wasn't surprised by Sir Anthony's interest in Eliza. Behind the tangled hair and dirty face of that Cockney flower girl he'd met last year, Higgins had discovered an exceedingly pretty young woman as clever and resourceful as she was attractive. Although Higgins viewed Eliza with affection, his feelings for her had never been romantic. For one, she was far too young. Two, he had little interest in anything aside from phonetics and language.

After bowing over Eliza's hand longer than necessary, Sir Anthony straightened. "Let me introduce my wife, Lady Annabel. Although I still think of her as my bride, even after three years of marriage." Sir Anthony touched the shoulder of the woman deep in conversation with Clara and the countess. "My dear, I'd like you to meet Miss Doolittle and Professor Higgins."

The woman hesitated before turning around. "But I know Professor Higgins," she said with an astonished smile. "I'd no idea you were a guest of the Ashmores. How have you been?"

Higgins found himself speechless. Literally. His mouth opened as if to speak, but he couldn't form any words. Eliza kicked him in the shin. He heard himself say something in response and hoped it was English.

The country house gods grew merciful just then. Philippe Corbet had finally made his way across the lawn, prompting everyone to crowd around him.

Eliza started to follow the others, but Higgins grabbed her arm.

"We need to make our goodbyes," he said in a furious whisper.

"Excuse me?"

"We have to leave. Immediately." He threw a desperate look in Lady Annabel's direction. "I am quite serious, Eliza. We must go!"

CHAPTER 6

"*L*eave!" Eliza fought to control her exasperation. "Honestly, you have even less manners than my blooming stepmother. We can't leave for no reason. Stop being rude."

Higgins glanced over at Sir Anthony's wife, now speaking with Lord Ashmore. "I don't care how rude it seems, I refuse to spend another minute at Banfield Manor. Not with Lady Annabel in residence. I mean it, Eliza. We can't stay. The woman is quite mad."

"I think you've gone mad. We've only just arrived. They haven't even taken our bags into the house."

"Perfect. That means they can be loaded back into the car." Higgins felt around in his jacket pocket. "I have the train schedule right here. We can catch the next train to London."

Eliza restrained herself from muttering a few Cockney curses. For two weeks she had played nursemaid to Higgins. Then the fool had almost burned the house down, forcing their temporary eviction. It was a blessing they'd had the Ashmore invitation to fall back. She now looked forward to enjoying pampered country life in a splendid manor house, and she had no intention of letting Higgins's rudeness get in the way.

"I'm not going anywhere. But if you're so afraid of this lady, go back to Wimpole Street. Only you'll be there without a kitchen. And there won't be a servant in sight. I'd like to see how you'll fare without some woman waiting on you hand and foot."

"You're right." His expression turned pensive. "Perhaps I should move in with my mother at her flat in Chelsea. She may not welcome the idea, but I don't think she'd refuse to take in her own son. After all, I am homeless at the moment."

"You are not. There's a house as big as Windsor Castle right behind us, and it's got a bedroom prepared just for you." Eliza straightened his tie. "Now stop being such a spoiled baby. I don't know what happened between you and that lady but—"

He leaned closer. "She's in love with me. At least she was seven years ago. I had to leave England to get away from her. The woman was determined to marry me."

Eliza found his declaration hard to believe. "Well, she's married to someone else now. And he's here, too. So your honor —or what's left of it—should be safe." After a warning look at Higgins, she joined the others clustered about Corbet.

Luckily, the aviator's dramatic landing of his plane right in front of everyone had overshadowed Higgins's odd reaction to Lady Annabel.

When Clara introduced the Frenchman to her, Eliza discovered he was even more attractive in person than in the newsreel. He certainly looked dashing in his flying gear: olive cardigan sweater coat, trousers tucked into brown leather boots, and buckskin gloves. Since he had removed his tight-fitting helmet and goggles, she could also see that Philippe Corbet boasted a distinguished profile, large brown eyes, and a thick mane of black hair. He was tall, too, a good three inches over the Professor. Best of all, he spoke with an enticing French accent.

She nearly swooned when he said, *"Enchanté* to meet you, Mademoiselle Doolittle."

Eliza felt torn between admiring the handsome aviator and examining the woman who had upset Higgins. Lady Annabel seemed an intense woman, prone to gesturing with her hands, tossing back her head, expressing amusement with a low laugh. Her coloring proved just as dramatic. Green eyes, copper red hair, creamy white skin. While it didn't quite add up to beauty, she was attractive. Yet Eliza found her unappealing. Lady Annabel reminded her of a jungle snake she'd once seen at the London Zoo: sinuous, alert, hypnotic. She began to feel sympathetic toward Higgins. If this woman determined to have something, who could resist her? Higgins probably had. Given his alarm, it had left him shaken.

With a shiver, Clara hugged herself. "We should go inside. I didn't know we planned to remain out here so long, or I'd have changed into a warmer ensemble. Like Eliza."

Eliza looked down at her navy jacket and skirt. "I'm too warm in my tweeds."

Lady Annabel looped her hand around Eliza's elbow. "Charming suit, my dear. Poiret, I believe? One can always tell by the cut of the jacket. Rather fond of him myself, although I'm wearing Mr. Worth this morning." She smoothed her deep plum walking suit. "Although Monsieur Poiret created my hat."

Eliza smiled in approval at the stylish velvet and silk hat, trimmed with the designer's characteristic roses. "We share a love of Poiret."

She gave another guttural laugh. "It appears we share more than that." Pulling Eliza with her, Lady Annabel followed Clara into the house. "Lord Ashmore explained that you and Professor Higgins are fellow phonetics instructors. Of course,

Henry has been teaching since Victoria was on the throne, but you seem fresh from the schoolroom."

Eliza glanced over her shoulder and saw an unhappy Higgins being forced to converse with the countess and Sir Anthony. "In a way, I am. Last year I became a student of Professor Higgins. He and Colonel Pickering taught me how to speak so well, I'm now giving lessons."

Lady Annabel stepped into the great entrance hall. "Ah, so you are the Cockney flower girl I heard about when Sir Anthony and I attended the opera this spring. We don't get to London often enough to enjoy all the current gossip. I judged the tale of the flower girl at the Embassy Ball to be more myth than fact. But if Henry is involved, even the most outlandish event may be believed."

Eliza peeked over her shoulder at Higgins, who looked completely miserable.

"Tell me, Miss Doolittle." Lady Annabel lowered her voice. "Are you Henry's lover?"

Startled, she stopped in her tracks. "Blimey, no."

Countess von Weisinger cleared her throat behind them. "After your long journeys, you must all want to freshen up. Baxter and Mrs. Stewart will show everyone to their rooms." She gestured to the butler and housekeeper who stood waiting before the sweeping grand staircase. "Luncheon will be served in an hour."

Wringing her hands, Clara looked over at the housekeeper. "If you're too tired, we'll send up sandwiches and tea. Won't we, Mrs. Stewart?"

Mrs. Stewart waited to answer until the countess nodded. "Of course, madam."

Her reply sent a ripple of activity through the hall as servants bustled about with luggage, and Lady Annabel conferred with the maid who'd traveled with her. The count and countess made their own stately promenade up the grand staircase, Sir Anthony between them.

Eliza was about to join Higgins, now skulking by the door, when Lady Annabel caught her sleeve. "We shall speak later, Miss Doolittle. No doubt we have fascinating tales to tell, especially concerning the elusive Henry Higgins."

With growing unease, Eliza watched as Lady Annabel followed Philippe Corbet upstairs. "What the devil was that woman saying to you?" Higgins hissed in her ear.

Eliza jumped. "Don't sneak up on me like that."

He whipped off his hat. "What did she say?"

"She asked if you and I were lovers."

"Damnation! This is intolerable. What did you say?"

"What do you think I said? And keep your voice down." Eliza sighed. "I must say your choice in women is puzzling. Perhaps it's because you don't have much experience with them."

"If I were fool enough to allow a woman in my life," he said with disgust, "you can't imagine I'd choose that Messalina in a corset, do you?"

"Who in the world is Messalina?"

"Stop whispering together." Clara tapped them both on the shoulder. "The two of you quarrel like a married couple."

Richard grinned. "Not that we've had a quarrel yet. Although I'm sure we will."

"Don't be silly," Clara said with a giggle. "We aren't like other married couples. Look how desperately in love we are. Why should we ever quarrel?"

"I can think of a hundred reasons," Higgins muttered.

Eliza shook her head at Higgins. "Don't listen to him. He wouldn't recognize romantic love if it stepped out of a Rolls Royce right in front of him."

Higgins let out a strangled cry.

Still feeling warm, Eliza removed her gloves. She looked about the entrance hall, its tiled floor and gilt framed portraits on the wall familiar from her visit last month. "How long will

Freddy will be at his riding lesson? Should we send someone to the stables to fetch him?"

"They'll be in shortly," Richard said, exchanging glances with his bride.

"They?" Eliza asked. "Who's riding with Freddy?"

"One of our guests. She arrived three days ago." Clara's expression turned disapproving. "A bit shocking, coming early like that. Then again, she is a cinema actress. An American, too. That makes her even more unconventional."

Eliza gasped. "A cinema actress? Here? Who is it? Alice Joyce?"

"No, not Miss Joyce," Richard said. "Lily Marlowe."

"Lily Marlowe? But I adore her! I've seen all her movies. She's a great actress, even though she's only a year older than me. I cried all the way through *The Pirate's Daughter*. Do you know Lily Marlow appeared on the cover of last month's issue of *Photoplay*? Freddy's seen her movies, too. He must be as excited as I am to meet her."

"Rather too excited," Clara snapped.

"Of course he is," Eliza said. "This will be the best party ever. I wonder if she knows the Gish sisters. Oh, I can't wait to meet her. Maybe I should go to the stables myself."

The sound of laugher and voices from outside met their ears. "No need for that," Clara said with irritation. "Here's Freddy and Lily now."

Trembling with excitement, Eliza turned as the front door banged open. But her happy greeting to Freddy died on her lips as the couple entered the house. It was obvious they had been at the stables. Freddy and Lily Marlowe wore riding habits. It was also clear they'd grown quite close. Literally. Freddy had his arm slung over the actress's shoulder, while she hugged him about the waist. They were wrapped so tight about each other, Eliza wondered how they managed to walk to the house without tripping over their feet.

"This looks rather interesting," Higgins muttered to Eliza. "Freddy?"

The young man looked up at the sound of Eliza's voice. For a moment, he seemed both startled and embarrassed. But in the wink of an eye, he'd recovered. A familiar wide grin now creased his face. "Eliza, how lovely of you to join us at Banfield."

"Freddy, is this your friend Eliza Doolittle?" Lily Marlowe finally took her arms from around Freddy. With a charming expression that Eliza had seen her wear in *The Pirate's Daughter*, the actress walked over to her with an outstretched hand.

"I'm Lily," she said with a dimpled smile. "Freddy says you're keen on my movies. If so, I'm delighted to meet another fan. Your countrymen have treated me marvelously well during my stay here." The actress waved in Freddy's direction. "Especially that countryman. He's been killer to me since I arrived. Absolutely killer."

"Don't you love how Americans talk!" Freddy said as he rushed to Lily's side. He looked down at the actress with the ardor and adoration he had formerly bestowed upon Eliza.

Not that she blamed him. Shorter than Eliza, Lily Marlowe had a petite but curvy figure which her snug riding habit enhanced. The cinema screen hadn't done justice to her perfect little nose, hazel eyes, and bow-shaped mouth. Lily reminded Eliza of a Dresden doll she'd once seen in an Oxford Street shop window. And her mass of wavy dark hair plaited and pinned to the back of her head in the new Grecian style exactly matched Eliza's own coiffure. They shared the same taste in men *and* coiffures.

Eliza suddenly felt like the fairy tale's ugly stepsister. And her prince had been stolen away.

"Isn't she splendid, Eliza?" Freddy asked, his attention focused on the woman beside him. "I told her how we'd seen every one of her films. Even *The Rose of Riverton*."

Richard Ashmore cleared his throat. "Excuse me, but I would

be remiss to let this conversation continue before I've had the pleasure of introducing Miss Marlowe to Professor Higgins." While he introduced Higgins to the actress, a stunned Eliza stared at Freddy.

It hurt her to the quick to see him avoiding her gaze. Physically he appeared the same, with golden hair and blue eyes like his sister Clara. What had clearly changed were his feelings for Eliza. Freddy had pursued her since the spring. He'd proposed so many times, Eliza had lost count. She knew that she'd frustrated him by insisting she wasn't ready to marry. But she was deeply fond of Freddy. Maybe she even loved him. Because she'd never been in love before, how was she to know for certain?

Yes, there were times his slavish pursuit got on her nerves. And he wasn't a favorite of Higgins. Yet she never imagined the passion he displayed for her could be transferred so easily to another woman.

"How have you been, Freddy?" Eliza asked while Higgins and Lily Marlowe exchanged pleasantries.

Freddy finally looked at her. "I've had the devil of a good time here. Beastly of me to not ring you up. But you were busy playing nursemaid to your cousin and the Professor."

Higgins must have heard that. "That doesn't excuse you from not phoning Eliza," he said.

Freddy turned stubborn. "It's unlikely she missed me. Eliza is always busy teaching. Or chasing after some murderer."

"Freddy told me that you and Professor Higgins are amateur gumshoes." Lily's lovely eyes sparkled even more. "The two of you sound like Sherlock Holmes and Dr. Watson. I insist on hearing all about it, but not at the moment. Freddy acted like a real goop at the end of our ride and startled my horse. I fell right into a muddy ditch." Lily turned around, revealing mud spatters on her forest green split skirt.

"Are you hurt?" Richard asked. "Would you like me to call a physician?"

"I've ridden horses in some of my movies. I'm no Calamity Jane, but I do know how to sit a horse *and* topple off one." Her laughter sounded as musical as wind chimes. "Only I must get out of these muddy things. If you could have one of the maids draw a bath for me."

Clara took Lily by the arm and walked with her to the staircase. "Let me apologize for my idiotic brother. I may take his riding whip and thrash him for upsetting your horse."

Freddy followed after them. "I say, Clara. That's a bit much."

Clara glared back at her brother. "And so are you. Why don't you catch up on things with Eliza while Lily goes upstairs. You've quite worn her out with your stupid antics."

Eliza's heart sank further when Freddy shook his head. "I'm worn out myself. In fact, I wouldn't mind a bath as well."

Lily lifted a gracefully arched eyebrow at him. "I hope you don't imagine we'll be sharing that bath."

He put his hands over his heart. "A man can imagine, can't he? And dream."

Eliza noticed that Higgins, Richard and Clara looked as uncomfortable as she felt.

"The baths will have to be brief," Richard said. "Luncheon is served in an hour."

"Unless you'd rather I have the kitchen send something up." Clara bit her lip, the job of society hostess seemed to weigh heavy on her.

"That would be perfect," Lily told Clara. "I need a nice long soak, and maybe even a nap. But I promise I'll be ready to dazzle at dinner."

"Me, too." Freddy grabbed Lily by the hand. "Although you dazzled me the moment I set eyes on you three days ago. Now let's get you out of those muddy clothes."

Giggling, the pair of them ran up the stairs hand in hand.

A long silence followed. "Maybe they both fell off their horses," Higgins finally said. "Only Freddy fell right on his head."

"He's got a bit of a crush on the girl, but it won't last. A mere infatuation." Richard gave Eliza a sympathetic look. "You can't blame him. After all, Lily is a cinema star."

"And she's beautiful." Eliza couldn't help sounding resigned.

"I do blame my fool of a brother," Clara declared. "He acted a perfect beast to Eliza just now. And I won't let this continue. In fact, I'm going up there right now to tell him if he doesn't behave, I'll send him packing. But first, I may box him about the ears." She picked up her skirts and ran up the stairs, looking for all the world like an angry little girl rather than the baroness of Ashmore.

"Excuse me. But I need to keep the family feuds to a minimum this week." Richard hurried after his wife.

Left alone in the great hall, Higgins and Eliza stared at each other. "You're right," she said. "We can't stay. I refuse to watch Freddy moon over some actress for the next week."

"Now you know how I feel." Higgins gave a loud sigh of relief. "All we need is to find a footman to get our luggage back to the car. Once we're ready to leave, we'll make the briefest of farewells to Richard and Clara."

"The sooner, the better."

Before either of them could search for a servant, the front door once more swung open. A woman dressed all in black gazed at them in silence.

"Can we help you, miss?" Higgins asked.

"Madame," she replied in a low voice, which betrayed a slight accent. "I am Madame Evangeline. The baron and baroness are expecting me. Please summon them."

Since Eliza had no wish to retrieve Clara or Richard upstairs, she decided to play hostess. She was also curious about this woman who spoke with ghosts. "As a family friend, allow me to welcome you." Eliza hurried over to the door. "Please come in. I'm Eliza Doolittle and the gentleman is Professor Henry Higgins."

Peeking over the shoulders of this new guest, Eliza spied a chauffeur and a muscular, swarthy man removing luggage from a large black touring car.

"Thank you," the woman said. "The drive from Salisbury has been long and tedious."

Eliza stepped back, allowing her to enter the manor house. She took note of Madame Evangeline's striking features. Her pale skin contrasted with mahogany brown hair pulled tight from her face and piled in an old-fashioned manner atop her head. Despite a sharply defined profile, high cheekbones, and an intimidating manner, she was pretty.

Young, too. No more than thirty. What impressed Eliza most were her enormous blue eyes. They were a chilly dark blue, which brought to mind a wintry sky. Her piercing gaze sent a shiver down Eliza's spine. Maybe that was because she knew Madame Evangeline consorted with the spirit world.

Without warning, the woman halted and shut those unsettling eyes. She remained silent while Eliza and Higgins exchanged puzzled glances.

"Are you all right?" Eliza asked finally.

"I see that you wish to escape this place," she replied in a deep, commanding voice. "Do not leave. That will lead to disaster. Death and darkness surround this house. The future of the world hangs in the balance."

Madame Evangeline opened her eyes and gave them a steely look. "You *must* stay."

CHAPTER 7

*E*liza had been right to dread the first formal dinner at
Banfield Manor. The table was set with more plates
and silver than the china department at Harrods. Exactly how
many courses were they expected to eat? Ten? Twenty? Cor, but
she pitied the poor scullery maid who had to clean up after such
a meal.

The footman paused beside Eliza and set a crystal dish
before her on the gold charger. She stalled for time by rear-
ranging the napkin on her lap. What if she used the wrong fork,
or mistook the finger bowl for soup? Last year, both Mrs.
Higgins and Colonel Pickering taught her proper dinner party
etiquette, but she'd never attended any as formal as this. Eliza
dreaded making a mistake and having these people view her
with contempt. She had quite enough of that when she sold
violets outside Covent Garden.

Philippe Corbet sat beside her. She peeked over and saw him
choose a small silver spoon from the endless flatware that
extended on either side of their plates. When the shellfish appe-
tizer had been served earlier, she kept her eye on Richard
Ashmore, who sat to her left. If she continued to shift her gaze

as each course was served, the guests might not realize she was watching everyone to see what to do next.

Eliza dipped her tiny spoon in the bowl of consommé before her. Tasteless as water. Then again, she didn't expect to enjoy dining in a stately room that boasted a plaster ceiling over-decorated at every corner with clusters of fruit and curlicues. Every time she glanced up at the gilt chandeliers which hung from red velvet-covered chains, she wondered if they were in danger of falling. If so, she hoped one of them fell on her.

Despite her anxiety, Eliza did admire the pristine linen tablecloth, the delicate crystal arrayed to the right of her plate, the red-patterned china and the gleaming silver. And as a former flower seller, she approved of the table's lush floral centerpiece flanked by tall glass candelabras. Clara sat on the other side of that centerpiece of asters and mums, looking even more miserable than Eliza.

The reason for Clara's misery was clear. Against every standard of etiquette Eliza had been taught, the Count and Countess von Weisinger presided at either end of the table, proclaiming themselves the official host and hostess. Eliza felt outraged on Richard and Clara's behalf, both now relegated to sitting among the other guests. It didn't help that the countess eyed Eliza's every move with disdain.

With Richard engaged in conversation with Lady Annabel beside him, Eliza turned to the Frenchman on her right.

"I hear you bought a camera," she said. "May I ask if it is easy to operate?"

"*Mais oui.* A vest pocket model of the Kodak Eastman. The camera, it is first sold last year. Modern and—*comment dites-vous?* how do you say?—compact. But it is not so easy to load the film spools. But once the process is learned, it is *vite comme l' éclair.*"

While he described the camera's chromatic meniscus lens, her attention wandered to Freddy and Lily, who sat on the other side of the table near Count Rudolf. Freddy hung on Lily's every word, but Rudolf looked bored.

Lily must have sensed the count's indifference. She batted her long lashes at him. "I just completed my twelfth moving picture. We movie actors are sure to become more famous than any stage actor or actress. Even Elenora Duse and Mrs. Campbell."

"You will never be more famous than Lucie Höflich," he said with finality.

Eliza assumed he referred to a German actress, since the count was enamored of all things German.

"I don't know who this Höflich lady is," Lily replied, "but I live in New York City. All the pictures in America are made there. That's how I was able to begin my career when I was only sixteen. A man saw me walking down Third Avenue, stopped his motorcar, and insisted I meet a director that he knew." Her smile seemed to falter a bit. "The rest is history."

"*Photoplay* put Lily on the cover," Freddy boasted. "She looked like an angel. Although is it even possible there are angels as beautiful as Lily?"

Eliza turned back to Philippe, who launched into a history of photography, beginning with Louis Daguerre. Evidently, photography and aviation were passions of his. She wouldn't have to do anything but let him expound for the rest of the dinner.

Conversation eddied about the table, none of which interested her until Sir Anthony announced, "I doubt anyone here has encountered the marvels that I did in the Amazon. Take the predatory assassin bugs who coat themselves with the carcasses of ants and tree sap in order to disguise their real nature. They snatch bees right from the air with their claws. There isn't an ant or a bee that can elude these tiny carnivores."

Since the explorer sat beside Clara, she obviously felt

compelled to respond. "How interesting. I've not been farther than the Continent, but I'd love to travel more."

Sir Anthony smoothed his extravagant beard and mustache. Eliza noticed how his bald head reflected the warm glow of the chandeliers above. "Exploring the wilds of South America is not for the faint of heart. Especially not for delicate ladies such as yourself. And the jungle heat is punishing, Lady Ashmore. You'd swoon after just one hour in a Brazilian dugout canoe."

"I know something of extreme heat myself," Richard said. "When I was stationed in India with the Hussars, temperatures sometimes exceeded a hundred and ten. The tropical heat felled a number of my fellow soldiers."

Sir Anthony shrugged. "True, we have both sweated through torrid summers. But I have faced dangers you cannot comprehend, Lord Ashmore." He seemed to swell with his own importance. "Man-eating plants, snakes seventeen feet long, natives who kill with poison darts. Nothing in India compares with the challenge and perils of the Amazonian jungle. You and your Hussars had it far too easy." He sipped his champagne. "The greatest danger you faced was trying to keep the Governor General happy."

Richard flinched at the veiled insult. Irritated, Eliza pushed away the tasteless consummé. She'd had quite enough of this course. And Sir Anthony's bragging.

"Maybe you only think it was dangerous because you got lost," she said.

Everyone stopped eating and looked at her.

"I beg your pardon, Miss Doolittle." Sir Anthony looked indignant.

She stared back. "You got lost, didn't you? In fact, you were lost for two years. That's a long time, especially for someone who's supposed to be a mapmaker. I'm sure that's why you thought the Amazon was so dangerous and hard. You didn't know where you were." Eliza gave him a reassuring smile.

"Don't feel bad. I'd be scared if I got lost, too. And if I stayed lost for two years, I'd be blooming terrified."

Farther down the table she heard Higgins sniggering. Richard hid his own grin behind a napkin.

Sir Anthony flushed crimson. "You are a most impertinent young lady."

"Thank you, Sir Anthony. I find you impertinent as well."

The stunned explorer was spared having to make a response when Lady Annabel asked, "Did anyone attend the Chelsea Flower Show this past May? Sir Anthony and I found it delightful. We arrived shortly after Queen Mary, who seemed quite impressed by the anemones."

"The Treaty of London was signed that month," Count Rudolf said. "A good thing, too. Well past time for Albania to be independent. And time for the fighting in the Balkans to end."

Sir Anthony grunted. "Didn't last long. Those Bulgarians attacked their Serb allies in June, although maybe your countrymen in the Austro-Hungarian Empire don't mind. Be careful about picking sides in the Balkans. That will lead to trouble, especially since the Hapsburgs and the Germans have their eyes on the Ottoman Empire."

"And the British do not? What about your meddling in Thrace?" the count asked.

The countess cleared her throat. "No politics during dinner. I insist."

An uncomfortable silence followed while footmen removed the empty bowls. Eliza prayed there wouldn't be endless courses, particularly if they were as bland as the consommé. The next course was a dainty pastry with bits of seafood in a creamy sauce. Eliza would have preferred a newspaper filled with fresh fried fish and chips.

Philippe returned to lecturing Eliza on daguerreotypes. Madame Evangeline now joined the conversation. Apparently, she also liked photography. Or Frenchmen.

Bored, Eliza reached for a wine goblet. One of the footmen eyed the flute instead and gave a surreptitious nod. Eliza noticed everyone else sipping champagne. The footman winked. He looked familiar, with those wide eyes, a freckled nose, and sandy brown hair slicked back. Was that Charlie Kenton, from Whitechapel? It had to be.

Charlie smiled at her before heading out with a silver tray. He looked so smart in his black footman's uniform that Eliza hadn't recognized him at first. How comforting that someone from the old neighborhood was here. She relaxed at the thought of a friend willing to guide her in the complicated rituals of a country house party.

A bell-like laugh rose up from the babble of voices. "You don't mean that, Henry," Lady Annabel said. "Then again, I forget you are possessed of a scathing wit."

Eliza leaned forward in time to see Lady Annabel tap Higgins on the shoulder. He pushed her hand away.

"I mean everything I say. Especially if the remark is scathing, so have a care." Higgins gazed up at the ceiling with an exaggerated sigh. Eliza knew he must be more desperate for the dinner to end than she was.

The older woman smoothed a coppery wisp that escaped her elaborate coiffure, unperturbed by the Professor's refusal to be charmed. And Lady Annabel did hold a cunning allure. She certainly knew how to dress to best advantage in a green silk gown with a twisted serpentine collar that drew attention to her creamy shoulders. And the triple aigrette feathers in Lady Annabel's auburn hair lent her a sensuous majesty. But although Sir Anthony declared his love for his wife earlier that day, he seemed oblivious to her efforts to flirt with Higgins.

Eliza realized Freddy was just as indifferent to her. He was too busy fawning over Lily Marlowe. But could she blame him? The actress outshone every female at the table. Her lively charm and gaiety brought to mind Lily's performance in *A Lady's*

Honor, one of Eliza's favorites. Lily could have discouraged him, of course, but she seemed to enjoy his attentions. No surprise. Freddy's dashing looks might have made him a cinema star as well, if he had any talent to go along with them.

"Her latest film is ripping good," Freddy told Madame Evangeline.

The actress giggled. "Freddy sounds like my press agent, who calls me 'splendiferous' in all the press releases. I'm just grateful to have the work."

"I believe you are the most talented and beautiful creature on the screen. Ten times more lovely in person," His cheeks reddened with the force of his ardor. "And you were already ravishing enough."

"Thank you, but I have competition tonight." Lily gestured at the other ladies.

Eliza could tell Freddy didn't believe that, nor would any other man here. Clara looked like yet another pretty girl who boasted an English rose complexion and the freshness of youth. Although she wouldn't admit it aloud, Eliza thought her own looks rivaled Clara's, and wouldn't fade once girlhood disappeared. But neither she nor Clara were any match for Lily Marlowe.

As for Lady Annabel, in her youth she must have been a tempting siren. However, a cold, calculated air now spoiled her charm. Eliza judged Madame Evangeline to be Lily's only real rival. If the medium changed her hair style and wore a more revealing gown, even Freddy's eye might wander. Certainly, Philippe seemed to enjoy speaking with Madame Evangeline. Maybe because she was fluent in his language. She seemed pleased by his rapt attention, too. But Eliza had no idea what they were now discussing in their rapid-fire French.

That left the countess, who had not inherited the good looks of her younger brother Richard. Instead, she was saddled with a high forehead, receding chin, a long nose and large teeth. Eliza found her profile remarkably horse-like. Even her dark blonde hair, coiled and pinned behind her head, resembled a thick horse's tail. The saving grace was her figure. Tall for a woman, with wide hips, she had a buxom bosom and a small waist. She also boasted dainty feet, which tonight were shown to advantage in gold embroidered slippers that matched her silk and lace gown.

"Miss Doolittle?" Lady Annabel waved a hand to catch Eliza's attention. "Is it true you support women's suffrage?"

"Oh yes, I've attended quite a few rallies with my friend Sybil."

"I don't see how you can join those awful women," Clara said with a shudder. "They've thrown bricks through windows at Westminster, and burned post boxes."

"Indeed," the countess said. "What if you are arrested, Miss Doolittle?"

"They'll have to catch me first," Eliza replied. "And I run nearly as fast as the racehorse I own. Especially if the police are after me."

"*Guter Gott,*" Count Rudolf muttered.

"But if they did catch you," his wife insisted, "they'd jail you. Of course, the primitive conditions in prison might not be so different from life in Whitechapel. Is that not where you are from, Miss Doolittle?"

Lady Annabel jumped to her defense before Eliza could react to such a rude comment. "I find it admirable that she supports such a noble cause," Annabel said. "As do I. Life as a woman in the literary arts also has its challenges."

"Noble cause?" The countess sniffed. "It's hardly noble to be trampled to death at the Derby. Or to be force fed in prison, like geese tortured to make liver paté."

Eliza raised an eyebrow at her. "Is it more noble to let men have the final say in everything, as if women are as stupid as geese?"

"Some women *are* as stupid as geese," Count Rudolf said. "And as silly."

"And some men are thoughtless, selfish brutes," Eliza shot back.

"I'd advise everyone not to debate Miss Doolittle," Higgins said with a wry grin. "She'll win."

"Can we please not talk about the suffragists?" Clara asked.

Richard looked over at Philippe. "Some of our guests may not be aware Mr. Corbet broke the world speed record."

"*C'est vrai*, but it is Louis Bierot who crosses the Channel first. I did hope to attempt such a feat, but it is *difficile* to obtain funds."

"Your speed record is more impressive, Monsieur," Madame Evangeline said.

"I saw your flight at Juvisy-sur-Orge, south of Paris, where you broke the speed record," Lady Annabel added. "Most exciting."

The Frenchman gave another slight shrug. "Such records will be broken by other aviators, and soon."

"Let us not forget that people may prefer to travel by zeppelins, which are faster than the fastest train," Count Rudolf said. "Germany has proven their reliability."

"Is that so?" Higgins asked. "I believe inclement weather caused the deaths of several zeppelin crew members of the Imperial Navy. Their airship was blown down into the North Sea during a storm, or did you not see that report in the newspapers?"

"A chance accident, Herr Higgins. Something no one could predict."

"But any windstorm or lightning strike could cripple a zeppelin far easier than it could a train. To say nothing of passengers in the zeppelin gondolas, who must bundle themselves in fur coats and blankets to keep warm."

Count Rudolf glowered at him. "All travelers suffer inconveniences. After crossing the Channel on the way here, my wife and I were treated to a wretched dinner in Dover. Dry Cornish hen, stale bread, a port wine as flat as the Rhine. And the car we hired broke down thirty miles into the journey. A British car, I might add. You'd never see that happening with a German motor wagon manufactured by Mr. Benz."

"Now, now, gentlemen," Lady Annabel interrupted. "It appears zeppelins are as perilous a topic as women's suffrage." For the first time at dinner, she addressed Clara. "Did you enjoy Paris, Lady Ashmore?"

"Oh yes!" Clara visibly perked up at being called by her title. "So romantic."

With childlike enthusiasm, she described how she climbed the steps of Montmartre to see the city spread below. Eliza had already heard the details of the Paris trip after lunch. She and Clara had stolen some time away together, although much of their conversation focused on Clara's fear of her formidable sister-in-law.

Eliza didn't dare tell Clara that she and Higgins had wanted to return to London. Nor did she reveal the warning Madame Evangeline had given them. A warning Higgins dismissed, but Eliza took to heart. How could she leave poor Clara to deal with whatever disaster might be threatening everyone? So Eliza persuaded Higgins into remaining at Banfield Manor, too. With luck, he would forgive her one day. Although Clara's endless description of her Paris visit now made Eliza regret staying.

Lady Annabel must have shared her opinion because she changed the topic. "Is it true that you and Miss Doolittle have solved several juicy murders?" she asked Higgins. "Do tell us all about them."

"That is not a suitable dinner table subject," Count Rudolf remarked.

"I agree," said Higgins. He bent forward in order to catch the eye of Madame Evangeline "Madame, I am curious as to your origins. I can usually pinpoint a speech pattern within a few minutes, but yours intrigues me. Where are you from?"

"I am a citizen of the world. I have lived in many places."

"We met Madame in Paris at a soiree," Richard said, "She gave a most convincing demonstration of table tipping."

"Oh yes, we were all thrilled," Clara added. "And a little bit frightened. One of the guests refused to believe Madame had tipped the table without tricks. He tried to lift it himself, but failed. Not even Madame's manservant could lift it, and he is quite strong."

"That manservant of yours seems an interesting fellow, too," Higgins said. "His name, Zoltan Batur, is a common one in the Ottoman Empire. However, I heard him speak with the butler this afternoon. His accent does not sound especially Turkish. Has he lived in Egypt?"

"I believe he spent his boyhood in Cairo and Alexandria," she replied.

"Why do you employ such an odd-looking fellow?" the countess inquired. "Most ladies are accompanied by a maid."

"I am a widow who travels widely. Some of the places I visit require protection, especially as a woman. Zoltan Batur is my bodyguard."

"I have never heard of such a thing," the count said. "And certainly not on the Continent. Although if you travel to the Middle East, you might well need protection."

"I knew an archaeologist who was killed in Mesopotamia," Sir Anthony said with grim satisfaction. "And all because someone didn't like the way he drank his coffee."

"That doesn't make sense at all," Eliza said.

"It does if you have been to Mesopotamia," he snapped. "Which is why I understand Madame Evangeline employing a manservant to protect her. He seems a fellow well able to defend himself, too."

Madame Evangeline nodded. "He has many skills, from

fencing and stick fighting to wrestling. Zoltan has helped me avert disaster several times."

"You mentioned disaster when you arrived this afternoon," Higgins said. "I've been curious about that. Why did you warn Eliza and me not to leave?"

She looked surprised. "Excuse me? I did what?"

"You said that if we left the house party, it would lead to disaster," Higgins said.

"And that death and darkness surrounded this house," Eliza added.

A gasp went up from the other guests.

Madame Evangeline grew paler than usual. "But I have no memory of saying any such thing. I must have fallen into a trance."

"A trance?" Eliza asked.

"Yes. It comes upon me at unexpected times."

"You fall in and out of trances?" Higgins looked amused. "Seems most inconvenient."

"Seems like bloody nonsense," Sir Anthony grumbled.

"My gifts are a mystery even to me." Madame Evangeline said, unmoved by their reactions.

"Oh, what does it matter?" the countess said. "You are a guest at Banfield Manor, madam. And my husband and I are honored to have you here."

"Richard and I are, too," Clara said in a small voice.

"If trouble does befall us," the countess continued, ignoring that remark, "it can be laid at the feet of my sister-in-law."

"I don't understand what you are talking about." Eliza was at the end of her patience.

"She invited Madame Evangeline without my approval, Miss Doolittle, and I was not informed until this morning. Such rudeness is unforgivable. It has put me in a difficult position as hostess. After all, if our remaining guest, Mr. Pentwater, had arrived on time, think of the social disaster that would have taken place tonight."

"What the devil do you mean, Louise?" Richard demanded.

Calling his sister by her first name revealed how irritated he was. Eliza hoped this didn't descend into a family argument. She had enough of that whenever she visited her father and Rose.

"I can explain." Madame Evangeline's distinctive voice held everyone's attention. "When Mr. Pentwater arrives, our number will be thirteen."

"Thirteen at the dinner table is an unlucky number," Clara said with obvious dismay. "How awful. What if it leads to the death and darkness you spoke of?"

"Superstitious claptrap," Higgins reassured her. "Besides, this Pentwater fellow may never turn up."

The butler appeared behind the countess's chair. "I beg your pardon, but an American gentleman has arrived. A Mr. Dwight Pentwater."

"Oh no!" Clara glanced at her husband. "What shall we do?"

"Set another place," Higgins said with a grin. "Our thirteenth guest has arrived."

CHAPTER 8

*D*wight Pentwater surveyed the room and its occupants with the typical brash regard of an American. Higgins judged him an American with means, however. His three piece lounge suit of dark gray wool looked bespoke, and his silk necktie boasted a jeweled stud. But despite his elegant suit, Pentwater seemed careless of his appearance.

His wavy, light brown hair reached past his collar and looked as if he hadn't bothered to comb it all day. Pentwater's goatee and mustache were also untrimmed, giving the impression of a shaggy animal. A lean and hungry animal, too, to paraphrase Shakespeare. It made Higgins curious. And wary.

Count von Weisinger rose to his feet in welcome, followed by the other gentleman. Except for Higgins. He'd been adjusting his sling and didn't get the chance to stand before everyone sat down again.

"Perhaps, Mr. Pentwater, you'd first like to change upstairs?" the countess asked.

"Thank you, no." He nodded at Higgins. "Glad to see one of the gentlemen here isn't in evening clothes either. So I won't be the only guest who's not dressed for dinner."

"I confess I'm not normally one to dress for dinner. Seems a waste of time." Higgins pointed at his sling. "But I have a legitimate excuse. There's a plaster cast on my broken arm. Can't fit my best tailcoats over the damned thing, which means I don't have to get decked out like a penguin."

The American laughed. "I have an excuse as well. I'm starving. Haven't had a bite since lunch. English pork pie, as cold and tough as Lizzie Borden's heart."

The countess looked mortified by both Higgins and Pentwater.

Pentwater nodded his thanks when the butler directed a footman to set another place next to Lily Marlowe. Oddly enough, the actress didn't look pleased; she avoided the man's easy smile, keeping her eyes fixed on Freddy. Then again, Pentwater's smile appeared rather lupine, like a hungry wolf sizing up a tasty lamb.

The next course was brought in, ironically a lamb cutlet, as the countess introduced each guest sitting around the table to Pentwater.

"How rude," Lady Annabel murmured to Higgins. "He ought to have forgone dinner, arriving so late. But we shouldn't expect much from an American. I spent several years in the States. Most of them possess the manners of Irish urchins."

"I've enjoyed pleasant encounters with Americans, even if they do mangle the English language. And they make delightful dinner companions. Far more enjoyable than a doddering duke, or a marchioness with too many jewels and not enough brains."

"You're being perverse, Henry." Lady Annabel turned her attention to the cutlet with mint sauce on her plate.

"How did you injure your arm?" Pentwater said. "Sorry, sir. I've forgotten your name."

Higgins looked up. "Henry Higgins. Professor of phonetics. And I broke my arm in a motoring accident in Putney." He nodded at Eliza. "Despite what Miss Doolittle may tell you, it was not my fault. I turned the corner and was met with an unhitched wagon in the middle of the road. Impossible to avoid crashing into it with my roadster."

"What a rum piece of luck," Pentwater said.

"He was also driving at about a hundred miles an hour," Eliza put in.

"Don't listen to her. I pushed my Hudson Mile-A-Minute to sixty that day."

Pentwater whistled. "You have an American roadster. Good choice. And a Hudson, too. What year?"

"The 1912 model manufactured in Detroit." Higgins lifted a forkful of tender lamb. "Bright blue color, too. Can't miss it on the road."

"A pity it was destroyed in the crash," Lady Annabel said with a sigh.

"The devil it was. Even as we speak, my roadster's undergoing repairs at Scotland Yard. Eliza's cousin works for the Metropolitan Police and he suggested their mechanics work on it. A detective plans to bring it here once it's finished, hopefully before the end of the week." He frowned. "I do miss my Hudson."

"He's mad for motorcars," Eliza said. "Sometimes, I think he's just plain mad."

"Insolent cabbage leaf," Higgins said under his breath.

"I do hope I'm at Banfield Manor when your car is delivered," Pentwater said. "That model Hudson is my favorite. The three-speed manual gearbox is a wonder."

"Have little interest in motorcars myself. I let my chauffeur deal with the Rolls." Sir Anthony sat back. "Now what brings you to England, Mr. Pentwater?"

"Business with the count. And others. I run a financial consulting firm, but also invest in companies that need an infusion of cash. Many I buy outright in order to improve their management and production. I've got my eye on a shipping firm in Leeds."

"It is my wish that you stay away from aviation," Philippe Corbet said.

The American seemed confused by his statement. "Why should I? Anyone who doesn't try to make a buck in aviation is a fool. Tons of money to be made."

"Money is not everything," Philippe replied. "Or perhaps a businessman such as yourself does not understand that."

Pentwater gave him a suspicious look. "Are you being rude? Or simply French?"

"Monsieur Corbet holds the world speed record in aviation," Richard explained.

"Well done," Pentwater said. "I may invest my money in building an aeroplane faster than anyone has ever seen. You might fly one of my aeroplanes someday."

"That is a thing I will never do." Philippe turned to Madame Evangeline.

Pentwater's expression wavered between confusion and anger. Higgins didn't blame him. Why did Philippe seem so hostile to the American?

"I wish you had called ahead, Mr. Pentwater," Clara said. "We could have waited dinner." She gave him a proud smile. "We have a telephone in its own little closet, and anyone can call us. Isn't it the most modern thing?"

"Don't know how I'd do business without a telephone," Pentwater agreed.

Polite conversation continued while the footmen brought in the next course, a joint of roast venison, accompanied by caramelized onions and diced butternut squash. Higgins realized he'd have a difficult time cutting up the tougher meat, given his injury. And he'd rather cut off his arm than ask for help. He didn't have to. Lady Annabel reached over and swiftly sliced his venison.

Embarrassed, he muttered, "Thank you."

"You're welcome, Henry," she said in a low, seductive voice. "After all, someone must look after your needs."

Higgins wanted to sink through the floor. He also wanted to pour his flute of champagne over Eliza's head for forcing him to stay at Banfield Manor.

"I hear you have an interest in moving pictures as well, Mr. Pentwater," Countess von Weisinger said. "Have you invested in any?"

"Yes. Eight. Or is it nine? They've all paid off more than expected, especially the ones I had a hand in at Vitograph Studios. But Miss Marlowe can tell you more about that. She starred in several." Pentwater glanced over at Lily.

The actress ignored him and continued her whispered conversation with Freddy. But Higgins knew she'd heard Pentwater by the way she held herself. Stiff, defensive. Possibly even fearful. What was going on? Why would both Lily Marlowe and Philippe Corbet act so antagonistic toward the American?

"Then you and Miss Marlowe know each other?" Lady Annabel asked.

"I visited the studio whenever I could. Sometimes I was there at the same time she was performing." He shot Lily another amused look. "We were together this past April when the Woolworth Building opened in Manhattan. To help celebrate the completion of the tallest building in the world, several famous people were invited to appear. Miss Marlowe was one of them."

"Is that true?" Eliza asked. "What fun. I read about the Woolworth and it sounds amazing. A building sixty stories high."

"With over five thousand windows," Pentwater added. "I took the elevator all the way to the top. And yes, before you ask, the Woolworth does seem to scrape the sky."

This caught Freddy's attention. "Did you go to the top of the Woolworth Building, too, Lily?"

She sat silent, a stubborn set to her jaw. "Yes," Lily finally said.

"What did you think?" he asked.

"Some buildings rise too high." She picked up her goblet. "Some men do as well."

Pentwater grinned. "On that cryptic note..."

"Is it true you helped finance one of Will Barker's Bulldog Films, Mr. Pentwater?" Richard asked. "The one called *Sixty Years A Queen*. I hear they're filming it at Ealing Studios in west London."

"I only dabble in film. George Samuelson financed that, not me. A pity American audiences won't be able to see it when it opens next month." Pentwater ate the last of his cutlet. "Blame Thomas Edison, who's muddied things up with his patent lawsuits. It's a long and complicated story. Doesn't concern me any longer."

"Lost your interest in cinema, have you?" Sir Anthony remarked. "Don't know how. Beautiful young actresses like Miss Marlowe would seem to be attraction enough. Who cares about patents when pretty girls decorate the screen?"

Lily pointed her fork at Sir Anthony. "Actresses are also talented. Unless you think any old person can be dragged in front of a camera and move an audience to tears or laughter. I'd like to see you try, Mr. Explorer. You'd be as lost in front of the camera as you were in that jungle."

Higgins and Eliza burst into laughter. Freddy snatched up Lily's hand, which still clutched the fork, and kissed it. But she pulled away.

"Enough, honey. Let a girl finish her dinner."

Pentwater raised his wine glass. "That should teach everyone not to mess with anyone from Brooklyn."

She finally smiled and exchanged a knowing look with Pentwater, which aroused Higgins's curiosity further. Sir Anthony resumed eating, muttering under his breath.

"This dinner is pretty swell, Baron Ashmore," Pentwater said. "Only I was hoping to see game hen on the table."

Higgins thought someone should have told Pentwater that the correct way to address his host was "Lord Ashmore." Although rich American businessmen probably cared as little about such things as former Cockney flower sellers did.

"The shooting begins tomorrow," Richard replied. "We'll be after hares. Later in the week, we'll take to the fields for grouse and pheasant. Our dinners will include whatever we bag during the day."

"Looking forward to it," Pentwater said. "Always did like pheasant."

Count Rudolf pushed his empty plate away. A footman quickly removed it. "A shame we are not on my estate in Bavaria. This is the season for hunting stag."

"These English country house shoots are famous for the number of kills," the American said. "I look forward to bagging more game than you gents."

Higgins let his attention wander while the conversation dwelt on bagging birds and skinning deer. An unappetizing dinner table subject. He didn't perk up again until he heard a comment by Richard Ashmore.

"—about that cricketer being killed. Samuel Cody's float-plane broke up over Hampshire," Richard was saying to Philippe Corbet. Higgins turned to hear more.

"Flying aeroplanes does seem a risky endeavor," Lady Annabel said.

"Every new technology has its problems," Pentwater said. "People forget there were plenty of boiler explosions when trains first began to run."

"Cody hoped to win the five thousand pound prize in the Daily Mail race that day," Richard said. "He'd flown his bi-plane several times without any trouble."

"I wonder if the craft had a structural weakness," Sir Anthony mused.

"*C'est possible*. No matter how careful we are, *la situation* cannot always be controlled. The worst does happen." Corbet bowed his head. "So it was with Henri Vennard. His plane fails off the coast of France, between Calais and Dieppe. I am sorry to say *mon ami s'est noye*. My friend drowns."

"How horrible," Eliza said. "Didn't your friend know how to swim?"

"*Mais oui*, but one must survive the crash before one can swim to safety." He paused. "The aeroplane breaks into many pieces."

"And no one found his body?" Eliza asked.

"*Non*," Corbet said stiffly. "Many ships went searching. Nothing is found." Higgins tried to recall anything he'd read about this accident. "Was the weather a factor? Storms come up fast as lightning over the sea."

"It is not the weather. Henri's aeroplane fails him." His expression grew grim. "Or rather, the men who manufacture the aeroplane. They are responsible."

"Lots of people have a hand in building trains, motorcars and aeroplanes," Pentwater said. "Hard to figure out exactly who's to blame if something goes wrong."

"Sometimes." Philippe drained his wine. "Other times it is not difficult at all."

Footmen delivering dishes of apple crumbles, a variety of cheddar and other cheeses, plus savarins with Chantilly cream, interrupted this somber conversation. This was followed by iced plates topped with tiny glass cups of pink sherbet shaped like a rose. Trays of fruit and nuts finished the dessert course.

"Delicious," Lady Annabel said, although she'd barely touched any of the desserts. "An exquisite dinner, Lady Ashmore."

"Thank you." Clara sounded forlorn.

The countess rose to her feet. "If the ladies will join me for coffee in the drawing room, we'll leave the gentlemen to their after dinner conversation."

Lady Annabel did as requested, followed by the other women. Freddy looked like an abandoned puppy when Lily left. Higgins almost expected him to whimper.

Count Rudolf signaled for brandy and cigars, but Higgins refused to smoke. He preferred his pipe, a comfortable armchair, and wittier companions. Instead, Higgins nursed his brandy while the others discussed the unrest in Ireland and the recently approved Army Expansion bill in Germany—which the count supported, and the others opposed.

Something about a stolen ancient artifact caught his ear. Philippe Corbet flicked ash from his cigar. "Whoever this thief is—"

"There's been no confirmation that the tip of the spear was stolen," Count Rudolf said, "but if true, it must be returned immediately."

Richard chuckled. "About as likely as finding the Holy Grail."

"The whole thing sounds made up." Pentwater laughed. "I've certainly never heard of this so-called Holy Lance."

"I have," Higgins said. Everyone seemed startled. It was the first thing he'd said since brandy and cigars were served. "It's also known as the Spear of Destiny and the Spear of Longinus."

"Who is this Longinus?" Philippe asked.

"Legend claims one of the Roman centurions at the crucifixion of Jesus was called Longinus. He was the soldier who pierced the side of Jesus with his lance. The lance is said to still be in existence."

"My father was a lover of ancient history, so I heard this story as a boy," Richard said. "I dreamed of finding the spear one day and presenting it to the Crown." He laughed. "Savior of the country and all that."

Pentwater shook his head. "I'm still stumped."

"Some people believe whoever is in possession of the Sword of Longinus will rule the world," Higgins explained. "That's why it's also referred to as the Spear of Destiny. Of course the lance is no longer in one piece." He shrugged. "After all, it would be nearly two thousand years old. And subjected to a lot of wear and tear during that time." Higgins took a sip of brandy. "I only know this because I had a classics teacher at Eton with a whimsical turn of mind."

"Are you saying this ancient lance is still floating around?" Pentwater asked.

"Pieces of it," the count said. "In Rome, Vienna, the Holy Land."

Sir Anthony snickered. "With enough pieces spread about, dozens of countries could rule the world."

"One needs the entire spear for such a thing to occur," the count said.

"There are other legendary objects rumored to confer power," Richard informed them. "The sword of Excalibur, the Golden Fleece, the cross of Charlemagne, David's Harp."

The count and Sir Anthony now returned the conversation to politics, specifically the intransigence of Montenegro in the Balkans. Higgins yawned and glanced at the clock. Only half past nine, but he was ready for bed. He stood, prompting a restless Freddy to also rise to his feet.

"Gentlemen, if you'll excuse me," Higgins said. "It's been a long day."

"Already?" Richard asked. "But I forget you are recuperating. I envy you. The rest of us will soon discover what parlor games my wife and sister have planned for our entertainment."

"I hear the piano." Freddy looked like he was about to swoon. "That must be Lily singing. Isn't she marvelous? I think she sounds as good as Ada Crossley."

Sir Anthony and Richard raised their eyebrows at that. Miss Crossley was one of the most gifted singers of the age. Higgins quickly exited the dining room before Freddy subjected them to more insane drivel about Lily. He also looked forward to the peace and quiet of his bed. But after climbing the stairs, he let out a yowl as his foot hit a narrow table along the hallway's wall.

"Professor, is that you?" Eliza stuck her head out of one of the bedrooms. She had changed into her favorite dressing gown, the one with the Oriental print. Her long hair now hung in a braid down her back.

He gritted his teeth while the pain in his stubbed toe subsided. "Why aren't you with the others in the drawing room?"

"As if I want to listen to Lily Marlowe sing for the next hour, then watch her dance the turkey trot with Freddy. I brought lots of fashion magazines to read this week. Along with a marvelous new novel called *The Mystery of Dr. Fu-Manchu*. I need to relax after being at your beck and call since the accident. Although I feel bad that Sybil is still playing nursemaid to Jack. I hope his leg heals soon."

"I hope my arm heals quickly too, because it's giving me fits." Higgins squinted at the oak door. "What's the name of the bedroom they put you in. I'm in Mallard."

"Mine's Sparrow. I don't know why all these bedrooms are named after birds. There's not a single thing involving birds inside."

"Some baronial birdbrain probably came up with the idea."

"What about the hunt? You can't possibly shoot with your arm in a sling."

"I'll decide in the morning. For now I need to collapse into bed. Good night."

Higgins lurched past her, heading to the end of the hall. When he reached the Mallard bedroom, Higgins twisted the brass knob with a relieved sigh. Luckily, a footman had unpacked his luggage.

He groped for the light switch, but couldn't find it. Higgins fumbled his way to the wardrobe in the dark and found his dressing gown. He struggled out of his sling and tweed coat, loosened his tie and undid his shirt collar. Before he could don his dressing gown, a whooshing sound startled him, as if a match had been struck. Candlelight suddenly glowed behind him. Next, he heard linens rustling. He slowly turned.

Annabel smiled coyly from the middle of the enormous four-poster bed, looking comfortable under the bedcovers. She nestled against the feather pillows plumped against the massive headboard. Her coppery hair tumbled over one bare shoulder.

"High time you arrived, Henry. I hoped you would retire early."

"Have you lost your bloody mind, woman?" Afraid Sir Anthony would find his wife in Higgins's bed, he pointed to the door. "Get your clothes on and leave. Now! Before your husband discovers you are not where you belong."

"Is that all you're worried about?"

"Madame, you are trying my patience. Go."

"I don't see why I should. My husband will not be looking for me." She laughed softly. "You ought to see how funny your eyes look. As if they're ready to pop out of the sockets, but surely you've seen a woman in your bed."

Anger now rose in him. "If you don't leave of your own volition, I shall physically throw you out of that bed."

"I'd like to see you try with a broken arm," she replied in a purring tone, "Henry, be a sport and let's have some fun. But silly me. I should have realized you need help undressing with that arm of yours." Annabel slid out of bed, letting the covers fall behind her. The woman was stark naked!

Higgins flattened himself against the wardrobe. If her husband chose to come looking for his wife. . .

Cursing under his breath, he fled into the hallway and rushed to Eliza's room. Higgins pounded against the carving of two birds on a branch. Eliza flung the door open.

"What is it now?" She looked exasperated. "Don't tell me there's another fire."

"You must come deal with her. I cannot. She is simply impossible. Found her in my bed, naked as Lady Godiva. Her husband may come upstairs any moment, and that red-haired madwoman refuses to leave. Eliza, you must throw Lady Annabel out."

Eliza doubled over with laughter.

"Quiet. I don't want anyone else to hear us. And this isn't funny."

She tried to get her laughter under control. "Actually, it is."

"Eliza, please." Higgins wasn't often heartfelt or reduced to begging for favors. But he'd get down on his knees if it would do the trick.

"Blimey, you are upset." Eliza patted him on the shoulder. "Don't worry. I'll handle this."

Tightening the belt on her dressing gown, Eliza marched down to his bedroom. He followed a few paces behind. When they entered his room, Lady Annabel was once more languishing beneath the covers. She looked stunned to see Eliza.

"Miss Doolittle, what are you doing here?"

Eliza braced her hands on her hips. "Lord, love a duck! You 'ave nerve, Lady Annabel, I'll give you that. And no shame bein' in yer Adam and Eve's togs, to boot!"

"You assured me that you and Henry weren't an item," she hissed. Higgins peered over Eliza's shoulder.

"And so we ain't," Eliza retorted. "That doesn't mean you can come waltzin' into any gent's bed like some Whitechapel light-skirt. You're off yer chump, you are. Now listen, 'cause I'll not be sayin' it twice. He don't want you, Lady A. That should be clear as mud."

"But it was the countess's idea to put me right across the hall—"

"Save it. I'm bettin' you asked her to do that ten minutes

after you got here. Now move yer bloomin' arse and find yer own bed."

"I won't!"

"Think you got 'im by the bollocks, do you?" Eliza took her by the wrist and pulled her off the bed. Lady Annabel let out a shriek.

"Keep quiet or you'll have everyone up here," Higgins warned, his nerves strained to the breaking point.

Eliza snatched the woman's clothing from a reclining chair. "Take these and get out. Now! Otherwise I'll be callin' Professor Higgins's friend at the *Times*. I'm thinking he'd like a juicy bit of gossip about a famous explorer's wife."

Lady Annabel bit her lip. "You wouldn't."

"I would." Eliza gestured toward the door. "Now use yer loaf and get along with you. Go on. Toodle pip!"

With her clothes clutched to her chest, Lady Annabel ran out of the room. Higgins held his breath until he heard a door slam.

He finally relaxed. "You're a wonder, Eliza. What would I do without you?"

"In this instance, I believe you would have been at the mercy of Lady Annabel."

"Thank you."

"You're welcome. Although I do admit it was fun to act like a proper Cockney cabbage again."

"More like an improper one." Higgins shot her a grateful smile.

"Go to sleep. You need it. You also need a little light in here." Eliza walked to the night table and switched on the lamp. "Lord, she even lit candles for you. Lady Annabel seems a hopeless romantic."

"Hopeless, for certain." Higgins sat on the edge of the bed, exhausted. "I could sleep for days, but now I'll have to rise at dawn."

"Why?"

Higgins looked at her in disbelief. "You don't think I can stay behind while the men go off shooting? Not with Lady Annabel in the house."

"Be careful and try not to get shot." She laughed again. "But knowing you, you'd prefer that to facing a love-struck Lady Annabel again."

"You know me too well, Eliza." He sighed. "Too well."

CHAPTER 9

*F*or the first time in her life, Eliza regretted not being a married woman. The sentiment had nothing to do with romance. The talkative maid sent to dress her hair this morning informed Eliza that married ladies were not expected to come down to breakfast at country house parties. Instead, they stayed warm and cozy beneath the covers as toast and tea were served to them in bed. But unmarried women had to get themselves to the breakfast room between nine and half past ten. And the only other unmarried female guest at Banfield Manor was Lily Marlowe.

Eliza gritted her teeth at the prospect of sharing a meal with the woman who was now the object of Freddy's rabid attention. And what if Freddy had preferred to stay with Lily instead of joining the hunting party? That prospect sank her spirits further. Glancing out the windows as she walked through the drawing room, she noticed the skies matched her gray and dank mood.

Higgins probably felt worse. After discovering Annabel in his bed, he chose to watch men shoot furry animals rather than remain behind with the ladies—especially *that* lady.

Eliza heard Lily give a tinkling laugh, echoed by a much deeper one. So Freddy was here. Pasting a smile on her face, Eliza breezed into the breakfast room. She welcomed the warmth from the fire crackling in the fireplace along the far wall. Banfield Manor held almost as many drafty corners as it did rooms. She suspected the manor house grew as chilly in winter as her shabby Angel Court flat where she'd lived during her flower selling days.

Lily and Freddy sat at the table, heads bent together as if sharing some private joke. They were so caught up with each other, they didn't even see her.

Eliza took one of the plates stacked on the oak sideboard. Her stomach growled at the sight of kippered herring, toast, curried eggs, sliced ham, fried bacon, mushrooms, cranberry muffins, and tea cakes. Embossed trays held pears, apples and grapes artfully arranged. A silver coffee urn sat on an adjacent tiered table, the aroma of fresh coffee permeating the air. While Lily and Freddy continued their whispered conversation, Eliza heaped food upon her plate, certain today would try both her stamina and her patience.

A footman standing at attention near the window cleared his throat. "If you require tea or hot cocoa, miss, it can be brought up."

"Thank you, no. Coffee will do just fine."

"There you are, Miss Doolittle," Lily sang out. "Freddy and I worried you might miss breakfast." She seemed especially animated this morning: eyes sparkling, cheeks rosy, lipstick expertly applied to her bow-shaped mouth. And the turquoise bandeau wound through her dark curls matched the color of her day dress. She looked even prettier than she had yesterday. Eliza wanted to strangle her with that bandeau. Then do the same to Freddy.

Eliza chose a seat as far away from them as possible. "The

maid informed me this was an informal breakfast. And that we didn't need to all eat at the same time."

"Seems rather a neat excuse for everyone to be lazy." Freddy chuckled. "We thought you'd never get yourself out of bed."

Eliza rolled her eyes at the "we" both of them were using. A cozy couple already. Would wedding banns be read next? She felt irritated and disappointed. Most of all, she felt jealous. Only she didn't know if her feelings were hurt—or her pride.

"I don't understand your concern. It's barely half past nine." Eliza unfurled her linen napkin with a snap, then placed it on her lap. "Besides, I'm sure the married ladies won't stir from their beds until after ten. Knowing Clara, it could be much later than that."

"Oh, but you're mistaken, Miss Doolittle." Lily flashed a dimpled smile. "The countess left for the hunt this morning with the men. At a gruesome hour, too. I heard her in the hallway outside my room asking that guns for both her and the count be readied. She also yelled at some poor servant for not polishing her walking boots. What a battle-axe."

"Lady Annabel went hunting, too," Freddy added.

"Lady Annabel decided to take part in the hunt?" Eliza asked. If true, Higgins might end up turning a gun on himself.

"Yes, she came down to the breakfast room for coffee and a tea cake," Lily said. "All dressed up in the sweetest gray walking suit. Said she felt cooped up in the house and thought the hunt might amuse her."

"She mentioned she'd like to try her hand at shooting. But I think she was joking. The lady doesn't seem the sporting type." Freddy sliced the kipper on his plate in half.

"I think she prefers stalking men, not rabbits," Lily announced. "That woman is a born flirt. I saw how she kept looking at Professor Higgins during dinner last night. A bit scandalous, with her husband right there."

"Haven't you heard the tales about English country house

parties?" Freddy winked at her. "People love to sneak into each other's beds at night. Like a game of musical chairs. And who knows where everyone ends up once the music stops?" He took Lily's hand. "I know where I plan to be when that happens, Lily."

"And what if my door is locked?" she teased.

"I shall break it down of course." He kissed her hand.

Eliza considered sticking a fork in Freddy's back. "From what I witnessed at dinner, it looks like Freddy might have competition from Mr. Pentwater." Actually, Pentwater had shown Lily little attention last night, but anything that upset Freddy seemed worth the effort.

Freddy turned to her, puzzled. "Mr. Pentwater?"

"I don't know what you mean," Lily said. "He and I barely know each other."

Eliza spread butter on her muffin. "You're both American, both from New York City. He also told us that he helped finance several of your films."

"That means nothing," she protested. "You heard him brag about his business ventures at dinner. He invests in lots of things. As for my motion pictures, Dwight is simply one of many investors in Vitograph Studios."

"Dwight?" Eliza raised an eyebrow. "You're on a first name basis?"

Freddy asked, "Lily, are you and Mr. Pentwater an item?"

"Don't be silly. I've met him a few times when he visited the studio in Brooklyn. And why shouldn't I call him by his first name? Americans aren't as stuffy as you Brits. Besides, he's not anyone important like D.W. Griffith. Dwight is just another money grubbing American. My country is filled with them." Lily's laugh sounded mocking.

"I'm relieved to hear you and Pentwater aren't involved romantically," Freddy said.

"Don't be crazy. The man is married with two children. Or is it three?" Lily shrugged. "Even if he were single, I wouldn't find him attractive. He's short and skinny, his nose is too long, and he needs to trim his hair. It hangs past his collar. Makes him look like a Bowery hobo." She stroked Freddy's smooth cheek. "I prefer tall, blond, muscular men with blue eyes and dreamy English accents."

"You darling girl," he murmured.

But Eliza wasn't done upsetting their apple cart. "If you and Mr. Pentwater are little more than acquaintances, why did the countess invite both of you to the house party?"

"What do you mean?" There was an edge in Lily's voice now.

Eliza ate a roasted mushroom before replying. "I'd understand Clara asking a cinema star to the party. She's young and modern and enjoys someone exciting to liven things up. But she and Richard told me that his sister handled the invitations, except for Madame Evangeline. So why did the countess ask you and Mr. Pentwater?"

Her expression remained innocent. "Didn't the count mention that he had business dealings with Mr. Pentwater?"

"That doesn't explain why the countess invited you. After all, there are lots of English cinema actresses she might have asked instead."

"I say, Eliza, what is this all about?" Freddy asked.

"I'm curious about how the guest list was compiled."

"I don't think curiosity has anything to do with it. I believe you're jealous." Lily cocked her head. "Freddy led me to believe that you and he were friends, nothing more. However, given how you've acted toward me, I'm guessing it was more than friendship."

"On his part, certainly. Or hasn't he told you how many times he's asked me to marry him?" Eliza looked at Freddy, who scowled. "And that I turned down each proposal."

She could see this surprised Lily. "Is that true, Freddy?"

"I admit I lost my head over Eliza for a time. When she wants to, she can be a charmer," he said, clearly exasperated.

"But she cares far more about playing detective and being an independent woman. I believe she cares about a certain Scotland Yard detective as well. A chap she's known a lot less time than she's known me."

"Colin Ramsey and I are nothing more than friends." Eliza felt her cheeks burn.

"As Lily and I are," Freddy shot back.

Eliza and Freddy glared at each other for a tense moment. The only sound in the breakfast room was the crackling of the fire.

Lily stood up. "I'm going upstairs to change. Lady Annabel had the right idea. I also need a bit of fresh air. I know we're supposed to wait to join the men for an outdoor luncheon, but listening to gunfire would be more fun than listening to the two of you bicker."

Freddy scrambled to his feet as she swept out the door. "Lily, wait!"

Eliza watched him run after her. The footman stepped to the table and cleared away the plates left by Lily and Freddy. She realized with a start that he had overheard the entire conversation. What secrets the servants must know. A pity the footman she recognized last night at dinner wasn't in the breakfast room with her. She'd love a chance to catch up on old times without the rest of the guests around.

"Excuse me," she said while he stacked empty cups. "Do you know where the footman called Charlie Kenton is? He and I are old friends."

The footman looked surprised. "Charlie is serving as valet to the American who arrived last night, miss. Mr. Pentwater did not bring a servant, and Lord Ashmore assigned Charlie the task of waiting upon the gentleman. I can inform Charlie that you'd like to speak with him, but he may be busy with his duties at the moment."

She smiled at him. "Please don't bother. I'm sure we'll find a chance to talk. Thank you."

"Of course, miss." After placing the plates and cups on a tray, he soundlessly left the room. She wondered if servants wore especially quiet shoes. Eliza also wondered why both Pentwater and Lily Marlowe were invited to this country house party. The count had business dealings with Pentwater, but no one brought up the reason for Lily's invitation. And Lily had avoided answering the question when Eliza asked her.

Eliza mused over this as she finished breakfast. Unlike the rest of Banfield Manor, the breakfast room felt warm and cozy. She could almost pretend she was mistress here. The sound of distant gunfire prompted her to look out the window. The stained glass prevented her from seeing anything but the mist shrouded outlines of shrubbery. A shame there was no sun today to make the colorful window glow.

A rustle of silk skirts broke her reverie as Madame Evangeline entered the breakfast room. She looked striking in a high neck dress of deep purple. She again wore her hair pulled back in a style more suited to Queen Victoria's time, but its severity was softened by an intricate amber comb.

"Good morning, Miss Doolittle. I hope I am not disturbing you."

"Not at all. Although I'm surprised to see you. I thought married women were served breakfast in bed."

"A foolish custom. The only people who should take meals in bed are invalids." Madame Evangeline inspected the sideboard before placing an apple and one slice of toast on a plate.

Since Eliza often woke up ravenous, she marveled that the spiritualist had so little appetite. The woman also required neither cream nor sugar in her coffee.

After Madame Evangeline took a seat across from her, she devoted her attention to peeling her apple with a paring knife. Eliza grew uncomfortable with the silence, but what did one talk about with a woman who spoke to the dead? If not for the occasional log falling in the dying fire, the room would be as silent as a tomb. A thought that sent a chill through Eliza.

Scrambling for a topic of conversation, Eliza finally spoke. "This is my favorite room at Banfield Manor. It's smaller than the others, with a much lower ceiling. Cozy for a manor house. I wonder why it's different that the others."

"I believe it is one of the few rooms that hasn't been tampered with since it was first built." Madame Evangeline waved her paring knife at the oak panel walls, leaded glass windows, and white plaster ceiling. "The style is known as Jacobean."

"Jacobean," Eliza repeated. "What does that mean?"

The woman turned her full attention on her now. Eliza felt nervous under the scrutiny of those unblinking slate blue eyes. "An era named after the Scottish King James, who later ruled England in the seventeenth century. My father schooled his children in history. Because he was Scottish, we were also instructed in the lives of the Stuarts." Madame Evangeline frowned. "Such an unlucky family. Ill-starred, every last one of them."

Eliza knew about the Stuarts. Colonel Pickering had given her a number of books about British history; she'd been especially moved by the tragic story of Mary, Queen of Scots.

"You don't sound Scottish."

"I'm not Scottish. My father is." Finished paring her apple, Madame Evangeline now cut it into crescent shaped slices. "Or was. He died a decade ago."

"Last night, Professor Higgins said you spoke like a woman who'd lived in a number of countries. You never mentioned which ones."

She nibbled at an apple slice. "Too many to name."

"France, for certain." Eliza might not be as expert as Higgins at gleaning a person's background from their speech, but she recognized the woman's hint of a French accent.

"I am often in Paris. And my mother was born and raised in North Africa. French Algiers. I spend a great deal of time there since I am fond of the desert. There are fewer spirits in the Sahara. It is why I feel at peace amid the shifting sands."

"My friend Colonel Pickering says the Sahara is positively scorching."

"It is. But I enjoy the sun and heat. I don't know how you live in such a cold country as England. The cold makes me uneasy."

Eliza grinned. "It only makes me want to put on a warmer dress."

"You don't understand. When the spirits of the dead are near, they chill the air with their presence. If one is sensitive to them—as I am—that makes it difficult to stay warm."

Although the fireplace had turned the room toasty, Eliza had felt chilled in every room in the house since last night. "When we feel cold, it's because a spirit is present?"

"Sometimes. But most people are not aware of the spirits who surround us." Madame Evangeline allowed herself a tiny smile. "If you feel cold this morning, I daresay it is due to the hoarfrost, and not a melancholy ghost."

"Are all ghosts melancholy?"

"Oh, no. Some are irritated. A few are convulsed with rage. Most spirits are confused because they do not understand how to get to the Other Side. I try to help them."

Eliza lowered her voice. "Are there any spirits in the room with us right now?"

Madame Evangeline shook her head. "We are quite alone for the moment. However, the ghost of a woman woke me last night. From her clothing I guessed she had lived during the time of the Prince Regent. She seemed unhappy to find me asleep in her bed. It took almost an hour to convince her to leave."

Eliza's mouth fell open. "I would have screamed my blooming head off. How did you not die of fright?"

She shrugged. "I am accustomed to it. On my way to the breakfast room just now, the spirit of a former servant walked past me. He seemed bent on still performing his duties and paid me no attention at all. It is possible he was not aware that I could see him. But I could, even down to his straw blond hair and crooked teeth."

"Blimey." Eliza sat back in dismay. She'd be looking over her shoulder every minute until she left Banfield Manor. And she'd never get to sleep tonight, not with the prospect of an annoyed spirit standing over her.

"Don't look so frightened, Miss Doolittle. If you have not yet encountered a visitor from the Great Beyond, it is unlikely you will start seeing them now."

"I wouldn't be so sure about that. Maybe I've never been in a place as haunted as Banfield Manor."

"Spirits are everywhere. Even at your London residence. On Wimpole Street, is it?"

Eliza got to her feet. "Please don't say that. And you've made me nervous to stay indoors. Especially with everyone at the shoot. I may walk out to the woods and join them."

Madame Evangeline's calm expression turned troubled. "That would be unwise."

"Why? Are there even more spirits in the forest?"

"No. But I sense danger." She closed her eyes. "Anger is in the air around us." Her voice dropped several octaves, almost as if a man were speaking, not her. "More than anger. A dark fury which ends in death. That fury lies waiting in the forest. A murderer awaits in the forest."

"Who's in danger?" Eliza grabbed Madame Evangeline by the shoulders. "And who is the murderer?"

The spiritualist's eyes fluttered, then opened. She looked at

Eliza with a surprised expression. "Why are you shaking me, Miss Doolittle?"

"You told me someone will be murdered in the forest! Who is it?"

"I said that?"

"Yes. Just now. How can you not remember?"

Madame Evangeline's gaze grew even sadder. "It is as I said at dinner. Professor Higgins asked why I announced that only you and he could prevent death and disaster from visiting this place. I don't recall saying that. Nor do I remember saying there is a murderer in the forest. My trances come upon me unexpectedly. I can neither control nor explain them."

"These things you say in your trances, do they ever come true?"

She paused. "Always."

"I need to tell Higgins. He might be the one in danger. Or perhaps Richard." Eliza bit her lip. "Or Freddy. He's out there now, too. I must warn them."

"It's too late, Miss Doolittle," she called after her.

Eliza paused in the doorway. "Has someone already been killed? Please tell me!"

"It is written."

"What? What is written?"

"Some events cannot be stopped. It is fate. Destiny." Madame Evangeline's severe expression and dark purple gown gave her the appearance of an angel of death.

"Of course we can stop it."

"No. Fate cannot be changed. Someone will be murdered in the forest."

In the four hours he'd been tramping about the forest, Higgins learned that hunting was even stupider than he guessed. The weather had turned cold and damp; it felt more like early winter than mid-October. And because the day began on a frosty note, a mist wafted among the trees, making it nearly impossible to discern a hare from a tree stump. Luckily, the gamekeeper, beaters, and loaders spotted the animals for them and instructed the gentlemen where to shoot. Otherwise the shooting party would likely have shot each other. Or one of the hunting dogs.

He was also grateful to the gamekeeper and his men since their speech patterns were the only ones of interest out here. The broad vowels and West Country cadence of one young fellow revealed that he hailed from the Forest of Dean. Higgins regretted not being able to spend more time conversing with him. Instead, he had to listen to Count von Weisinger order everyone about as if he were a Hapsburg general. Even worse, the countess had joined the party. Both never stopped complaining or shooting. Even with the gamekeeper's help, they had only bagged a dozen hares. But it had taken about two hundred shots to accomplish even that. Richard Ashmore seemed resigned to paying second fiddle to his sister and her husband, wandering off on his own like a young boy eager to run away from home.

Higgins felt no compunction to stay near either Ashmore or his dreadful relatives. He did enjoy an amusing hour with Philippe Corbet, who spoke in equally admiring terms of aeroplanes and a certain mademoiselle from Trieste.

Sir Anthony also proved an interesting companion—until Lady Annabel showed up unexpectedly. Higgins would have preferred to see Medusa emerge out of the mist to that woman, and he quickly took his leave.

For the past half hour, Higgins had accompanied Dwight Pentwater. Higgins knew exactly how much time he'd spent with each member of the shooting party; he checked his pocket watch every ten minutes. Now he couldn't wait for luncheon and the chance to stop terrorizing bunnies in the damp forest. Enough food was stored in the Banfield Manor kitchens to keep the county of Kent fed for the next year. Hunting for anything other than sustenance offended Higgins's sense of justice. Every time another one of these well fed blighters killed a forest creature, he wanted to give them a swift kick in the arse.

He toyed with the idea of leaving the shooting party. After all, with Lady Annabel now in the forest with her husband, she couldn't chase after him in the manor house. But every beech tree in the forest looked like the next, especially in the mist. And from every corner shots rang out. If he set off on his own, one of these bunny killers might shoot him. A bullet would no doubt already be lodged in an arm or leg, if not for the eagle eyes of the gamekeeper and his men.

Beside him, Dwight Pentwater lifted his shotgun and fired. Of course he missed. Higgins gave him credit for one clever thing. The American wore a crimson scarf about his neck and a red feather in his hat.

"I admire your sartorial choices this morning," Higgins remarked. "Given the low visibility, you probably assumed everyone would be shooting at anything that moved."

"Exactly." Pentwater lowered his gun. Unlike the other men in the party, he preferred to reload the ammunition himself than rely on someone else. "In America, we often wear red to prevent any accidents. You Brits don't take the same precautions, I guess."

"You don't have much faith in hunters?"

"I certainly don't have any faith in this gang. Wasting their time shooting at rabbits."

Higgins shrugged. "We prefer to call them hares."

"I don't care what you call them. Might as well be shooting squirrels. I own a hunting lodge in Pennsylvania. Every autumn I invite friends and fellow businessmen to shoot whitetail deer. That's how a man hunts. Not this nonsense." He snorted. "And the loaders have done everything but pull the trigger for these idiots. I'll never understand the English."

"No more than my fellow countrymen can understand the American love of hot dogs."

"I blame the Germans for that," Pentwater replied. "I blame the Germans for a lot of things. For example, I'm sure it was Count Rudolf who came up with this tedious rabbit shoot. Lord Ashmore doesn't have the guts to stand up to him, even if this is his property."

"Count von Weisinger is an Austrian," Higgins reminded him.

"Don't see any difference between a German and an Austrian." Pentwater raised his gun once more. Gunfire sounded all around them. He let off another shot. "Neither is to be trusted."

"And yet you do business with the count."

Pentwater sent Higgins a cynical look. "I do business with lots of people I don't trust. Profit is my only concern, like it is for every good businessman. That's why I don't consider the count a businessman."

"What is he, then?" Higgins fell into step with Pentwater as he set off toward another clump of trees. Fallen leaves crunched beneath their feet.

Pentwater thought a moment before replying. "A fabulist."

This intrigued Higgins. "Which definition of 'fabulist' does he fit? A liar who invents complicated, dishonest stories, or a person who passes on fables?"

"Both." Pentwater raised and shot his gun once more. Higgins saw a brown shape twitch in the shadows of a tree. "Got 'em." He whistled to alert a beater to collect the animal.

"The count isn't interesting enough to warrant anyone's curiosity," Pentwater went on. "There are other house guests a lot more entertaining. Lady Annabel, for one." He chuckled. "That one has her eye on you. I have a feeling she wants to bag you like I bagged that rabbit."

Higgins grunted. "I'd rather meet the rabbit's fate."

"She isn't bad. I have a fondness for redheads, but I don't blame you for not being thrilled. Women who pursue men are vulgar." Pentwater came to a stop, cradling his gun in his arms. "Men should be the ones who go after women. And it makes the chase more fun if they don't want you."

"I don't see how." Higgins found the fellow increasingly unpleasant. He understood now why no one else in the shooting party chose to hunt with Pentwater.

"Because then you bend them to your will."

"A man can end up in jail for that," Higgins said in a harsh voice.

"There are other ways of persuading a woman to give her favors other than physical force. Especially if you have money and power."

"And no conscience." Higgins shook his head. "Is that how you win over women, with physical force and fear? If so, I pity the woman who marries you."

"Save your pity. I've been married for some time. And Alice lives quite well."

Higgins would love to hear Alice Pentwater's side of the story. It was certain to be a dark tale.

He'd heard enough from Pentwater. And he'd also had his fill of hunting. No matter the risk of being shot in this fog, he planned to head back to Banfield Manor. Once he got there, he would insist to Eliza that they return to London. They could stay at his mother's Chelsea flat until the fire damage was repaired at Wimpole Street. But it was madness to remain closeted here with Lady Annabel, the unpleasant count and countess, and the even more tiresome American.

As for Madame Evangeline's dire warning the day they arrived, Higgins felt foolish for allowing Eliza to convince him to stay. Madame Evangeline was an obvious fraud, one of many spiritualists who sprang up to take advantage of a credulous public. The only disaster he could foresee was enduring another week in close contact with the houseguests at Banfield Manor.

"I'll take my leave, Mr. Pentwater." Higgins briefly doffed his fedora. "Hunting has proved as dismal as I expected, and your conversation far worse. My only hope is that one of the hares learns how to shoot a gun before this hunting party comes to an end."

"You English say the damnedest things," Pentwater muttered.

Higgins set off in what he hoped was the direction of Banfield Manor. But he hadn't gone more than twenty steps when he heard Eliza calling him, "Professor, where are you? It's Eliza! Can you hear me?"

"I'm over here! Follow my voice!"

Higgins strained to catch sight of her through the trees and smiled when he saw a slender figure dressed in yellow emerging from the mist. Just then, a loud gunshot fired, followed by a strangled shout. He spun around and ran back to where he had left Pentwater.

With a startled cry, Higgins stumbled over the unmoving body on the ground. Blood stained the front of Pentwater's hunting jacket.

Higgins crouched down and felt for a pulse. After a moment, he released the man's wrist. The red feather and scarf had not protected him after all. Dwight Pentwater was dead.

CHAPTER 10

*H*iggins needed a distraction, something to keep him from remembering the blood-spattered corpse in the forest. Only there was little hope of that. The county police had been summoned and the day promised to be filled with endless unpleasant questions. All of them leading back to the dead man.

He scanned the room they had been asked to assemble in, a fancy chamber known as the blue parlor. Well, he certainly felt blue sitting here among the delicate furnishings.

While Chief Constable Sidney Brakefield studied his notes, Higgins forced himself to stare at the ivory plaster busts perched above the parlor's elaborate pediments. Probably ancestors of Richard Ashmore, as were the subjects of the oil portraits hung every few feet on the walls. He might have a better chance at distraction if he were allowed to thumb through the aged tomes displayed in two Chippendale break-front cases. Then again, he doubted it.

When he'd knelt beside Pentwater's body, Higgins was reminded of a similar scene this past summer. His friend and colleague, Colonel Pickering, had been shot right in front of him. Only by the grace of God—and a fine surgeon—did he survive. But the horror of that shocking moment had never left him. Witnessing Pentwater's death from a bullet not only reawakened those unhappy memories, it left Higgins shaken.

"Their shoes are muddy," someone said in a furious whisper.

Higgins looked up. Clara sat on a divan with her husband. She seemed distraught, only he wasn't certain if it was because of Pentwater's death, or the mud streaks left on the Persian carpet from the parade of witnesses the policemen had questioned. Knowing Clara, it was probably both.

When the Kent police first arrived, the chief constable interviewed the beaters and loaders from the hunting party. Of course, their boots had been muddy. As were the boots of the gamekeeper, Mumford, who stood before Brakefield with flat cap in hand.

"Aye, the gen'lmen all had guns. 'Cept for him, due to his arm in a sling." The man gestured toward Higgins. "But I didn't see when the American gent was hit."

"Then you couldn't say where the shot came from?" the chief constable asked.

He shook his head with sorrow. "Didn't even 'ear it, sir."

Chief Constable Brakefield's craggy features spoke to years of hard work, as did his prominent worry lines and calloused hands. Higgins bet those sharp brown eyes didn't miss much. He once more turned to Richard Ashmore. "Tell me again, Lord Ashmore. Why did you decide to host a hunt this week?"

"This was the first of our autumn house parties," Richard said. "The Ashmores have held shoots and fox hunts every fall for generations. As the newest baron, it was my duty to do likewise. The county expects it. Especially the fox hunt and the accompanying ball. Over forty people will be attending."

"But you weren't hunting fox," one of the constable detectives said. "Or grouse."

"No, I decided to begin this first house party by letting the guests shoot hares in the forest." Richard frowned. "Actually, none of this was my decision. For this party, I relied on the advice of my brother-in-law, Count Rudolf von Weisinger. And my sister, his wife. They had several shoots planned. Some in the forest, others in the fields. With the fox hunt closing off the week."

"The weather this morning was not agreeable for hunting." Countess von Weisinger's voice came from the depths of a blue wingback chair. "By the time we realized the light mist had turned into a fog, it was too late. Someone accidentally turned their gun in the wrong direction. It has happened before at Banfield Manor."

"It has?" Brakefield asked, his voice sharp. "When?"

"Eight years ago," the gamekeeper said. "The old baron presided over things then. Best shot I ever saw. During a pheasant shoot one of the beaters got hit. Never found out who pulled the trigger. Hard to know with two dozen guns going off."

"Did the beater die?"

"No, but the bullet tore up his leg pretty bad." Gamekeeper Mumford winced at the memory. "The doctors ended up cutting it off."

"My father saw to it that the man had work on the estate," the countess added, "and provided a cottage for him and his family. They're still here, if you wish to speak with the man. The Ashmores take care of their own."

"That's true," Richard said. "And there have been other hunting accidents over the years. Sometimes a gun misfires and causes harm to the shooter."

"When I first began to work for the Ashmores as a lad, a misfired gun killed some marquis from France. Terrible thing it was." The gamekeeper shook his head.

The last thing Higgins wanted was to hear descriptions of other men who had been shot. He glanced at his pocket watch.

Three hours had passed since Pentwater had been killed. Was the body being held somewhere in Banfield Manor until a local doctor or coroner pronounced accidental death? Or had it already been taken to the village? Higgins suspected the body was still here. Although he hated to sound as fanciful as Eliza, it felt like a dark heaviness hung over the house. A shroud.

He caught movement out of the corner of his eye. Eliza paced from one end of the parlor to the other. She looked as upset as Clara, but with more reason. Eliza had been the first person to join Higgins when he discovered Pentwater's body. She had also witnessed Pickering being shot. Bending over another bloodied victim had upset her as much as Higgins.

"Plenty of bullets go astray," the gamekeeper continued. "One of my beaters, Tom Moray, has a scar three inches long. Happened last year. On a day as clear as can be."

Brakefield frowned. "That's what bothers me. Why hold a shoot when a man can't see more than ten feet in front of him? Is it usual to go shooting in a thick fog?"

"It is not," Sir Anthony declared from where he sat with his dirty boots propped up on a footstool. He puffed on his cigar. "Fool decision, if you ask me."

"Then why were all of you out there shooting?"

"I believe my wife has explained." Count Rudolf stood by the door, as if he planned to leave at the first opportunity. "When we left this morning, there was no more than a *nebel*—a mist— over the grass. It was warmer yesterday, but a frost came during the night. Such things draw mists from the wet ground. It is common in the country at this time of the year. As the day goes on, the *nebel* lifts. It vanishes. Poof."

"Only this time it didn't," Brakefield reminded him.

"*Ja*, the mist became thick. A fog. And I tell my wife, we should end the hunt."

"He is correct," the countess said. "Shortly before Mr. Pentwater was shot, my husband informed me that it made no sense to continue. The fog had grown worse and he feared someone might be hurt. He left me to find the gamekeeper and give orders that the beaters were to round up everyone and lead them back to the house."

The count nodded in agreement. "I had difficulty finding Mr. Mumford. But I saw Sir Anthony. He was upset because his wife had come to join him in the hunt, and he had lost sight of her. I informed him the hunt was over and we must return."

"And so he did," Sir Anthony said. "I asked one of the loaders to point me in the direction of the house. Along the way I spotted Annabel, who seemed to be doing just fine." He winked at his wife, who perched on the edge of a nearby Hepplewhite chair. "She had just bagged two hares. Amazing woman."

"Lucky shots," she demurred.

"Women were shooting?" one of the constables asked in shock.

"It's not unheard of for women to shoot with the men," Richard said. "But it is uncommon. My sister has always hunted. She's an excellent shot, better than me."

Brakefield turned to Clara. "Lady Ashmore, were you shooting as well?"

She looked at him as if he'd just asked if she danced naked on London Bridge. "Good heavens, no! I never left the house. In fact, I was still in bed when I heard about the shooting." She made a face. "I can't imagine anything I'd fancy doing less than tramp about shooting at animals. Beastly business."

Literally, Higgins thought, trying not to chuckle. Clara might end up being his only distraction.

Richard clasped her hand. "My wife doesn't shoot or ride."

"I'm afraid of horses." She leaned forward as if imparting a secret. "They're so big."

The chief constable glanced down at his notes. "Miss Doolittle? Did you participate in the hunt?"

Eliza stopped pacing. "There's enough violence in the world

without me trying to find sport in it. But I did go out to find the Professor."

Higgins cleared his throat to get the constable's attention. "As I mentioned before, Eliza arrived at the exact moment I heard the gunshot. She was not carrying a weapon."

"I saw the young lady in the woods," the gamekeeper said. "Couldn't hardly miss her, seeing as she was dressed in that yellow skirt and jacket. Bright like the sun, she was. And she weren't holding a shotgun."

Brakefield consulted the list of guests again. "Freddy Eynsford Hill?"

Freddy raised his hand from where he slouched on the sofa. Lily sat beside him, fiddling with her charm bracelet and swinging a dainty foot back and forth.

"Mr. Eynsford-Hill, did you see Mr. Pentwater in the forest this morning?"

He shook his head. "I didn't see anyone at all, except for Lily. The two of us decided to join the hunt after everyone else had left. By the time we got dressed and found guns, the fog had turned into a real pea-souper."

"Didn't you think it pointless to go hunting when you couldn't see anything?"

"Actually, we thought it would be something of a lark. And it was." He peeked over at Lily, who shot him a quick smile. "We chased each other about for awhile. The fog made everything so mysterious and exciting, didn't it?"

"It felt like we were the only people around for miles," Lily said. "Except for when we heard the guns."

"What the devil did the two of you do out there?" Brakefield demanded.

They exchanged another conspiratorial look. "Oh, we shot at things once in awhile. Trees mostly." Freddy grinned. "And played hide and seek."

"Then you weren't always in sight of each other?" one of the detective asked.

"Oh, Freddy couldn't see me when I hid, but I always knew where Freddy was." She tousled his hair. "How could I miss him with such a golden mane as this? He was almost as hard to miss as Eliza in her sunny ensemble." The pair nudged each other.

Brakefield looked like he regretted asking them anything. "Where is Mr. Corbet?" He mistakenly pronounced the name to rhyme with "orbit."

"*Oui?*" Philippe stood leaning against the window.

"Professor Higgins states that he was with you for the better part of an hour during the shoot. After he left, did you join up with anyone else?"

"I begin the hunt with Lord Ashmore, Count Rudolf, and his wife. Then I spend time shooting with *Professeur* Higgins. After that, I shoot alone." He looked out the window. "And no, I do not see Monsieur Pentwater when I was in the forest. At least not until I hear the shouting and run to where the man is lying dead."

"I believe everyone has told you what happened this morning," Richard said. "I also believe Mr. Pentwater's death was an unfortunate accident. And tragic. If I had more information about him, I'd contact his family." He turned to Lily. "Do you know where Pentwater lived in America?"

She shrugged. "Somewhere in New York City."

Richard hung his head and sighed.

Brakefield took pity on the young baron. "Given the weather this morning, I must agree with Lord Ashmore. Mr. Pentwater's death appears to be an accident. Plenty of hunting accidents in the countryside, I'm afraid, and this isn't the first this season, either." He gestured to the gamekeeper. "That will be all for now, Mr. Mumford. You can dismiss your men as well. Thank you."

With a nod, the gamekeeper shuffled toward the door.

"I can't imagine anyone here had a reason to kill Mr. Pentwater," Richard said. "I'd never even met him before last night."

"I met him several years ago in Berlin," the count told Brakefield. "The Grand Duke of Hesse hosted a trade conference. Herr Pentwater spoke on investment opportunities in America. Because I found him an informed man, I have sought his advice on occasion. But he is no more than a business acquaintance."

"Yet you invited him to your house party," Brakefield said.

"*Ja*. Of course. He rang me up and said he would be in London soon. When he asked if I wished to meet in The City and talk business, I thought inviting him to this party would be *sympathischer*."

"More congenial," the countess translated.

Brakefield looked down at his notes. "Miss Marlowe knew him."

"Again? How often do I have to hear about Mr. Pentwater and me? Give a girl a break." Lily threw herself back on the sofa in a most unladylike position. Her brashness entertained Higgins. She sometimes reminded him of an American Eliza.

"A break?" Brakefield asked, puzzled.

"Honestly, doesn't anyone here speak English?"

Higgins bit back a grin.

"Would you understand me better if we spoke at the station, Miss Marlowe?"

Lily pretended to consider it, one finger on her chin. He understood now why she made such a convincing actress. "Okay. What do you want to know that I haven't already told you? I'm an actress. I make movies at Vitograph Studios in Brooklyn. Pentwater invested in some of them." She raised an eyebrow. "The movies, not me."

"You're a pretty girl, Miss Marlowe. Did Mr. Pentwater think so, too?"

"Probably. But I'm not the only pretty actress at Vitograph.

Let me tell you, actresses are used to fellas on the make for them. And some of them are real heels."

"Heels?"

She ignored him. "What you should be asking is if I was keen on him."

"Were you?"

Lily gave a dramatic sigh. "He never combed his hair and had a long nose. So what do you think? And I don't deserve to be called on the carpet with these questions."

The chief constable appeared completely confused by her American slang. "Right, then," Brakefield said. "Aside from the count and Miss Marlowe, it appears that Mr. Pentwater had no important connection to any of the guests."

"I can tell you something important," Eliza announced.

Brakefield motioned for her to come closer.

"Madame Evangeline predicted a death this morning at breakfast," Eliza began in a somber voice. "That's why I went off to the forest. To warn the others."

Clara's eyes widened. "Oh, Richard! Your sister was right about thirteen guests being unlucky. To think Madame Evangeline knew Mr. Pentwater was about to die."

"Darling, please," Richard said. "It's impossible to predict the future. Even if you are Madame Evangeline."

"Except she blooming well did," Eliza told him.

Brakefield cleared his throat. "And who is this Madame Evangeline?"

"One of our guests," Richard said. "She is both a spiritualist and a medium."

"A medium," the chief constable repeated. "Is that like a person who holds séances?"

"Yes, she communicates with ghosts. And she falls into trances," Eliza said eagerly. "When she's in them, she tells the future."

Higgins wanted to stop her from making a fool of herself,

but didn't bother to interrupt. Once Eliza was set on a course, nothing could stop her.

"She doesn't have a clue what she says afterward either. But I heard her, plain as day in the breakfast room. She told me that she sensed danger." Eliza thought a moment. "Her exact words were, 'Anger is in the air around us. More than anger. A dark fury which ends in death. That fury lies waiting in the forest. A murderer awaits in the forest.'" Eliza gave the chief constable a pointed look. "I have a sharp memory."

"I can vouch for that," Higgins said. "Eliza forgets nothing."

"Impressive," Lily remarked. "With a memory like that, Eliza could make a living on the stage." She giggled. "Or as a spy."

"None of that matters. What does matter is that Madame Evangeline told me a murderer was about to kill someone in the forest. And it happened."

"What a frightful thing for Madame Evangeline to say." The countess seemed offended. "It is most improper for guests to be predicting death in the breakfast room."

Clara put her head in her hands. "This must be England's worst house party!"

No one disagreed.

"Stevens?" Brakefield crooked a finger at one of the junior constables, who leaned down to hear his whispered command. The young man hurried off. The chief constable wrote in his notebook until Stevens returned with Madame Evangeline, who was accompanied by her manservant.

Due to her dark purple gown and severe expression, Madame looked suitably grim. But Higgins found Zoltan Batur a more forbidding sight in his black silk jacket and turban, although gold embroidery decorated his black slippers. He wondered if that was the typical footwear worn by a fellow accustomed to living in Turkey and Egypt. Or was it just peculiar to this manservant, entrusted with the protection of Madame Evangeline? Slippers might mask the sound of his footfall, an asset if he wished to surprise anyone perceived as a threat. Higgins would certainly be wary of meeting this fellow in a dark alley.

Although not tall, Batur made up for it with a broad chest and muscular arms that strained at the sleeves of his jacket. His ominous presence was further enhanced by his jet black hair, beard, and striking eyes, almost amber in color. Higgins couldn't help but notice how he held his hands in perpetual readiness, fingers slightly curled, as if coiled to spring at any moment and throttle someone.

"Why am I here, sir?" Madame Evangeline asked before Chief Constable Brakefield had a chance to speak. "I was told that only those who were at the hunt this morning needed to be questioned. And I never left the house."

"I wasn't at the hunt," Clara offered, "but he wanted to speak with me, too. I'm not happy about all this either. I'd much prefer to be in my bedchamber. Or bathing."

Higgins shook his head. At some point, the girl needed to learn how to act like the lady of the manor.

"Miss Doolittle told us something that involves you, Madame Evangeline."

Brakefield eyed the manservant with suspicion. "First, who the devil is this fellow?"

"My manservant, Zoltan Batur. He assists me in my work. And protects me if the need arises."

Zoltan bowed his head toward her. "It is my honor to look after Madame and see that no harm befalls her."

"How long have you looked after Madame Evangeline?" Brakefield asked.

"Since the death of my husband several years ago," she replied for Batur.

"I see," Brakefield said. "Mr. Batur, have you witnessed these trances?"

"Of course."

"What happens exactly?"

"The trances take Madame unawares. But when the spirits speak, she must listen. They speak through her. Whatever she says, it is the truth. Those from the Great Beyond have no need to lie."

That may be so, Higgins thought, but plenty of people on this side of the Veil did. "I've known Madame no more than a day," he said, causing her to turn that disturbing gaze upon him. "But I have noticed she only imparts dark and distressing things. I wonder why the spirits never have anything cheerful to share with us."

Her enigmatic smile reminded him of the Mona Lisa. "As you said, Professor, you have only known me a day. If we had a longer acquaintance, you would learn that I also bring happy news. Or so I have been told. Sadly, I never remember my utterances."

Sir Anthony gave a derisive snort.

"All I know is that if I were a spirit and able to communicate to people, I'd want to warn them if they were in danger." Eliza shot Higgins and Sir Anthony an exasperated look. "I can't see how none of you understands that. Madame Evangeline is trying to help."

Brakefield raised an eyebrow at that comment. "She wasn't able to help Mr. Pentwater."

"That saddens me far more than it does you." The medium stared at him with an air of annoyance. "I am only a conduit. Sometimes a poor one."

"You have a gift, Madame," Zoltan reassured her. "A great gift. One not worthy of the people in this room."

"I think it's fair to say neither of us believe in spirits predicting the future." Higgins bowed his head at Evangeline. "My apologies, but I must speak the truth as you claim your spirits do. From what I have heard so far, you have done little more than make vague predictions about danger and darkness."

"Is no one blooming listening?" Eliza asked. "She foretold that someone would be murdered in the forest. And it came true."

"Ah, yes," Sir Anthony said. "A forest shrouded in fog where the lot of us were firing guns in all directions. It's a miracle more of us weren't killed."

"Exactly." Higgins ignored Eliza's angry looks.

"I believe we are in agreement, Professor Higgins." Brakefield turned to Richard. "We should be able to close the case tomorrow. By then, we will have spoken with the coroner and decided whether this was indeed an accidental death."

"Are we free to go?" Higgins got to his feet.

"You are free to leave the parlor." Brakefield buttoned up his jacket. "However, until Mr. Pentwater's death has been officially ruled an accident, I must request that everyone remain at Banfield Manor. As I said, our decision should not take long."

"I don't know why it should take any time at all," Lady Annabel said.

"I need to make inquiries into Mr. Pentwater's past. See if there is anything he has done which might incite murder."

"What bother and nonsense." Lady Annabel nervously re-pinned a decorative clip in her hair. "All this fuss over a hunting accident. How could it be anything else? And I don't see why we should all be detained here like prisoners in the dock."

Brakefield didn't bother to reply.

Higgins wondered why Lady Annabel cared if they had to remain at the manor another night. Maybe she felt upset at being in such close proximity to a sudden death.

Whatever the reason, Higgins was grateful. He'd feared that seeing her after last night's farce in his bedroom might prove uncomfortable. But when she joined Higgins and her husband in the forest, she gave not the slightest indication that anything unusual had transpired. If Higgins were a religious man, he'd offer up prayers of thanks.

"I instructed the servants to lay out the picnic luncheon in the dining room," Richard announced. "We shall eat in one hour. That will give everyone time to change."

"It might be fun to gather in the drawing room afterward for cards," Clara suggested. "Or maybe charades."

"I bet we can convince Lily to sing us a tune," Freddy added.

The constables exchanged disbelieving looks before leaving. Higgins didn't blame them. A party guest had been killed, and they were already eager to move on to lunch and charades. Perhaps Madame Evangeline also felt offended because she and her manservant quickly left the parlor.

"Clara, don't you think games and music are inappropriate?" Eliza said.

"You're right. Afternoons at a country house party should be devoted to reading and walking in the garden. We'll save the music and games for tonight." Clara's face lit up. "Maybe Madame Evangeline can tell our fortunes, too."

Higgins headed for the door. He didn't need anyone to tell his fortune. He could already predict this would be a long, tiresome day.

ELIZA TUGGED ON HER SILK EVENING GLOVES, WISHING TO BE anywhere but at Banfield Manor. It seemed so long ago when she'd looked forward to this country house party. She expected to have fun with Clara and Freddy, and had been excited to meet the other guests. Her hopes about Freddy were quickly dashed. Even if he came to his senses—which seemed unlikely— she would not take him back. As for Lily Marlowe, Eliza swore to never watch another one of her films again. And she loved her films. Drat!

She couldn't even enjoy playing dress up in her new gowns. Not after that terrible scene in the forest today. As soon as she heard the gunshot and a man cry out, she raced to join Higgins. She found Dwight Pentwater motionless on the ground, blank eyes staring up at them. And there was so much blood! Eliza fought to put the sight out of her mind. But she feared her dreams tonight would be as haunting as the nightmares after her dear Colonel Pickering was shot.

At least she was holding her own with the other ladies where fashion was concerned. Although Lady Annabel's jade satin Poiret creation did set off her vibrant coloring to perfection. The countess looked a bit dowdy in a russet velvet gown that had seen too many seasons. Eliza wondered if the von Weisingers were having money problems. She knew an impressive title did not guarantee an impressive income. And the death of Pentwater had upset Clara's fashion sense. Her ruffled white dress, embellished with pink roses, was more suited to spring than fall.

All Eliza cared about was that her own outfit tonight, a Worth gown, compared well to that of Lily's. With a black silk skirt topped by an ivory and black bodice, Eliza outshone the actress's deep blue confection with a too fussy lace overlay. They had also both changed hairstyles; Eliza had twisted her dark hair and pinned it up beneath a wide gold headband; Lily wore a simple chignon with a spray of silk flowers. But after the death in the forest, pretty gowns and stylish coiffures seemed trite and silly.

Restless, Eliza moved toward the shelves of books. Nothing interested her. Maybe she should retrieve the Fu-Manchu mystery book from her room. She'd like to converse with Higgins, but he seemed completely engrossed in some weighty volume propped up on his lap.

Eliza glanced over at the card tables. Freddy and Lily had paired up with Clara and Count Rudolf to play whist; at the other table, the countess, Philippe, Lady Annabel, and Sir Anthony were engaged in a highly competitive game of bridge.

Only the shuffle of cards and pops from the crackling fire broke the silence, with an occasional murmur from the card players.

"Why don't you play something, Eliza?" Clara suggested, eyeing the cards in her hand. "A ragtime piano piece. They're ever so much fun to hear."

"Lenzburg's *Hungarian Rag* is more suitable." The countess nodded toward the piano. "I believe there is sheet music beneath the piano bench."

"No, play *The Aviator Rag* instead," Richard said from where he sat nursing a brandy by the fire. "Philippe might enjoy that."

"*Bien sûr,*" the Frenchman murmured, "but it is not necessary."

"Or *The Racehorse Rag*." Clara turned to Lily. "Did you hear about the music hall singer Marie Lloyd? The police arrested her when she arrived in America to begin her tour. She and a jockey claimed to be husband and wife when they applied for entry visas. They charged him under the White Slave Act for bringing a woman who is not his wife!"

"I read he was threatened with deportation or what they termed 'moral turpitude.' We Americans can be such Puritans." She gave a careless shrug. "At least Miss Lloyd hasn't been hurt by the scandal. The tour's been a real smash, despite all the publicity."

Sir Anthony played a card. "There is no such thing as bad publicity. At least that is what the American showman P.T. Barnum was fond of saying. Is that correct, Miss Marlowe?"

"Mr. Barnum said a lot of things. That sounds like him. The man was known as the king of hucksters."

Eliza pulled out a chair at a small polished table by the window, in no mood to play the piano and entertain them.

"May I join you, Miss Doolittle? You seem sad and might enjoy some company."

She looked up to see Madame Evangeline. "Yes, please. I am

in need of a little distraction. It was a terrible morning. Just as you foretold."

"It is my tragedy that I often cannot prevent such things. But the hand of fate is a heavy one." Madame Evangeline sat in the chair across from her. She smoothed down her black lace gown, which seemed fitting for such a glum day.

"You wore black as I did," Eliza observed. "I didn't really know Mr. Pentwater, but wearing black tonight seemed the right thing to do."

"We should cover ourselves in dark colors to honor the dead. They take offense when we do not."

Eliza stiffened. "Are there any ghosts in the room with us right now? And are they offended? Is Mr. Pentwater here?"

"I sense only the ghost of a child. He is playing by the fireplace."

Eliza looked over at the fireplace in alarm, but saw only a crackling fire and Richard Ashmore sipping his brandy. "Should we tell the others?"

"Why? They will not be able to see the boy any more than you can. And the child is not aware of us." Madame Evangeline rummaged in her lace drawstring bag and pulled out a thick deck of cards. They did not resemble those used by the other guests.

Trying to put the thought of the ghostly child out of her mind, Eliza watched her shuffle the worn cards. Madame Evangeline cut them several times, reshuffled, then set the deck in the middle of the table with a casual wave.

"Please shuffle the cards," she said in a soft voice. "They may tell you there is no need to remain sad. Although I believe it is time you learn that men can be inconstant."

"Looks like I've had that lesson." Eliza regarded her with interest. "You can read my future with playing cards?"

"These are Tarot cards. The information gleaned from a reading can help you in decision making. While you shuffle the cards, think of a simple but important question. But do not tell me what is in your mind until I am finished with the reading."

Eliza picked up the deck. "There's more than fifty-two playing cards here."

"Seventy-eight in number. They are not playing cards. Each has a meaning and a reversal. You will see once I do the reading. When you finish shuffling, hand me the first six cards. Or choose any six out of the deck."

After Eliza followed her instructions, the medium placed the first of the six cards she'd chosen in the table's center and arranged the others around them in a pattern. Evangeline turned them over and studied them for several minutes before tapping the middle card.

"This represents you—the Querent, or one who questions. Temperance refers to the soul, and you see the angel mixing water as if blending energies. But I believe this card represents a tempering, like metal which forges anew." She held up her hand when Eliza started to speak. "Do not interrupt. We will discuss afterward."

Eliza's excitement grew. She did feel as if she'd been hammered at a forge. Professor Higgins's laboratory, in fact. Forged into a new person. She'd left the Cockney East End flower seller behind, along with poverty and hunger, to become a lady. How extraordinary to be able summarize her life in one card!

"This card, the Four of Cups, represents the Earth element of stability and also security," the woman added, her voice soft. "The Four of Cups may point to a longing for change, a restless-ness you feel. But see here. In the Air element position is the Queen of Swords. Your feminine side. That shows indepen-dence and non-reliance upon others. Perhaps it is advising you to leave sentimental attachments behind."

Madame Evangeline tapped the next card. "In the Fire element position, which can both create and destroy, is the Ace of Wands. Hmm. Trust your instincts, Miss Doolittle. You may need to spring into action at a crucial moment. But here, for the Water element, is the Two of Swords. It reflects conflicting ideas. Mixed signals."

Eliza suddenly thought of the fickle Mr. Eynsford Hill.

Evangeline touched the next card. "Wait until the time is ripe. Be patient. And the last position, Spirit, is the Six of Wands. You shall celebrate a victory, earning respect from someone important." She tore her attention from the cards and looked at Eliza. "Now, what was your original question?"

"Will there be another suitor in my future? Someone more worthy of romance, I mean. You said men are inconstant. Are they all inconstant?"

"No. And this last card indicates a victory in winning a better man's heart." She smiled. "A promising future, Miss Doolittle."

"Thank you. But it doesn't clear up what you said at breakfast. About how a murderer waited in the forest. And it came true."

"I do not remember saying such a thing. I never do. Only I am not sure if that is a blessing or a curse." Madame Evangeline gathered up her cards.

Eliza nodded at the Tarot deck. "How will I know if any of this will come true?"

"Pay attention to everything and everyone around you. Look for signs. The cards are open to more than one interpretation, as are the events of our lives."

"Excuse me. What's this?" Lily appeared at their table in a swirl of blue silk, her trademark scent of lily of the valley accompanying her.

"Are you reading the Tarot cards for Eliza?" Lily asked with an excited smile. "I once had my fortune told in Coney Island. Could you read the cards for me next?"

Madame Evangeline stood up. "I never give more than one

reading at a time. And the cards still bear the imprint from Miss Doolittle. Tomorrow will be better." She quickly hid the Tarot deck in her lace and silk bag.

Disappointed, Lily turned her attention to Eliza. "If you tell me what she told you, I'll tell you what the gypsy fortune teller in Coney Island said." She laughed. "Although the woman sounded like she came from Bushwick, New York, not Romany."

"Excuse me. It's been a tiring day. My energy is nearly gone. I must retire." Madame Evangeline nodded gravely, then left the room.

"A bit of a crepe hanger, that one," Lily said. "A real looker though. She'd do well in the movies. The camera loves actors with big eyes. Only hers are a little scary, don't you think?"

Eliza had to agree. Even scarier was the presence of a ghostly child in the room. And who knew how many other ghosts were floating around the house? Maybe Dwight Pentwater was now one of them.

She needed to think of something else. "I believe I will sing," she announced.

Higgins looked up from his book with a puzzled expression.

Clara clapped her hands in delight. "*The Racehorse Rag,* please."

Eliza walked over to the piano. She'd sing a dozen songs for them tonight. If it took her mind off dead bodies and ghosts, she'd bloody well give them a music hall performance. Because if Madame Evangeline's prediction about a murder in the forest was true, the murderer was in the room with them right now.

CHAPTER 11

"You look as if you've seen a ghost," Higgins declared when he saw Eliza the next morning.

"Shh." Eliza scanned the empty hallway with a nervous expression. "We don't want to attract their attention. Madame Evangeline saw the ghost of a child by the fireplace in the music room. She says ghosts are all over the house. One of them woke her up the other night."

Higgins snorted. "Lucky her. I'd rather have a ghost disturb my sleep than Lady Annabel. I'd even welcome three of them, like Ebenezer Scrooge."

"Don't joke. I believe her." Clutching her shawl tight about her, she whispered, "What if Mr. Pentwater is a ghost now? He could be around the corner, listening to us."

"If he's eavesdropping on this conversation, the afterlife is duller than I imagined." Higgins pointed in the direction of the breakfast room. "Can we discuss ghosts while having our coffee and poached eggs?"

"I'm not hungry. You go ahead. I'll wait in the library."

Ignoring his rumbling stomach, he followed her. Luckily, the library's floor to ceiling windows provided much needed light on such a rainy morning. The only other illumination came from the coal fireplace where Eliza now stood, warming her hands.

"If you're not hungry, the Apocalypse is imminent. What the dickens is the matter?"

"That should be obvious," Eliza replied. "Madame Evangeline told me someone was about to be murdered in the forest. And she was right."

"Not again. The fact that it came true probably surprised her as well. It's like the old saying, 'even a stopped clock is right twice a day.'"

"This has nothing to do with broken clocks. She sensed someone was about to be murdered and it happened. Don't pretend I'm not right. You should be ashamed of yourself for not agreeing with me when the police were here." She shook her head. "We failed."

"Failed at what? And why are you shivering? Every room in this mausoleum has a blazing fire." Higgins looked at her fringed paisley shawl. "The only time I've seen you wear that Indian shawl Pickering gave you is in the dead of winter. It's nowhere near that cold now."

"Speak for yourself." Eliza shivered again, despite the heat radiating from the coal grate. "And don't use words like mausoleum and dead."

With a resigned sigh, Higgins chose a seat on a brown leather settee. It gave him an excellent view of the raindrops streaming down the windows. Only an hour ago, he'd been awakened by a torrential downpour, but it had slowed to a shower. He suspected the rain would cease soon, leaving only gray skies and a chill wind. Foul weather for a hunting party week.

"What's this all about? How have we failed?"

"On the day we arrived, Madame Evangeline warned that death and darkness surrounded the house and only we could stop it." Eliza abandoned the warmth of the fireplace and walked over to him. "But we didn't stop it. Mr. Pentwater is dead."

"Eliza, listen to me. Madame Evangeline is a fraud. A predatory spiritualist who lines her pockets by telling the fortunes of gullible, rich people."

"I'm neither rich nor gullible. She foretold a death. It came true. Unless you believe Mr. Pentwater's death was an accident."

Higgins stretched out his long legs. "Please remember how thick the fog was. And hundreds of bullets were flying about. Although, I do agree it looks a bit suspicious. He was shot as soon as I left his side, almost as if someone waited until I was out of the way."

"Exactly. The murderer probably followed Pentwater through the fog until the perfect moment. I only wish Madame Evangeline had told me earlier. By the time she did, it was too late. She said I couldn't prevent the death. It was destiny."

He raised an eyebrow. "Now the death and disaster were fated? I guess Madame Evangeline changed her mind about how we were the only ones who could avert it."

Eliza sat down beside him. She closed her eyes and leaned her head back. "You're right. I hadn't thought about that. But I've been so anxious since she told me about the ghosts. I kept the covers over my head all night. I barely slept."

"You do look rather awful." Higgins now noticed the dark circles beneath her eyes.

"I can't stop thinking about what Madame Evangeline told me. Ghosts are everywhere. She also said people sensitive to the presence of spirits often feel cold when they're around."

"So?"

"I've felt cold from the moment I set foot in this house," she wailed. "They're probably following me. What if they start to appear? I shall go stark raving balmy if they do."

"And I'll go balmy if we stay here a moment longer." Higgins readjusted the sling about his left arm. "I knew this visit would turn nightmarish the moment I saw Lady Annabel."

"How do you think I feel having to watch Freddy throw himself at a cinema actress?"

"The boy's made a complete fool of himself." Higgins had never thought much of Freddy Eynsford Hill, but the chap's behavior the past two days had exceeded even his low expectations. "Freddy's done everything but serenade Miss Marlowe outside her window. Although he'll probably do that tonight. Right after he bays at the moon."

Eliza's expression turned stubborn. "I don't care what he does any longer. Yes, he hurt my feelings, I'll not deny that. But Freddy's been a nuisance for months, always begging me to marry him And he flew into an awful temper each time I said I wasn't ready. It will be a relief to not have him badger me." She sighed. "I'll miss him though. He was my first sweetheart."

Higgins grunted. "You can do better. As for Pentwater, let the police decide if it was murder or not. It's nothing to do with us. That's why I've already packed."

"Poor Clara. Once the police give their approval, I'm sure her guests will leave."

"As should we. Life will be calmer for us at my mother's flat in Chelsea. No ghosts there. Only a cook with a talent for steak and kidney pie." Higgins looked at the shelves of books lining the room. Two wooden ladders stood propped against the wall, an aid to the top shelves which reached to the fresco painted ceiling. "A pity. Under normal circumstance, I might have welcomed my stay here, especially with a library such as this to explore. Except for the hunting. Bloody useless activity unless one is a character in a James Fenimore Cooper novel."

"Speaking of novels, have you read any of the ones Lady Annabel has written?"

"I struggled through several. I wanted to understand the

byzantine workings of her brain. It left me further convinced I needed to stay clear of her."

"What exactly happened between the two of you?" she asked. "Is it a scandalous tale?"

"Maddening, but not scandalous. Seven years ago my *Universal Alphabet* was about to be published overseas. The publisher threw a reception at the Criterion in London to celebrate. Not just my book. Four other authors had books scheduled for release, too."

"Including Lady Annabel?"

"Yes. I think it was the latest in what they call her 'sensation' novels: *The Daring Sin of Julia*. Or something like that. She was known as Mrs. Annabel Taggart then, the widow of some wretched fellow who died a year earlier."

"Why was he wretched?"

"From all accounts, he became mired in debt and drank himself to death. I believe the only thing keeping them afloat financially were her novels."

Eliza looked puzzled. "But why did Lady Annabel take such a fancy to you?"

"Ask *her* why she pursued me up and down the length of England. I went on a lecture tour and that bloody woman turned up at every stop for three months. I had to flee the country like a felon. I spent five tedious weeks traveling through Switzerland. Deadly dull people, the Swiss. The only worthwhile things they've ever produced are cuckoo clocks and chocolate."

"What happened to Lady Annabel?"

"When I finally dared return to England, my publisher informed me she had embarked on a speaking tour of America. Her novels always did create excitement, proving that one should never underestimate the taste level of the reading public."

"Was she in America long?"

"Long enough for me to put the lurid escapade out of my mind. For all I know, she spent years there. I've no idea. I certainly wasn't aware she had married Sir Anthony Dennison."

Eliza sat up, excited. "Maybe she knew Pentwater while she was in America."

"They gave no sign of it at dinner."

"If she had a reason to murder him, she might pretend not to know him."

"But why would Pentwater pretend not to know her?" he asked.

"For the same reason. Lily, too. She doesn't sound truthful when she claims that she barely knew Pentwater. I think both women are hiding something. We need to look into this."

"You need to get some sleep." Higgins stood up. "And I need coffee and breakfast."

"Someone deliberately shot Pentwater yesterday." Eliza got to her feet, too. "Someone filled with anger and fury, according to Madame Evangeline. And the murderer was in the forest with all of you. I doubt it was a gamekeeper or any of his men. That leaves the guests."

Higgins's stomach growled once more. He had no wish to become involved in another murder investigation. At least not until after he had eaten a proper breakfast. Besides, this past year he'd seen enough dead bodies. But he found it hard to ignore Eliza's pleading gaze.

"Who do you think is the prime suspect?" he asked.

"I wouldn't mind the murderer being the count or the countess. They're so disagreeable, like sausage gone bad. Plus Clara would be thrilled if that awful pair weren't around."

"How about the Frenchman? Unless you believe handsome men are always innocent."

"Oh, no. Philippe Corbet is a suspect along with the other guests. Except for Freddy, of course. Philippe acted cold to Pentwater at dinner, didn't you think? Especially when he brought up the death of his friend. The one whose aeroplane crashed."

Higgins decided her instincts could well be correct. "Let's wait until we return to London. I have a cousin who works at the *Times*. I'll ring him up and ask him to look into this dead French aviator. See if there's any connection to Dwight Pentwater."

"I believe I can save you the phone call, Herr Higgins."

A figure stood in the doorway. Even in the dim morning light, Higgins spied the gleam of medals pinned to the man's jacket. He wondered how long Count Rudolf had been listening to them.

Eliza whispered, "Do you think he heard me compare him to spoiled sausage?"

Higgins nodded, then pointed to a chair. "Perhaps you could enlighten us, count."

Instead of taking a seat, Count Rudolf walked over to a large terrestrial globe attached to a walnut pedestal. He stood beside the globe as though posing for a portrait, one arm held behind his back. "We do not have time for a lengthy conversation. I actually came in search of you and Fräulein Doolittle. The local police have returned and wish to speak with all of us again."

"Have they learned anything important about Mr. Pentwater?" Eliza asked.

"That I have not been told. But it seems likely, otherwise why would I be asked to gather the guests. Neither of you appeared for breakfast. It is fortunate I heard your voices." He scowled at them. No doubt he'd overheard their whole conversation.

"You mentioned you could save me that phone call to the *Times*," Higgins reminded him. "How? All we know about Philippe's friend is that his name was Henri Vennard and that he died in an aeroplane crash two years ago."

"We wondered if Pentwater was involved somehow," Eliza said.

"Herr Pentwater involved himself in many things. Some less successful than others. One of his failures was Argo, a company which made parts for aeroplanes." The count spun the globe. "Pentwater made unwise decisions. And he *schneiden Sie finanziell ab*. How do you say? He cut corners where financing was concerned."

"Does that mean some of those machine parts were defective?" Higgins said.

"*Ja.* Three aeroplanes built with those parts made emergency landings. A fourth aeroplane crashed. The one Henri Vennard was flying." He abruptly stopped the spinning globe. "Vennard was a man much respected and liked. Of course his death would be looked into. When the results of the investigation became known, Argo ceased operation."

Eliza looked thoughtful. "It's possible Philippe blames Pentwater for Henri's death."

"I think it is more than possible, Fräulein Doolittle. If the police have come to tell us Pentwater's death is no accident, it should be easy to solve." The count shrugged. "No matter. It is of little import, except his death has spoiled the first house party of the baron and baroness. This reflects badly on my wife and me. Our friends and acquaintances will assume we had to manage things here because of the newlywed's lack of experience. For someone to die during a hunt is an embarrassment. And a great inconvenience."

"Especially for the person who died," Eliza reminded him.

He gave Eliza a withering look "The English should teach their children manners."

"And where are your manners, Count Rudolf? A man was killed yesterday and all you feel is embarrassment. That's blooming wrong."

His cheeks flamed red as he turned to Higgins. "I have saved you that phone call to the *Times*, Herr Professor. Now I must join the others in the gold drawing room. I suggest you and Fräulein Doolittle follow me." He clicked his heels and took his leave.

Higgins chuckled. "Be careful, Eliza. I believe he'd like to wring your neck."

"Great. I'm already looking over my shoulder for ghosts. Now I'll have to keep an eye out for an angry Austrian."

Higgins didn't upset her further by warning that if Pentwater had been murdered, that angry Austrian might well be the killer.

ELIZA WELCOMED THE SUMMONS TO THE GOLD DRAWING ROOM. IT was one of the prettiest rooms at Banfield Manor, filled with creamy white furnishings, gold figurines and candelabra, velvet flocked wallpaper, and a dazzling decorated ceiling that Higgins told her was called "vaulted." Crowning it all was an enormous, glittering chandelier which resembled a crystal sun. Eliza had never been in a palace before, but she thought this room would fit quite nicely in one.

The blazing fire, coupled with the number of people scattered on various chairs and divans, also made the room far warmer than the library. The count and countess sent her icy looks, however. No doubt he had told his wife about their conversation. Eliza was also grateful they hadn't been asked to meet in the music room where they had played cards last night. What if that poor ghostly child was still there, sitting all alone by the fireplace?

Clara waved at Eliza. She had saved her a seat on one of the damask sofas. Because Higgins chose to sit on an ottoman by the door, Eliza went to join Clara.

"Isn't this dreadful?" Clara said as she watched the chief

constable and two fellow policemen speak among themselves. "The whole county will know the police have turned up once again. Why would they do that for a simple hunting accident?"

"Maybe they've come to tell us the death has been officially ruled an accident." While Eliza meant to reassure Clara, she thought it unlikely. A simple confirmation of accidental death shouldn't require the presence of three policemen.

Clara appeared on the verge of tears. "I've heard the servants whispering about the house party. I can't blame them. The party should have begun with a grouse hunt, not shooting hares in the forest. And why didn't Richard's sister include more people on the guest list? People with a proper English title. We've hardly any guests, and now one of them is dead!"

Richard, who stood beside the marble fireplace, sent his bride an anxious glance. "Keep your voice down," Eliza said. "No need to make the police more suspicious than they are."

Clara squeezed her hand. "I don't know what Richard and I would do if you weren't here. You're the only guest I can trust. My only friend." She glanced at Higgins. "I'm grateful for the Professor, too. The count and countess are a little afraid of him."

Being Clara's only friend at the house party had proved exhausting to Eliza. Since the death of Pentwater, Clara had rarely left her alone. Their recent conversation in the library had been the first time Eliza was able to speak with Higgins in private.

"With luck, this will be the last time the police visit," Eliza said.

"I certainly hope so," Clara whispered back. "I blame them for almost ruining the carpet in the blue parlor. It took the servants hours to clean up. The carpet is still damp."

Chief Constable Brakefield cleared his throat, silencing the room. Even Freddy and Lily looked up from where they sat whispering on the piano bench. Eliza marveled that so many of the rooms held a piano. Especially since she had yet to hear any of the Ashmores play a note.

"Ladies and gentlemen, I regret having to bother you again," Brakefield said. "But neither the circumstances nor the weather seem favorable at the moment." The rainstorm had left the cuffs of his trousers wet. Drops of water beaded his thinning hair.

Eliza worried about Percy, although Richard assured her the estate peacocks slept in a large coop when the weather turned rainy. She decided to check on Percy once this police visit ended. She'd be most upset to find her pet peacock soaked and chilled in some tree.

Brakefield scanned the room. "One member of your party is not here. The Frenchman."

"I could not find him," the count replied. He sat to one side of an inlaid writing desk, his arm draped over the polished wood surface. The countess occupied an identical tufted chair at the other end of the table, completing the impression of two monarchs perched on their thrones. Even her tawny brown silk dress matched the color of his suit.

"Philippe received a telegram while we were at breakfast," Richard said. "He left the table to read it. I have not seen him since." He turned to the butler, who stood at attention near Higgins. "Baxter, please find Mr. Corbet and inform him that his presence is required."

The butler bowed, then took his leave.

"Must we wait for him to show up?" Lady Annabel asked. Eliza thought she looked quite attractive this morning in an amber dress of faun silk and velvet, trimmed with metallic gold cord. Combined with her red hair and creamy skin, Lady Annabel seemed the personification of autumn. Perhaps Higgins should have let her catch him a time or two.

"Yes, can we get on with it?" Sir Anthony said.

"All right then." The chief constable looked down at his notes. "We spoke with authorities in America. A warrant for

Dwight Pentwater's arrest was issued in July. He left New York before he could be arrested and we believe he entered the country illegally last month. Probably under an assumed name, given that he was a wanted criminal."

A sudden discordant sound from the piano drew attention to Lily and Freddy, who sat on its bench. "Sorry," Lily said, clearly flustered. "I accidentally leaned forward and hit the keys."

"What did they want to arrest him for?" Higgins asked.

"Fraud," Brakefield said. "Pentwater operated an investment company known as Pentland Inc. He formed the company in February 1912 with Gilbert Landis, a stockbroker turned financial adviser. After both men set up shop in Manhattan, they circulated flyers nationwide to attract investors. Not only did they guarantee a ten per cent return on each dollar invested with them, they promised such gains on a weekly basis."

Sir Anthony guffawed aloud, but the chief constable ignored him.

"In less than a month's time, more than three hundred thousand dollars had been invested with Pentland Inc.," Brakefield went on. "Each subsequent month saw an increase in investors. People from all over the country wanted to give their money to Pentwater and Landis, believing they would see a quick and sizable profit. At the end of the first year, Pentwater and Landis had netted over a million dollars. However, their investors weren't so fortunate."

When Sir Anthony laughed once more, the chief constable turned to the explorer, who sat in a loveseat opposite Eliza and Clara. "You find this amusing, Sir Anthony?"

"It's always amusing to learn how foolish greedy men can be. I may not be a financier, but I recognize a con game when I hear it." He fished a handkerchief from his jacket and loudly blew his nose.

Lady Annabel, who sat beside him, shot her husband a disapproving look.

Sir Anthony stuffed his handkerchief back into his pocket. "If people are stupid enough to fall for such schemes, they deserve to lose their shirts. They lost their money, didn't they, Constable Brakefield?"

He nodded. "Except for those who first invested with them."

"I'm confused," Eliza said. "After people gave Pentwater and Landis their money, what did they invest that money in?"

"Stocks and bonds, most likely," the count sniffed. "Or business ventures that required capital investment."

"Actually, Pentwater and Landis never invested in anything. They kept most of the money for themselves." Brakefield closed his notebook. "To keep up the pretense, they only paid those who first put money into the company. They made certain those returns were impressive enough to convince the other investors to be patient."

"A brilliant ruse," Higgins said, "but not one they could continue indefinitely."

Now it made sense to Eliza. "So when enough people wanted to know why their investment never paid off, Pentwater and his partner realized the game was up."

"Probably when they decided to escape, too," Higgins added.

"Both men fled the country in July," Brakefield informed them. "Landis was discovered two weeks later in Toronto as he tried to book passage to Europe. He was brought back to New York where he's now standing trial for grand larceny. If convicted, he could be sentenced to ten years in prison. A prison I believe they call Sing Sing."

"To think that terrible man was a guest in our house! And it's all your fault." Clara pointed an accusing finger at the countess.

"What an absurd accusation," she said in outrage. "I demand an apology."

Count Rudolf frowned. "*Ja.* You must apologize to my wife."

"I will not apologize." Clara lifted her chin in defiance. "You should apologize to Richard and me for inviting Mr. Pentwater. And to think you had the nerve to object to my inviting Madame Evangeline. At least she is a perfectly respectable person."

Everyone turned their attention to Madame Evangeline, who lounged on a sofa by the window. Her ivory silk gown matched the sofa's fabric so well, she seemed to blend in with its cushions. By her dreamy expression, Eliza wondered if she was even paying attention to the conversation. She found it curious that Madame had not worn one of her dark and somber gowns. Then again, Eliza had not chosen black today either. How sad that no one mourned Dwight Pentwater. But he was little more than a stranger.

"But you both invited a criminal," Clara continued. "If Mr. Pentwater hadn't died, who knows what he might have stolen from the house?"

"I agree," Richard said. "You have placed us in a difficult position. After news of his crime and his death become public, how do we explain Pentwater's presence in our home?"

Count Rudolf's right eye began to twitch. "*Es ist nicht unsere Schuld*," he muttered.

"My husband is right," the countess said. "It is not our fault. How could we know about the nefarious deeds of this man?"

"A proper hostess should be aware of what their guests have been up to," Clara snapped. "They don't allow any old scoundrel to sit at their table and sleep under their roof."

Eliza had never been prouder of her young friend.

"Herr Pentwater was a well known businessman," the count said. "As I told you yesterday, we met in Berlin a few years ago."

"Had you much contact with him since?" the chief constable asked.

"Not in person. By letter. An occasional phone call."

"Regarding what?"

The count fidgeted in his seat. "Politics. Business."

"Please be more specific."

"He has done nothing wrong," the countess insisted.

"I will be the judge of that after you have answered my questions. And not just Count von Weisinger. All of you are to be questioned again today."

"Everyone seems to be getting steamed up over a simple hunting accident," Lily said.

Lady Annabel tugged at the locket on her long gold necklace. "Exactly."

"The interviews will take place in the study," Brakefield said, ignoring their comments. "Each of you will be questioned separately. What I learn shall remain private." He paused. "Unless it has direct bearing on the case."

Sir Anthony grumbled aloud. "Is this necessary? The fellow died because of a stray bullet. The fog was thick as custard yesterday. I've taken part in dozens of shoots. This wouldn't be the first time someone has been killed by accident, usually one of the beaters. Pentwater happened to be standing in the wrong place at the wrong time."

"Perhaps, Sir Anthony. But Pentwater was also a criminal whose company bankrupted people. Many investors saw their entire fortunes lost. Two investors committed suicide."

Eliza didn't blame Clara. To think such a vile thief had sat at table with them.

"Pentwater made enemies," Brakefield went on. "Enemies who might feel they had nothing to lose now that their money was gone. Enemies who might want Pentwater dead and were prepared to make that happen."

"Well, it's not me," Lily said in a strained voice. "Constable, I don't mean to grouse, but I'm just an actress. I don't see what I can tell you."

"I won't know that either, Miss Marlowe, until we have our interview."

Freddy put his arm around Lily's shoulders and hugged her close.

"I never met Mr. Pentwater," Madame Evangeline suddenly announced. "But perhaps when we speak, Constable, the spirits will come through. They may tell me something important. All secrets are revealed on the Other Side."

Brakefield ignored this pronouncement. "It is possible Mr. Pentwater's death was accidental, despite his criminal past. If so, all of you will be free to go. But at this time, everyone is to remain at Banfield Manor until inquiries are completed."

Eliza heard Higgins muttering. She didn't blame him. It felt like they were prisoners.

The butler re-entered the room. "Excuse me, sir."

"Yes, Baxter?" Richard asked.

"I have been informed by one of the footmen that Mr. Corbet left the house twenty minutes ago. He was carrying his traveling bags."

"His traveling bags?" Richard repeated. "Why would he do that?"

Eliza thought the answer was obvious. So did the police constables.

"Didn't Corbet fly here in his aeroplane?" one the constables asked their chief.

Before he could answer, the sound of a plane's rumbling engine met their ears.

Eliza sprang to her feet and ran to the window. The rain had stopped and there was no morning mist. She had a clear view of Philippe Corbet about to make his escape.

CHAPTER 12

"*B*loody hell!" Stuffing his notebook into his jacket, Chief Constable Brakefield ran out of the drawing room. His men raced after him. Higgins hoped they wouldn't be too late.

"What's going on?" Freddy asked. "Why is Corbet leaving without telling anyone?"

"*Dummkopf.*" Count Rudolf shook his head at him. "The Frenchman is escaping."

The countess sighed. "It appears Monsieur Corbet has taken fright. He would not do so without reason. Which means his reasons must be criminal."

"At least it's livened up the morning," Sir Anthony said with a laugh. "And I feared we faced a dull day cooped up in the house. Things have turned rather amusing."

"What a ridiculous thing to say, Anthony. There's nothing amusing about murder." Lady Annabel pulled on her gold necklace so hard, the locket broke off.

"Wait. Did Philippe Corbet kill Mr. Pentwater?" Clara rushed over to her husband and threw herself in his arms. "Richard, this is horrible."

Richard looked as miserable as his bride. Higgins felt miserable himself. Corbet may have had a reason to hate Pentwater, but would the Frenchman commit murder? Corbet was an admired aviator, a pioneer, and a decent and intelligent man. Higgins took no pleasure in thinking him a killer. But if he was guilty, he must face justice.

"None of this seems real," Lily said. "I feel like we're all actors in one of my movies."

Higgins joined Eliza at the window. "I'm going out there."

She tore her attention away from the scene outside. "Why? The police are better able to capture him than you are." Eliza gave a pointed glance at his injured arm.

"I want to be there when they pull Philippe out of that plane. He may be too upset to concoct a proper lie. If so, I need to hear what he has to say."

"But he's not in the aeroplane yet. He's still on the ground, trying to spin that thing you call a propeller."

"Good." Higgins strode out of the room.

Eliza followed him. "Wait! I'll go with you."

He stopped her in the hallway. "Stay here. Pay attention to what everyone says and does. If Philippe didn't kill Pentwater, one of them certainly did."

For a moment, he feared she might object, Instead, Eliza gave him a slight push. "Then you'd better hurry."

Higgins did just that, and almost knocked down a chambermaid busy with her dustpan in the foyer. He didn't stop until he reached the front door when he realized he had no quick way to reach Philippe's aeroplane on the estate. It would take a good fifteen minute walk. And the police were already speeding across the lawn in their four-seater Daimler.

"How long will it take to have a car brought up from the garage?" Higgins asked the butler, who surveyed the scene from the front steps.

"The chauffeur can bring the car within five minutes, sir."

At that moment a black and white delivery van appeared from around the side of the house, apparently having made a delivery to one of the back entrances. The words 'Lisle Milk Service' were painted on its sides.

Flipping the collar of his suit jacket up against the brisk chilly wind, Higgins ran down the steps. "Hold on! I say, chap!" He waved at the driver with his good arm.

The van rolled to a stop. The driver peered at Higgins through the open door. "You wantin' more milk? I just delivered it to the kitchen, along with the daily cream."

"No. I need you to drive me over to where that aeroplane is." Higgins jumped into the van, causing the driver's eyes to widen.

"Aeroplane?"

Higgins pointed over the fellow's shoulder to where the plane sat in the distance.

"Would you look at that?" the driver said in wonder. "I never seen a flying machine."

"If you want to see one up close, step on the gas. Now!"

The driver gave Higgins a shrewd look, clearly sizing up his status and importance. He must have passed muster because a moment later, Higgins was headed in the van toward Philippe and his aeroplane.

"Don't stay on the drive," Higgins instructed. "Cut across the grass, like the police did."

"The police?" The driver's expression turned suspicious. "Does Lord Ashmore know about the police and flyin' machines on his front lawn?"

"His lordship is well aware of the situation." Higgins sat forward as he watched Brakefield and his constables draw closer to the aeroplane. Philippe had started the motor and was climbing into the cockpit. Any second, he'd taxi across the lawn and achieve altitude. Higgins gauged the distance they still had to cross and feared Philippe would make his escape. As the delivery van got closer to the aeroplane, Higgins heard the horn honks from the police vehicle, as if trying to get his attention. The noise of the aeroplane motor was louder. Philippe might be unaware the police were chasing him.

"Can't you go any faster, man?" Higgins asked.

"Not without tipping the blooming truck over and busting my milk bottles." To prove his point, the delivery van hit a depression in the lawn, rattling the glass bottles in back. "You're lucky this wasn't a year ago. Lisle Dairy had us make deliveries by horse in a 'milk pram.' Course there weren't no bottles to bust then, just tin cans. Everything changed when Mr. Lisle bought motor vans. I miss my horse somethin' awful."

The sound of the aeroplane motor grew louder. The delivery van had gotten close enough, glass bottles rattling. Now Higgins had a good look at Philippe in the cockpit. He wore his flying goggles and a leather helmet.

"If you don't mind me askin', sir, why are we driving around out here with the police?"

"We need to stop that aeroplane from taking off."

The plane began to move. "Look at that," the driver yelled. "They're trying to outrace that monster flyin' machine!"

Actually, the police were putting themselves in the plane's path. Higgins cursed under his breath. If Philippe didn't see them in time, that crazy idea might get them killed. And if the Frenchman had murdered Pentwater, it could be exactly what he had in mind.

"Follow the plane," Higgins ordered.

"As long as you're not wanting me to win any race. This here's a milk wagon, not a bleedin' horse at Ascot."

They had no hope of doing more than trailing the plane at a respectable distance. Not so the police, who drove a much faster vehicle. Now they had caught up with it, like two runners almost at the finish line. Suddenly, Brakefield's motorcar sped up and overtook the plane. Their car's horn had been blaring nonstop. One of the constables hung out the window and waved at Philippe, who appeared not to notice.

Higgins tensed up as the police motorcar turned left. By Jupiter, they meant to cut directly across the path of the plane! He didn't know whether to admire Brakefield's courage or pity his foolishness.

"God Almighty!" Higgins cried out. The plane headed straight for the car. He shut his eyes, dreading the sight of the impending accident.

He heard the delivery driver say, "Never seen such damned foolishness in my life! If I were that gent in the aeroplane, I'd be giving those coppers a ticket."

Higgins opened his eyes in time to see Philippe swerve to the right, narrowly missing the motorcar. After a fishtail spin, the plane mercifully came to a stop. By the time Philippe cut the motor and its propeller slowed, Higgins was running toward the plane. Brakefield and his men jumped out of their own car and took up positions around the machine.

"Mr. Corbet, I order you to surrender," Brakefield shouted.

The Frenchman shook his head at the constable, but obeyed. By the time Philippe climbed out of the plane, Higgins had joined the others.

"*Avez-vous perdu votre esprit?*" Philippe yelled at Brakefield, clearly in a rage. "*Vous aurais pu être tué!*"

"He wants to know if you've lost your mind," Higgins translated for Brakefield, who looked confounded by Corbet's French. "And that you could have been killed."

"You've lost *your* mind, trying to escape in your aeroplane!" Brakefield seemed as enraged as Philippe. "Did you think to make a quick getaway because you killed Pentwater?"

Philippe turned to Higgins. "This man cannot be serious!"

Higgins frowned. "The police came to Banfield Manor this morning with information about Pentwater. It appears he committed fraud in America and was a fugitive from justice."

"Until we learn if there is any connection between Mr. Pentwater and the members of the Ashmore house party," Brakefield said, "no one is allowed to leave. I thought I made that clear last night."

"In all fairness, yesterday you only asked the guests to remain at Banfield Manor until the death had been officially ruled a hunting accident," Higgins reminded the chief constable. "It seemed a polite request, not an order."

"I changed that to an official order this morning."

"True. But Mr. Corbet was not in the room at the time." Higgins felt Brakefield was being unreasonable.

"He wasn't in the room at the time because he was planning his escape," one of the other policeman chimed in.

"Exactly," Brakefield said. "Don't you find it suspicious that this man decided to leave without letting anyone know?"

"I may leave whenever I want." Philippe pulled off his flying goggles. His dark eyes regarded the three policemen with hostility. "I am a French citizen, Chief Constable. You and your gendarmes have no power to stop me."

Higgins feared that statement would not be well received.

Brakefield nodded to his two men. "Oh, we don't? Take Mr. Corbet into custody. I'm arresting him on suspicion of murder."

The two constables took hold of Philippe's arms, effectively restraining him.

"*Mon Dieu*! I have done nothing," Philippe protested. "*Je suis un homme innocent*. You have no right to arrest me! None! And I must return to France. I must!"

"What's so urgent in France that you didn't bother to tell your hosts you were leaving?"

"The chief constable has a point, Philippe," Higgins said. "To fly off without telling any of us does look odd."

"It looks damned suspicious," Brakefield added.

"It is a private matter." Philippe spoke to Higgins, ignoring the police. "During the hunt, I speak to you about a certain young lady for whom I have much affection."

Higgins remembered the conversation. "The woman who lives in Trieste."

"*Oui*. Mademoiselle Ardant. We are secretly affianced since the spring."

"Then you were flying back to France to get married?" Higgins asked.

"Likely story," one of the police constables muttered.

"No. I fly back to prevent her from getting married."

"You just said the two of you are engaged," Brakefield said.

"We are, but her father does not wish it. That is why we keep it secret. He is a deputy cabinet minister, with ambitions to rise as high as Raymond Poincaré. Monsieur Ardant insists his daughter marry a man who is rich or has influence. I am only an aviator."

"A famous one," Higgins remarked.

Philippe shook his head. "Fame is not as important as riches and power, not to Bernard Ardant. And a widowed government minister wishes to marry Nathalie. The telegram this morning is from my Nathalie. She is most upset."

"I assume her parents demanded she no longer see you," Higgins said. This whole escapade further convinced him that romantic love only led to trouble.

"*Bien dit!* Her parents insist she marry the deputy minister in three days!" He swore in French. "Everything is arranged: the church, the priest, the menu for the wedding breakfast. Her *belle-mere*—stepmother—has ordered the flowers and white gown. They wait until I leave France to put this into action. Now Nathalie, my only *amoureux*, will be forced to marry unless I return and take her away!"

Brakefield shrugged. His men seemed unconvinced as well. Higgins didn't share their skepticism. Yesterday, Philippe spoke at length to Higgins about his love for a mademoiselle called

Nathalie. He even recalled she was twenty, the same age as Eliza. According to Philippe, the young woman possessed the profile of Nefertiti, the allure of Helen of Troy, and the figure of the Venus de Milo. In other words, he was behaving like every other passionate Frenchman in the throes of love.

Higgins turned to Brakefield. "I believe him."

"Well, if you believe him, I guess that's good enough for the police." Brakefield's voice dripped with sarcasm. He gestured to his men, who tightened their grip on Philippe's arms. "Get him into the car. We're taking him back to the house."

"But I must return to France!" Philippe struggled against their hold. "I cannot allow my Nathalie to marry another man!"

With a heavy heart, Higgins watched the constables shove the Frenchman into their black Daimler. Once they learned about the death of Philippe's friend Henri, they would be even more convinced of Philippe's guilt. Despite that, Higgins's instincts told him otherwise. As the police drove off, Higgins became aware of the delivery van driver. He stood a few feet away, tapping one foot on the wet grass.

"Are we done here, sir? I'll drop you off, but I must get back to work. Don't have time for all this stuff about murder and French ladies. Not with deliveries to make."

"Thank you. You've been most accommodating." Higgins reached for his wallet and pulled out a pound note. "For your trouble."

He tipped his cap. "I appreciate it, sir, although I should be thanking you. After all, I ain't never had such a morning. I got to see a flying machine up close *and* a murderer."

Higgins hoped only half of that statement was true.

"THE POLICE STOPPED THE AEROPLANE FROM TAKING OFF," ELIZA informed the others in the drawing room. She pressed her forehead to the windowpane. "Now it looks like Philippe is arguing with them."

Madame Evangeline joined her at the window. "This is terrible."

"Let's hope they clap that murderous frog in irons," Sir Anthony declared.

"One should never trust the French," the count agreed. "Remember Napoleon."

"I believe Mr. Bonaparte was a Corsican," Lady Annabel said in a haughty tone.

"Corsican. French. What does it matter?" Sir Anthony replied. "Corbet is guilty."

Madame Evangeline spun around. "How can you say such a thing? Monsieur Corbet is one of the finest men I have ever met. None of us know why he has decided to leave. But I am sure his reasons are sound."

"I'm not sure *your* reasoning is, madam," Sir Anthony said with a chuckle. "The man up and leaves without a word to any of us. And just happens to do so when the police are here. Looks like an escape to me. And only the guilty try to escape."

"*Mais non,*" she protested. "Sometimes the innocent must flee to protect themselves.""That sounds like the silly plot of one of Miss Marlowe's films," the countess remarked.

Clara stamped her foot. "You are not to be rude to my guests."

"Your guests?" the countess shot back. "My husband and I are the ones who invited most of them. And we are the only people trying to prevent this house party from descending into complete chaos."

"Doing a pretty poor job of it, too," Eliza muttered.

When Sir Anthony once again blew his nose, Lady Annabel almost bit her husband's head off. Those left behind in the drawing room were anxious and on edge. Lily even asked for brandy. But the count had to ring for a footman; the actual master of the house sat with his head in his hands. Richard seemed overwhelmed by the situation. Meanwhile, Clara had resumed blaming her sister-in-law for this latest escapade. The new baroness had finally lost her fear of the countess, but Eliza found her timing ill-advised. What was the point of bemoaning the guest list when a man's freedom lay at stake?

"How can you all argue when the police may arrest Monsieur Corbet?" Madame Evangeline reminded them. "This is not the time for silly arguments. I fear a miscarriage of justice is about to unfold."

Eliza noticed that the spiritualist trembled slightly. Had Madame Evangeline been moved by the Frenchman's dashing looks and adventurous feats?

"I like our Frenchman, too," Lady Annabel said with a weary air. "He is an accomplished and cultured young man. However, he must be guilty of something."

"He killed Herr Pentwater," the count announced. "That is clear."

Madame Evangeline stiffened. "That is not true. I spoke with him last night at dinner. He carries much sadness with him and is guilty only of caring too much. If he had committed a crime, my spirit guides would have told me."

No one bothered to dispute this comment. With a heavy heart, Eliza continued to watch out the window. She, too, had found Philippe Corbet a charming, likable young man. It saddened her to think that he might be a murderer. Yet he did have a motive: revenge for the death of his friend. How tragic if he were tried and found guilty. A man accustomed to flying as free as a bird would instead be locked away in a damp, filthy jail cell.

"The police are driving back to the house," Eliza reported. "They have Philippe in the car. And Professor Higgins is following them in a strange motorcar. Looks like a milk van."

"In my country, a great estate keeps their own dairy cows,"

the count said. "We have no need of milkmen from the village. The English do not know how to live like proper gentlemen."

"If you don't like it, go home to Austria." Clara shot back. "Richard and I didn't ask you to stay. In fact, I wish you were the ones flying off in Philippe's aeroplane."

"Common upstart." The countess fumed. "You disgrace the Ashmore name."

Before the argument escalated, Madame Evangeline cried out, "They are almost here!" Picking up her skirts, she rushed out of the room.

An uncomfortable silence followed as they all looked at each other.

"Did a secret romance spring up between Philippe Corbet and Madame Evangeline in the past two days?" Lady Annabel asked with a sly smile.

"If so, I suspect it's also a secret to Philippe," Eliza said.

"I can't be the only one who thinks our ghost lady is looking all fresh and girlish today," Lily said from her perch on the piano bench.

"Dressing up to attract the attention of that murderous frog," Sir Anthony muttered.

Eliza's heart sank when she saw the police pull up in front of the house. A second later, Philippe was hauled out of the car. Two constables kept hold of his arms as they pushed him toward the house. He was already being treated as a common criminal.

"They're bringing him inside," she said. "Madame Evangeline could be right. He could have a logical explanation for leaving."

Even Clara regarded her with a pitying expression.

Loud voices erupted from the front hall, along with a woman's scream.

Eliza raced out of the drawing room, hearing the others follow close behind. When she reached the entrance foyer, she saw two detectives wrestle Philippe to the floor. Pieces of a broken vase lay scattered on the tile.

A red-faced Brakefield gripped Madame Evangeline by the arm. She clutched part of the vase. "By heaven, get that man under control!" yelled the chief constable.

"You will hurt him! Stop," Madame Evangeline begged. "Please stop!"

"And I'll hurt you, Madame, if you try to interfere with an arrest again." He gave her a shake. "Do you understand me?"

"What has she done?" Richard asked in distress.

At that moment, Higgins walked through the open front door. He looked as stunned as everyone else. "What the devil is going on here?"

"The Frenchman resisted arrest," said one of the detectives restraining Corbet. "And that woman tried to stop us by braining us over the head with a bloody vase."

Cor, Eliza wished she'd been here to see that.

"That is not the truth," Madame Evangeline said. "I only wanted to draw the policemen's attention. So they would listen to what my spirits wish to say." She winced. "And you are hurting me, Chief Constable. Let me go!"

The door to the servants' quarters flew open, revealing an angry Zoltan Batur.

"Take your hands off Madame! If you harm her, I will cut out your tongue!"

"I advise you not to threaten the police," Brakefield warned.

"This is no threat. It is a promise." Batur drew a shiny dagger from his jacket.

As Eliza gasped, he advanced toward the police constable with the raised dagger.

CHAPTER 13

"*E*veryone, get back!" Higgins shouted.

"He has a knife!" Freddy stated the obvious.

"This is unacceptable behavior," the countess announced. "Disgraceful!"

Brakefield pushed Madame Evangeline behind him in a protective gesture. "Take one more step, Mr. Batur, and my men and I will break both your arms."

"Zoltan, please stop," Evangeline pleaded. "You will only make this worse."

"Why does he hurt you? I heard you scream from downstairs." Batur pointed his dagger at the chief constable. When the two detectives who had wrestled Philippe to the floor slowly stood up, he included them in his threatening gaze. "Don't move!"

"*Er ist ein verrückter,*" Count Rudolf warned. "A madman. Stay back!"

A shocked Philippe sat on the floor watching all this unfold. Higgins felt shocked himself but was helpless with his arm in a sling.

"If I only had one of my pistols with me," Sir Anthony grumbled.

"I could really use that brandy I asked for," Lily said from the drawing room doorway.

"Mr. Batur, I must ask you to stop before someone is injured." Richard took a few steps forward. Clara stood behind him, clinging to Eliza's arm. "I will see to it that the police do not distress Madame Evangeline further."

"Stay out of this, Lord Ashmore." Brakefield's eyes never left Batur and his dagger. "This is a police matter."

"And this is Banfield Manor and I am its lord." Richard's voice took on a new gravity. "I would advise you not to forget our respective stations."

If the situation hadn't been so tense, Higgins might have clapped the young baron on the back. Someone needed to defuse this situation; Ashmore had a better chance of doing that than the agitated policemen. And while Higgins had no regard for class distinctions, his countrymen cared far too much. Chief Constable Brakefield knew his own position in Kent would be in jeopardy if he offended the new lord of the manor. Some things hadn't changed at all since Jacobean times.

"Fine, sir," Brakefield said. "Let's see you handle this angry savage."

"He is no savage," Evangeline protested. "Mr. Batur is only trying to protect me."

"She's right," Eliza said. "After all, the man is her bodyguard. And he heard her scream."

"Madame Evangeline also shouted that you were hurting her." Richard frowned at Brakefield. "The chap ran up here and saw you restraining the young woman. How do you expect him to respond? Please remember that he is paid to guard her."

"It appears that everyone is just doing their jobs." Higgins walked closer to the assembled group. Out of the corner of his eye, he noticed a terrified chambermaid pressed against the wall.

Batur stood frozen in the same position, dagger raised.

"Put your knife away." Richard told him. "No one will harm you or Madame Evangeline. You have my word."

Zoltan Batur scanned everyone in the entrance hall, his gaze uncertain. He began to lower the knife when a flurry of footsteps sounded behind him. As he pivoted, two footmen ran through the doorway leading to the servants' quarters. Before he could raise the dagger once again, both men grabbed him. The knife clattered to the tile floor. Brakefield snatched it up.

"Thank heaven that's over," Lady Annabel murmured.

Higgins thought her declaration premature, since Batur still struggled with the footmen. Higgins recognized one of them as the young man called Charlie, a friend of Eliza's from the old neighborhood.

The butler emerged from the servants' stairway. "My lord, I heard the commotion and thought it best to ask Charlie and Albert to be of assistance. Both men have had boxing experience."

"Thank you, Baxter. But I believe we have the situation in hand." Richard nodded at the two strapping footmen who had a firm grip on the Turk. "Release him."

The footmen looked as skeptical as the police constables, but Charlie and Albert stepped back. A disgruntled Batur straightened the sleeves of his jacket.

"Can someone explain what the devil is going on?" Higgins asked.

"I told the police it was a mistake to arrest Monsieur Corbet," Madame Evangeline began. "He is not guilty of the death of that American. It is an impossibility. Such a fine, sensitive man could not be moved to violence."

"*Merci mille fois*, Madame Evangeline." Philippe finally got up from the floor. He brushed at the dirt on his trousers.

"The police handled Monsieur Corbet most roughly." She shot an accusing look at them. "As if he were a wild animal. When they threw him on the floor, I screamed. They might have hurt him. So I picked up the vase and hit it against that." She pointed at the marble-top table behind her. "I had to make them stop. To pay attention to what I must say."

"Why do you care so much about the Frenchman?" Constable Stevens asked her. "Are you and he old friends? Relatives?"

"Your lover perhaps?" Brakefield narrowed his eyes at her.

She lifted her chin. "Absolutely not. I only met Monsieur Corbet two days ago."

"You seem to be awful upset up over the fate of a man you barely know," Stevens said.

"Everyone should be upset to see a miscarriage of justice. He is innocent of any crime. My spirits have told me."

Brakefield looked suspicious. "I think there's something you're not telling us."

"And I think you and your men have behaved like brutes." She went to Philippe and gently touched his arm. "Did they harm you?"

"No, madam. But I am most grateful for your assistance and your faith in me. *Merci encore.*" Philippe took her hand and kissed it. She smiled.

Higgins and Eliza exchanged curious glances. If there hadn't been a young woman called Nathalie in Trieste, he wondered if Monsieur Corbet might have lost his heart to the lovely spiritualist with the haunting blue eyes.

Her bodyguard must have felt the same. "I believe you care so much because he reminds you of another Frenchman."

She stiffened at his disapproving tone.

"Hold on." Sir Anthony chuckled. "Is there another Frenchman we have to worry about?"

"Who is he referring to?" Brakefield asked Madame Evangeline.

She remained silent.

"Maybe you can tell us." Higgins turned his attention to Batur.

"The Frenchman was called Aristide Robichaud." He stared at Madame Evangeline, who averted her gaze.

"Was?" Eliza asked.

"He died eight years ago," Madame Evangeline said in a voice barely above a whisper. "He drowned. I had known Aristide since childhood. It was a great blow."

"Madame blames herself for his death," Batur added. "She is wrong to do so. It was an accident. But she has never forgiven herself."

"He would not have been on the river that morning had I not asked him to meet me. Aristide was in love. He always did as I asked." She bit her lip. "His death was my fault."

"Were you in love with him?" Eliza asked.

Madame Evangeline shut her eyes, as if the memory was too painful.

"Of course she was in love with him," Batur said in a gruff voice. "No man will ever compare to Aristide Robichaud. Not even the man she ended up marrying."

"So Robichaud wasn't your husband? The one who died?" Eliza looked almost as sad as Evangeline.

She shook her head. "Aristide and I planned to marry, but fate had other plans. My spirits said not a word to warn me, to prepare me for the tragedy. Perhaps they knew my heart would be so broken, I might die before he did."

Higgins glanced at Corbet. Young, handsome, and full of life. "Does Philippe resemble Robichaud, by any chance?"

"There is a great resemblance," Evangeline said, her voice breaking.

"That is why she carries on about *this* Frenchman." Batur waved a hand at Philippe.

"A touching story," Brakefield said. "But not touching enough to make me forget Corbet tried to escape in his aeroplane."

"Yes, why did you leave without telling us, Philippe?" Richard asked.

Philippe glanced at Higgins. "Please tell them."

As Brakefield gave a sigh of exasperation, Higgins quickly told everyone about the telegram and Philippe's love for Nathalie. When he was done, Lily remarked, "Sounds like the plot of my first motion picture, *Love's Struggle*."

"A pretty tale," the countess observed. "But how do we know it is true?"

"I can prove it." Philippe unfastened his leather flight jacket and pulled out a crumpled paper. He handed it to Higgins. "This is the telegram I received at breakfast."

Higgins looked over the telegram, written in French, from a girl called Nathalie. "It asks him to hurry back to France before she is forced to marry."

"Do you mind?" Brakefield took the paper from him. "This is police evidence."

"Evidence of what?" Higgins asked. "Why do you insist Pentwater was murdered?"

"Because he was a fugitive from justice."

"Does that mean he couldn't also die in a hunting accident?" Higgins avoided looking at Eliza. He knew she believed the ghostly prognostications of Madame Evangeline.

"Herr Higgins, you surprise me." Count Rudolf said. "We spoke an hour ago about the death of the American. And I told you why Corbet had a good reason to want him dead."

"What in the world do you mean?" Richard wore a perplexed expression.

"Enlighten us, count," Brakefield ordered.

Instead of replying, the count gestured for Higgins to inform the chief constable. Bloody hell, how had he become the resident teller of tales? Trying to keep his own temper in check, Higgins explained how the death of Philippe's friend Henri occurred because of the defective aeroplane parts manufactured by Pentwater's company.

Philippe seemed as pained to relive his friend's death as Madame Evangeline had been over the drowning of Aristide.

After Higgins finished, Brakefield nodded. "As I thought," he said with an air of satisfaction. "Motive and opportunity. Add to that his attempt to escape just as the police arrive on the scene." He snapped his fingers at the other two constables. "Arrest him."

Madame Evangeline cried out in protest.

"But I did not kill Monsieur Pentwater," Philippe said as the detectives came to stand beside him. "*Je suis innocent.*"

"Do you deny Pentwater's company was responsible for your friend's death?" Brakefield asked the Frenchman.

"I do not deny that. When I hear his name announced at dinner, I know it is the man who owns the company called Argo. But I did not expect to see him. How could I know?"

"Maybe you didn't know ahead of time, but here he was. The man who basically killed your best friend. It must have put you in a blind rage."

"But Henri dies two years ago. His friends, his family—we are angry to learn it is the fault of a greedy man's company. A company that saves money by making machine parts that fail. A lawsuit is brought. The company goes bankrupt. We mourn Henri. But we move on. We must."

"Only here is the man behind your friend's death," Brakefield pressed. "Brought right to the dinner table. The next day there's a hunt, and everyone has a gun. Including you. The perfect chance to deliver justice."

He shook his head. "It would not be justice. I am not a

gendarme. Or a judge. It would be revenge. I am not a vengeful man."

"Leave him alone," Madame Evangeline spat at the police. "He has done nothing. It is you who are the monster, Constable Brakefield."

Brakefield looked at his detectives. "Until we're finished here, keep this woman away from the pottery."

Higgins crossed his arms. "See here, I must agree with the lady. First, I am not convinced Pentwater was even murdered. Second, anyone in the forest could have shot the American."

"But did they all have a motive?" Brakefield looked like he wanted to smash a vase over Higgins's head.

"I think the frog did it," Sir Anthony said. "So let's bring this to a conclusion."

"*Ja*," agreed the count. "*Der Mann ist schuldig*. Guilty."

Philippe shook his head. "*Mon Dieu*, why will no one believe me?"

"Chief Constable, I don't think Philippe did it either," Eliza said. "And for all you know, there's another person in the house party who had a reason to want Dwight Pentwater dead."

"Don't be absurd, Miss Doolittle." Lady Annabel gave her a reproving look.

Evangeline let out a mournful cry.

"Madame!" Batur rushed to her side. He grabbed her about the waist before she could slump to the floor in a faint.

"Is she all right?" Clara asked.

Evangeline shut her eyes. "Those who wish to deceive are here. They are among us."

"She is in one of her trances." Batur gave her a gentle shake. "Speak."

Higgins noticed how Eliza seemed riveted to what was unfolding.

"A man who was lost," Evangeline spoke in a monotone. "A

man in the jungle. A man who wanders alone. Desolate. Angry. A man much honored. Knighted by his king."

"I wonder who that man can be," Sir Anthony said in a sarcastic voice.

"Indeed," Lady Annabel added.

Eliza turned to them. "Shh!"

Madame Evangeline cocked her head to one side. "The spirits tell me this man thought he would be rescued quickly. Rescued by the man who sent him. A rich American."

"How long do we have listen to this folderol?" Sir Anthony asked. "Damned nonsense."

"But the rich man did not care." She paused, as if listening to spectral voices once more. "Even though he had paid for the expedition, he spent no money finding the knight. And the knight knew he had been abandoned. When he was rescued by chance, he swore to never forget who left him to die in the jungle." Evangeline sighed. "Such anger. Such unending rage."

"That is quite enough!" Sir Anthony's deafening shout startled Madame Evangeline. Her eyes fluttered open.

"Did I say something?" she asked, puzzled.

"You know damned well what you said about me!"

Eliza looked impressed. "You spoke about Sir Anthony being lost."

"I did?"

Although Higgins didn't believe in Madame Evangeline's spirits, he did believe she had looked into the histories of everyone on the guest list. And that impressed him.

"Did Pentwater fund your Amazonian expedition?" Higgins asked.

The older man flushed red with anger. "Don't tell me you believe this charlatan."

"A simple yes or no will suffice."

"It's an easy matter to verify, Sir Anthony," Brakefield said.

"Why don't you save us the trouble and answer the question. Did Dwight Pentwater fund your expedition to the Amazon?"

Everyone stared at him, waiting.

He stroked his plush mustache, as if hoping it was a genie's lamp and he could make a wish to disappear. "Yes," Sir Anthony said finally. "Dwight Pentwater paid for my expedition to the Amazon. I met him years ago when he was in England for the racing season, hobnobbing with new money at Ascot and Epsom Downs. He'd read about my latest exploration in Bolivia, and was interested in the tin reserves I had discovered. When he learned what I planned to explore next, he offered to back me."

"Why didn't the Royal Geographical Society sponsor your expedition?" Higgins asked. "Haven't they funded those you have undertaken in the past?"

"Yes, but those were for the purpose of surveying. Making maps. This time I wanted to search for something different. A legendary city of gold. The lost city of Mato Matlan. The Society had no interest in what they called treasure hunting."

"But Pentwater did?" Brakefield said.

Sir Anthony smirked. "Anything that involved treasure or gold interested him. He gave me the money I needed, expecting I would find something of value. If not gold, then precious metals. What neither of us expected was that my expedition team would die of disease or misfortune in the jungle. Or that I would become ill and hopelessly lost."

"Surely when you went missing," Higgins said, "search parties were sent out."

"It took months before anyone realized we'd gone missing. And I had only five men with me. Two Portuguese, two natives, and a *mestico de indio*. Men who had led dangerous and uncivilized lives. They had no one to mourn them or care about their whereabouts. No family or friends to go looking for them if they disappeared."

"But you're a man with important friends," Higgins reminded him.

"No one knew where to look for me." His expression turned hard. "Except Pentwater.

We agreed I should tell no one where I surmised the lost city was."

Higgins shrugged. "That makes sense. After all, when one goes off to discover a fabled city of gold, it might be best to keep those plans a secret."

"Adventurers and treasure seekers can be found behind every wimba tree in the jungle. I did not want rivals stumbling upon my lost city before I did."

Lady Annabel took his hand. "My husband has written of his travails in the Amazon. No need to press him on it. It's common knowledge that he lost one team member to dengue, two to sleeping sickness, another to an infection from a cut leg. As for the *mestico,* he suffered from malaria. While delirious one night, he ran off into the jungle where a coral snake bit him." She looked at Sir Anthony. "Isn't that right?"

"Yes, my dear." He gave her a grateful smile.

"Were you married to Sir Anthony when he went missing?" Brakefield asked.

"No, I did not meet Sir Anthony until three years ago. We married soon after." Her manner grew haughty. "But like any educated person in Britain, I knew of his exploits."

"You said Pentwater had knowledge of where you planned to look for this lost city," Higgins said. "Why didn't he send out a search party when too much time had elapsed?"

"I assumed he did. That hope kept me going as I wandered ill and alone in the jungle. Often pursued by hostile natives. A Christian missionary found me near death and brought me back to his village. He sent word to the nearest outpost of civilization. By the time I was brought to Recife, two years and five months had passed since I set out on my expedition."

"Did you wire Pentwater to let him know you were alive?" Brakefield asked.

Sir Anthony shook his head. "When I recovered my strength, I sailed for New York. He was shocked to see me. And amused. I was far from amused, however. I had learned in Brazil that one of the men who had outfitted my expedition wired Pentwater to let him know we had not been heard from in a long time. Pentwater told him to do nothing, that the lack of communication had been agreed upon due to the secrecy of our expedition."

"Was that true?" Eliza asked.

He snorted. "A self-serving lie. Pentwater assumed my men and I had died. And he didn't want to send search parties in case they discovered Mato Matlan themselves."

Higgins snapped his fingers. "A couple of years ago I read about some Americans looking for a lost city in Brazil. Didn't pay much attention to it. Thought it was one more futile search for El Dorado. But I wager Pentwater paid for that expedition, using the information you had given him."

"He did. But they never found anything, thank God."

Higgins doubted anyone would. Legendary lost cities usually remain no more than that.

He looked over at Brakefield. "It seems Monsieur Corbet is not the only guest who had motive and the opportunity to put an end to Dwight Pentwater."

"That is a lie!" Sir Anthony shouted. "How dare you insult me in such a manner?"

Lady Annabel looked offended as well. "What a beastly thing to say, Henry. I thought you were a scholar and a gentleman."

"A scholar, for certain. As for being a gentleman. . ." Eliza shrugged.

"My wife and I will not remain at Banfield Manor a moment longer." Sir Anthony glared at Higgins. "You have impugned my reputation. And dared to call me a murderer!"

"I simply said you had a reason to wish Mr. Pentwater ill. As

Philippe did. But that does not mean either of you killed him." Higgins gave a rueful smile. "Indeed, I'm still not convinced the chap was murdered. It seems more likely that one of you is simply a terrible shot."

"And I am not convinced that one of Lord Ashmore's guests did not deliberately aim their gun at the American." Brakefield regarded Philippe for a long moment. "An arrest at this time would be premature. The information about Sir Anthony has shed new light on the investigation, since both men had a reason to want Pentwater dead." He put up his hand to prevent either one from protesting. "I came here today to interrogate each one of you privately. That seems more urgent than ever. Especially if I learn another of you also nursed vengeful feelings against the American."

Philippe looked relieved. Sir Anthony did not.

Brakefield turned to his men. "Stevens, take Sir Anthony into the study. Detective Foster, put Corbet in the library. Remain with him until I am finished with Sir Anthony."

The two detectives took Sir Anthony and Philippe away.

The chief constable now directed his attention to the rest of the house party. "Each of you will be questioned. Wait in the drawing room until I call for you." Brakefield gave a brief nod to Richard, mindful that he was giving orders in another man's house. No one spoke until he left.

The butler gestured for the two footmen to return below stairs, then asked Richard, "Can I do anything, my lord?"

"Tea in the gold drawing room, please," he said. Baxter bowed.

"Scones and teacakes, too," Clara added. "It's almost time for elevenses."

"Isn't this a fine kettle of fish," Eliza said. "I wonder who else might have wanted to put Mr. Pentwater in the ground."

"It wasn't my husband," Lady Annabel said curtly. "Of that I am certain."

"And I know Monsieur Corbet is innocent." Madame Evangeline leaned against Mr. Batur for support.

"Madame Evangeline, why don't you ask your spirits?" Freddy suggested.

"I believe she has told us quite enough." Higgins laughed. "In fact, her latest revelation should keep the police occupied with Sir Anthony for hours."

"That is not funny, Henry," Lady Annabel chided him.

"It is not up to me, Mr. Eynsford Hill." Madame Evangeline sounded exhausted. "The spirits choose the time and place to come through. As they did just now. Otherwise I must implore them to show themselves by holding a séance."

"Let's have a séance then," Freddy said. "Sounds like a bit of fun."

"What a ghoulish idea." Lily shivered. "Who wants to talk to a bunch of ghosts?"

"Freddy's right." Eliza ignored her. "Who knows what else the spirits may say during an actual séance?" She looked over at Richard and Clara.

Like her brother, Clara appeared delighted by the idea. "What a splendid plan."

Richard seemed less delighted, but nodded. "Madame Evangeline?"

She took a deep breath. "Yes. I sense that my spirits will welcome the chance to speak again. We will have a séance tonight and let the dead join our company."

Although Higgins didn't put much faith in séances, he thought the "dead" might prove entertaining. Like a skilled magician, Madame Evangeline probably had more tricks up her sleeve. He also suspected she possessed a few secrets she had yet to reveal.

CHAPTER 14

*A*n anxious Eliza waited to see if Madame Evangeline approved of the room she and Clara had chosen for the séance. Banfield Manor's tapestry room certainly seemed appropriate for communing with the Other Side. Rich tapestry hangings on the wall not only lent an intimate air, they muffled sounds from the other parts of the house. And the candlelight which played over the scrolled plaster ceiling made one think of an earlier century.

"This room will do very well." Madame Evangeline nodded. "I hope you don't mind that my assistant has turned off the electric lights. I prefer candlelight when I contact the spirit world."

Higgins wore a cynical grin. "Should we expect the ghosts to blow them out at the proper time?"

Eliza kicked him in the shin. "Is there anything else you need, Madame?"

"No, Miss Doolittle. I only hope the policeman will not interrupt us."

"He shouldn't," Richard said. "Constable Stevens is only staying the night at Banfield Manor to make sure no one attempts to leave again." He avoided glancing at Philippe, whose face flushed red.

Now that Zoltan Batur had finished lighting the candles set into the hanging chandelier, he positioned himself beside the door. Garbed once again in black, he looked like a dark phantom. Eliza wondered if some of the ghosts were afraid of him. She also wondered if he'd reclaimed his knife from the police. A sulfuric scent from the matches he had used lingered in the room. Or maybe he was the source of the unsettling aroma.

The medium scanned the house guests who waited around the table. Like her assistant, Evangeline also wore black, but her lustrous moiré silk gown shimmered in the candlelight. And while her hair was swept back in her usual bun, tiny red satin roses were pinned along the crown of her head. A crimson cashmere shawl was draped over her shoulders as well.

Evangeline raised her hands. "Welcome, everyone. Please sit." A huge round table sat in the room's center with a dozen needlepoint-cushioned chairs. "Tonight, I shall attempt to cross the divide between the living and the dead with the help of the Cardinal, my spirit guide. Perhaps Richelieu himself may make an appearance."

Her words puzzled Eliza, who didn't understand why a bird would be a spirit guide. And who the devil was Richelieu?

Clara and Richard chose seats beside each other. Philippe Corbet claimed the chair beside Evangeline, while Freddy and Lily sat across from them.

"Are you sure about this?" the actress whispered.

"Relax, Lily," he said. "I'll protect you from any ghosts."

Eliza hoped a ghost would appear and send Lily screaming like a banshee back to America. Lady Annabel took the chair next to Higgins. Because Sir Anthony and the von Weisingers were already seated, Higgins had no choice but to sit on the other side of Evangeline.

Eliza settled herself in the chair beside Richard. "What do we do now?"

"Prepare yourselves, take a deep breath, and be open to whatever comes tonight." Evangeline's always dramatic voice intensified. Higgins snorted, but the medium appeared untroubled by his reaction. "If we fail to ready our minds, we may cause anguish to those beyond, and much sorrow."

"Utter nonsense—"

"Professor," Eliza interrupted, "behave yourself."

"He will soon learn the power of spiritual realities, the unseen intermediate place between Heaven and Hell. Please, everyone must hold hands," Evangeline said. "A firm grasp, Professor. But not too tight, Lady Ashmore."

Clara relaxed her hold on Richard's hand, although her blue eyes remained wide. Eliza wasn't happy to have Sir Anthony on her right. And he seemed even less thrilled to be here.

"Before we begin, everyone should know that I do not believe a single thing that is about to take place." Sir Anthony's voice was filled with resentment. "However, given what happened this afternoon, I decided it was wise to be present. Especially if Madame Evangeline decides to drag me into the conversation again."

Evangeline only gave him a serene smile.

"I am not a man who believe in ghosts either," the count said. "But as the host, it is my duty to see things proceed without mishap."

Eliza heard Richard mutter something under his breath, the last sound she heard until the medium's strong and commanding voice suddenly rang out.

"Close your eyes," Evangeline ordered. "Place your joined hands on the table. Do not break the circle."

"Hold on tight." Higgins chuckled. "The table may tip."

Evangeline leaned forward so far that the flickering lights

danced on her pale skin. "You must cooperate, Professor Higgins," she said sternly. "I am unable to concentrate on reaching through the fissure to the departed if you or anyone else displays a negative attitude in our circle. The spirits are not to be trifled with. A restless ghost might become aware of someone who is vulnerable—or insulting—and latch onto them."

Clara gasped. "Oh, no."

Evangeline frowned at Higgins. "Contrary energy dampens the atmosphere. It is important to remain neutral. Or polite, at the very least."

"I do apologize, madam," Higgins said stiffly.

Eliza wanted to congratulate Evangeline for putting him in his place.

The countess cleared his throat. "I, too, am uneasy about participating. 'Regard not them that have familiar spirits, neither seek out wizards, to be defiled by them.' Leviticus, chapter nineteen."

"Verse thirty-one." Evangeline nodded. "I know that passage and I do recognize God's authority over every living thing and of the dead. Do you not believe that the Almighty also has powers over the supernatural beings and commands them? That He did mighty works in the past, and is capable of doing so now?"

"That may be true, but—"

"I am a mere channel, countess. God uses me to assist those who seek solace and hope. For good and not evil. So I believe. As does my priest."

"You are Catholic?" Philippe asked, sounding relieved.

"*Oui.*" She smiled at him and pressed his hand. Eliza heard Zoltan Batur mutter by the door. "Before we begin, we must decide on our purpose. What is it you seek?"

"You mean, like asking the spirits a question?" Clara asked.

"Richard and I once used a Ouija board, with letters and numbers on it."

"No, Lady Ashmore. I refrain from using the Ouija or its planchette," Evangeline said. "It can be too easily manipulated. We have several skeptics already present. I do not wish to be accused of falseness or influencing the spirits in any way."

"We wouldn't want that to happen," Lady Annabel said. Eliza couldn't tell if she was being sarcastic, despite the candles' glow on her face "When does this game begin?"

"It is not a game," Evangeline said sharply.

"I've no wish to offend," she replied. "But I do view this as a parlor game."

Eliza wanted to box the ears of some of the people at this table. She had witnessed one of the medium's predictions come true, and respected Madame Evangeline's talents. A séance was serious business, not a game. Eliza had no doubt this woman would succeed in contacting the beyond—and without using tricks or devices.

"Let us continue," Evangeline closed her eyes. "Do not panic if anything untoward happens. Again, do not break the circle. That is vital. If the spirits wish to send a message, we must accept whatever method they will use to communicate."

"Yes, please. Let's all concentrate," Clara said, wriggling in her chair. "Aren't we here to contact Mr. Pentwater in the beyond?"

"Excuse me, but I must break the circle for a moment." Richard let go of the hands of Clara and Eliza to reach inside his inner jacket pocket. He pulled out a red feather. "I've read that using a possession of the deceased may help form a connection."

Eliza recognized the red feather Pentwater had worn in his hat the morning of the hunt.

"Thank you. Lord Ashmore." Madame Evangeline took the red feather and placed it on the table's center.

Everyone once again clasped hands.

Closing her eyes, she began, "We beseech the spirits and request protection for those in our circle here. I seek the Cardinal, my guide in the spiritual realm. We wait, patient but eager, until he signals his coming."

She now swayed back and forth, each movement more pronounced. Eliza was fascinated. Would Pentwater speak to them soon? Evangeline's head bobbed as well, accompanied by a low moaning. Since no one but Evangeline had her eyes closed, Eliza could see the expressions on everyone's faces. Clara, Richard and Philippe looked concerned, Lily and the countess distinctly nervous. But the remaining people at the table seemed suspicious. Eliza hoped their suspicions didn't ruin the séance.

Eliza heard a small movement somewhere in the darkened room and strained to see where Zoltan Batur stood. His bulky figure, a dark mass against the ivory paneled wood, shifted a little in the candlelight.

A breeze stirred the tapestry hangings. Evangeline stiffened. "Cardinal, is that you? Give us a sign if you are here."

Eliza shivered when one flame of the candelabra sputtered and died. Blimey, how could only one candle have blown out? Zoltan wasn't anywhere near the table, either.

"I see. . . flames." Evangeline's gravelly tone sounded even odder than usual. "A blazing fire and pages burning within it. The manuscript is destroyed. A life's work."

At a sharp intake of breath, Eliza glanced over in time to see Lady Annabel's stricken expression.

Evangeline moaned. "Such malice. wanton destruction. The man had no right to burn it. No right." She gave a great shudder. "Wait. Another fire? Yes!"

Higgins glanced at Eliza and mouthed silently, "Our fire?"

"I see a broken teacup. Smoke, flames. People waking in the middle of the night to escape." She cocked her head. "This, too, was malicious."

Was the woman referring to the kitchen fire at Wimpole

Street? Only there was nothing malicious about that fire. If Higgins had accidentally caused it, such behavior could be termed careless. But not malicious. Eliza shrugged. Maybe the spirits got details wrong now and then.

"A motorcar." Evangeline's already deep voice lowered even more. She scarcely sounded female. "A motorcar black as night. The driver watches and waits. The Cardinal tells me this car meant to harm someone."

Eliza sat bolt upright. Was that the black motorcar she'd seen driving up and down Wimpole Street the week before they arrived at Banfield Manor? The car she'd been so worried about, the one that may have belonged to some criminal her cousin Jack may have crossed.

Evangeline spoke again, but in a flat tone, more feminine. "So many secrets."

"What about the black motorcar?" Eliza asked.

"Forget that," Freddy said. "What about Pentwater? Was he murdered?"

"Murdered," the medium moaned. "Yes. The Cardinal believes it is so."

"Look at the feather," Clara said in a shocked voice.

Eliza watched as the red feather trembled on the table's surface. It moved slightly from one side, then the other. The feather shook once more before it lay still again.

"Blimey, did you see that?" Eliza asked. Everyone looked stunned.

"It must have been a breeze," Higgins finally said.

Eliza shook her head. A breeze from where? The windows were all closed behind the heavy velvet draperies. She stared at the feather, wishing she could touch it. But she dare not break the circle of closed hands.

Without warning, Madame Evangeline cried out. Her hands, linked with Higgins and Philippe, jerked forward into the table's center. Their joined hands quickly moved to the left, back to the center, down to a spot closer to Higgins, and then across the table three times.

Suddenly the table trembled, as the feather had. Eliza held her breath as her side of the table lifted off the floor. Not much. Maybe an inch, but she saw and felt it move. She didn't know whether to be excited or frightened.

"*Mon Dieu!*" Philippe whispered.

"That was incredible!" Clara exclaimed. "It tipped!"

Richard and Freddy seemed delighted, but Lily pulled away from the table as much as she could without letting go of anyone's hand.

"What trickery is this?" Sir Anthony hissed.

Evangeline slumped in her chair, as if resting, then the threesome's linked hands moved across the table in the same order as before. To the left, then right, and straight across three times. She stopped and sat back. Everyone waited.

A throaty groan now arose. It hadn't come from Evangeline, or anyone else at the table. Chills ran up Eliza's spine.

"The Cardinal speaks of regret and sorrow." She kept her eyes shut. "But it is too late to recover what was foolishly lost."

"What was lost?" Lily asked Freddy in a low voice. "Honestly, this Cardinal needs to be more specific."

"Don't interrupt," Eliza said.

Clara leaned forward. "Excuse me, Mr. Cardinal, I have no wish to offend. But can you tell us what was lost?"

"What is usually lost when one gambles," Madame Evangeline said in a monotone. "Money. A great deal of money. I see the number thirty-five."

"What? Thirty-five pounds?" Sir Anthony smirked. "Maybe he means thirty-five dollars or francs. The Cardinal's a frugal fellow if he thinks those sums are a great deal of money."

Count Rudolf let out an exasperated breath. "Maybe that is how much this séance will cost us."

"Could we please bring this to en end?" the countess asked in a shaky voice. "I find none of this amusing."

"We still haven't learned who killed Pentwater," Freddy reminded her.

"Who cares about that dreadful man?" the countess cried. "We are fools to waste a minute more on his life or death."

"I can't argue with that," Higgins said.

"Let Madame continue." Philippe glowered at everyone.

Evangeline took a sharp breath. "The gold of the great king. The king who unites many." Her voice had once more turned low and masculine. "A talisman of gold. It passes—like power—through many hands. The payment is high. In blood. And war. But it gives power, too."

"What does this have to do with Pentwater?" Freddy seemed bored now.

"What is hidden shall be found," she continued in such a slow voice, Eliza feared she would soon stop. "And there the danger lies."

Eliza now glimpsed something over the medium's head, a pale strange substance that shimmered, almost dancing in the air. As it dipped toward Evangeline's head, Higgins broke free of the medium's hands. Jumping to his feet, he grabbed hold of whatever it was. In response, Evangeline fell off her chair in a noisy tumble.

All the candles guttered out, sending the room into pitch darkness. The only sounds were Clara and Lily's screams.

"Gauze! I knew it," Higgins said in a triumphant voice.

Someone turned the electric lights on, revealing Higgins waving a thin material.

Eliza stared in shock. "What's that?"

"It's a common trick used by mediums," he told her. "This

ghostly looking material was attached to a thin filament of fishing line. Her bodyguard must have hidden it up in the chandelier and rigged it so he could lower the fabric at the proper time." He snatched up the red feather. "And I bet he lowered another filament to make this move."

Zoltan Batur stomped over to them. "I did nothing of the sort."

"Madame, Madame! *Qu'est-ce qui ne va pas?*" Philippe knelt beside Evangeline.

Batur shoved him aside. "Don't touch her! Get away. Give her room to breathe."

She stirred and sat up. "What happened?"

"You conveniently fainted," Higgins replied. "You probably planned to swallow this gauze and then pretend to regurgitate it. I believe this is called ectoplasm in your trade."

"Madame is not a trickster," Philippe protested. "You must not say such things."

"What gauze are you talking about?" Evangeline appeared startled when Higgins held up the bit of fabric. "I have never seen that before—oh!"

"Here we go again," he muttered as the medium began to thrash, struggling against both Philippe and Batur. "Blast and damn."

Everyone gathered around the trio crouched on the hard parquet floor. Evangeline actually foamed at the mouth; Higgins guessed that Batur must have broken open an ampule of something to give her that physical effect, a clever ploy to distract her audience.

As he suspected, the séance was no more than fraudulent dramatics. Melodramatics, given the extremes to which Madame Evangeline was willing to go in her tricks. During the séance, Higgins had heard faint footsteps behind his chair. No doubt when Zoltan Batur snuck around the room to tug at the nearly invisible fishing line.

He also guessed that when the medium manipulated their hands around the table, it acted as a diversion for Batur to create a ghostly breeze and lift the red feather.

"I don't know whether this woman is having a scizure or acting," Lady Annabel said in indignation. "Whatever it is, I demand you stop it this instant, Mr. Batur." She kicked him to get his attention.

Batur threw her a surly glance. "I have seen this before. She recovers quickly." He paused. "Unless there are people nearby who have evil in their hearts."

"My patience is at an end with this nonsense." Annabel turned to her husband. "Let us retire, my dear. Things have become too grisly."

Sir Anthony ushered his wife out of the room, but not before throwing everyone a look of seething contempt. The countess hurried after them. Higgins thought she might be weeping, but that made no sense.

Clara wrung her hands as she watched Evangeline slowly revive. "We should ring for Baxter. Ask him for water or brandy."

"I shall find a pitcher of cold water." A concerned Philippe quickly left.

"Brandy might help Madame feel better," Batur said. "So will one of my tisanes."

Lily perked up. "I'm keen for some brandy myself. Freddy and I will go to the drawing room and bring back a snifter for her." She and Freddy hurried out.

"Will Madame Evangeline be all right?" Richard asked Batur.

"Yes. But she is exhausted after such exertions." He looked down with love at the woman cradled in his arms. "When her strength returns, she may explain what the Cardinal revealed."

"I can figure it out for myself," Higgins said. "Your employer uncovered a few secrets about the guests here. And her trances allowed her to throw out hints of these secrets. Spare me your outraged looks, Batur. The pair of you are frauds."

"You know nothing," Batur snarled.

"I agree with you, Herr Higgins," Count Rudolf said stoutly. "And I am ashamed my brother-in-law thought such people were suitable for polite company." After the customary click of his heels, the count left the room.

"Excuse me," Richard said with irritation. "I need to have a word with Rudolf."

"I'd best go with you," Clara told him. "Your quarrel may turn into fisticuffs and I don't want to miss that."

Higgins shook his head in resignation after they left. "The Drury Lane Theater witnesses less drama than this house."

Eliza laughed. "Not always." She no doubt recalled the explosive climax she and a murderer had presented at that very theater this past spring.

Evangeline moaned again. "I'm fine now, Zoltan," she said. "Please help me stand."

Eliza assisted the bodyguard in getting the medium back on her feet. She appeared tired, but calm. Higgins judged her a superb actress, one of the best he'd seen.

"I recall that you waved something at me, Professor Higgins." She leaned against Batur. "You called it ectoplasm. But I assure you that ectoplasm looks nothing like that."

"Forgive me if I don't put a lot of faith in your assurances."

"He's a skeptic," Eliza said, "but he hasn't yet seen the truth of your gifts."

"Barbarian," Batur muttered.

"Shh, Zoltan. He simply does not understand the great mysteries."

Eliza's face creased in a wide smile. "Just like in *Hamlet*, 'There are more things in heaven and earth than are dreamt of in your philosophy.' Act One, scene five."

Higgins groaned. "I curse the chap who gave you a copy of that play."

Evangeline gave him a penetrating look. "You believe in curses then?"

"Absolutely not." He paused. "But if this house party gets any worse, I may start believing in them."

CHAPTER 15

*H*iggins looked over his shoulder as he went downstairs for breakfast. Not for ghosts. He left that sort of idiocy to Eliza. Instead, he searched for any sign Madame Evangeline and her exotic manservant might be lurking in a corner.

The medium's revelations yesterday left him convinced she and Zoltan Batur had spied on the guests before their arrival. Evangeline's network of informers could be spread around the world. She was, after all, a highly sought medium invited into the homes of Europe's privileged classes. He blamed this public interest on Sir Arthur Conan Doyle's well known fascination with spiritualism. Some said the author of Sherlock Holmes even believed in thought transference.

Higgins had no faith in telepathy or talkative spirits. But he did believe Evangeline came to her séances armed with information about everyone at the table. How else could she have known Pentwater abandoned Sir Anthony in the jungle? Along with the reference to a manuscript being burned in a fire. From the reaction of Lady Annabel, he assumed this related to some painful event in her past. What troubled him more were the hints during the séance that she had investigated Higgins.

He needed to talk this over with Eliza. Before coming downstairs, he knocked on her bedroom door; there was no answer. A peek inside revealed an unmade canopy bed but no occupant. Eliza's ravenous appetite had probably led her to the breakfast sideboard. As he approached the breakfast room, he was met with the clatter of silver against plates. But only Richard, Philippe, and the count sat at the table. None of the men spoke while they ate.

Higgins retreated before anyone spotted him. No matter how much he wanted coffee and eggs, he had no desire to sit down with that taciturn trio.

Uncertain, he paused in the library. Maybe he should wait here until Eliza showed up. Then again, she might be upstairs in Clara's bedroom, giving endless sympathy to the overwhelmed baroness. And the windows revealed a sunny morning. Their enforced stay—combined with foul weather—made Banfield Manor seem more confining than Wandsworth Prison. But it looked like the rain and brisk winds had disappeared. A walk might do him good.

On the way to the front entrance, Higgins passed the butler walking in the opposite direction. In his hand he held a salver tray with a stack of mail on it.

"Good morning, sir. Off for a walk, are we? It's a splendid day for it."

"Good to hear. By the way, have you seen Miss Doolittle?"

"Yes, sir. She went out riding over an hour ago."

"Riding? As in horses?"

"I believe so. The young lady wore a riding costume."

When did Eliza learn how to ride? Confused, Higgins nodded. "Thank you, Baxter."

He headed for the stables, curious as to why he'd never heard of Eliza's equestrian endeavors. Cockney urchins who sold fruit and flowers in the street weren't likely to have much opportunity to mount any horse other those hitched to a vegetable wagon.

The day had indeed brought fine weather. Despite the hoarfrost earlier in the week, the temperature this morning felt better suited to May. By the time he reached the paddock, he'd even unbuttoned his tweed Norfolk jacket. While looking for a groom to question, Higgins heard the sound of galloping hooves.

Eliza, mounted on a white horse, not only cantered into view, she jumped a fence!

She lifted her riding crop in greeting as she rode past. Two grooms waited for her by the stable door. Higgins watched as she dismounted, then spent a moment stroking her horse.

Higgins leaned against the paddock fence as she made her way over to him. "When did you become a lady jockey?" he asked.

"Since I became part owner of a racehorse this summer. All that time spent at the track watching the Donegal Dancer win gave me horse fever. Like you have motorcar fever. Only horses are much more beautiful than any car." Eliza looked back at her mare, now being led away by a groom. "Especially that one. She's the only white horse in the stable."

"How did you learn to ride so well? You sat that horse as expertly as my sister Victoria, and she's the best rider in Buckinghamshire."

"For the past two months, I've spent every Friday taking lessons."

"I thought you went to the cinema on Friday."

"Not when the weather is agreeable. Instead, I take the train to the horse farm in Windsor for my lessons. I also go on the days when I don't have students."

"You've never said a word to me. Does Pick know?"

"Oh, yes. He's been most encouraging. Colonel Pickering

believes every woman should know how to sit a horse. We thought it best not to tell you, at least for awhile." Eliza waved her riding crop at him. "You can be an awful tease."

Higgins felt offended at being left out, but refused to show it. "From what I saw, you're a quick study. And you certainly dress the part."

"It is a fine costume, isn't it?" Eliza slowly turned to give him a better look at her two-piece outfit. The black riding habit boasted a notched collar, slightly puffed sleeves, and a split apron skirt which concealed the breeches underneath. As customary, a top hat sat jauntily upon her head. "Special ordered from Charles William Davis."

Although not a rider himself, he knew Davis was London's most sought after tailor of riding outfits. Higgins also recognized proper riding attire. This was up to the standards of the Bilsdale Hunt, England's oldest fox hunt. "A pity you can't ride to hounds while we're here."

"What do you mean? I have every intention of doing so."

"Because the Ashmore Hunt is supposed to take place in two days. An event which seems unlikely to occur, given that a member of the house party has died."

Eliza laughed. "The Ashmores will not cancel the hunt. Clara would go into hiding if the hunt didn't go as planned. Richard, too, most likely. The death of a houseguest won't stop them."

"You make them sound as insensitive as Count Rudolf."

"Not really. They'd never even met the American until two nights ago. You can't expect them to go into mourning for a stranger. Anyway, I've spent hours talking about this with Clara. The hunt and the ball formally introduces the couple to every snob from here to London. Their reputation is at stake." She pointed at the manor house. "If you don't mind, I need to change out of these clothes before they clear the sideboard in the breakfast room. I'm starving."

As they walked past the stables, hounds barked from a

nearby kennel. From somewhere on the grounds, peacocks shrieked. One of them was certain to be Percy. "We must speak about last night before we go in. I'm troubled by what Madame Evangeline said during the séance."

Eliza looked at him with wide eyes. "She was blooming amazing yesterday. I wonder who in the house party is connected to the money she mentioned. And the number thirty-five. As for that manuscript destroyed in a fire, it must be related to Lady Annabel. Your redhead's eyes popped open when Madame Evangeline talked about that."

"Lady Annabel is not my redhead," he snapped.

"You were also rude last night to Madame Evangeline. Accusing her of fraud."

"She is a fraud. So is that bodyguard. Or didn't you see the fishing line hanging from the chandelier? That clearly exposed their trickery."

"Who cares about fishing lines? She saw Pentwater's death. That should impress you."

"I'm more impressed by something else she said. Something about me."

Eliza stopped and faced him. "You mean when she spoke about the fire in the kitchen and the teacup? She was right about that, too. How can you not see she has a real gift?"

"A gift for ferreting out information, certainly. Please remember everyone in the house party is aware we suffered a kitchen fire before our arrival. I'm not referring to that." He lowered his voice although no one was in sight except for a stable boy with an armful of hay. "She spoke about a black motorcar that meant to harm someone."

"Yes. I was shocked she knew about the motorcar I kept seeing on Wimpole Street."

"What?" This jarred Higgins. "When did this happen?"

"During that endless week when you and Jack drove me and

Sybil crazy with all your demands. I saw a black motorcar go past our house at least three times a day."

"Blast it all. You never told me. I don't like this at all."

Eliza shrugged. "At first, I assumed the man was lost. Or maybe he'd recently bought the car and was learning how to drive. Then I worried he might be watching our house."

Higgins grabbed her arm. "You said a man was driving. Can you describe him?"

She shook off his grip. "Calm down. You'll be having the vapors next. I assumed it was a man by the hat. However, he wore goggles so I have no idea what he looked like."

"Eliza, a few days before my accident in Putney, a driver in a black motorcar attempted to race me. I thought he was simply another motorist eager to push his machine to the limit. He drove damned recklessly, forcing me to do likewise. And don't give me that look. I realize I do not always drive with caution."

"According to Jack, you drive as if every detective in Scotland Yard is after you."

"This fellow was worse. He couldn't catch up with me because he took a sharp turn and spun about. I didn't see him again that day. Only now that I look back, I believe the same car trailed me from a distance at least twice that week."

Eliza chuckled. "Maybe that spin taught him to drive slower."

They resumed their walk to the manor house. "Madame Evangeline said the person who drove that black motorcar intended to harm someone," he said. "But neither of us mentioned a black motorcar to anyone here. Or even to each other. So how did she know I encountered such a vehicle? Or that you saw a black motorcar drive past our house?"

"She knew because the spirits told her. Honestly, how much proof do you require?"

"What I require is an explanation. Why would someone want to pursue me in such a manner, and did he have sinister intentions? Was he the same man motoring up and down Wimpole Street?" Higgins didn't like where his thoughts were leading him. "Even more troubling, was there anything sinister about the kitchen fire?"

"That kitchen fire was caused by a grumpy elocution professor who didn't pay any attention and left the gas jet burning on the stove." Eliza kicked at the graveled path with her boot. "You're nervous because Madame Evangeline and her spirits know the past and future."

"She knows something about us. I think we need to talk with someone not connected with the house party." Higgins remembered Clara boasting about a telephone room in the house. "I'll ring the exchange and put a call through to Jack. He's staying with Sybil's family, right? I assume they have a telephone."

"Oh, don't bother Jack. My cousin needs to relax and get better. Tales of dead Americans and mysterious black cars will only rile him up." She raised an eyebrow at him. "And if Jack gets upset, it makes things much worse for poor Sybil."

Just then, they came upon Freddy and Lily, arm in arm.

"What a surprise." Lily glanced down at her own riding habit. "We're going riding, too."

Although the couple wore expectant smiles, both Higgins and Eliza only nodded and walked past them. He heard Freddy mutter, "I say, that was a bit rude."

"You may be right about Jack," Higgins said. "I won't ring him."

"I'm glad I was able to talk sense into you."

Higgins didn't tell her that he decided to ring Detective Colin Ramsey instead. He'd use the repairs on his car as an excuse. And after he inquired about his motorcar, he would see what Detective Ramsey thought about this Pentwater business. Maybe have him look into Madame Evangeline's background. Too many people in this house had a reason to hate Dwight Pentwater, including Sir Anthony, Lady Annabel, and Philippe.

Were there more? And was Madame Evangeline privy to their secrets?

Higgins now agreed with Eliza. Pentwater's death was not only unfortunate and unexpected. He also believed it was murder.

ELIZA WISHED IT WASN'T REGARDED AS RUDE TO EAT BREAKFAST IN dusty boots and a riding habit. As she passed the breakfast room, her stomach growled at the aroma wafting into the hallway. A quick peek revealed a footman clearing the table. She cast a longing look at the food laid out on the sideboard. Maybe she should wrap a scone and boiled egg in a napkin to bring upstairs. Something to fortify her until after she changed and came down for a proper breakfast.

The footman turned around and saw her in the doorway. A wide grin crossed his face. "Milady Doolittle, as I live and breathe."

"Charlie Kenton!"

She rushed over and embraced him. He quickly stepped away.

"Need to be careful the swells don't catch me actin' cozy with the guests. I'd be sacked for sure. But I'm glad to see a friendly face, even if it does belong to someone upstairs."

"I'll never really belong upstairs," she told him. "I've only learned how to act as if I do. How long have you been working for the Ashmores?"

"Lord Ashmore hired me when he and the missus got back from their wedding trip."

"I heard you'd taken up boxing."

"Not for long." He pointed at his left shoulder. "Shattered the bone two years ago during a bare knuckle match in Holborn. Mum carried on like I'd been run over by a bus. Certainly felt like I had. Took me a year to recover. When I did, the shoulder and arm weren't the same. Never goin' to be a featherweight champ like Jim Driscoll now."

"Do you like being in service?"

"Beats starvin'. At least I get to wear clean clothes with shiny gold buttons." Charlie smoothed down his crisp black uniform. "Also don't have to get my hands dirty or bloodied. Thinkin' I might join the army. That way I can wear a uniform *and* carry a gun. Mum don't want me to join up, worried I'll get killed. But I'm nineteen and make my own decisions. Like I be tellin' her, how can I get killed if there ain't no wars goin' on?"

"I don't know how long that will last." Eliza bit her lip. "Now that I live with Professor Higgins and Colonel Pickering, I've started to read the newspapers. I have to, if I hope to keep up my end of the conversation. There are rumblings of war, Charlie. And they're getting louder."

He looked delighted at the thought. "Even better. Could be my big chance to win a medal. Ladies love a soldier what's got medals on his chest, Lizzie." He frowned. "Can I still call you Lizzie? Or should I call you 'Miss Doolittle' even when we're alone."

She laughed. "Call me anything you like, only don't call me late for a meal, as Da always says." Eliza looked over at the sideboard. "And I'd love to have a meal right now. Except the countess would have a conniption if she saw me eating in the breakfast room while still in my riding habit. However, I might snatch a scone or two to take upstairs."

Charlie leaned closer. "Not much chance of the countess findin' you here. Ain't never seen her near the breakfast room. Go on. Sit down and I'll make a plate for you."

"I don't know if I should." But even as she said this, Eliza pulled out a chair. She whipped off her riding gloves, then unpinned her hat. Cor, she was hungry. She wondered if Higgins had eaten yet. In fact, she wondered where he was. If he had lied to her and went off to place a call to Jack with the phone exchange. . .

Eliza soon forgot all that as Charlie put a plate of eggs, smoked salmon, and toast in front of her. A moment later, he'd also brought her coffee. She dropped three sugar cubes into the cup.

"Let's catch up while I eat," Eliza said between mouthfuls. "We haven't seen each other for at least eight years."

"Dorset Street Ragged School." He sighed. "Never did take to the classroom meself. You was a sharp though. Smarter than any teacher we ever had." Charlie walked over to the entrance to the breakfast room and peered out. "Think I'll keep an eye out while you eat. Don't want the guests or that foreign count to hear me jawin' with you like we was old friends."

"We are old friends. The count can hang himself."

"Ain't so easy to say if your livelihood depends on pleasin' the bluebloods. And they're damned hard to please. Same with famous people, which is what this house party seems filled with. A few right odd ones, too. Like that lady what talks to ghosts."

"She has a gift, Charlie." Eliza turned solemn. "Remember Old Mary who read palms in Angel Court."

He nodded. "Old Mary told me sister she'd marry a fisherman from Cornwall. We thought she was daft. A girl in the East End ain't likely to meet a fishermen from so far away. But two years later, Mabel up and marries a pilchard fisherman from Sennen Cove. He'd come up to London for his uncle's funeral. They been married five years now. Three children." Charlie snickered. "Not a one of them ever stops cryin' or eating."

"Madame Evangeline is even better than Old Mary," Eliza assured him. "She revealed secrets about Sir Anthony she couldn't possibly have known if her spirits hadn't told her."

He looked as skeptical as Higgins. "Don't know about any

spirits, but that foreign fellow she brought with her bears watchin.'"

"What do you think of Zoltan Batur? You know him better than I do since he's staying below stairs."

"We all keep our distance from him. Ruder than the countess, he is. Treats us like we're his servants. He reminds me of the Geary boys in Whitechapel. They'd crack your head open just for smiling at 'em."

Eliza nodded. She remembered the notorious Geary boys all too well.

"I wasn't surprised when Batur turned a knife on the police yesterday," Charlie continued. "Sure was glad Mr. Baxter sent both Albert and me to restrain him. I couldn't have done it on me own. Not with this shoulder. Also don't think it was right he weren't arrested. If I'd pulled a blade on a copper, I'd be trussed up in a cell. Because he's the servant of some fancy guest, he gets away with it. And a foreign bloke, too."

Eliza ate the last of her eggs and salmon. She'd eaten so quickly, she feared a stomachache would follow. "He's more than a manservant. Mr. Batur is Madame Evangeline's bodyguard. He protects her. That's why he came to her rescue when he heard her cry out."

Charlie peeked his head out the doorway to scan the hallway again. "If you ask me, he's a damned sight more than her bodyguard."

"What do you mean?"

"He talks about the ghost lady like she was something he owned. He won't even let the housemaids press her clothes. Batur does it himself. Same as he cleans her shoes. He also don't trust the maids to make his lady's evening tea. Some herbal brew they call a tisane. He prepares it, then gives it to one of the maids to bring to her bedroom."

"Sounds like he's obsessed with her." If true, Eliza feared that made him even more dangerous than he looked.

"That he is. If I was any of the gents here, I wouldn't get too close to Madame Evangeline. Her bodyguard's the jealous type, he is. I think he'd put a fella in the ground just for standin' too close to her."

This worried Eliza. Madame Evangeline had made no attempt to disguise her warm feelings for Philippe Corbet. What if Batur grew jealous and tried to harm the Frenchman? Poor Philippe had been through quite enough for one house party.

"If Mr. Batur posed a danger to anyone, Madame Evangeline's spirits would warn her." Eliza said this more to convince herself than Charlie. "When we had breakfast the other day, she foretold the death of Mr. Pentwater in the forest. He was killed within the hour."

Charlie shot her a rueful smile. "Bad luck for him *and* me. Lord Ashmore asked if I'd serve as the American's valet. Thought it was my chance to get more responsibility. And a little more pay. Then he gets himself shot."

"That's right. You were Mr. Pentwater's valet, at least for one evening," Eliza said. "Did you notice anything unusual about him?"

"Didn't have much chance. I did unpack his bags. Lots of fine suits with New York labels on them. He had some of the nicest cufflinks I ever laid eyes on. Gold, mother of pearl, black onyx. Even finer than the ones worn by Lord Ashmore."

"How did he treat you?"

"Like any gent. Polite, but expected me to know what he wanted before he did. Typical rich man." Charlie paused. "Maybe not typical, now I think about it. He acted strange when I helped him undress. Kept laughing to himself, like he was in on some private joke. I even asked him what was so funny. If I'd said that to the count, he would have reported me to Mr. Baxter for talking above my station."

"What did Mr. Pentwater do when you asked him?"

"Said he found the English amusing because they cared more about how things appeared instead of how things really were." He shrugged. "Don't know what he meant by that."

"Did he mention any of the other guests?"

"Let's say he had a private encounter with one of them." His smile grew into a leer. "A most private encounter."

"With who?"

"That pretty cinema star. Lily Marlowe. I was right jealous of Mr. Pentwater that night."

Eliza sat back. "Wait. You saw Mr. Pentwater and Lily having a private conversation?"

"A lot more than a conversation. After I helped him get ready for bed, he asked me to take a shirt down for pressin'. He wanted to wear it the next morning for the hunt. I brought it back up, past midnight, but he told me that he'd still be awake. I heard a woman's voice in his room right before I knocked. Then Pentwater opened the door. Said he'd take the shirt from me. No need for me to put it away. But before he shut the door, I caught a glimpse of her."

"You saw Lily in his bedroom?"

"In his bed. And she didn't have a stitch on."

Eliza's mouth fell open. "Are you certain, Charlie?"

"Hard to mistake a naked girl for anything else."

"Did she see you?"

"Indeed she did," he said. "Looked right upset about it, too. Can't say as I blame her. Like I said, she was naked as a jaybird."

"Lily must have been so embarrassed." Eliza almost felt sorry for her.

"That she was. She turned red as a strawberry. No need for it neither. Mr. Pentwater didn't have to open the door as wide as he did to take the shirt from me. I think he wanted me to see the lady. Maybe he planned the whole thing to embarrass her. Don't know. I can't figure out half of what these rich swells do."

"Blimey." Eliza had always assumed Lily knew more about

Pentwater than she let on. Only she didn't suspect the actress knew him *that* well. "Was she still in his bed when you woke him the next morning?"

Before Charlie could answer, footsteps sounded from overhead. Muffled shouts followed. Something banged. More footsteps as if people were running.

"What the devil are the maids doing up there?" Charlie looked at the ceiling.

"Mr. Baxter! Mr. Baxter," a woman cried out. "Something awful has happened!"

Eliza ran into the hallway in time to see a frantic maidservant by the staircase.

"What's wrong, Dora?" Charlie hurried to meet her. Eliza was only a few steps behind.

The maid looked as white as her apron. "She's dead! I have to find Mr. Baxter."

Eliza grabbed her before she could leave. "Who's dead?"

"Madame Evangeline," she wailed. "I went in to help her dress and found her cold as ice in her bed. She's dead. She's dead!" The maid tore free of Eliza's grasp and ran off.

"That can't be true," Eliza told a stunned Charlie. She raced upstairs to the bedrooms. Two housemaids held each other for comfort in the hallway. The door to Madame Evangeline's bedroom stood open.

When Eliza rushed inside, she saw the countess standing at the side of the bed, her fingers on Madame Evangeline's wrist. The countess looked at Eliza. "The maidservant was correct," she told her in a flat voice. "She's dead."

Aghast, Eliza looked down at Madame Evangeline. There were no signs of blood. No marks of violence that she could see. Just a pale young woman lying motionless, like a sleeping beauty waiting for a prince to wake her with a kiss.

The countess appeared grim. "I heard the maids making a commotion in the hall and came in to find her like this."

"What is going on, Eliza?" Clara stood in the doorway. She wore her nightgown and a panicked expression. "Why are the servants so upset? And why are you and the countess in Madame Evangeline's bedroom?"

"Prepare yourself for a shock, Clara," Eliza said. "Madame Evangeline died during the night."

Clara screamed and collapsed to the floor in a faint. Muttering under her breath, the countess went over to her unconscious sister-in-law. Eliza, however, drew closer to the bed and the still figure lying on it. Poor woman. She would never hold a séance to speak to the spirits again. Then again, she didn't have to.

Madame Evangeline was now one of them.

CHAPTER 16

$\mathcal{H}$iggins watched an agitated Eliza stride about the drawing room. Muttering to herself, she smacked her boot several times with her riding crop, as if wanting to use it on something other than leather. Everyone kept their distance. A wise decision.

Clara's teacup rattled whenever she set it down on her saucer. Faced with the house party's second death, the poor girl appeared numb. He wondered what would happen when gossip spread beyond this small circle of guests and servants. Would it reflect badly on Richard and Clara's hosting abilities, or would it increase interest in the new baron and baroness? The aristocratic class could be unpredictable. Higgins knew any hint of mystery or intrigue titillated his older brother's network of society friends. Boon or bane, as one would say.

Sir Anthony and Lady Annabel sat at opposite ends of one sofa. Both seemed distracted. Higgins wished he had more details about the burned manuscript Madame Evangeline mentioned during the séance. Given Annabel's reaction, the lost book must have been hers. Was the malicious man Pentwater? If so, that may have been a reason to murder him.

Certainly, her husband was justified in hating Pentwater after being abandoned to an uncertain fate in the Amazon. Philippe also had reason to despise Pentwater. Was the same true for Lily Marlowe? Higgins agreed with Eliza. It couldn't have been a hunting accident. Too many people here hated the dead man. The fog, combined with dogs, loaders, beaters, and so many people firing guns, served as perfect distraction for whoever aimed that lethal shot.

A shame Madame Evangeline never gave any hints as to who killed Pentwater at the séance. Especially since his death had been the whole reason for that farce. Apparently, her 'spirit guide' hadn't finished his research before they sat down at the table.

"This house party is driving me batty," Lily complained. "People dying. Police everywhere. I'm afraid some cat burglar will make off with my jewelry next."

"Hush, darling." Freddy took her hand. "I'll take care nothing happens to you." The couple huddled together on their loveseat.

Lily whispered something to him, prompting Freddy to kiss her on the forehead.

At that moment, Eliza strode past the couple, still swinging her riding crop. It barely missed hitting Lily in the cheek. Higgins bit back a chuckle. In a way, Freddy and the actress were well suited. Two pretty faces—and not much else. At least Lily was reputed to be talented, which is more than could be said for Freddy.

Loud shouting came from upstairs. "Good heavens," Lady Annabel murmured. "What is going on?"

They heard Zoltan Batur yell at the top of his lungs, half in Turkish, and presumably at Chief Constable Brakefield. A bit unsettling. As were the policemen who now guarded every door in Banfield Manor. The entire constabulary must have been summoned to assist Brakefield and Constable Stevens in investigating this latest death.

"I do wish Richard would come down," Clara said. "Why must he remain upstairs with the chief constable? It was the maid who found Madame Evangeline."

"It's his house, Clara" Eliza said. "He has to oversee things. If anyone isn't needed upstairs, it's Count Rudolf and his wife. They stick their noses into everything."

"This whole business is dreadful," Clara moaned. "I simply can't believe it. And did you see how distraught Philippe was by the news?"

Indeed, the Frenchman appeared in a state of shock when he learned Madame Evangeline died during the night. The police were no doubt questioning him again; Higgins suspected they still believed Corbet had killed Pentwater. But it seemed ludicrous the aviator would have had any hand in Evangeline's death. Despite his fiancée, he seemed fond of the spiritualist, clearly enjoying their private tête-à-tête's in French.

Clara gulped her tea, then shakily poured herself another cup. "Madame Evangeline was so young. And ten minutes after she had that fit, she sat in the parlor drinking brandy with us. She seemed perfectly fine. How can she be dead?"

"The Turk did her in," Sir Anthony growled. "He had that knife, after all."

"That depends on how she was killed." Higgins tugged at the sling supporting his casted arm. "Madame Evangeline had never met any of us before her arrival, except for the Ashmores. She didn't have time to make enemies. Of course, she didn't endear herself to anyone either."

"Except for Monsieur Corbet," Lady Annabel reminded him.

"I meant that her trances exposed several secrets," Higgins said. "She may have investigated everyone's past, pretending the details came from her so-called spirit guide. It's possible someone here felt threatened and decided to silence her."

"I say, how dare you accuse one of us of murder," Sir

Anthony shot back. "Just for revealing a secret or two? Preposterous."

Eliza waved her riding crop. "Madame Evangeline knew things from the Great Beyond. Secrets. Maybe more than one person here feared Evangeline might expose them next in one of her trances."

Lily laughed. "What bunk. Freddy has no secrets. Nor do I."

"That's not what I've heard. It appears that games are sometimes played at house parties after everyone is in bed. Occasionally those games are witnessed by servants. Like a housemaid." Eliza paused. "Or a footman."

"Is that an accusation?" Lily asked, her cheeks growing flushed.

Freddy jumped up. "How dare you accuse Lily of anything! You're to blame for everything that's happened here. You bring death wherever you go. Look at the debacle in the maze at Clara's wedding. And don't forget how it all started with the murdered Hungarian last spring. Clara and I had the bad luck to be with you then. My sister still has nightmares."

"I do not," Clara objected. "I'm not a child, after all."

He put up a hand to silence her. "Or how about the dead man at the Henley Regatta, Eliza? Bloody horrible that was. I'm not even including the other dead bodies you keep stumbling across. You and Professor Higgins. I swear, the pair of you are ghouls."

Eliza gasped. "How can you say that? We've helped the police."

"Your idiocy knows no bounds, Freddy," Higgins said with contempt.

But Freddy had gotten himself all worked up, like an excited terrier. "You're a dark cloud, Eliza. You spoil everything you touch. And here's the proof. You've spoiled my sister's first house party."

"That's unfair. I had nothing to do with the deaths of Mr. Pentwater and Madame Evangeline."

Higgins wanted to smack the fellow. Eliza was far too superstitious and didn't need accusations that she brought bad luck to people.

Clara stamped her foot. "How dare you say such things to Eliza? Apologize now."

Freddy sat down again and grabbed Lily's hand. "After she apologizes to us for these latest dead bodies."

Eliza burst into tears and ran out of the room. Higgins knew that Eliza rarely cried. Damn and blast that blighter Freddy! He got to his feet, intent on punching him in the nose. But Clara got there first. She marched over to where Freddy sat and dumped the contents of her teacup over her brother's head. Then she ran after Eliza.

"What the devil," Freddy spluttered as tea dripped from his clothes and face. Beside him, Lily looked stunned.

"You selfish, ignorant blackguard." Higgins was glad to see how his harsh words cut the young man, who recoiled in surprise. "I'd thrash you if my arm wasn't broken. But the devil take you for being such an ungrateful ass. Eliza was your friend. And your sweetheart. *Was*, I say, because I doubt if she'll ever speak to you again."

Now Freddy seemed close to tears. Lily poured herself a cup of tea as a diversion.

Brakefield entered the drawing room before Higgins could rain more abuse on Freddy's sorry head. Richard trailed the policeman. He assumed Zoltan Batur was under guard upstairs.

The chief constable rubbed his hands together. "Things are coming along nicely."

"What does that mean?" Sir Anthony asked, still petulant.

"We believe the dead woman was smothered," Brakefield said. "With a pillow."

"How can you tell?" Higgins asked.

"Her face was bluish-red. We noticed a bit of froth at her mouth, too." The chief constable shrugged. "Seen it before in another case. An old woman, whose grandson wanted her money quicker than waiting around for her to go natural. Some feathers from the pillow were in the throat, too, but the victim didn't appear to struggle. Too sleepy from her evening cuppa."

"Bedtime tea wouldn't keep her from fighting for her life," Higgins said.

"We believe her bodyguard slipped a drug in it. According to the maid, he always prepared her 'ti-zahn', a tea with bark and herbs. We'll search his things next. I'm sure we'll find something." Brakefield scanned the room. "First we need to question that Frenchman again. Where has he gotten off to now?"

"We thought he was upstairs with you," Higgins glanced at Richard, who shook his head. "He must be somewhere. You have every door and window guarded."

Brakefield cursed under his breath. "If he's slipped out from under our noses for the second time, I'll have someone's head."

"I'm all right." Eliza pocketed her damp handkerchief and leaned against the carved staircase post. "It's not your fault, Clara."

"But I feel horrible. How could Freddy act like such a beast?"

"It was a terrible shock to hear him speak to me like that," Eliza admitted. "I guess Lily has made him lose every last drop of sense."

"And he never had much sense to begin with."

"Only he acted as though he hated me. Why? I've done nothing to him."

"He feels guilty about throwing you over." Clara patted Eliza's hand. "I know my brother. Whenever he behaves badly, the first thing he does is blame someone else. He's also frightened by this latest death." She sighed. "We're all frightened."

"But to accuse me of bringing bad luck and death! He knows that's not true. Why, I thought he loved me. He told me many times. Too often."

Her voice trailed off as the drawing room doors banged open. Chief Constable Brakefield stormed into the hall. "Where's Philippe Corbet?" he barked at a junior policeman guarding the far end. "And why isn't Stevens at the front door?"

"He's upstairs, sir, with Mr. Batur," the young man replied.

"Corbet must be in the house," Higgins said, hot on Brakefield's heels. "It's impossible for him to escape with every door guarded."

"I know where he is." Clara rose to her feet. "When everyone came down to the drawing room, Philippe asked if he could place a telephone call to France. I sent him to the telephone room down the hall. A small cubby to the left."

"Moore, go and make certain he's there. Stay with him if he is." Brakefield snapped his fingers at a second policeman standing near the door to the servants' staircase, who came running. "Bring Batur downstairs to his room and hop to it. I don't want him complaining to my superior that we planted evidence, in case we do find anything."

"I will accompany you," Clara announced, despite Brakefield's obvious displeasure. "Richard, would you please check on our guest in the telephone room? I don't want Philippe to feel threatened."

"Of course, darling," he said, squeezing her shoulder before he left.

"We'll go with you, too." Higgins held out his good hand to Eliza, who quickly rose and joined him. She assumed her eyes were red and puffy, but she had recovered.

"Better to have as many witnesses as possible during the search," she said.

Brakefield frowned, but held his tongue.

"I can also tell you what I've learned about Mr. Batur." Eliza repeated what Charlie Kenton told her. "The maid took the tisane to Madame Evangeline's room every night. But Zoltan Batur always made it."

"Then he'd find it easy to add a drug without her knowing it. And no one else would have had the chance." Brakefield led the way to the door that opened into the baize-lined servant's passage.

"Why is there green cloth on the walls?" Eliza murmured to Higgins.

"Muffles the sound, like on a billiards table," he said before they descended a narrow staircase. "Wouldn't do for all the servants' footsteps to be heard. Or their voices."

A string of foreign words rang out behind her. She glanced over her shoulder and saw a grief stricken and furious Zoltan Batur being hauled down the stairs after them.

Eliza had been curious to see how Charlie and the other servants lived in comparison to the lush surroundings above stairs. Everything seemed neat as a pin, but stark; a long wooden table and chairs in the servants' hall, a common parlor with worn chairs grouped near a fireplace, narrow passages between the kitchen and pantries plus other rooms. She also saw supplies for cleaning lamps or knives, pressing and mending clothes, plus rooms devoted to storing luggage and guns. Living quarters for the butler, cook, and housekeeper must be here, too.

Mrs. Stewart bustled toward them. "May I help you with something, madam?" The housekeeper looked at Clara.

"The police have questions," she said in her newly acquired lady of the manor voice. "I'm sure you will cooperate fully."

"Are these the footmen's bedrooms?" Brakefield asked Mrs. Stewart, who nodded. "What about Zoltan Batur? Where did you put him up?"

"We had to move Charlie in with Albert for the week," the housekeeper said.

Brakefield waited for Mrs. Stewart to unlock the door, then brushed her aside. A narrow bed, covered with a brown wool blanket, took up half the windowless room no bigger than a broom cupboard. A leather valise sat beneath it.

"What about the maids?" Eliza hissed at Higgins. "Where do they sleep?"

"Most likely in the attic rooms."

She raised an eyebrow at that. Probably as tiny, too. Hot and stuffy in summer, but freezing cold in winter. Just like every place she had ever called home until Wimpole Street.

Brakefield drew out the valise and unfastened the straps. Inside, beneath a change of clothing, lay a narrow case which held various bottles of dried herbs. The chief constable triumphantly held up a small bottle with a worn label.

"Aha—"

"That is mine," Zoltan Batur cried out, struggling against Constable Stevens's hold. His black coat looked wrinkled and worse for wear under the policemen's rough handling. One sleeve was ripped at the seam. "Do not touch it."

"You added this to her tea," Brakefield said. "Is that correct?"

"Yes. Last night. It is valerian root mixed with passionflower, and steeped in a cup of chamomile. I brew it for Madame when she cannot sleep."

"So she wouldn't wake when you smothered her—"

"You lie! *Bu bar yalan,*" Batur yelled. "I am innocent! There was nothing bad in the tisane. She trusted me to brew it, and no one else. After all, she is my wife!"

Eliza was stunned. His wife? It didn't seem possible. Everyone except Higgins stepped back in shock, especially the policemen. Batur shook off Constable Stevens.

"Madame would never have been invited to all these grand houses if they knew the truth," he said, his voice rife with grief.

"My darker skin kept me from being accepted by the lords and ladies who want her services. You aristocrats look down on the people I come from, Turks and Egyptians. We could not even live openly as man and wife, for fear of being rejected by them. It is your bigotry that is to blame for her death. Otherwise I would have been beside her in bed last night. I would have kept her from harm."

"Let's not forget you were jealous of Philippe Corbet," Brakefield reminded him. "The other servants claim you were extremely possessive."

"Why not? She was my wife and I had to protect her! She was vulnerable because of the Frenchman."

"But Philippe has a fiancée," Eliza said gently.

"It did not matter," Batur sobbed aloud. "Evangeline never forgot her first love."

"All the more reason to take your revenge. To maintain your hold on her and prevent her from taking up with another Frenchman." Brakefield took a deep breath. "Zoltan Batur, I am arresting you on suspicion of murder."

Batur dropped to the floor, wailing in his native tongue. Eliza felt sorry for him, but sorrier for Madame Evangeline. Why didn't Madame's spirit guide warn her at the séance? Instead, a murderer had outwitted a woman who spoke with ghosts.

If Madame Evangeline could be taken unawares, no one else was safe either.

CHAPTER 17

"*I* didn't kill her. I didn't! But I'd like put a knife in both of you!"

Higgins watched as two constables pushed Zoltan Batur into their motorcar. The count and countess stood beside Higgins on the front steps.

"I knew the man was a beast!" the count exclaimed. "But I find the dead woman even worse. Married to her Turkish servant. Part Egyptian, too. *Beschämend!*"

"Shameful indeed." The countess shuddered. "To think we have Clara and my brother to blame for their presence here."

Richard, who was conversing with Chief Constable Brakefield near a second police motorcar, overheard them. "I blame both of you for inviting that despicable American. And I'll hear no more accusations directed against my wife or me." His normally benign expression turned stormy. "Or you may leave my house. Immediately."

The count looked away. His wife pretended she hadn't heard and instead turned to Higgins. "I must apologize for what has been a most unseemly house party. Such things never happened at Banfield Manor when my parents were baron and baroness. I am only glad my mother chose to spend the autumn in Baden-Baden, rather than attend Richard's first attempt at a hunting party. She will be most aggrieved when I write her." The countess raised a scornful eyebrow. "But not surprised."

"It has differed from country house parties I've been subjected to in the past," Higgins agreed. "At those I was merely bored to death. Here, two guests have actually met their death."

Ignoring the displeased faces of the count and countess, Higgins made his way over to Brakefield and Richard. The men watched as Detective Constable Stevens energetically turned the crank on the police motorcar. When the engine started, he straightened up, visibly relieved. It had taken over thirty tries. Petrol fumes filled the air.

"I'm glad we can put this latest death behind us," Richard said as Higgins joined them. "It's clear the man killed his wife in a fit of jealousy."

"Exactly." Brakefield nodded. "An open and shut case of—"

"I disagree," Higgins broke in. "Why would the fellow kill a woman whom he claimed to love obsessively?"

"Because he *was* obsessed with her," Brakefield replied. "I've dealt with jealous husbands before. The wife gives an innocent look at another chap, and an unhinged possessive spouse beats her senseless. Or puts her in the grave. I'm guessing Mr. Batur would have killed the Frenchman, too, had be been around when that rage came upon him."

"Professor, you heard Madame Evangeline talk about her lost love," Richard added. "A Frenchman, no less. One who resembled Philippe. And Batur claimed she had never loved any man as much as this Aristide, not even her own husband. Little did we know Batur was talking about himself."

"But he seemed sad when he said that, not angry," Higgins said.

"Did he seem sad when he threatened me with a dagger

yesterday? Or when he swore he'd love to put a knife in the police just now?" Brakefield scowled. "Batur is a brute."

"A brute obsessed with a pretty young wife, who dare not acknowledge him as her husband." Richard threw Higgins a pitying look. "That pretty wife then tries to protect a handsome Frenchman who reminds her of a former lover. I'm not prone to jealousy, but such a circumstance might put even me in a contrary state."

"A contrary state is far different than a murderous one," Higgins insisted. "I do not believe there is sufficient evidence to arrest Mr. Batur."

"The sleeping drops—"

"Only show that Madame Evangeline required a tisane to help her sleep. My own mother takes a nightly tisane of valerian, honey and oatstraw."

Brakefield seemed unperturbed by Higgins's interruption. "Such a tisane not only brings on sleep, it deepens it. Just what a murderer would require if he planned to smother his victim. After all, the less noise and struggle, the better."

"Herr Professor, why do you not believe the Turk killed his wife?" Count von Weisinger commented from his vantage point on the stairs. "It is obvious to everyone but you."

"Mr. Batur proved he has a violent temper and a jealous nature," Richard said.

"Motive. Opportunity." Brakefield turned to Stevens, who was busy pulling on driving gloves. "Wouldn't you agree, Stevens?"

"That I would, sir. And the sooner he gets properly charged, the sooner we can clap him behind bars. Good riddance." Stevens got behind the wheel.

"But what about Dwight Pentwater's death?" Higgins grew more frustrated by the second. "We've had two dead bodies this week. How do you explain that one?"

"Hunting accident," Richard and his sister said at the same time.

"I agree," Brakefield said. "I thought so from the beginning. It was only the discovery of Pentwater's criminal activities in America that made me hesitate."

"And so it should," Higgins said. "Too many people in the house party had reason to hate Pentwater."

Brakefield clapped Higgins on the shoulder. "You're a professor, aren't you? Used to London streets and city life. I'm a country man, the son of farmers. Tracked hares and birds while growing up. People who shoot game sometimes end up getting hit themselves. Nothing murderous about it though. Bad aim, unlucky shot. And in this instance, a fog thick as treacle." He winked. "Count yourself fortunate you left Pentwater's side when you did. Otherwise, you might have been the one with a bullet through the chest."

"One more thing, Chief Constable," Richard said. "The Ashmore Hunt."

"The fox hunt takes place the day after tomorrow, with the hunt ball later that night," the countess added. "The event cannot be canceled."

"Surely, the deaths of Pentwater and Madame Evangeline would explain the decision to cancel." Higgins often felt as baffled by the upper classes as Eliza.

The count sighed. "No one will be alarmed by news of a simple hunting accident."

"Especially someone who was not a member of our circle," his wife said. "An American, besides."

"It's true," Richard told Higgins. "I've already received calls from friends who learned of Mr. Pentwater's death. They wanted to know if the hunt will proceed as planned."

"And the death of Madame Evangeline?" Higgins asked. "She was a well known figure."

"Known for speaking with ghosts." Richard shrugged. "An

intriguing woman, but rather lurid. Once news of her death and the arrest of the jealous husband becomes public, it will be viewed as scandalous. But the sort of scandal that society enjoys."

"A scandal which tarnishes the victim and the murderer, but not us." The countess wore a regal expression. "After all, what do such people have to do with the Ashmore family?"

"There's your answer, sir." Brakefield straightened his gray Homburg. "The Pentwater death will be ruled an accident later today. And Mr. Batur has been charged with the murder of Madame Evangeline. That means your guests are free to leave Banfield Manor whenever they like, Lord Ashmore." He smirked. "Even that irritating Frenchman."

Richard shook the man's hand. "Thank heaven things can get back to normal."

But two dead bodies proved there was nothing normal about this house party.

After the police left, Higgins remained outside. He'd expected the count and countess to view the recent deaths as nothing more than sordid annoyances. But while he assumed Richard had more common sense, it appeared Eliza was right. Richard and Clara wanted to prove they were fit to be the new baron and baroness. That meant proceeding with the Ashmore Hunt, even though one man had been shot in their forest two days ago, and a woman smothered in her bed last night. Bloody fools, the lot of them.

Maybe a brisk walk would put his thoughts in order. Madame Evangeline's warning about the black motorcar nagged at him. How did the medium discover that he and Eliza had encounters with just such a suspicious vehicle? Were they in danger? And were the deaths here connected to the car?

Deep in thought, Higgins was surprised to find himself in a walled garden on the estate. Thank God he hadn't wandered into the famous Rose Maze. He and Eliza became lost within minutes during their one and only visit to the maze during Clara and Richard's wedding. A most alarming occurrence, given that a killer also lurked along its verdant paths.

He looked out over a garden ablaze with autumn color. Viburnum berries, bright yellow hickories, purple cyclamen flowers. The October breeze carried the scent of burnt sugar; an indication the fallen leaves of Katsura trees lay nearby. Another scent also caught his attention. Cigarette smoke.

A lazy swirl of smoke appeared above a tall hedge. Probably Philippe, who often retired to the music room to smoke his Gauloises. But when he rounded the corner of the privet hedge, Higgins was met by the sight of Lady Annabel sitting on a stone bench. Smoke from her cigarette swirled about the green and brown feathers of her hat. He'd forgotten that Annabel also had a taste for French cigarettes.

Poised to make a quiet retreat, Higgins recalled how Madame Evangeline mentioned a burning manuscript and the malicious man who destroyed someone's life work. The pronouncement must refer to the authoress. And possibly Pentwater.

Higgins cleared his throat. She started at the sound, throwing him a quick glance.

"I am not in the mood for polite conversation. Or in your case, Henry, impolite conversation. So I suggest you move along." Annabel took a long puff of the cigarette in her quellazaire. He noticed the color of her jade cigarette holder exactly matched her walking suit. The woman had a fondness for the color green. Probably because of her green eyes, which even Higgins admitted were rather lovely.

He ignored her suggestion and sat down on the stone bench.

She scooted a few inches away. Annabel must be irritated if she did not want to be in close proximity to him.

"Have I done something to offend you?" Higgins asked.

Exhaling another stream of smoke from her cigarette, she refused to look at him. "Where should I start? How about soliciting a former flower girl to toss me out of your bed?"

"I asked you more than once to politely leave."

"You're a cold-blooded monster."

"And you are a married woman. Unwise to forget that your husband is a guest, too."

"Don't be absurd. Sir Anthony and I have separate bedchambers here, as we do in our own residences. Husbands and wives are not expected to actually sleep together, except for the first delirious months of marriage. Everyone in society knows that." Annabel drew on her cigarette. The distinctive Gauloises's aroma overwhelmed the other garden scents. "My husband would have been none the wiser if you and I had spent the night together. Nor would he have flown into a jealous rage if he had known, as that terrible Turk did. It is not our way."

"You may be mistaken about Sir Anthony's forbearance." Higgins said. "He appears to be most fond of you."

"He has grown far fonder of politics this past year. I believe he is obsessed with it, as Mr. Batur was with his unfortunate wife. His days are filled with reading newspapers and the latest dispatches from the Continent. When we're in London, he spends every night dining with men who have the ear of Prime Minister Asquith. Deadly dull situation for me, I must say."

"Does he plan to run for Parliament?"

"Good gracious no." Annabel finally turned those lovely green eyes in his direction. "He plans to save the world."

Higgins was confused. "Whatever do you mean?"

"My husband is convinced there will be war soon with Germany. And he is correct. The pieces on the geo-political chessboard are in place and only require a final event to trigger a declaration of war." She frowned. "I've tried to convince him to spend an extended time in Canada or America. Somewhere to wait out the inevitable slaughter. Instead, he harbors dreams of being able to prevent the conflict. Foolish man. Although I can't fault his patriotism."

Higgins knew enough of the current state of politics to doubt that any one man could curb the militarism of Kaiser Wilhelm II or assuage the fears of England, France, and Russia over the growing naval power of Germany.

"How does Sir Anthony believe he will be able to prevent war?"

Annabel's laugh rang hollow. "You wouldn't believe me if I told you. The idea is wild and mad. Then again, the idea of war is mad, isn't it? It is why we are at this deranged house party. Count von Weisinger is determined to save the world, too. Only he wants to save it for the Germans. My husband and the count are battling among themselves for the chance."

Her answer only increased his confusion. "You speak in riddles, madam."

"Actually, I speak the truth. Or at least hint at it. If you want the full story, ask Sir Anthony or the count. Perhaps they will tell you." She shrugged. "But most likely not."

Even though he sat in a walled garden, Higgins felt as if he had wandered into the maze instead. "You continue to mystify," he said. "I don't believe I have ever understood a single action of yours. Starting with your inexplicable pursuit of me seven years ago."

She took another long puff on her cigarette. "Why inexplicable? You are an attractive man, Henry. Tall, slender, with a noble profile and rust brown hair that shows little sign of thinning." Annabel peeked over at him. "You also possess the liveliest pair of eyes. The same color blue as the ocean on a blustery day."

He winced. "Please confine such purple prose to your novels."

"However, it wasn't your looks that drew me to you," she continued. "Nor was it your scholarly achievements. I am not a superficial woman. Substance matters to me. And I'd heard you were a true gentleman, with the soul of a romantic."

"What are you talking about? I am the least romantic man in England. And proud of it."

"That is not what I was told." Annabel finished her cigarette. She pulled it from the jade holder, dropped it onto the ground, then stamped upon it with the toe of her leather boot.

"May I know who has spread mad rumors of my fictional romantic nature?"

"Catherine Marsh Stanton, sister to the Duchess of Waterbury."

Higgins cringed, feeling as if he'd been punched in the stomach.

"No need to look stricken," Annabel chided him. "It was told to me in confidence."

"But how? Why?"

"Months before we met, I was invited to a dinner at the London home of the Duke and Duchess of Waterbury. As I'm sure you know, the duchess is a devotee of literature. A number of novelists were in attendance, including myself and Mr. Galsworthy, whose first book in the Forsyte trilogy had recently been published. I had occasion to speak at length with the younger sister of the duchess. Sweet girl, but unhappy in her marriage to an English marquis." Her expression turned cynical. "Her tale didn't surprise me. For years, American millionaires have sold their daughters to debt-ridden English aristocrats."

Higgins's thoughts were in a turmoil. Had Helen told her sister Catherine about them?

Annabel took mercy on him. "Dear man, you look as if you're about to faint. If I'd known this might upset you, I would have remained mum. And I've never uttered a syllable to anyone of your romantic past with the Duchess of Waterbury. Nor will

I." She shook her head at him. "However you should not be ashamed to have expressed such love and chivalry."

"What do you mean?" Higgins asked in a hoarse whisper.

She turned an almost maternal smile upon him. "How could you not have been captivated by the young American heiress betrothed to the most powerful duke in England? Helen Marsh, as she was known then—beautiful, intelligent, kind. Flawless, in fact, except for her dreadful Boston accent. That required the instruction of an expert language instructor, a prodigy by the name of Henry Higgins. Being so skillful, he quickly improved her speech so when she married the duke, she sounded as English as Princess Alice. By that time though, the professor and the future duchess had fallen desperately in love."

Higgins stood up. His head swam. "That was a long time ago," he said.

"Yes. I believe the duchess was only one and twenty, while you were a stripling of twenty-three." Annabel's smile turned rueful. "I would have loved to have known that young, impetuous Henry Higgins."

"What is your purpose in saying this?" Higgins's shock changed to suspicion. "That romance occurred seventeen years ago. It is long past. The Duke and Duchess of Waterbury have a respectable marriage and an admirable young son. Scandal has never touched their family. And I will do all in my power to prevent it from happening now."

Annabel stood as well. "I would never malign another woman, especially in matters of love. Catherine told me of your youthful affair with Helen because she envied her sister's more prestigious marriage. She was jealous because Helen revealed to her that she had discovered real love with you."

Higgins held up his hand. "Enough."

"Don't blame Helen for confiding in her sister. She did so because Catherine was involved in a liaison with another man and felt guilty about betraying her marquis, even if he was a violent imbecile. Catherine said Helen wanted her to know she wasn't the first woman in the family to seek love outside marriage." Annabel sighed. "I've always regretted not having a sister. My brothers have all the sensitivity of a brick wall."

Higgins didn't give a damn about Annabel's brothers. He reeled from the knowledge that Helen had confessed their romance to her sister, who foolishly confided in Annabel.

"If Catherine told you about my relationship with the duchess, I must assume she told others." Higgins felt a mixture of fear and anger.

"Not at all. She only told me because I confessed the details of my own wretched marriage, which thankfully my husband's death put an end to the year before. And you are making too much of this. After all, your romance with her is ancient history. Who in the world would care now? Or even be able to prove it?"

Her statement showed how little Annabel and Catherine really knew. After Helen married the duke, a desolate Higgins assumed their relationship was over. However, their love for each other only grew stronger when the duke turned out to be a cold and inattentive spouse. Higgins and Helen resumed their romance, only this time with utmost care and secrecy. What no one knew—not her sister, Annabel, Eliza or Pickering—was that their affair continued to this day.

"I only tell you this because you asked why I pursued you," Annabel said. "It was because I knew you to be an honorable man. After falling in love with an engaged woman, you dutifully prepared the bride for her new life. Then stepped aside when the time came for another chap to claim her." She placed a hand over her heart. "Honorable, romantic, and gracious. How could I not want to win the affections of such a man? Especially since you have remained single since then. It must be a lonely existence."

Higgins hoped his guilty expression hadn't given him away.

"I thought I might be the one to tempt you from your solitary scholar's life, but alas." Annabel shrugged. "When I heard about Miss Doolittle, I assumed she was your paramour. However, after watching both of you, it is obvious your feelings for each other are not romantic."

"Good lord, no. Eliza is my friend. A damned irritating one at times, too," Higgins said. "But don't underestimate her. She's cleverer than the devil."

"I have no intention of doing so. Any more than I will utter a word about your youthful romance with the American heiress."

In the distance, Higgins heard the shrieks of peacocks, which reminded him that he was still at this blasted house party. "We have discussed my past quite enough. But since we are speaking of Americans, why don't you tell me about your relationship with Dwight Pentwater?"

This time Annabel looked startled. "I don't know what you mean."

"I mean that you were upset when Madame Evangeline spoke about a burning manuscript during the séance. And about the malicious man who destroyed it." He narrowed his eyes at her. "I don't need a fake medium to tell me it was your manuscript which was destroyed. Was Pentwater the disagreeable fellow behind its destruction?"

Annabel scanned the surrounding flowers and shrubbery, as though looking for a gardener or guest within earshot. After satisfying herself that she and Higgins were alone, she said, "I met Mr. Pentwater six years ago, many months after your speaking tour in England."

"The one in which you dogged my every step."

She rolled her eyes. "Most men would have been flattered by such attention. I learned you went off to Switzerland to elude me. I can't imagine you found that stimulating."

Higgins couldn't help but smile. "You had provided more than enough stimulation for one year. I needed to recover." He gestured at the pebbled walk. "Shall we take a stroll?"

Annabel and Higgins began to walk toward the beds of chrysanthemums, now in glorious bloom. "After you escaped to the Alps," she began, "I proceeded with my scheduled tour of America. Dwight Pentwater introduced himself at one of my readings."

"He didn't seem like the bookish type."

"He wasn't. However Dwight did have a passion for redheads." She patted her coiled auburn hair for emphasis. "And if we were famous, so much the better. The New York papers showered me with a great deal of laudatory press. They called me the 'Vixen of Fiction.' Photos of me everywhere. I was as big a sensation as Anna Held, the star of *A Parisian Model*, that year's hit show on Broadway."

"Pentwater pursued you?"

"Relentlessly. It made me regret having hounded you the way I did. I led him on quite a chase, too. Dwight was not an attractive man, personally or physically. But after a few months, his determination wore me down. I found him rather entertaining in the beginning." Annabel brushed a large yellow chrysanthemum as they strolled past. "Dwight had his hands in almost every enterprise in New York City. His friendship helped me secure a lucrative contract with an American publisher. It is why I remained in America for years."

"You became his mistress?" Higgins found it hard to imagine Annabel with Pentwater.

She gave a mocking laugh. "We had encounters, but both of us led separate lives. Also Dwight had a wife, and I had the memory of my husband, who drank himself to death only two years earlier. Matrimony held little appeal for me until I met Sir Anthony."

"How did he come to burn your manuscript? Seems a vindictive measure for a lover, even a sporadic one."

"It was done out of arrogance. The act of a selfish child who wanted his own way."

"But why?"

Her brow furrowed. "The manuscript he destroyed told a story unlike any I had attempted before. As you know, my novels are filled with sensation, melodrama, heightened emotion. I know how to entertain an audience, hence my success. But it is not a success meant to last. Despite my bank account, I knew no one would read *The Daring Sin of Julia* or *A Scandal in Sussex* after I died. It would be as if I never existed. No children. No works of art to lend me even a little immortality." Her voice trailed off.

"But the destroyed manuscript was different?"

"Yes. I titled it *The River*. I began writing it when my first husband was still alive."

"Fiction?"

She nodded. "I worked on it for almost a decade. Never let it out of my sight when I traveled. I was near to completing it when I lived in New York. Dwight had read parts of the manuscript. He found it too dark and thought me a fool for wasting so much time on it. Tragically, he was right. Years of work were destroyed in minutes when he tossed it into the fire." She tried to laugh, but it came out a sob.

Perhaps he had misjudged Annabel. Beneath her worldly, vivacious exterior lay an industrious and somewhat melancholy woman. "Why would he do such a thing?"

"He was toying with the idea of being a theatrical producer. Said there was money in it. And fame. Both were irresistible to Dwight Pentwater. He viewed my popular novels as perfect vehicles to be adapted for the stage. And he wanted me to adapt them. I told him I was close to finishing my novel. I needed to spend the next few months doing only that."

"I assume he disagreed."

Her face grew hard. "He asked for wine. Said he hoped a glass or two might make me reconsider. After I left the room to get the bottle, he threw my manuscript into the fireplace.

When I saw my pages burning, I tried to retrieve them. Dwight pulled me away before I became severely burned. But I still bear the marks." She pushed up her sleeve, revealing white scars on the inside of her forearm. "My palm is scarred, too. So is my soul. I knew I would never be able to recreate the manuscript, you see. It was my only copy. And it was lost. Forever."

"I am sorry," Higgins said with genuine regret.

Annabel pushed her sleeve back down. "Even with my arms seared with pain, I grabbed the poker and struck him. It left a large scar on the back of his neck. That's why he always wore his hair long." Her eyes glittered with hatred. "I clawed him like a tiger. Bit him. Threw a lamp right at his head. He literally ran for his life, because had he remained a moment longer, I would have killed him."

A long silence followed. "Did you?" Higgins asked finally.

"No. But I wish I *had* been the one who shot him in the forest. I would have derived enormous satisfaction from it."

Higgins raised an eyebrow at her. "You and he gave no indication you knew each other."

"Why should we? Neither of us felt the need to acknowledge each other. Or our past."

"Did Sir Anthony know of your relationship with Pentwater?" he asked.

"Of course. I'm a woman of the world. Sir Anthony would not be attracted to some shy maiden with neither accomplishment nor adventure to her name."

"You told him about the manuscript?"

"That was hardly a secret. I was quite vocal to my friends in New York about what Dwight had done."

Higgins lifted a finger for emphasis. "You realize this means Madame Evangeline could have learned about the destruction of your manuscript before she came here?"

"Probably." She shivered. "Although I did find her words

unexpected. I never believed my past would factor into her séance. Most unnerving."

"I assume Sir Anthony told you how Pentwater left him to die in the jungle?"

Annabel seemed exasperated. "He's my husband. Why would he keep such a thing from me? Especially since he knew how much I hated the man. Indeed, our mutual antipathy toward Pentwater was one of the things that first drew us together."

Higgins remained silent.

"And no, my husband did not kill Dwight either."

"I didn't say anything."

"You don't have to. Suspicion is written all over your face. It appears the rumors of you and the Cockney flower girl being the new Holmes and Watson are true."

"Those rumors should also have told you that we've caught several murderers."

"And you think to do so here?" Annabel curled her gloved hand about his uninjured arm. Higgins surprised himself by not pulling away.

"If possible. Eliza and I believe someone deliberately shot Pentwater. And each guest here possesses a motive for doing so."

"Your list of suspects include my husband and me, of course," Annabel said with an air of amusement.

"Yes, along with Lily Marlowe and Philippe Corbet." Higgins thought a moment. "It's possible the count and countess have ties to Pentwater as well. That needs looking into. As does the death of Madame Evangeline."

Annabel looked surprised. "I thought a jealous husband was responsible for that."

"Perhaps not. Whoever killed Pentwater also killed Madame Evangeline. Only I am not certain about motive. Since you don't appear to have a reason to want the spiritualist dead, you're not on my current list of suspects."

She chuckled. "Thank heaven for small favors."

"Then again, you may be keeping something from me. No doubt you are."

"Oh, no doubt." She squeezed his arm. "You do amuse me, Henry."

"I wish I felt amused by this situation. Instead, I fear justice will not be served."

"For someone so clever, you can be rather thick," she declared. "After forty years, you should have realized there is no justice in the world."

Higgins didn't agree. Justice could be served if people were determined enough to fight for it. However, seekers of justice also needed courage. After all, both he and Eliza had come close to dying for their efforts this past year.

He only hoped their lives wouldn't be in danger once again.

CHAPTER 18

*E*liza woke early on Friday morning after another
uneasy night worrying about ghosts in her bedchamber. After she washed and dressed in her riding habit, she
slipped downstairs. Luckily no one noticed her—not the maids
hurrying to tidy rooms and open draperies, nor the footmen
lugging urns of coffee to the breakfast room. Although Charlie
Kenton did wink at her while he carried two racks of toast.
Eliza flashed a cheery wave and headed outside.

Last night at dinner she overheard Lily tell Freddy about her
plans to ride before breakfast. He had declined; apparently he'd
been thrown from his horse, but didn't want to speak about it.
All Eliza cared about was that there had not been a moment
when Freddy wasn't right beside the actress all week. This
would be her best chance to catch Lily alone.

Eliza smiled as she breathed in the familiar scent of horses
and saddle soap inside the low brick stables. One groom tipped
his cap to her and brought out the white hunter she usually
rode. While waiting, she glanced back at the house and was
elated to see Lily heading in her direction.

By the time the actress strode into the stable, Eliza was safely atop her side saddle. Lily looked surprised to see her.

"Happy to see you," Eliza called out to her. "Now we can ride together."

Lily turned to the groom. "Please saddle the chestnut stallion."

"Yes, miss," he replied, then hurried off.

"Go on ahead," Lily told her. "I'll catch up."

"Don't be silly. I'll wait for you out in the paddock."

When Eliza walked her horse past Lily, the actress looked like she didn't know whether to be irritated or nervous about this outcome. But Lily had recovered by the time she joined Eliza. Indeed, she wore a dazzling smile, one Eliza had seen in all her films. Lily also looked quite at ease on her mount. Although Eliza thought the woman's deep green riding habit far less smart than her own.

"Why don't we follow the fox hunt route?" Eliza suggested as she made certain her left leg was hooked securely around the pommel of the saddle.

Lily regarded her with amusement. "How are we supposed to guess where the fox will go tomorrow? Once the dogs catch his scent, that little ol' fox will be running for his life. Probably going every which way. Impossible to predict where. And from what I've seen, Lord Ashmore's property is as big as Dutchess County." She must have seen Eliza's puzzlement because she added, "That's a county in New York."

Eliza laughed. "You're right. I've never been on a fox hunt before. How about you?"

"One of the movie producers in New York owns a big spread in Virginia." Lily gave a slight kick to her horse's flank and steered him out of the paddock. Eliza followed.

"Every fall for the past three years, he invites a ton of us from Vitograph to come down for the hunt. I had to learn how to ride for my first three movies, so I thought it might be fun."

She threw Eliza a mischievous smile. "And it was. Especially the jumping. Like being on the roller coaster at Coney Island."

"I like jumping, too." Eliza rode alongside of Lily as they crossed the open pasture. "Horses are the most beautiful creatures. Can't believe how lucky I am to own one. I only wish I had the time to ride everyday. Is there anyone who doesn't love horses?"

"Freddy. He's been trying to get comfortable in the saddle all week, but he's gotten worse. I swear, that boy is gonna fall off as soon as the hunt master blows the bugle. He landed right on his backside yesterday." Lily giggled. "In a pile of manure, too."

"Maybe Freddy will use his fall as an excuse not to ride tomorrow."

She gave Eliza a smug look. "He knows I expect him to ride with me, so he will. Freddy will do anything I ask. But you must have guessed that already."

"Indeed," Eliza said with clenched teeth. "It wasn't too long ago when Freddy was willing to do anything I asked him."

"Men are fickle," Lily said with a sigh. "We women are fools to ever trust them."

She suddenly kicked her horse's flanks into a fast trot. Eliza easily matched her pace, then urged her horse into a canter. They raced across an open glade, letting their horses expel some energy. Lily slowed her horse when they reached the woods where the path narrowed; Eliza angled her mare into a trot beside her.

"Do you want to talk about yesterday?" Lily asked. "You seemed pretty upset. Just let me say that I think Freddy was an ass to make you cry like that. No one blames you for these stupid deaths. But Freddy got scared and needed to take it out on someone." She frowned. "You just happened to be there when he did. After all, he certainly wasn't going to turn on me."

"Freddy is quite taken with you, isn't he?"

Lily looked amused again. "Most of my fans are."

"Is that all he is to you? A fan?"

She thought a moment. "No, he's more than that. I find him so much fun. Far more polite than American men. And oh, I love that English accent of his. Makes me swoon."

"I believe Freddy's in love with you, or he thinks he is. Only last month he thought he was in love with me. I'm glad I never accepted his marriage proposals. Think what a unreliable husband he'd make." Eliza threw Lily a pointed glance. "Something for you to keep in mind."

"He's already proposed to me. But the last thing I want is a husband, no matter how divine his accent. After all, I'm only twenty-one, and a cinema actress, too. Why should I tie myself down right now? It's time for adventures with all sorts of handsome and passionate young men." Lily slowed her horse further. "Right now that includes Freddy. I hope you don't hate me too much for that."

"I don't hate you at all." Eliza was surprised to discover that was true. Lily may not have discouraged Freddy in his attentions, but he'd doggedly went after another woman. And right in front of Eliza. "I don't hate Freddy either. He's been an important part of my life this past year. I feel sad." Her voice hardened. "And angry. I won't forgive him for how he's behaved. Not ever."

Lily flashed her a look of admiration. "You shouldn't. Men think they can treat women according to their mood. Some of them are real cads. Keep it light, I say, and don't let them stay too long. Trust me, I won't keep Freddy forever. Just until the fun starts to run out."

Although Eliza resented Freddy's cavalier treatment, she still didn't want to see him hurt. And Freddy was such a unsophisticated fool, he was certain to get his heart broken many times. It bothered her that Lily would be the first woman to do so.

Having slowed the horses to a walk, they entered the woods. The autumn beauty silenced the women for a few moments.

Eliza drank in the resplendent hues of the rich gold and copper of the oaks, beeches, and chestnut trees, now swaying in a refreshing breeze. Birds trilled overhead, while the scent of pine and moldering leaves along the path perfumed the air. The path soon dipped into a hollow where a small bridge crossed a stream. The horses climbed a steep rise and emerged once again into an open meadow.

A dewy spider web stretched between a gap in the hedgerow. "Be careful you don't ride through that spider web," Eliza pointed at the silky strands. "It would be a pity to destroy it. Looks like a fairy spun it overnight."

Lily moved her horse away from the spider web. "It may look pretty," she told Eliza, "but it's a trap. Spun to catch its next victim."

"That reminds me. Are you ever going to tell Freddy that you spent the night with Pentwater just hours before he was killed?"

She reined her horse to a stop. "What are you talking about? I did no such thing."

"A footman said he saw you in Pentwater's bed. 'Naked as a jaybird' was how he put it. The footman is an old friend of mine, so of course he passed the story along."

Lily looked off in the distance with a resigned expression. "Oh, all right. I suppose it's no use trying to deny it. I went to Dwight's bed that night, but not because I wanted to. You have no idea the kind of man he was. Filthier than a sewer of rats. He didn't leave me much choice." She swore under her breath. "He never gave me much choice. Always threatening me."

"What could he threaten you with?" Eliza asked.

"Exposure. Lies, half truths, anything that would make for dirty gossip, the type that papers and magazines live for." For a second Lily looked older than her twenty-one years, like a woman weary of battling the world. "Dwight's the reason I got into movies, you know."

Eliza thought back to dinner the first night here. "You said some man saw you walking in the street when you were sixteen and insisted you meet a director that he knew. Was that Pentwater?"

Lily nodded. "I was on the way to Wilton's. That's the hosiery and notions shop where I worked in Brooklyn. Six dollars a week, for a fifty hour week. I hated the place. Anyway Dwight drove past in a snazzy roadster, all red and gold. It dazzled in the sunlight. When he saw me, he stopped cold, skidding the tires. Jumped right out, ran over and promised to make me an actress. Begged me to see a friend who had started to direct movies. But only if I did exactly what he wanted." She shrugged. "I was sixteen and naive. He was more than twenty years older and rich. I never stood a chance."

"I see," Eliza said softly. Being from the rough streets of the East End, she didn't have to imagine what Dwight Pentwater might want of a pretty young girl, whether or not he had a wife and children. Growing up, she'd turned down plenty of "opportunities" from prowling men who thought a poor girl would be eager to lose her virtue for a pound note, or a pretty dress.

"At least he made good on his promise after he got what he wanted from me," Lily went on. "Unlike other girls he seduced. Dwight used to pass them on to his friends, then discarded the poor things, like worn out shoes. Most of those girls never got beyond walk-on parts." A look of pride came over her face. "But I was talented. The camera liked me. I could act. I was smart." She paused. "And tough."

"What did your parents think about Pentwater? Weren't they concerned?" Even as she asked this, Eliza remembered how she'd been left to fend for herself at a tender age.

"Dwight charmed my mother, which wasn't hard to do. She was a looker when she was young, but not very clever. As for my dad, he was thrilled. For my first film, I earned five times what he did in a month at the factory; double that with the second and third films." She sighed. "No, they didn't object. Especially once I earned enough to pay all their bills."

"But you said he moved on to other girls. And you became a famous actress. Was he still part of your life after that?"

"He never let go, not completely. Sometimes a whole year went by and I wouldn't see him. Then he'd show up at the studio or my apartment, arms filled with gifts and scandalous stories." Lily's horse danced a bit, but she quieted him with a pat. "I was Dwight's favorite. He told me that often enough. I think he liked that I had spunk, fire. I always told him exactly what I thought of him. No other woman dared do that, especially his mouse of a wife."

"Maybe he was in love with you," Eliza said.

Lily laughed so hard, tears came to her eyes. "Love? That's rich. Dwight never loved anything but himself. And money. He lusted after me. That was all. I was his pet, his living breathing doll. He liked to tell me what to wear, what to eat, what to say, what parties I was allowed to go to. And only if he could be there to keep an eye on me."

Eliza saw a shadow flit deeper into the woods, no doubt some creature frightened by their proximity. "Then you let him control you."

"He threatened to spread nasty rumors if I didn't cooperate. That would have killed my career. Journalists love a good scandal, and they don't care if anything's true or not." She looked disgusted. "Oh, I knew Dwight dabbled in shady business practices, but I never asked questions. The less I knew, the better."

"Were you shocked when you realized he was invited to the house party?"

Lily gave her a strange look, as if deciding what to tell her. "I may as well be honest. I'm only here because Dwight told the count and countess to invite me."

Eliza reined her horse to a halt. "He did?"

She smiled. "Why so surprised? You've been suspicious

about me from the beginning. Asking me at our first breakfast why an American actress had been invited to the house party instead of a Brit. I thought for sure you'd put it together, with Dwight and me both being from the States."

Lily was right about that. Her presence at the house party had puzzled Eliza from the start. "Did you know he was wanted by the police?"

"I sure did. I was in New York when the Pentland Inc. story hit the papers. Everyone who ever knew Dwight was questioned by the police, including me. I didn't know where he'd gone to until he sent me a letter. He wrote that he was never coming back. But if he was forced to be on the run, he didn't want to be alone. I was ordered to sail to England as soon as possible and join him at Banfield Manor. He'd wrangled an invitation for me. He also warned that if I didn't turn up, those fake rumors and stories about me would be given to the press."

"And you agreed."

"I did. But meeting up with him bought me time, until I could figure out what to do."

What if her solution involved murdering Pentwater? Eliza looked around. There wasn't a person to be seen. If Lily was a killer, it may not have been wise to go riding off alone with her.

Eliza kicked her horse, turning back in the direction of the house. "So you arrived early." She felt a pang of regret. Freddy might not have fallen so hard for Lily if she'd come as late as Pentwater. "Days early, in fact."

Lily brought the stallion alongside her. "Dwight got delayed in London."

"But you didn't seem so welcoming when he finally arrived."

"I knew he couldn't do anything to me while we were at dinner. I should have known he'd be irritated that I snubbed him so publicly. He wanted to get back at me." Lily leaned toward Eliza. "Letting that footman see me naked in his bed was his revenge. It was meant to show me that he was still in charge. And that I couldn't do a thing about it."

"You must have been relieved after he died. Grateful, even."

"Grateful?" She laughed. "Try giddy. I wanted to break into song when I realized he was dead. But don't get any ideas about me being the killer. There's a whole gang of people at this house party who wanted to see Dwight in the grave. I've heard the police finally ruled the shooting an accident. So it looks like no one cares how or why he died. Case closed, as reporters say who cover the crime beat."

"What about Madame Evangeline's death?"

"What about it? That brute of a husband killed her." Lily shivered. "Another reason not to rush into marrying anyone. I'm just glad this whole mess is behind us. I want to enjoy a real English fox hunt. And I've got a swell dress for the ball afterward."

"Will you return to America?"

"Oh no. I'm heading to Italy for a little sun and fun." She tucked a stray wisp of dark hair beneath her hat brim with a wide smile. "I've invited Freddy to come along. He'll go mad for the Mediterranean. And what mischief we'll get into when riding the gondolas in Venice. Although if those Italian gentlemen make eyes at me, I don't know how I'll be able to resist. I love their accents even more than English ones. Who knows? One of them may whisk me off to their villa and Freddy will have to make his own way home."

"Please don't play with his affections." Eliza tightened her grip on the reins. "Freddy is younger than his years. It won't take much to crush him."

"Don't know why you care. He's treated you terribly."

"I know. But I don't want to see him destroyed." She gave Lily a stern look. "Just be honest with him. Tell him the truth about you and Pentwater."

"Why should I? And stop acting like Freddy's mother. He's a

grown man. Time for him to act like it. I promise you, he'll have fun."

"If you don't tell Freddy about Pentwater, then I will."

Lily looked as if she didn't know whether to stick her tongue out at Eliza or slap her. Instead, she dug her heels into her horse's sides and galloped away.

Eliza's heart sank at the thought of Freddy going off to Italy with that woman. And she fully intended to warn him. Eliza had no idea if Lily was capable of murder, but she was certain of one thing. Lily was sure to break Freddy's heart.

CHAPTER 19

*E*liza knelt on the ground and gave Percy a hug. "You're such a darling," she crooned.

"I can't fathom why that bird lets you put your arms around him," Higgins said. "He'd peck my eyes out if I tried such a thing. Not that I ever would."

"Percy and I love each other." Eliza stroked Percy's handsome turquoise head. The bird closed his eyes in appreciation. "He took a fancy to me at Clara's wedding, and a good thing he did. I might not be alive at this moment if he hadn't."

Two peahens emerged from a nearby coop. One of them let out a piercing call. Percy's eyes flew open and he swept out of Eliza's reach. With a grand flourish, he unfurled his fan of tail feathers for his admirers. The peahens responded with loud shrieks.

"I feel like a drab guttersnipe whenever he does that." Eliza smoothed her pale rose fitted jacket and skirt. "I probably should have worn a feathered hat."

"You still wouldn't outshine Percy. And it's time to take our leave. This shameless display of male vanity might continue for some time. Similar to the way Freddy behaves around Miss Marlowe. A shame we can't get Percy to peck Freddy to death."

"Oh, stop." Eliza joined Higgins. "I fear Percy won't want to leave when we return to Wimpole Street. The gamekeeper says he's reached maturity. That means Percy now prefers the company of love-struck peahens to an English girl who feeds him cake." She looked out over the rolling lawns of Banfield Manor to the forest beyond. "And it isn't fair to confine him to our house in London. Not when he can roam free here."

"The peahens have won, then?" Higgins grinned.

She smiled back. "Indeed they have. Next year, there will be peachicks to prove it." Her smile dimmed. "It also appears Lily has won. But I expected as much."

As they walked back to the manor house, Eliza told him about her ride this morning with the American actress. Higgins wasn't surprised that a lurid relationship had existed between Lily and Pentwater. Or that Pentwater had treated her in such a threatening, self-serving manner. But hearing that Lily wished to continue her relationship with the empty-headed Freddy baffled him. More appealing young chaps could be found at every pub, cricket match or village lane in England. Women never failed to confound Higgins.

"Do you really think Freddy will go off to Italy with her?" he asked.

"Freddy always wanted to tour the Continent, only he lacked the money. But Clara's given him an allowance now that she's a rich baroness." Eliza shrugged. "I'll never forgive him for his behavior. Still, I don't want to see him get hurt."

Higgins thought she was being too kind. "He hasn't shown one whit of concern for you."

"True. But we both know Freddy isn't the most intelligent man in London."

He snorted. "There's an understatement. A duck in Hyde Park is ten times cleverer than Mr. Eynsford Hill."

"Exactly why I don't fancy the idea of Lily trifling with his affections. It's clear she enjoys his slavish attention. Something she probably gets from every man she meets."

"Not Pentwater. According to her, his feelings were proprietary, not slavish."

Eliza frowned. "And according to the guests here, he was a greedy, arrogant bully. Cruel for no reason, too. Why destroy someone's life work? Poor Lady Annabel. From what you told me last night, I'd have bashed him in the head. Pentwater was a bad penny, he was."

"I wonder if Lily killed him," Higgins mused. "Except for me, everyone in the hunt carried a gun, including her. Who's to say she couldn't aim it accurately? We learned this past summer that some ladies possess an uncanny ability to hit their target."

"Lady Annabel and the countess made no secret of the fact they've gone shooting before. It could be either of them as well." Eliza considered that for a moment. "Although why would the countess decide to shoot one of her guests? She's disagreeable, but I don't think she's off her chump. And only a madwoman kills someone for no good reason."

"Agreed. That's why the count isn't on my suspect list. No motive."

Eliza looked his way. "If the same person killed Mr. Pentwater and Madame Evangeline, we need to come up with a motive for both deaths."

"Blackmail perhaps. Our ghost lady seemed the bearer of secrets. What if she demanded payment to keep quiet?"

She wrinkled her nose. "But Evangeline never stopped revealing those blooming secrets. Doesn't sound like a black-mailer to me. We had a nasty run-in with one this past spring, so we should know."

"Maybe there were other secrets she had yet to reveal. One deadly enough to put her in danger. A common hazard in any fraudulent profession. And don't give me that look," Higgins warned her. "Madame Evangeline was a con artist. Albeit a most talented one."

"She was not!"

"Of course she was. Evangeline knew the names on the guest list ahead of time. Except for us."

That brought Eliza up short. "How?"

"Richard told me the house party guest list was compiled by his sister before he and Clara left on their honeymoon. Soon after, the newlyweds met Madame Evangeline in Paris and extended their own invitation to her."

"So?"

"Clara and Richard were afraid she might turn them down. Mediums are apparently in high demand this season. To tempt her, they mentioned the celebrated people invited to their house party. That gave our ghost talker several weeks to investigate the lives and foibles of those individuals. Which she did quite well."

Eliza nodded. "She probably asked her spirit guide about the guests."

"By George, I think you've gone off *your* chump. It's impossible to talk with ghosts."

"Then how did she know Mr. Pentwater was about to be killed? Explain that if you can."

"She and Mr. Batur were probably better detectives than we are. One of them may have heard something suspicious while they were here. Something that led them to believe Pentwater was in danger." Higgins shook his finger. "You served as the perfect gullible vessel for her to spout nonsense about a death in the forest."

Eliza seemed convinced. "You didn't see her that morning. Her trance was different than the ones where she talked about Sir Anthony. Or Lady Annabel's manuscript. Even the one where she brought up the number thirty-five. When she spoke about danger in the forest, it was in a different voice. Deeper.

Strange. Like the voice she spoke in at the séance, when she mentioned the gold talisman. Whatever that means."

"I do recall her saying 'a great deal of money,' and the number thirty-five."

"That makes sense," Eliza said. "Pentwater was on the run because he operated a criminal operation in America. What if someone here invested their money with Pentland Inc. and lost it all?"

He raised an eyebrow. "Our doomed spiritualist did her homework most thoroughly."

"But Count von Weisinger spilled the beans about Philippe, not her. In fact, the count seemed eager to blame Philippe for Pentwater's death. Why?"

"I don't think he cares for the French. And the shooting seemed like a great nuisance to him. The sooner he could blame someone for it, the quicker he and his tiresome consort could move forward with this house party."

"The motive for killing Pentwater is obvious," she said. "Everyone hated him. And fear of Madame Evangeline revealing the next secret seems the likeliest reason for her death. Poor woman. To have such a gift, only to be killed for it."

"Bloody hell, Eliza. You can't still believe that woman chatted with ghosts and foresaw the future like Nostradamus. She was an unmitigated liar who—" Higgins stopped as he caught sight of a familiar motorcar pulling up the drive. "Is that my roadster? By heaven, it is!"

"Did you know it was being delivered today?"

"Not for certain, but I hoped." He waved his good arm. "Over here! Hello! Over here!"

"Why don't we just walk to the house?" Eliza asked. "That's where they'll stop."

Higgins grinned as the blue roadster veered off the gravel drive and headed straight for them. "Because I want to see how well my Hudson Mile-a-Minute beauty handles uneven ground. And it's doing a damned fine job."

"Blimey, you're worse than my father. It's just a machine." She shaded her eyes from the sun. "Wait a minute. Is that Detective Ramsey in the passenger seat?"

Being an open-air car, they recognized that it was indeed Colin Ramsey. But the driver's identity remained concealed by large goggles.

"I rang him up yesterday morning," Higgins said.

"You what? Did you call Jack, too? I told you not to bother him and Sybil. You never listen to me. I swear, I should break your other arm." She didn't look happy.

"Stop screeching, I didn't bother Jack. But I wanted to check on my roadster's repairs." Higgins shrugged. "I also wanted Ramsey's opinion on what has been going on here."

"Oh." Eliza seemed placated by that. "What did he think?"

The roadster came to a stop a few feet away. "Ask him yourself."

Higgins tried to hide his amusement as Eliza quickly readjusted the ribbons on her hat. He had sensed a few romantic sparks between her and the recently promoted Scotland Yard detective this past summer, although he suspected both would deny it. But with Freddy out of the picture, perhaps Eliza's attention would drift to someone far more worthy of her. And he liked the young man almost as much as he liked Jack Shaw. He thought Ramsey smart, capable, and manly; his short, muscular physique brought to mind a pugilist. Eliza could do far worse. Indeed, she had proved that with Freddy.

As soon as the motor was cut, Colin Ramsey jumped out. "What do you think, Professor? Does she look good as new?"

Higgins ran his hand over the curve of the fenders, the rims, the gold-trimmed lamp. "Marvelous. Just marvelous."

"I believe he's swooning," Eliza remarked to Colin.

"So he should," Ramsey said. "I've never heard a four-cylinder engine so quiet."

"Like a large kitten, she is." The driver pushed his goggles on top of his cap, but Higgins still didn't recognize him.

Ramsey nodded at the fellow. "This is Officer Barnaby Lake of the Metropolitan Police."

The man smiled. "Pleased to make your acquaintance."

"He's also an expert mechanic," Ramsey went on. "Spends a lot of his time working on Yard vehicles. I've a background in mechanics myself. Given how pretty this roadster is, I didn't mind working on it with him whenever I could."

"Good as new, I suppose?" Eliza asked.

"Better." Ramsey gave her an appraising glance. Higgins could tell the detective liked what he saw. "And you're looking well, Miss Doolittle. All in pink, like a spring flower."

"Thank you." Eliza smoothed her ribbed silk skirt. "But the fashion magazines call this color dusty rose."

"Do they now? Whatever they call it, you look as striking as Professor Higgins's motorcar. Only I've heard you're not as quiet." Ramsey lifted an eyebrow. "Then again, I seem to recall you having a lot to say."

"I do." She threw him a challenging look. "But are you clever enough to listen?"

He laughed. "Perhaps you'd be willing to school me."

"Can we move on?" With his roadster ready for inspection, Higgins wasn't in the mood to listen to coy flirtations. "Have all the repairs been made?"

"Every last one," Barnaby Lake replied. "But we had to take the whole machine apart, then put it back together. Lots of small problems needed fixing."

"Runs smooth as cream now," Ramsey added. "And we fairly flew here from London. It gets amazing speed. No wonder they use the Hudson Mile-a-Minute for racing."

"Do you and Officer Lake plan to take the train back to the

city today?" Higgins asked while he inspected the white-rimmed tires.

"We have no immediate plans to return to London," Ramsey said. "In fact, I brought Lake here to watch over the motorcar tonight."

Higgins straightened. "Lord Ashmore has a garage. It will be perfectly safe there."

"I'm not convinced of that. Better to have one of us keeping an eye on it."

"And why does Professor Higgins's Hudson require a chaperone?" Eliza asked.

The detective glanced over his shoulder at the sprawling manor house, a lengthy walk away, apparently making sure they stood on a stretch of open lawn with no one close by. "It's safe to talk here."

"Safe?" Higgins and Eliza said at the same time.

"I've been looking into your accident all week. Some details bothered me." Ramsey shrugged out of his heavy driving coat, which had protected his suit on the open road. "Your accident in Putney seems to be anything but. Someone deliberately left the wagon in the middle of the road." He flung the coat onto the car's blue leather seat. "And I found a witness, an older fellow taking his daily constitutional in Wandsworth Park that morning. He claims he saw a man who unhitched a wagon, left it in the middle of the road, then led the horse away."

Eliza and Higgins exchanged troubled glances. "What did the man look like?" she asked.

"The witness is over seventy and near-sighted. What he saw was mostly a blur."

"Then his testimony is worthless," Higgins said.

"Even though he couldn't see details, he swears a man left the wagon on that road." Ramsey tapped his fingers on the car's bonnet. "I questioned the fellow and believe him. I also found a smithy who claims his horse and wagon went missing that

Sunday morning. Stolen right out in front of his business. The horse showed up two hours later. But not the wagon."

Eliza's eyes widened. "Someone wanted to cause an accident. How vicious to do such a thing for sport! Jack and the Professor might have been killed."

"I don't think it was for sport. Whoever left the wagon intended to kill or gravely injure your roadster's driver." Ramsey gave Higgins a pointed look.

"In other words, me," Higgins said. "After all, no one knew ahead of time that Jack would be my passenger."

Eliza gasped. "It must have been the man in the black motorcar."

"What black motorcar?" Ramsey sounded puzzled.

She told him about the black car she'd seen repeatedly driving down Wimpole Street. "It could have been the same one chasing Professor Higgins that day."

"Damn it all, for what purpose?" Higgins spoke more to himself than anyone else. "If they wanted my roadster, why cause it to crash?"

"We think the person wanted what we found inside the car."

Ramsey beckoned Eliza and Higgins closer and removed a small pouch from his inner suit pocket. He scanned the surrounding area again, then pulled an object from the pouch. A gold cross, no more than three inches long.

"You found that in my roadster?" Higgins shook his head. "Impossible. I inspected every inch of the car when I purchased it."

"Found it inside the auto-meter," Barnaby Lake said. "Well-hidden, too."

Eliza gave him a curious glance. "What's an auto-meter?"

"The round gauge near the steering wheel," he explained. "An auto-meter tells you how fast the motorcar is going, as well as total distance traveled. The crash caused the auto-meter to fall off. We wanted to see if the inner mechanism had been damaged, so we took it apart."

"It fit neatly inside the back metal cover," Ramsey said. "Clever spot."

"Is it valuable?" Eliza seemed dubious. "It looks old. I assume someone wore this around their neck. There's a small hole at the top for a chain or cord. Not very attractive though."

Higgins took the cross from the detective. The center held three dull red stones. Rubies? Garnets, perhaps? Whatever they were, they were too small to be worth much. He felt something on the other side. Turning the cross over, he spied an inscription.

"What does it say?" Eliza peered at the writing.

"Can't make it out. The letters are too small." Higgins looked up at Ramsey. "Have you or your men seen the inscription under magnification?"

"We have. DCCC AD is inscribed along the left arm of the cross. We assume it's Latin."

"DCCC is eight hundred. AD stands for Anno Domini, the year of our Lord."

Ramsey pointed at the cross. "The right side bears the inscription VAE VICTUS."

"Latin for 'Woe to the Conquered.' If I remember my classics courses, the Roman historian Livy claimed this was a phrase first uttered by Brennus." Higgins noticed their blank expressions. "He was chieftain of the Gauls. Brennus said this phrase about the citizens of Rome, the city he had just sacked." He ran a fingertip over the inscription that ran the length of the cross. "What's this?"

"MUNDUS MEUS," Ramsey said. "And there's a space before the next inscription which is CHARLES MAGNUS."

"'The world is mine,' followed by 'Charles the Great.'" The inscriptions now made sense to Higgins. "That last one refers to

Charlemagne. Pope Leo III crowned him Roman emperor in the year 800."

"I need to read more history books," Eliza said in a mournful voice. "I only know about the Stuarts. And a little about Marie Antoinette. She had her head chopped off, you know." Eliza suddenly grabbed both men by their sleeves. "The gold of the great king. That's what Madame Evangeline said during the séance."

"What séance?" Ramsey asked her.

"We had a séance the other night and her spirit guide spoke about a gold talisman. And a 'king who unites many.' Sounds like this Charlemagne cross could be the talisman she mentioned. The one that gives power."

Ramsey and Higgins looked at each other. "Good Lord, she's right," Higgins said. "But why would anyone hide it in an auto-meter?"

"Maybe as a way to protect the driver," Eliza suggested.

"Or it has a value we can't yet guess." He tried handing the cross back to Ramsey, but the detective waved him away.

"The cross is yours, Professor, since we found it in your vehicle," the detective said. "Someone wanted you to crash. Probably hoped you might be killed or knocked unconscious. If either had happened, whoever caused the accident would likely have removed the auto-meter from the car and fled."

"The Professor has a rock hard head," Eliza said. "And he probably stayed awake because he was more worried about the roadster than he was about himself."

Higgins didn't bother to contradict her. "Jack and I were lucky a carload of churchgoers happened upon us just then to rescue us. So what do you hope to accomplish here?"

"We're here to flush the guilty party out. There must be some connection between the motorcar and this house party."

"As Madame Evangeline warned us." Eliza poked Higgins in the chest.

"But what connection could there be?" Higgins asked Ramsey.

"When we found the cross three days ago, I looked into the background of the roadster. Contacted the ship's manifest from America, as well as the dealers where such a vehicle might be purchased there. I was especially interested in who owned the motorcar before you and Alfred Doolittle. Early this morning I learned the original owner's name."

"Tell us, man," Higgins demanded. "Who was he?"

Ramsey's expression grew stern. "Dwight Pentwater."

CHAPTER 20

Given her aggrieved expression, Countess von Weisinger looked like she objected to a Scotland Yard policeman sitting down to luncheon with them. But Eliza realized with pleasure that the insufferable woman could do little about it. After the deaths of two guests in less than a week, the countess's influence had waned.

Instead, Richard and Clara gave Colin Ramsey a warm welcome. The couple had been quick to remember his valiant presence at their recent wedding reception and insisted he join the guests at the dining room table. Officer Barnaby Lake took his meal in the servants' hall, however. Social rules could only be bent so far.

Eliza bit back a smile when Freddy scowled at Ramsey. He had been jealous of the young detective since he came on the scene during the wedding murders. Eliza had never given Freddy reason to be jealous, but from the beginning Colin Ramsey intrigued her. And he seemed interested as well. Both of which Freddy resented. Well, he could go to the devil now. If Colin's interest in her grew, she had no intention of putting a stop to it. In fact, she wondered what his kiss would be like. He seemed the passionate type.

"Are you daydreaming, Eliza?" Clara looked down the table at her. "I've asked you twice about your cameo. It's not the one your friend Sybil gave you as a bridesmaid's gift. Lady Annabel and I wondered where you purchased it."

"Italian, I'd say." Lady Annabel picked up her wine glass. "Seventeenth century."

Eliza touched the brooch pinned to her lace collar. She'd been so deep in thought, she hadn't heard the surrounding conversation. Ramsey sat directly across the table and shot her an impish grin. Had he guessed she'd been thinking about him?

"Colonel Pickering gave it to me for a birthday present. He told me it had been in his family forever. Back to the time of Queen Elizabeth." Eliza smiled, as she always did at the mention of her beloved Colonel. "I didn't want to accept it. After all, the cameo's a family heirloom, but he insisted I was his family now."

"Pickering is generous to a fault." Higgins speared a smoked sardine.

"He's the kindest gentleman in the world," she added.

"Given its antiquity, you should look into its provenance in my library," Richard said. "Although credit should go to my father and grandfather. As art collectors and antiquarians, they amassed endless volumes. You should be able to research any antique object in there."

Eliza exchanged an excited glance with Higgins and Ramsey. Had the same idea occurred to them?

"I assumed you brought the roadster so Professor Higgins and Miss Doolittle can drive back to Wimpole Street," Richard said. "Since the motorcar is only a two-seater, you and your fellow officer will need to make other arrangements for your return. I am more than happy to have my chauffeur drive you to the train station. This evening, if you like."

The detective set down his glass of burgundy. "With your

permission, Officer Lake and I plan to spend the night. Repairs on the roadster were extensive. We wish to make certain it's in full working order before we leave." Ramsey sat back as a footman removed his plate. "I'd hate to learn the Professor and Miss Doolittle were left with a defective motorcar."

"Where do you and your associate intend to sleep?" the countess asked in a disdainful voice. "The village? Or the garage, perhaps?"

"The garage will do fine. Your chauffer mentioned empty bedrooms above it."

Ramsey looked with approval at the plate of grilled mutton chops now set before him. Eliza thought it only polite if Detective Ramsey were invited to stay in the manor house, but she doubted even Richard and Clara were modern enough to suggest that.

"If you insist on staying, Baxter will see about readying the garage rooms." The countess threw a long-suffering look at the butler, who bowed.

"I'd love to take the Hudson Mile-a-Minute for a spin," Richard said.

"Let's do it after luncheon, then," Higgins suggested. "Wait till you see how it hugs the ground. And it's as fast as a cheetah. We'll scare all the peacocks."

"American, isn't it?" Richard took a bite of his mutton.

"Indeed it is. Like its original owner."

"Who was its owner?" Richard asked.

"Dwight Pentwater," Colin Ramsey said.

Lily froze, her hand poised in mid-air. The count's fork, however, clattered to his plate, while Sir Anthony choked on his peas.

"Mr. Pentwater?" Annabel gulped down her wine with a trembling hand.

"But it belonged to Eliza's father," Freddy said, "and he sold it to the Professor."

"He did," Higgins said. "Alfred bought it this past summer at one of the shipping line auctions. Baggage which remains unclaimed too long goes on the auction block, including cars. It's why Alfred got such a good price."

"*C'est vrai*," Philippe said. "I once bought a leather trunk at an auction in Calais."

Eliza was surprised to hear him speak. Until now, the Frenchman seemed preoccupied with his own thoughts and oblivious to the conversation.

"Professor Higgins's motorcar once belonged to Mr. Pentwater?" Clara bit her lip. "How strange. They hadn't even met each other until Monday night."

"A most peculiar coincidence," Sir Anthony grumbled.

"As a general rule, Scotland Yard doesn't believe in coincidences," Ramsey said. "A bit too neat. They make us suspicious."

"Are you saying there is no such thing as a coincidence?" Annabel still seemed shaken.

"I think he's saying that a coincidence is merely a term we give to something that defies logic or probability," Higgins answered.

"And most people are too lazy to figure out what's really going on," Eliza added.

"I couldn't have said it better myself, Miss Doolittle." Ramsey's smile deepened.

"What do you imply, *Offizier* Ramsey?" the count snapped. "That there is something suspicious about Herr Pentwater's motorcar? The American was chased by the police, *ja*? He escaped to Europe, and sent ahead his possessions. Including this motorcar."

"I wager Pentwater was unable to pick up his car, so it went on the auction block," Sir Anthony said. "Unlike you, Detective, I do believe in coincidences. Too many unexplained things have happened to me on my travels. Must have been a trick of fate that Miss Doolittle's father bought it. And that Higgins then bought it from him."

"Besides, who could have guessed the Professor would injure himself in a motorcar accident," Richard said. "Clara and I were disappointed when Eliza called to turn down our house party invitation. But soon after another unpredictable event occurred. A fire broke out at their Wimpole Street home, which necessitated their visit."

Eliza set down her fork as those words sunk in. Like Higgins and Ramsey, she didn't put much stock in coincidence. Except it was no trick of fate that a black car appeared on Wimpole Street, then followed Higgins on his drives. Especially since a mysterious cross had been found in the auto-meter. But she hadn't connected any of this to the fire until now. It all fell into place.

"Is something wrong, Eliza?" Ramsey asked in a low voice.

"No, I'm fine. Something just occurred to me. We can speak about it later."

This certainly wasn't the time to announce that whoever wanted the roadster enough to kill Higgins had also set the fire at Wimpole Street. The perpetrator had taken two big risks to get their hands on the car. If Higgins was gone, access to the roadster—and the cross—would be easier. Only they couldn't have guessed the roadster would be delivered right to Banfield Manor. Or maybe they did. Now she really was worried.

"A penny for your thoughts, Eliza." Higgins said.

Eliza picked up her fork once more. "They're worth far more than a penny."

"This has been a most unusual house party, Lord Ashmore," Ramsey said. "Two deaths."

"Both of them explained," the countess replied. "No need to dwell on them. Or on Professor Higgins's motorcar coincidence."

"What about the other coincidences?" Ramsey asked.

"Whatever do you mean?" She signaled for the footman to remove her plate, even though the countess had touched little of the main course.

Ramsey swallowed his peas first. "From what I learned, most of you here had past connections to Dwight Pentwater. Rather unpleasant ones."

"He was an unpleasant man." Lily's brusque tone suggested she'd gotten over her shock about Pentwater's car, and now seemed irritated.

"Monsieur Pentwater was also a criminal," Philippe reminded everyone.

"None of us knew about his past," the count said.

"I believe your wife did." Ramsey nodded toward Countess von Weisinger at the head of the table. "In fact, she has suffered at his hands. In a manner of speaking."

She stiffened. "What an ill-mannered fellow you are."

"Leave this house." The count rose to his feet. "You have insulted my wife."

"Sit down, Rudolf," Richard ordered. "We've heard how Pentwater caused injury to others here. If my sister was also affected, I demand to know."

Eliza looked at Ramsey in surprise. What did he know about the countess?

The countess flung her napkin onto the table. "Demand to know, Richard? I demand to know why you married a girl with no money, no property, and no sense."

Clara looked as if she hadn't decided whether to burst into tears or throw a plate of mutton at her sister-in-law. But Richard shot to his feet. If this kept up, luncheon might be brought to a close before the sherbet could be served.

"Louise, my tolerance is at an end." Richard appeared more formidable at this moment than both von Weisingers combined. "I will not remind you again that I am Ashmore's seventh baron and my wife is baroness. You will treat us with the respect we deserve. If not, you will no longer be welcome at Banfield Manor or any other family property."

"You cannot mean that. Mama and I have the right to—"

"Where the Ashmore holdings are concerned, you and the Dowager Baroness have only the rights which I choose to extend. It would be wise to remember that."

The countess paled at his words. "You wouldn't dare deny us."

"Don't tempt me, Louise." Richard also looked pale, but with anger. "I spent years being treated as an afterthought by our parents. Indeed, it would have suited everyone had I spent the rest of my days with the Army in India. But I am Lord Ashmore now. If you cannot accept that, I cannot accept you in my house."

Eliza had no wish for a ringside seat at a family argument. The other guests must be wishing to be elsewhere as well.

After an awkward silence, Richard turned to Ramsey. "Please continue. What was my sister's connection to Dwight Pentwater?"

The count sat down, looking at his wife with confusion. Eliza figured he had no knowledge about this either. Richard's sister flushed beet red but avoided his gaze.

"Professor Higgins rang me yesterday to ask about his roadster," Detective Ramsey began. "He also told me about the deaths which occurred this past week at Banfield Manor. The name 'Pentwater' seemed familiar. This past summer, Scotland Yard received a wire from New York authorities regarding an American fugitive by that name. After my conversation with the Professor, I contacted them. They gave me was a list of everyone who'd invested in Pentwater's company. Pentland Inc., to be exact. Countess von Weisinger was on that list."

"You invested with that dishonest man?" Richard asked his sister.

The count smacked the table. "*Mein Gott!* Tell them they are wrong, Louise."

She remained as immobile as the marble bust on a pedestal behind her.

Ramsey frowned. "Last year, the countess invested thirty-five thousand pounds. And lost it all when Pentland Inc.'s dishonest practices were exposed."

"Thirty-five thousand? Madame Evangeline mentioned thirty-five during the séance!" Eliza marveled anew at the deceased woman's abilities. Higgins groaned aloud.

"Is that true, Louise?" Richard asked.

"*Nein*, it cannot be," the count said to his wife. "Your dowry was not to be touched."

The countess stirred, as if she had fallen asleep and only now awoke. She turned her attention to Ramsey. "I was left to deal with our financial matters, since my husband is much preoccupied with politics. Though he has a respected name in Austria, it did not come with a fortune to match my family." Contempt crossed her face. "Richard bemoans his status as the third son. How tragic. At least he had the chance to one day be baron. As a female, any claim to the Ashmore estate was denied me."

With a heavy sigh, Richard once more sat down. "That is the law."

"Our expenses have grown as of late," she continued. "Last December, a friend returning from America told me they had invested in Pentland. The company reputedly paid tremendous returns on a small investment. My friend always made sound financial decisions, so I had no reason to doubt him."

"But thirty-five thousand pounds," the count said hoarsely.

"It seemed a gamble that carried few risks. I have not taken many risks in my life. This seemed like the moment to do so." She looked over at her husband. "I knew you had met Mr. Pentwater in the past. You spoke highly of his business acumen."

The count put his head in his hands. "*Wir lagen falsch.*"

"When did you learn you had lost everything?" Higgins asked her.

"In July. I hoped after my father died this year, there might be a bequest for his only daughter. Instead, everything went to Richard."

"I'm so sorry," Clara said, although the countess only sneered in reply.

Richard shook his head at his sister. "You should have told me."

"I saw no reason to publicize my folly."

"Did you speak to Pentwater about the money when he was here?" Ramsey asked.

"No. I feared he might recall my name as being one of his investors." She reached for her water goblet and took a long sip. "But so many of us handed our money over to him, we were probably nothing more than numbers in a ledger. I was appalled to learn my husband had invited him here on business. There was no way to disinvite him without revealing what I had done."

The atmosphere in the dining room had turned gloomy, despite the sunlight pouring through the tall windows. Suddenly a loud rumbling met their ears. It sounded like Philippe's aeroplane, but he still sat at the table.

"*Mon Dieu*, she is here!" With a jubilant smile, the aviator sprang to his feet. "Nathalie has arrived!"

"Your sweetheart from France?" Eliza asked.

"*Oui.* The other day on the telephone, I call Nathalie and my friend Jean-Paul. I ask him to fly Nathalie to me here, in secret. This way she will not have to marry the deputy minister, and we can be married. Maybe in Scotland." He looked so happy, Eliza thought he might able to take flight without the aid of his flying machine.

Clara clapped her hands. "You're eloping! How romantic."

The aeroplane's rumbling grew louder, as if landing nearby.

His eyes welled up. "Wait until you meet Nathalie. I wish you to meet Jean-Paul, but he must fly on to York today."

He raced out of the room. Everyone sat in stunned silence before the countess erupted in laughter. Eliza half-wondered if she'd grow hysterical before long.

"What is so amusing, countess?" Higgins asked.

"It appears we have come full circle. On our first night, we had thirteen for dinner. Of course, that was before our guest list was reduced to eleven. And now. . ."

"With Detective Ramsey and Nathalie, we will have thirteen once again," Eliza finished.

The countess sat back, as if exhausted. "I doubt things can get any worse."

Eliza hoped she was right. But until the murderer was caught, she feared yet another disaster lay ahead.

CHAPTER 21

*H*iggins shoved a leather-bound book back onto the shelf. "Damnation, but I'm sick of looking for any personal details left by Napoléon's secretary. Bourrienne was too much of a diplomat regarding his battle reports."

Colin Ramsey glanced up from a stack of books. "Probably wanted to make his boss look good. Happens all the time at the Yard. An easy road to promotion."

"He did write that a small gold cross had been brought to Napoleon during the Battle of Arcole, which ended in victory against the Austrians. The battle hadn't gone well for the general. Not until a French sympathizer presented him with this cross said to have been given to Charlemagne by the pope." Higgins shrugged. "I guess it did the trick. Still doesn't give us any history on the cross, though."

"Seems to have worked for the Corsican." Ramsey held up a book. "According to this, Napoleon fought sixty battles, and only lost eight. Most of them at the end of his career. Maybe he'd lost the cross by that time." He laughed. "Or the British just outfought him. Hey, maybe the cross fell into Wellington's hands. Was the Duke an admirer of Charlemagne?"

"Any sensible man would admire him." Higgins plucked another gilt-edged volume from the shelf. "Certainly, Napoleon idolized Charlemagne, along with Caesar and Hannibal. Studying their methods, learning how artillery was the key to success. I found one mention of the Charlemagne cross in a letter he wrote to Joséphine. Lucky break, that."

"Wasn't Joséphine his wife?" Eliza asked, curled up on the sofa with a box of daguerreotypes. She held up a magnifying glass to one grainy specimen and then tossed it aside.

"One of them. He divorced her in order to get an heir with his second wife."

Eliza muttered something churlish under her breath about men. Colin grinned. Higgins skimmed through the pages of his book. He felt hampered by his injured arm and the little amount of information they had uncovered so far.

After luncheon, Higgins, Eliza and Ramsey agreed that their best opportunity to learn about the cross of Charlemagne was in the Ashmore library. Only they didn't want anyone to know what they were doing. The clock had just struck ten when Higgins met Ramsey at the front door to let him in. Mercifully, the other guests retired early due to tomorrow's fox hunt. For the past few hours, the three of them had closeted themselves in the library, searching through every history book pertaining to Charlemagne, the late Middle Ages, and France.

"Too bad we can't ask Madame Evangeline's spirit guide about the cross," Eliza said.

Ramsey slouched further in one of the library's armchairs and yawned. "By the way, I haven't told you what I learned about your medium. Her real name was Esther Bezier Campbell. Born in the capital of French Algiers in 1886. The Beziers were French colonists who worked for the government. They've been there for decades. A lot of intermarriage with the locals, too. Her grandmother was a Moorish woman from one of the desert tribes."

"That makes sense," Eliza said. "She mentioned the Sahara, and how peaceful the desert was. What about the father? Madame Evangeline claimed he was Scottish."

"Angus Campbell, a lawyer from Glasgow. An expert on deeds and property law. A wealthy émigré family asked for his help concerning a land dispute. They paid for his passage to Algiers, where he settled the dispute, then fell in love with Sidonie Bezier, the daughter of a government clerk." Ramsey yawned again. "Sidonie made quite an impression on the Scotsman. He married her and made French Algiers his home until he died nine years ago."

"What about Evangeline's mother?" Higgins rifled the pages of a new volume.

"Alive and well in Paris, along with one of her sons. She moved there after Angus died."

Eliza sighed. "We should contact her family and tell them the tragic news."

"That's not our job," Higgins said gently. "After all, she had a husband. If anyone should inform them, it is Zoltan Batur." He paused. "Or more likely the police."

"What about the Frenchman who resembled Philippe Corbet?" Eliza asked. "That Aristide fellow who drowned. Who exactly was he?"

Ramsey picked up another book. "I'm guessing he was a member of the French colony in Algiers. He must have drowned in the Chelif River. Around this time, Esther had a nervous breakdown. After she recovered, she told people that Aristide's death had made her spiritualist 'gifts' stronger. That's also when she started to call herself Madame Evangeline."

"When did she marry Zoltan Batur? And who is the chap, anyway?" Higgins asked.

"Not a lot of information on him. It's not even clear if that's his real name. He spent a lot of time in Turkey and Egypt. Algiers, too. Batur acted as a strong man for important people.

When he met Evangeline, she was still known as Esther Bezier. He worked as a bodyguard for a rich family in Algiers. Probably had his eye on her. And after this Frenchman died. . ."

Eliza picked up another daguerreotype. "He loved her from afar. Then after her heart was broken due to Aristide's death, Batur picked up the pieces. It's actually quite romantic."

Higgins and Ramsey exchanged skeptical glances. "Don't know about that," Ramsey said with a chuckle. "They married in France, shortly after Sir Arthur Conan Doyle attended one of her first séances. That séance convinced him of her talents. Doyle urged his famous and wealthy friends to seek her out. His recommendation soon made her a popular favorite in the drawing rooms of Europe."

"Probably when Batur was introduced as her bodyguard, not her husband," Eliza said. "I know how snobbish the upper classes are. They wouldn't have welcomed someone like Batur into their homes as her husband. At least he made a convincing bodyguard."

"An even more convincing spy," Ramsey told her. "It's why she was successful. He paid off the servants of her rich clients for all the secrets Evangeline needed before going into those trances. Batur had contacts in Europe and America, who funneled information to him."

"Whereupon she pretended her spirit guide told her all that rot," Higgins said with disdain. "I don't want to say 'I told you so,' Eliza, but I told you so."

"What about the things she couldn't have known? Like the black motorcar." Eliza remained stubborn. "I never told anyone about that, except the Colonel. And don't forget her warning to us the day we arrived. She was right about the death and disaster."

"I spoke to a few people who believed Madame Evangeline did slip into an authentic trance on occasion," Ramsey added. "These trances reportedly were not under her control, coming upon her at unexpected times. She claimed to never recall what she said."

"Exactly." Eliza turned to Higgins. "And she also told us about the cross of Charlemagne during the séance."

He waved a hand. "Well, she cannot tell us anything more, being dead. No doubt killed for what she did learn, either from her spy or the spirit world."

Eliza looked down at the box of daguerreotypes. "There's nothing of use in here."

"Don't give up. Keep at it, you might find something."

Higgins jotted down a few notes from one book and then buried himself in the next for another half hour. The wind moaned against the mullioned windows while he read. He checked the time. Long past midnight.

Colin stood, stretching his back. "Has anyone found anything else about this cross? Who owned it before Napoleon? And where does the legend come from about its power?"

"Nothing beyond the letter to Joséphine, which mentioned how he always carried the cross but forgot to tuck it into his pocket during the second battle of Bassano," Higgins said. "His first defeat, in fact. He held onto it for years, according to his journals. As you said, his battle record is outstanding until Wellington defeated him at Waterloo. Maybe Napoléon no longer possessed Charlemagne's cross at that time. Not that I believe any of this nonsense about the its power. But Napoleon certainly did."

"The cross could have been stolen." Ramsey held out a book to him. "The Duke of Wellington had his headquarters at Waterloo. Napoléon was quartered far to the south."

Higgins looked up with interest. "Ah, you found the French account of the battle."

"This passage tells how locals pried out the teeth of dead soldiers and sold them to denture makers. And here it reads,

'Napoléon was in despair after the battle, pacing back and forth, pockets empty, until he regained his coolness.'"

Eliza rose and walked over to Ramsey. He pointed the passage out to her.

"Quite true about the Waterloo teeth, from what I heard," Higgins said, "and that's an interesting note about his empty pockets. It could be a deliberate reference that he no longer had the cross. If only we could find a definitive source."

"Was the cross something Charlemagne wore on a chain around his neck?" Eliza asked. "Or on a rosary? Maybe it was part of his crown."

"We only have to go through several hundred books to answer that," Higgins said.

Everyone went back to the bookshelves amid yawns and grumbles.

After another thirty minutes, Eliza announced, "I found something." She held out a book. "Charlemagne's crown was destroyed during the French revolution. Here's an illustration."

Higgins peered closely at it. "Hmmm. A simple circlet, four rectangular plates with jewels, and four fleur-de-lis. No cross on it at all." He snatched up a book that he'd set aside with a strip of paper to mark the page. "This is a drawing of Charles the Bald, grandson of Charlemagne. It shows him holding a scepter, passed down from his great-great-grandfather Charles Martel, who defeated Abdul Rahman Al Ghafiqi at the Battle of Tours—"

"Hold on." Ramsey thumbed through a third book. "The cross on that scepter looks exactly like this one, carried by Philip the Bold." He pointed at the illustrated page.

Higgins drew the cross from its leather pouch. An unprepossessing item, despite its history. The gold had a dull glow, making the small red stones appear black against the metal. He once more examined the Latin inscription, then glanced again at Philip the Bold's scepter.

"They could be the same. Difficult to tell, but possible."

"'Woe to the conquered,' didn't it say?" Ramsey picked up the last hefty volume of Bourrienne's Memoirs. "Napoléon talked about that phrase often, according to this."

"And I read that Charles the Mad struck the cross off the scepter during one of his rampages after 1392. Nearly killed his brother one time," Higgins said.

Eliza rolled her eyes. "And I thought my family was crazy."

"Historians have no idea why Charles suffered his bouts of insanity. The scepter was passed on to the next ruler. And so on, we must assume, until Louis the Sixteenth."

"So perhaps the cross was a talisman of sorts," Eliza said.

"I read earlier that Louis the fifteenth carried a cross at the Battle of Fontenoy in 1745. Also a French victory." Higgins rummaged through the pile of books. "Here, this volume. The cross can be traced forward from Charles Martel to Charlemagne and on to the last ruler before the Reign of Terror. It's no surprise the revolutionaries destroyed some of the royal regalia. But Charlemagne's cross survived. Napoléon could have come upon it at that time."

"I'm surprised he didn't use the cross when he had his own crown made." Ramsey thumbed through another book. "Look."

Higgins noted the simple cross atop the bejeweled gold crown, with its antique cameos—the center one of Bonaparte himself. "Ah, that is not the same cross. I doubt Napoléon would have entrusted such a precious item to any goldsmith, for one thing. And he needed to keep it with him at all times to ensure success in his doings. But it must have been stolen from him before Waterloo. He'd never have parted with it willingly."

"But how did the cross fall into Pentwater's hands?" Eliza asked.

"That, Eliza, is a question that may never be answered." Higgins frowned. "I suppose Pentwater ran across it during one of his business ventures here in Europe."

Ramsey scratched his chin. "I was in Paris once and visited a flea market. They had lots of valuable antiques there. Books, jewelry from the French nobility."

"Close to the Porte de Clignancourt station? Founded in the late seventeenth century from what I've heard. I found several treasured first editions there," Higgins said, recalling the place with fondness. "It's possible the cross ended up there, or a facsimile of it. Who can say if the cross is the one Napoléon had, or a fake?"

"That flea market sounds as good a place as any for someone to stumble upon Charlemagne's cross," Eliza observed. "When I sold flowers at Covent Garden, I watched all kinds of things being sold. If the seller spins a good yarn, he or she can make the buyer believe they were buying not only Charlemagne's cross, but every blooming thing he ever owned."

Higgins grinned. "Especially if the price was right."

"Pentwater certainly thought he could profit from it," Ramsey added.

"Yes, but perhaps no one in the States was interested," Higgins said. "Whatever the case, Pentwater wasn't about to lose it. When the authorities closed in, he must have chosen to hide the cross in the motorcar. That way Pentwater knew it would make it here to England."

Eliza nodded. "I'll bet he already had a buyer here."

"I think you're right." Higgins said. "And he tried damned hard to recover it."

"Pentwater was the driver in the black motorcar, wasn't he?" Eliza looked grim. "The one driving past our house on Wimpole Street, probably looking for the roadster. And he drove the black car that followed you."

Higgins adjusted his sling, wishing he no longer needed the prop, but his arm ached badly. "Undoubtedly. But we have no way of figuring out who else Pentwater might have told about the cross. Its history of bringing success to whoever possessed it seems a good draw for anyone with ambition. Especially knowing Napoléon's victories."

"Who wanted the cross badly enough to murder for it?" Ramsey mused.

"Someone who knew it would fetch a high price," Eliza suggested. "A person just like Pentwater. Someone greedy."

"Or patriotic." Higgins held up the cross. "A man determined to acquire the cross of Charlemagne to help his country. A man who wants his king—or his Kaiser—to hold the key to world power." He grimaced. "Especially with the drums of war growing louder each day."

Eliza's eyes widened. "Sounds like Count Rudolf to me. He never stops bragging about anything Austrian and German. And every time he says the Kaiser's name, he bows his head, like he just mentioned Jesus. I've never seen a person go on about their country so much."

A memory stirred Higgins. "When I spoke with Pentwater the morning he was shot, he called the count a fabulist."

"What's that?" Ramsey and Eliza both asked.

"It refers to a person who invents fables, or one who makes up complicated stories." Higgins nodded. "Or maybe someone who believes in such stories."

"If war breaks out in Europe," Ramsey said, "Kaiser Wilhelm and the whole of Europe is sure to be in the thick of it."

"England, too." Higgins lifted an eyebrow. "A fervent Englishman such as Sir Anthony might prefer such a talisman be in the possession of King George. His wife told me yesterday that Sir Anthony is obsessed with politics. He's convinced there will be war soon. She actually said he wanted to save the world. Count Rudolf, too. It's the reason they're at this house party."

Eliza stared at the cross Higgins held. "The count and Sir Anthony both want the cross because they think it will make their country more powerful."

Ramsey took a deep breath. "Pentwater planned to sell the

cross to the highest bidder. That's why all three men were here. Only the motorcar got waylaid somehow, causing Pentwater to try to get his hands on it."

"He caused the accident," Eliza said. "And then tried to burn our house down."

Higgins nodded. "But the fire seems a clumsy way to go about getting the car back."

"It bloody well worked, didn't it? We ended up coming to this house party, and Colin brought the car right to the front door."

"But how would Pentwater know that would happen?"

Ramsey laughed. "I hate to say it, but this may be one of the few times we can call something a coincidence. Although I doubt that was what Pentwater envisioned. By the time of the fire, he probably figured out your motorcar was in the garage at Scotland Yard. With you dead or injured from the fire, he'd have an easier time getting his hands on it."

"This means either Sir Anthony or Count Rudolf killed Pentwater," she said in a low voice. "He could have told them where the cross was hidden, and that he needed more time to get his hands on it."

"Once they knew where it was," Ramsey added, "they didn't need Pentwater."

Higgins swore under his breath. "At dinner that first night, Pentwater asked how I'd been injured. I told him about the accident. And that the car was being repaired at the Yard."

Ramsey shot him a rueful smile. "The killer was listening, too."

"What do we do?" Eliza whispered, as if someone were listening by the shelves.

"Nothing, for now," Ramsey said. "We have no proof."

"But we have to do something," she insisted. "This person also murdered Madame Evangeline. After she spoke about the cross at the séance, it probably got the killer nervous. They wanted to silence her before she said anything more about it."

Higgins looked unhappy. "Again, how do we prove it?"

Ramsey nodded at the cross. "That's our only hope. The killer wants the cross of Charlemagne bad enough to kill two people for it. Well, the roadster it was hidden in is now here. I suspect the killer will try to retrieve it. And soon. That's why Lake and I came."

"Until the killer shows himself, we must keep the cross safe," Higgins said. "I'll hide it in my room."

"That will be the first place someone would look if they discover it's not in the motorcar," Ramsey said. "My room would be the second place."

"Give it to me," Eliza told them. "No one will suspect me of having it."

Ramsey appeared dubious, but Higgins said, "She's right." He slid the cross back into the pouch and handed it to Eliza, who tucked it into the pocket of her skirt.

"Please keep it hidden," Ramsey told her. "If the killer even suspects you have it, you'll be in as much danger as Madame Evangeline."

"This isn't my first experience at outwitting a murderer, Colin."

"I know." Ramsey squeezed Eliza's elbow. "And let's make certain it isn't your last."

CHAPTER 22

*B*ecause he attended them rarely, Higgins forgot how exhausting country house parties were. Although such gatherings did not normally include a murder, guests were still subjected to idle conversation, charades, card games, ping pong, and amateur theatricals. All that before the fox hunt even began. When this party ended, he would need another week to recuperate.

"The dogs are loud," Eliza complained as they returned from the topiary garden.

She and Higgins had given Philippe and his fiancée a tour of the gardens after breakfast. They hoped to avoid the nonstop arrival of fox hunt participants and the excited barks from the hounds. But not even Banfield Manor was large enough to escape the noise and confusion.

"The hounds know they'll be let loose soon," Higgins told her. "It's blood fever, which the riders share." Indeed, the riders wore avid and hungry expressions—like the predators they were. Higgins had little affection for the ruling class or their leisure pursuits.

Nathalie clung to Philippe's arm as they approached the house. "Why do they chase after such a dear little animal," she said in charmingly accented English. "I cannot kill even the spider. And foxes, they are most beautiful. *Si triste*. So sad."

Eliza sighed. "Until today, all I thought about was how fun it would be to jump over hurdles and race through the country-side. Riding habits also make everyone look dashing." She glanced down at her sleek outfit. "But today I realized an inno-cent fox will be killed, too."

"Not a pretty sight," Higgins said. "Avert your eyes when the hounds catch up with it."

She shivered. "I'll ride back as soon as the poor thing is trapped."

"I do not wish to even think about it," Nathalie moaned.

"I would fly you away, *chéri*," Philippe said to Nathalie. "But I do not like the skies this morning. The wind, it is strong. And there are many low clouds."

"Will it storm?" Higgins scanned the overcast sky. Although windy, the day was warm.

"*Je ne pense pas*. I do not think so. A rain shower perhaps, but not a storm. Only to take Nathalie in the air would not be pleasant for her. We wait until tomorrow to leave."

"We stay in the house, *oui*?" She gazed up at Philippe with a worshipful gaze. A gust of wind tousled her blonde curls. "I do not wish to see any of the hunt."

"*Bien sûr*, of course. We listen to the phonograph. Maybe I shall sing to you."

Higgins had as little desire to witness that as the fox hunt. "Eliza, the master of hounds will sound his horn soon. You haven't gotten your mount yet."

"I told the grooms to saddle my favorite mare," she said. "A white Irish hunter. I don't want anyone else to take her. Luckily, the riders who live nearby brought their own horses and won't steal mine." With a grin, she lifted her riding crop. "Otherwise I'll use this on them."

"Perhaps you will join Nathalie and me in the music room, *Professeur.*"

"Thank you, Philippe, but no. I have matters to discuss with the detectives."

Philippe looked pained. "Detectives. Murder. Dead foxes. I cannot wait to take Nathalie away from here." He put his arm around his fiancée and swept her into the house.

"They make a beautiful couple," Eliza said. "I love French accents, too."

He snorted. "Give me a good Geordie dialect from Tyneside any day. And the girl is pretty, but insipid." Indeed, she reminded Higgins of a macaron: small, delicate and too sugary.

"I feel like a brute next to her. Not only am I inches taller, I'm about to take part in the slaughter of a little animal." Eliza smacked the riding crop against her leather boot. "First, I want to visit the garage. Our trusty detective never showed up for breakfast at the house."

"He probably wanted to avoid the feeding frenzy."

Higgins recalled how shortly after dawn, the hunt participants began to arrive. Some on their horses, others in motorcars. Because so many people were here for breakfast, the servants set up the sideboard in the main dining room. Higgins hadn't seen that much food since his niece's lavish wedding reception.

"I wonder if anyone tried to get to your roadster last night," Eliza said as they walked up to the manor house garage.

The long brick structure resembled a stables. Instead of horses, each walled partition held a motor vehicle. The partitions had no doors, so she could see each of the seven vehicles inside. All of them belonged to Richard, except for the shiny blue roadster.

"Colin?" Eliza called out. The smell of petrol and oil filled the air.

"Over here, Eliza." Ramsey's voice came from beyond an open door at the back.

He and Eliza walked past the parked motorcar, careful to avoid the tires which hung on the wall and a worktable cluttered with tools. The door opened onto a large space filled with metal parts. Windows on the back wall revealed a man tinkering with the engine of a green touring car. Higgins recognized him as Frank, the estate chauffeur. But where was Ramsey?

Eliza and Higgins stood for a moment, puzzled. Then they turned to see Ramsey and Barnaby Lake side by side on a bench. Lake held a towel to his forehead.

"Someone hit him with a heavy object," Ramsey told them in a low voice.

"Oh!" Eliza hurried over in concern. "Do you need a doctor?"

"Nah." He lifted the towel, revealing the large lump which protruded a few inches from his right eye. "Got the chauffeur to put some ice in a towel for me. Told him I slipped and fell."

"When did all this happen?" Higgins crouched before them, trying to mask his anxiety.

"Early this morning," Lake replied. "Detective Ramsey and I took turns watching over your motorcar. I'd been sitting on that stool near the front of the car for about two hours when I started to doze off. I didn't worry much about that. If I fell asleep, I'd slip from the stool and wake up. But as I started to drift off, I heard a sound in the garage."

"Did you see anything?" Eliza asked.

"Only a shadow moving quick as air, miss." Lake winced when he placed the towel of ice back on his forehead.

"I found him soon after," Ramsey said. "For a moment, I thought he was dead. I offered to send for a doctor, but he refused."

"Not the first time I've been knocked out. Usually after a

tussle with a sinister bloke or two. But all I want now is a lie down. Maybe some aspirin."

Ramsey looked over at the chauffeur bent over the green touring car. "Frank, can you see that Officer Lake gets safely up to his room?"

The man wiped his hands on a cloth. "Sure thing. I know what he feels like. Once had the hood of a Talbot brougham fall right on my head."

They remained silent until the chauffeur led Officer Lake away. As soon as they were gone, Higgins said, "Someone did try to get to the roadster. We're lucky they didn't kill him."

Ramsey looked somber. "Whether Lake lived or died didn't appear to matter to this blighter. And whoever attacked him got what they came for."

"But the Professor's motorcar is still there," Eliza said. "We walked right by it."

"They didn't come for the car." Ramsey marched over to the blue Hudson. "Look."

Eliza and Higgins peeked inside the interior of the roadster. "It's gone!" she cried.

"They took the auto-meter." Higgins shook his head. "Made a mess of my dashboard, too. Probably smashed at it with the same pipe or object used to strike Officer Lake."

Ramsey turned to the workbench behind him and picked up a metal wrench. "I'm betting it was this." He flung it back down. "As soon as I made certain Lake was fine, I searched the area. Questioned all the grooms, any servant I saw. I spoke to the early fox hunt arrivals as well. No one saw anything suspicious near the garage."

"When this person opens up the auto-meter and discovers the cross is gone, they'll be furious," Higgins said. "And even more dangerous. Who will they go after next?"

"You, Professor," Ramsey said. "Or me. The roadster is yours.

And I brought it to you and worked on its repairs. Thank heaven Eliza isn't connected directly to the car."

"What do we do now?" Higgins asked.

"I'll go into the village and speak with the constable. Only I don't want to attract attention from our assailant. Frank can drive me in one of Lord Ashmore's cars."

"What do you want from Chief Constable Brakefield?" Eliza asked.

"I want him to re-open the investigation into the deaths of Dwight Pentwater and Madame Evangeline. We need a heavy police presence here to flush the culprit out."

"Brakefield won't like that," she said.

"He'll like it far less if I go over his head and have the investigation handed to Scotland Yard. Which I will." Ramsey buttoned his jacket. "While I'm gone, Eliza should be safe. She'll be surrounded by dozens of people at the hunt. But I'm worried about you, Professor. I'd take you with me to the village, but what if the killer comes after us in his own car, as he did to you in Putney? Better that you remain here, but not alone."

"I'll hole up in my bedroom. I have a linguistics treatise to write."

"Absolutely not. Once the person who stole the auto-meter discovers the cross is missing, they'll likely search your room next. I don't want you to be a sitting duck."

The detective's stern tone told Higgins it would be futile to resist. Especially since sensible precautions did seem in order. "Philippe and his fiancée won't be in the hunt. I can join them in the music room," Higgins said. "Philippe plans to serenade the fair Nathalie."

"Good." Ramsey nodded. "That should keep you bored *and* safe."

"We're forgetting something." Higgins lowered his voice to a whisper. "We gave Eliza the cross last night. If this person searches her bedroom, they'll find it."

"No, they won't." Eliza reached beneath the collar of her riding habit and pulled out a thin gold chain. The cross dangled from it. "I figured it was too valuable to leave lying around, so I put it on one of my necklaces. There's a hole at the top for a thin chain. The cross is too large to conceal beneath ordinary clothes, but no one will see it under my riding habit."

Eliza tucked the cross and chain beneath her snug black jacket. She was right. There was no sign of it now.

Ramsey gave her a proud smile. "Well done. You can keep the cross safe while remaining safe at the hunt." His smile faded. "I need both of you to be cautious today."

"You'll get no argument from me," Higgins assured him.

"I'm more worried about you, Colin," Eliza said. "Whoever stole the auto-meter may decide to go after the other Scotland Yard detective here. Especially if they think you possess of the cross."

He shook his head. "They'll be in for a surprise then."

"You're the one who may be surprised. I'd rather you stay with the Professor until after the hunt. Call the constable from the house."

"I'd rather not risk eavesdroppers."

Eliza swung her riding crop in frustration. "You'd rather risk your life?"

"I appreciate your concern. But I'm perfectly capable of handling risky situations." Ramsey gently straightened her tall black riding hat. "Now it's time for you to join the hunt." He winked. "And try not to fall off your horse."

"He's right," Higgins said after the detective left. "Until Ramsey brings more police back into this investigation, we need to be cautious."

"Except he isn't being cautious himself. Blooming men. They never listen." Her mood now matched the color of her riding habit. "And if he thinks I'll simply gallop off to enjoy the hunt while he puts himself in danger. . ." Eliza marched away before finishing her sentence.

She didn't need to. Higgins knew Eliza to be both fearless and foolhardy. But he couldn't think of any trouble she could get into during the hunt. He wouldn't worry about her until after the fox had been caught.

If only it was as simple to catch a murderer.

ELIZA HADN'T HEARD THIS MUCH NOISE AND COMMOTION SINCE a runaway horse and wagon tore through the vegetable stalls at Covent Garden. She couldn't even count the number of riders. Most wore black riding habits as she did. Some were attired in navy, dark green or gray. The most striking were those men in scarlet jackets. She'd learned that only the master of the hunt, the whippers-in, and men who had earned their "color" were permitted to wear scarlet. Ladies were never accorded the privilege, no matter how skilled. She wondered if that would change when women finally earned the right to vote. Knowing men, most likely not.

The hunt officials began to place riders in proper order. Richard and his sister were already at the front of the group. Eliza sighed. Even at a sporting event, the upper class insisted on ranking everyone. Given her lack of "breeding," she would likely bring up the rear.

Conversation flowed about her as she scanned the group for house party guests. She felt relieved that Clara had remained behind at the house. Although she probably wouldn't be able to use her excuse of feeling under the weather next time. The girl needed to learn to ride.

Eliza stretched from her perch on the side saddle. Several riders moved, revealing Freddy astride a restless black gelding. He looked petrified. A much more relaxed Lily sat on the chestnut stallion beside him. Sir Anthony and Lady Annabel conversed on their mounts nearby.

She pulled the necklace from beneath her riding habit. When she let the chain fall, the cross sat atop her upper chest. Given its size and how the gold stood out against her black jacket, no one would be able to miss it. Especially the person who stole the auto-meter this morning. The same person who murdered Dwight Pentwater and Madame Evangeline. If this didn't smoke them out of hiding, nothing would.

When the house party officially ended tomorrow, the guests would disperse. Time was running out. Eliza didn't like the idea of having the murderer lie in wait for them on the way back to London. Or perhaps in London itself. Nor would she allow Colin Ramsey to be put at risk. Whoever killed Pentwater and Madame Evangeline was riding in the hunt, and they'd soon realize she possessed the cross of Charlemagne. There was little they could do about it while in pursuit of a fox. But afterward, they might grow reckless. Reckless people made mistakes.

"You seem most serious. This is your first hunt, *ja*? I am sure it makes you afraid."

Eliza turned to meet the antagonistic gaze of Count Rudolf. "Not at all. I only wish they'd start. It's rather dull sitting here. Nothing to do but listen to horses stamp their hooves."

The count's mouth fell open as he stared at the cross. "What is that you wear?"

"Oh, this." She lightly stroked it. "A gift."

"That cannot be. Impossible. Who gave the cross to you? I demand to know!"

His raised voice drew glances from the people around them. "As I said, it was a gift. And I see no reason to tell you who gave it to me."

He muttered in German, then nudged his horse closer. "Do not play games with me, *fräulein*. You are not clever enough. Tell me how much you want. *Jezt!* Now!"

She raised her riding crop. "I will not allow you to startle my horse, count. So back up and calm down. Otherwise, I may decide not to discuss my cross with you at all."

His face reddened with rage. "Foolish girl." After another shocked glance at the cross, he struck his horse's flanks. He rode up to his wife, who had been speaking with the master of the hunt. The count whispered to her. She threw an astonished look at Eliza.

Interesting. Did both von Weisingers know about the cross of Charlemagne? Nothing else could account for their reaction. Lily Marlowe rode up, blocking her view.

"What did you say to the Austrian?" she asked with a laugh. "Whatever it was, it sure got his trousers in a bunch."

Eliza didn't have time to answer. Lily now saw the cross, but her reaction was different than Count Rudolf's. She appeared amused. "What are you wearing around your neck? Are you so nervous about riding in the hunt, you're praying to God to protect you?" She laughed again.

"I thought it looked pretty against the black silk," Eliza said with a casual air. "I wasn't aware jewelry wasn't allowed at these things."

Lily regarded her with mild contempt. "Sweetie, if you wanted to wear jewelry today, you could have borrowed some of mine. Even my costume jewelry is better than that." She scrunched up her nose. "You look like one of those Catholic nuns. All you need is a veil."

"Thank you. I've always liked nuns' habits. Those lovely flowing robes."

"I'll never understand you Brits." Lily sighed. "Anyway, I'd better get back to Freddy. He's shaking so much, he may fall off his horse before the hunt begins. In fact, you should give him your cross. I think he's been praying ever since he got in the saddle. The boy is not a natural horseman." With a careless wave, Lily rode back to a frantic Freddy.

Eliza shifted her gaze to Sir Anthony and Lady Annabel. They looked in her direction and nodded. She smiled back, then kicked her horse forward.

"How are you both this morning?" Eliza asked when she drew up beside them. "I missed seeing you at breakfast. Then again, so many people showed up."

Sir Anthony's greeting to her died once he caught sight of the cross and his face flushed purple. Even his horse's ears flattened, as if aware of its rider's agitation.

"I never come down to breakfast," Lady Annabel said. "And my husband decided to take an early morning walk. He missed breakfast entirely. Isn't that right, dear?"

He ignored her. "I have not seen you wear that cross before, Miss Doolittle," he said gruffly. "Has it been in your possession long?"

"No, but I've already grown fond of it. Looks rather antique. I wonder if it's as old as my cameo brooch."

Sir Anthony seemed as if he were trying to keep his emotions in check. "Perhaps."

"If I sold it, do you think it would fetch much money?"

His expression turned wary. "Are you selling it? If so, I may be an interested buyer."

Lady Annabel rubbed her forehead with a pinched expression. "I fear I am not in the mood for riding today. My headache grows worse by the minute. And the noise from the hounds has driven me to distraction. I shall never be able to tolerate three hours of barking."

"Fox hounds do not bark, Annabel. They bay." Sir Anthony gave an impatient wave. "If you do not wish to take part, return your horse to the stable."

With a curt nod at both of them, Lady Annabel left. Eliza suspected that if it weren't so crowded with riders, she would have kicked her horse into a canter.

A horn blast sounded. Everyone stopped talking and steered their horses into place.

"We shall speak about your cross later," Sir Anthony said. "And you should decide on a price, should you wish to part with it."

"What if I decide to keep it?"

"You may be the one to pay the price then." He shot her a calculating look, then moved off. Just in time, too.

The hunt had begun.

CHAPTER 23

*H*iggins fought the impulse to cover his ears with a few sofa pillows. He had an even stronger urge to shove one into Philippe's mouth. Anything to keep the Frenchman from singing.

"*Buzz, buzz around, keep a-buzzin; around,*" Philippe warbled as he stood by the phonograph. He kept his gaze fixed on Nathalie. "*We'll be just as happy as can beeee.*"

Who knew music could be so excruciating? Philippe had sung along to a dozen phonograph discs in the music room. Nathalie sat on the loveseat, swooning with every out of tune note. None of the songs were in French, forcing Higgins to cringe at the chap's labored attempts to sing English lyrics.

"*Be my little baby bumble beeeee.*" Philippe's wretched voice grew stronger each time he reached the chorus.

They had listened to *Be My Little Baby Bumble Bee* four times. This popular hit of 1912 was the couple's clear favorite. But Higgins had already been subjected to tunes even more dismal. And if Philippe dared to play *Daddy Has A Sweetheart And Mother Is Her Name* once more, Higgins might smash the phonograph.

Higgins wished he had gone to the village with Detective

Ramsey. Even if someone did try to run them down with a motorcar, it would be preferable to this agony.

Philippe opened his arms wide and belted out, *"Honey, keep a buzzin' pleaseeeee."* Then he did a little spin.

Good grief. Choreography, too! Nathalie sprang to her feet and swayed to the music. If the pair broke into the can-can, Higgins would be not held accountable for his actions. He tried to focus on a history volume of medieval France he'd taken from the library. But the exploits of Louis XI were no match for a love-struck young couple with access to a phonograph.

Tossing the book aside, Higgins's thoughts drifted to Eliza and the fox hunt. It could take hours before the fox had either been caught, or successfully eluded the hounds. He refused to spend that entire time with Philippe and Nathalie. Not that they were aware of him.

A visit below stairs could prove distracting. He felt around in his suit pocket for his notebook. May as well take the opportunity to mingle with the servants and write down any interesting dialects a maidservant or footman might possess. He also hoped to persuade the cook to serve him a bowl of the cock-a-leekie soup he'd been smelling for the past hour.

As Nathalie joined Philippe in singing *"We'll be just as happy as can beeee,"* Higgins snuck out of the music room. He felt instantly better. So did his ears.

Higgins preferred the manor house emptied of people. The servants were below stairs, and Clara pretended to battle the sniffles in her bedchamber. Pausing in the grand foyer, he welcomed the peace and solitude. After his visit to the kitchen, he'd retire to his bedroom, despite Colin Ramsey's warnings. Who was around to threaten him? Except for Philippe and Nathalie, all the guests were at the fox hunt. And he didn't believe the French couple capable of murdering anything but song lyrics.

The front door swung open. "Where is that derelict butler?"

Lady Annabel demanded. "I shouldn't have to open the door myself. It's uncivilized."

"Why?" Higgins asked. "Have you lost the use of your arms?"

"Very funny, Henry." She kicked the door shut behind her, wincing at the noise. "A butler or footman should be here to greet us all the time."

"Baxter is below stairs, as are the other servants," Higgins informed her. "With most of the guests riding to hounds, it gives them time to get their other work done."

"I've never seen a household more haphazardly run."

She tried to walk past, but Higgins stopped her. "Did something go wrong at the hunt?"

"No. Why should it?"

"Because you're dressed for the hunt, yet you're here." He nodded at her black riding habit, silk top hat, and riding crop, identical to Eliza's. "Unless the fox surrendered himself rather than being run ragged."

Annabel threw him a pained look. "This morning I woke with a dreadful headache. I hoped the fresh air might help, but it only got worse. And those hounds. A person can't think once they start barking." She waved a hand. "Excuse me. They 'bay,' according to my husband. I simply could not face hours of listening to the dogs and jumping fences."

"But the hunt began on time?"

"I hadn't even made it back to the stable when the horn sounded." She rubbed her temples. "At least I said my goodbyes to my husband and your Cockney flower girl."

"Eliza and Sir Anthony planned to ride together?" Higgins asked in surprise.

"I have no idea. When I left they were discussing jewelry," Annabel said. "My husband found her gold cross most intriguing."

Higgins almost choked. "Gold cross!"

"Don't shout. Yes, Miss Doolittle wore a gold cross to the hunt."

"Damnation! I swear Eliza is incapable of sensible thought. That girl is maddening!"

"And you are deafening. I refuse to listen to you bellow a moment longer when my head is ready to explode." Pushing him aside with her riding crop, she marched up the wide marble stairs.

Eliza had deliberately let everyone see the cross! Oh, Higgins knew very well how her mind worked. She thought to use herself as bait during the fox hunt. A fox hunt that included the killer. So brave—and so foolish. She'd left him no choice but to haul her back.

Higgins took a few steps toward the telephone room, then stopped. It would take too much time to put through a call to the village constable; even longer before Colin and the chauffeur drove back here. And he knew enough about fox hunts to realize the riders would be traversing over a terrain not particularly hospitable to a motorcar.

He hurried back to the music room. Philippe and Nathalie twirled about the furniture to the strains of *The Road to Mandalay*.

"Excuse me, Philippe," Higgins said loudly.

The couple threw startled looks in his direction. "*Oui, Professeur?*" Philippe asked.

"I hate to interrupt this dance, but I am in desperate need of your aeroplane."

WHAT JOLLY FUN. ALTHOUGH SHE ENJOYED RIDING OVER THE estate this past week, it couldn't compare with the excitement of the hunt. She felt a thrill as she and the other riders cantered over fields, raced up and down grassy hills, then leaned forward as the horses jumped over yet another hurdle. It felt like flying. Who needed an aeroplane when one had a horse?

Being so windy, it was even easier to imagine herself airborne when she jumped another fence or hedge. And the fox had led everyone on quite a merry chase. She'd heard more than one rider complain about the shifting winds, which made it difficult for the hounds to track the scent. This suited Eliza. She hoped the fox would escape his gang of pursuers and live to face another fine October day.

Eliza had been so caught up in the hunt, she often lost sight of the riders from the house party. Richard was far out in front with the hunt master; she'd never catch him. However, she did pass Count and Countess von Weisinger when they reached the open pasture near the creek. Occupied with splashing through the water, she forgot to check if the pair were still close behind. Probably not. Despite their boasts of fox hunting experience, Eliza suspected she was the more naturally skilled rider. She was also lucky to be on such a splendid horse. The mare responded with only the lightest touch from Eliza's left leg and riding crop.

Sir Anthony, too, seemed fortunate in his mount, a dappled gray that jumped over each fence and hurdle with inches to spare. Even during the more hazardous parts of the chase, Eliza kept him in her field of vision. Or perhaps it was the other way around. He wanted to keep an eye on her—and the cross she wore. No matter what his intention, Sir Anthony rode well.

The same could not be said for Freddy. He either clutched his reins too tight, or loosened them too much. It confused his horse. And he went too fast, faster even than Eliza. She doubted that was Freddy's intention. He looked like he was clinging for dear life, hoping the horse would take control. Lily should have kept watch over him. The actress proved she was a skilled horsewoman during their ride yesterday morning.

But Lily rode ahead of Freddy, glancing over her shoulder

after each jump with a gleeful expression, as if taunting Freddy to follow. Eliza could have passed both of them, but she worried about Freddy. The fool didn't have an ounce of ambition or sense. And to impress Lily, he'd put his life at risk by riding in the fox hunt.

Eliza winced as he barely cleared the next fence.

Forget about Freddy, she told herself, as she and her horse smoothly sailed over the fence. Let him break his neck on the hunt. He was no longer any of her business. Eliza had just kicked her horse to pass him when Freddy yelled out. She heard him even over the hounds and the pounding hooves.

His horse suddenly veered right. Along the edge of the pasture ran a line of trees, and the horse darted through them. Freddy almost fell off twice.

Eliza raced after him. She no sooner cleared the trees and emerged into another open glen when she saw Freddy tumble to the ground. Eliza whipped her horse and quickly overtook the frightened gelding. Once the horse stopped, she reached over and grabbed the bridle. After she'd calmed the poor animal with soothing words, she led him back to Freddy, who'd gotten back on his feet. His hat had been knocked off; grass and dirt streaked his riding breeches. When he walked over to remount, Eliza saw that he limped slightly.

"Are you hurt?" she asked once he climbed back in the saddle.

He shot her an accusing look. "Why did you chase after me? You spooked my horse."

"Ungrateful idiot. If I hadn't caught him, you'd have had to limp back to Banfield Manor. And you have no business taking part in a fox hunt. You can't ride at all."

He brushed off the grass from his sleeves. "I've been riding longer than you, Eliza."

"Yes. All of it spent in a pony ring. I watched you today. I'm amazed you stayed on as long as you did. You could have been killed." She shook her head at him. "Did you think to impress the movie actress by breaking your neck?"

Freddy glared at her. One side of his face was bruised from where he'd fallen, and his blond hair held clumps of dirt. "I don't have to impress Lily. She's already quite taken with me. Haven't you noticed?"

"Oh, we've all noticed," Eliza said. "The two of you have done everything but tear each other's clothes off in the drawing room."

"Why shouldn't we? I'm in love with her. And she feels the same. That's why we're going to Italy." His gaze grew cold. "Some women don't pretend to care for a man, then keep him at arm's length."

"Freddy, you're an amusement to her. Nothing more. Once your adventure in Italy is done, she'll be done with you. Sooner, if she finds an Italian gentleman more entertaining."

He flinched. "You're jealous."

"I was when I first saw the two of you together. But not now."

"Hah! You got over your jealousy in a few days? Not likely."

"It's true. I swear on the Colonel's life."

Freddy's eyes widened. He knew how much Colonel Pickering meant to her.

"You were my first sweetheart, Freddy," Eliza went on. "Even though you didn't have a title or a vast estate, you treated me as a gentleman treats a lady. And you helped me to think of myself as a lady. It wasn't only Higgins's lessons and the Colonel's gracious behavior which was responsible for that. It was your romantic devotion as well. So thank you."

For a moment, the love he once professed for her seemed to shine in his eyes. Then he turned away. "Is that detective devoted to you now?"

"Time will tell." Eliza took a deep breath. "Freddy, I want you to find happiness with another woman. I truly do. But Lily is not right for you. She's much too worldly, for one. And I don't think she's been honest about her past. You should know—"

"You know nothing about Lily or her past. Don't embarrass yourself by pretending you do." Freddy gathered up his reins in preparation for leaving.

"I know she was Dwight Pentwater's mistress," Eliza said before he could ride away. "And I know they were together the night before he died."

"You're a jealous liar! Lily hated him. Pentwater pursued her for years. He badgered her to become his lover, but she refused. A brave decision, given that she was afraid of him. Afraid of his power, his money, and how he could ruin her career if she made him too angry. That's why she couldn't ignore all his demands. But she was never his mistress!"

So Lily hadn't been honest with him. Eliza patted her horse, who took a few steps. The mare seemed eager to rejoin the hunt. "What demands?"

"She persuaded people to invest with him. She delivered letters for him. Packages, too." Freddy sighed with exasperation. "That's why she's in England. He told her to travel in the ship bringing that blasted motorcar across the ocean. But the police in America stopped her before she could board. They had questions for everyone associated with Pentwater."

"Lily was supposed to deliver the motorcar to Pentwater in England?"

"Yes. She said when Pentwater fled America, he didn't have time to bring anything but his clothes. But he loved that roadster and insisted she deliver it herself. Only the police delayed her own arrival in England. By the time she got here, your father had bought it at auction." Freddy smoothed back his hair. He looked surprised when he realized his hat was gone.

"How long have you known this?"

"She told me everything after dinner last night. It only proves Pentwater was a rich man who loved to order people about. And it proves how little you know Lily." He kicked his horse.

"When exactly did she arrive in England?" Eliza shouted after Freddy as he galloped back through the line of trees toward the hunt course.

"When did Lily get here?" Eliza asked aloud, only this time to herself.

She heard the hounds in the distance. Anxious to rejoin the hunt, and possibly catch up with Lily, Eliza resettled herself on the saddle. The sound of approaching hooves made her look back toward the trees. Did Freddy change his mind and decide to finish their conversation?

But Freddy wasn't riding toward her. It was Lily Marlowe.

Before Eliza could call out a greeting, Lily whipped the flanks of her horse. The chestnut stallion snorted.

And galloped straight at Eliza.

CHAPTER 24

*W*ith a horrified yell, Eliza kicked her horse and wheeled out of the way. It was close, though. The tail on Lily's horse brushed against Eliza's leg when she galloped past.

"What are you doing?" she shouted at Lily.

The other woman responded by reining her horse, who whinnied. Lily turned around.

Did the actress intend to charge her again? No doubt, given how she raised her crop high.

Eliza refused to be an easy target. Instead, she sent her white hunter into a prancing trot, in preparation for full-out flight. "Are you insane? You almost slammed right into me."

Lily had her horse under control, but the brown stallion was nervous. He snorted and danced along the grass. "I wanted to get your attention."

"Bloody foolish way to go about it. The horses could have been injured." Eliza moved even further away. "If you're looking for Freddy, he's rejoined the hunt."

"Freddy's whereabouts are of no interest to me." Lily moved

her horse closer. "But I did notice you were no longer part of the hunt."

Given the unfriendly expression on Lily's face, Eliza doubted the actress had been worried about her. "I'm fine, but Freddy took a spill. Not that you seem to care."

"I don't. It's you I care about. Well, not you." She pointed her riding crop at Eliza's chest. "That's what I want."

Eliza looked down at the gold cross she wore and grew even more uneasy. "My cross? I though you considered it unattractive, little more than costume jewelry. And worthless."

Lily narrowed her eyes at the cross. "You know very well what it's worth. And I'm guessing you or that handsome detective who arrived yesterday took it out of Professor Higgins's motorcar." She smirked. "Dwight stuck it in that gauge thing. What he called an auto-meter. I was up before dawn so I could sneak into the garage and take it. Only I didn't expect to see one of the English gumshoes napping in there."

Eliza's anger warred with fear. "Hit him with a wrench, didn't you? You could have killed him."

"What did you want me to do? It was my only chance to get to the car. No matter how much the cop snored, the noise taking apart the auto-meter would have woken him up," she said. "And what's your beef? He lived. I'm the one who wasted my time. Let me tell you, I got pretty steamed up when I saw the cross was gone. That meant the police got there before me." Lily shook her head. "Now I see that you took it."

"They found it when the car was still at Scotland Yard." Eliza backed up her horse, until they were almost through the line of trees. She had to return to the fox hunt course. Somewhere they could be seen. "Detective Ramsey brought it here. That's when the Professor and I first saw it. Along with the inscription on the back. The one that says it once belonged to Charlemagne. We've done a little research on it since then."

"I'm sure you did." Lily whipped her horse to follow Eliza through the trees.

"Stay back!" Eliza lifted her riding crop. "Or else you and me will be racing over these fields faster than any fox. Eventually we'll meet up with the other hunters. I'm sure some of them will be interested to hear about the cross. And what you were willing to do to get your hands on it." She paused. "Murdering Dwight Pentwater, for one."

The other woman flinched. "That was a hunting accident."

"I don't think so. You admitted you did Pentwater's bidding. After all, you went to his bed when he crooked his finger. And Freddy said you convinced people to invest with him."

Lily shrugged. "Suckers who deserved to lose their money."

"You made deliveries for him, too. Letters, packages." Eliza's voice grew hard. "And motorcars. Specifically, the blue roadster you arranged to ship across the ocean for him. The one you were supposed to travel with, before you were delayed by the police investigation."

"Yeah, that didn't go as planned. Dwight wasn't happy I missed the boat." She laughed and patted her horse's mane. "Literally, in fact."

"Why didn't he pick up the motorcar himself?"

"Dwight wasn't in England when the ship docked. He initially sailed to France. Had some deals cooking in Strasbourg or some other fancy French town. By the time we both got to England, your father had bought the car. Then he sold it to Higgins. That put Dwight in a rotten mood. This house party was coming up and he'd promised to bring the cross with him."

"Rotten enough to kill the Professor? First the accident, and then the house fire—"

"Calm down, it was only a little kitchen fire. Dwight needed to get Higgins out of London. By that time, he'd tracked the motorcar to Scotland Yard. Bribed some copper who told him the roadster was being repaired at their garage."

Eliza's jaw dropped. "What!"

"You think stuff like that is tough to find out? Rich people can buy information as easy as we could buy a pair of gloves."

"So our coming to Banfield Manor was arranged by Pentwater?"

"He asked Countess von Weisinger to arrange it. Told her Higgins was interested in buying the cross, too. That's why you got the invite a couple days before Dwight set the fire. He'd learned the repairs on the car were almost complete. Dwight guessed someone from Scotland Yard would deliver it to Banfield Manor. He was right, too."

"What a bloody maniac! That fire could have killed us all."

Lily urged her horse closer to Eliza. "Blame Higgins for the fire. He didn't give Dwight a chance to steal the roadster. Your professor never let it out of his sight." She reined in her restive mount. "Like the saying goes, 'desperate times call for desperate measures.' All I did was come to the party early and keep an eye on things until Dwight arrived. We also agreed to pretend not to know each other. At least not as well as we really did."

"You did whatever he asked." Eliza scanned the surrounding trees and meadow. The strong winds shifted again, bringing the distant sound of the baying hounds. If the fox had changed direction, perhaps the hunters would head back here. "Whenever he asked."

"Was I supposed to let him ruin my career—my whole life!—with rumors and dirty gossip? Yes, I did as he asked. Didn't have much choice."

"So you've said before. A likely excuse," Eliza said with contempt.

"I didn't have a choice," she repeated dully. "And Dwight trusted me. That's why he wanted me to join him. And told me about the Charlemagne cross, how there was a legend connected to it. Whoever owns the cross will be granted victory and power. Bunch of bunk, if you ask me. Dwight thought so, too, but he knew there was always a sucker who'd fall for a story like that. Sometimes, more than one sap."

"I figured out he planned to sell it during his visit to Banfield Manor." Eliza saw a flash of movement within the trees behind Lily. Was it a horse and rider? She couldn't be certain due to the wind riffling through the forest's russet leaves. "Just wondering who was interested. Count Rudolf or Sir Anthony?"

"Whoever paid Dwight's asking price, which was steep." Lily's smile turned smug. "I've decided to raise it even higher."

"Did you really have to kill Pentwater?"

"You're loony. Freddy and I stayed together during the hunt."

Eliza huffed in disbelief. "That's not what you told the chief constable the morning Pentwater was shot. I recall the pair of you saying how much fun it was to play hide and seek in the fog. And you mentioned how Freddy couldn't always see you. I'm sure that's when you snuck away to shoot Pentwater."

"I forgot about that sharp memory of yours." Lily's pout resembled how a pretty child might look when caught in a white lie. Only this lie was as black as murder.

"How fortunate it was foggy. No one saw you take the shot."

"A lucky break," she admitted. "I had no plans to shoot him that morning, but the opportunity was too good to resist."

Eliza stroked the mare's thick mane, her reins tight in her left glove. "I guess you viewed it as sweet revenge after all his mistreatment."

"More like justice." Her face twisted with hatred. "Dwight should have suffered a lingering death. I aimed for his gut at first, but he might have recovered. I couldn't take that chance. He taught me to shoot at his hunting lodge in Pennsylvania. How ironic is that? A shame Dwight never saw me aim the rifle at his foul, rotten heart."

"Are you certain you can sell the cross?" Eliza gauged the terrain. She had to make a break for it soon. "What if they won't pay what you ask?"

"Both Sir Anthony and the count want it so bad, one of them will. I'm betting on the explorer fellow. The count might not have as much cash to throw around since his wife lost her money investing in Pentland, Inc."

"What about Madame Evangeline?"

Lily looked amused. "What about her?"

"She spoke about the cross at the séance."

"The ghost lady knew too much," Lily said, "and I can't figure out how she knew unless she paid people off, like Dwight. Although it gave me a helluva turn when she brought up the cross at that table. Scared me more than any spirit. Couldn't risk her saying anything else I needed to keep secret. Like me shooting Dwight. She left me no choice but to kill her that night."

Eliza couldn't conceal her horror. "You smothered her. Did you drug her, too?"

"I didn't want her waking up to find a pillow over her face." Lily laughed. "I have trouble sleeping sometimes, so I travel with a bottle of chloral hydrate. A few drops of that in the tea her husband brewed every evening did the trick. I went to her room to say good night. Told her I was worried, given that fake seizure she had. It was easy as pie to slip the drops in her tisane."

If she'd been closer to Lily, she might have struck her. "You did all this just for money?"

Lily shot her a pitying glance. "I can't think of a better reason. You're too naïve, Eliza. Freddy always said so."

"Perhaps I am." Eliza again saw movement in the nearby trees. But if it was a person, why did they remain hidden? "However, I'm not naïve enough to give you this cross."

"I'll just take it." She gave a dramatic sigh. "After you're dead, of course."

"How? You don't have a gun. And if you have a knife tucked in that riding habit, you'll never get near enough to use it."

"This is my weapon of choice." Lily patted the chestnut stallion. "Hannibal is the fastest horse in the stables. All the grooms and stable boys agree. He and I will catch up with anyone I chase after. Even your pretty mare."

Eliza's horse tossed her white mane, no doubt sensing her nerves. "And when you do?"

"Run you down, or spook your horse so she throws you. The fall might break your neck. If it doesn't, I'll make sure Hannibal does." Lily surveyed the meadow. "We may as well begin. I wanted to make sure the hunting party was farther away. Our conversation has been amusing, but I'm getting restless." Her stallion whickered. "So is Hannibal. Ready?"

Lily suddenly whipped her horse's flanks.

"Go, girl!" Eliza cried.

Her mare whirled beneath her with only a slight pressure of one knee and broke away at her urging. She suddenly recalled Madame Evangeline's tarot reading, about having to take action at a crucial point. This had to be what the cards meant. Even if the stallion was the faster horse, Eliza refused to make it easy for him. A stiffer wind blew, tearing her hat free of its pins. She heard Lily curse behind her.

"Come on, girl, come on," Eliza coaxed.

The sound of pounding hooves told her that Lily was getting closer. Eliza had to push her mare to the limit. All they had to do was catch up with the hounds and hunters.

Because right now she was in more danger than the fox.

HIGGINS SHIVERED IN THE COLD AIR WHIPPING THROUGH THE narrow confines of the aeroplane. If only he'd donned a heavier coat. At least he'd wound a woolen scarf around his neck and wore a leather cap with goggles. Only they kept steaming up, so Higgins pushed them on top of his head. And the blasted seat was rock-hard. The jarring bumps at takeoff had been unnerving—and uncomfortable.

But words failed to encompass the experience. Only a poet could do justice to the scope of the sprawling landscape spread below them. The brilliant gold, scarlet, and flaming orange of the autumnal forest combined with the adjacent meadow's varying hues of green and russet. From this height, Banfield Manor and the other estate buildings looked Lilliputian. Far in the distance, Higgins glimpsed the village church spire.

Philippe Corbet pointed to the left and shouted something to him, although Higgins could not make out a single word above the driving wind.

When he peered below, Higgins spied the huntsmen and hounds. Eliza had to be somewhere among the group. Since the riders still raced after the dogs, he assumed the fox had not yet been caught. Many of them glanced up at the aeroplane, but that didn't help Higgins. There were too many, and half rode sidesaddle. Not that he could spot Eliza from this height. Everything appeared normal at the hunt. But what if she was no longer with the group?

He leaned over the side, then sat back with a thunk as the plane banked again.

Damnation. He'd expected a smoother ride even though Philippe warned him today's strong winds could make for a bumpy flight. But Higgins was grateful the Frenchman quickly agreed to take him up in his aeroplane so they could look for Eliza.

The aeroplane now dipped sharply, forcing Higgins to grip the sides. His stomach felt a bit queasy. Well, more than a bit. He wished he had eaten a lighter breakfast.

"*Professeur!*" Philippe shouted. "*Regardez!*"

Battling nausea, Higgins looked down when Philippe banked the plane again. Two single riders, both with a trailing skirt, cantered across the field. The rider in front rode a white horse and wore black. And the woman's hat had fallen off, revealing nut brown hair. By George, that must be Eliza. He remembered her riding a white horse the other day.

Who was the woman close behind her? The green riding habit looked similar to one he'd seen on Lily Marlowe. Why were the two of them off by themselves? Philippe flew low enough so that he noticed how Eliza looked over her shoulder, then whipped her horse forward. If Lily was chasing Eliza, there could no other reason except the cross.

"Land the aeroplane!" Higgins shouted. "*Vous devez faire atterrir l'avion,* Philippe!"

The Frenchman answered, but the wind tore his words from him. Philippe pointed to a flat clearing ahead in front of the women and began their descent.

The biting wind stung Higgins's watering eyes. While Philippe circled, Higgins now spotted a third horse and rider gaining on the women. A man this time, and unable to control his mount. The black horse careened in such a wild gallop, Higgins marveled how the chap stayed in the saddle at all. Were the women fleeing from him? Or was Eliza eluding Lily? What the devil was going on?

The aeroplane dropped lower. Higgins now saw it was a terror-stricken Freddy who fought with the reins. He and the animal zigzagged one way and then the other. Leave it to Freddy to end up on a runaway horse. That bloody idiot.

Freddy's horse careened alongside Lily, and far too close. Frantic, Lily waved at him with her riding crop, as if warning him away. But too late. Lily's horse shied violently and sent the actress toppling from her saddle.

Powerless to do anything but watch, Higgins lost sight of the riders as the aeroplane descended further. The rough ground rose to meet them. With a bump and a shudder, the flying machine finally halted. Philippe tore off his helmet and goggles.

"*Comment était-ce pour une course folle?*" the aviator called out, laughing. "You are all right, Professeur? I hope you enjoyed the ride. A little crazy, *non?*"

"A bit, yes." He struggled to free his legs and scramble onto the wing. Philippe caught him before Higgins fell to the ground. "We must reach Eliza. She may be in danger."

Together they ran toward the horses and riders. Lily lay sprawled on the ground. Freddy knelt by her side. Eliza had already looped her mare's reins around a sapling and was attempting to calm Freddy's horse. Higgins caught sight of Lily's stallion as it galloped away.

Eliza ran to meet Higgins and Philippe. "When I heard the aeroplane, I knew it was you." She gave him a quick hug, then did the same to Higgins but was careful to avoid his broken arm. "How did you know I was in trouble?"

He gave her a disapproving look. "Lady Annabel told me that you were wearing the gold cross. Obviously, you meant to provoke the killer."

"It worked." Eliza pointed at Lily, unconscious on the ground.

"*Mon Dieu*, is Mademoiselle Marlowe dead?" Philippe asked.

He followed Higgins and Eliza when they rushed over to the fallen woman. "No," Freddy said in a grim voice. "Just knocked out. She's coming round."

Lily began to moan and slowly move her arms.

Philippe crouched down and took her pulse. "I do not see blood. Unless a bone is broken, I think she will be good."

"Lily is anything *but* good," Freddy said with disgust. He looked up at Eliza. "I heard what she said to you. How she killed Pentwater and Madame Evangeline."

Higgins and Philippe exchanged startled glances. "But did not the jealous husband kill Evangeline?" Philippe asked.

Freddy stood. "No. Lily did. I heard her confess, and all because she wanted that cross Eliza is wearing." He stabbed a finger at it. "Apparently, Lily planned to sell it to Sir Anthony or the count because of some legend connected to it. I don't know. It all sounds mad to me."

"How did you hear this?" Higgins asked.

"I fell off my horse during the hunt and Eliza came after me to help," he said. "Lily hadn't even noticed I was gone. When I rode back to rejoin the hunt, I saw Lily and waved to get her attention. I thought she'd come looking for me, but she rode right past. So I followed." He glanced at Eliza. "Once I reached the trees where I'd left you, I realized something was wrong. I heard Lily say terrible things. Things I would never have believed possible."

"I thought I saw a horse and rider among the trees," Eliza said. "That was you all along."

He nodded. "I didn't want to let Lily know I was there, not until I heard every evil thing she confessed." Freddy looked miserable. "You were right. She was Pentwater's mistress. And worse." Another moan sounded from Lily. "Far worse."

"What's happened?" Lily cried out. "Where's my horse?"

"Probably near the village by now," Higgins said in a wry voice. "He's that fast."

"Did I fall?" She bolted upright. "What are all of you doing here?"

"Listening to tales of your murderous crimes," Higgins answered.

Lily shot an angry look at Eliza. "I don't know what she's been saying about me, but it's not true. She's jealous about me and Freddy. She'll do anything to keep us apart, even make up stories about how I killed people."

"Does Monsieur Freddy also make up these stories?" Philippe's expression had turned icy. "He tells us how he hides among the trees and hears you confess to the murders of Madame Evangeline and the American businessman. You are most despicable. To take the life of such a dear woman as Madame."

"I did no such thing! What a ridiculous story. Freddy's lying." Wincing, Lily rose to her feet. No one helped her. "So is Eliza."

"I haven't had a chance to explain anything yet," Eliza said. "But I will now. Freddy heard you confess to the murders of both Evangeline and Pentwater." She stroked the gold cross. "With two witnesses, no one will be buying this from you now."

Lily's wary expression turned fearful. She looked at Philippe, then Higgins. "Don't you see? Freddy and Eliza are trying to frame me for murder. They're the ones who want that cross. And they've set me up as their patsy. You can't believe them. You can't!"

Freddy swore under his breath. "What a fool I was to imagine you loved me."

"I'm innocent!" With a frantic cry, Lily sprinted toward Eliza's mare. Philippe and Freddy quickly caught her. Each man held firmly onto her arms.

"How will we get her back to Banfield Manor?" Eliza asked, watching Lily struggle against them to break free.

"Colin and the local constables should be here soon," Higgins told her. "Before Philippe and I left, we instructed Baxter to ring Chief Constable Brakefield." He looked past her. "Indeed, I believe I spot several motorcars now."

The others turned their attention to the three vehicles in the distance. "Damn all of you!" Lily cried. "I hope you all die terrible deaths!"

Freddy tightened his grip. "I hope you spend the rest of your life in prison."

Higgins believed this was the first time he'd ever agreed with Freddy. But Eliza gave a startled cry. "What's wrong?" he asked her in alarm.

She pointed and said in a hushed voice. "Look."

A breeze blew the leaves of a nearby downy willow bush, revealing the white tip of a plush orange and black tail. The fox stood still, half hidden, as if listening to the baying hounds in the distance.

"Who cares about the stupid fox?" Lily spat. "Let me go!"

Eliza ignored her and made a shooing motion to the fox. "Run away, it's your chance to escape. Go!"

The animal didn't have to be told twice. It vanished, rustling the bush's leaves.

"Well, this is what I call a successful hunt." Eliza appeared delighted. "The killer was caught, not the fox."

"Agreed. The fox lives to see another day." Higgins winked. "And so do you."

Eliza waved her riding crop at the approaching police and smiled. "Tally-ho!"

CHAPTER 25

*E*liza wiped away tears after she hugged Clara and Richard goodbye. She wasn't sad about leaving the Ashmores. And the tears were certainly not over Freddy, who returned to London two days ago. Eliza wept over saying farewell to Percy. A noisy farewell, too, given how his fellow peacocks and peahens shrieked as Eliza embraced the bird one last time.

"I didn't realize you minded so awfully about leaving Percy here." Richard handed her a handkerchief. "We'll take good care of him."

She blew her nose. "I know. Percy will be much happier with his fellow peacocks. And all this space to run around in. It's only that he reminds me of a pet canary I had years ago. Little Petey died of the cold one winter when I didn't have enough money for coal."

Higgins leaned against the blue roadster parked in the drive. "Don't let her go on about Petey. The waterworks will get worse. She still refuses to get rid of his empty birdcage."

Clara patted Eliza on the shoulder. "We're only a short train ride from London. You can come for a visit whenever you like."

Her mood brightened. "And now that I've learned how to drive a motorcar, I can borrow Professor Higgins's roadster. After all, I'll be driving us home today."

Colin Ramsey, who stood next to Higgins, frowned. "At the risk of starting another argument, that's a bad idea. Let's not forget the Professor still wears a plaster cast on his arm from a motoring accident."

"Due to sabotage, not my driving abilities."

Ramsey ignored Higgins's protest. "I'm not convinced Eliza is ready to drive forty miles by herself back to London."

"She won't be alone. I'm riding with her. Although I am tempted to take the wheel." He nodded at his arm. "By Jupiter, but I'm weary of this fool cast. Once I arrive home, I shall insist Dr. Bettancourt remove it."

"You are not driving with one hand," Eliza said, "and I don't know why you'd be so uncertain of my abilities, Colin. You and Richard spent the past week teaching me." She pulled on her brown leather gloves. "Both of you remarked that I was an excellent driver."

Richard chuckled. "She has us there."

Indeed, whenever Eliza hadn't been occupied with giving testimony to the police about Lily Marlowe's crimes, she drove about the estate and along the adjacent country lanes. She'd even persuaded Richard to let her drive his red Stutz Bearcat a time or two. After some initial nervousness, Eliza found herself enjoying the experience. No wonder Higgins made such a fuss about his roadster.

Eliza fastened the brass buttons on her duster coat and then joined Higgins and Colin by the cars. It had been over a week since the fox hunt, more than enough time to ring up Whiteleys department store and order a motoring costume. Colin had been a dear about delivering it during one of his trips to Banfield Manor. Because he'd been involved in the murder investigation, he had an official reason to come to Kent.

Although Chief Constable Brakefield had grown suspicious of the Scotland Yard detective's near constant presence. Especially since Colin spent far more time with Eliza than the constabulary detectives.

Not that resolving this case was difficult. In addition to Lily's confession in front of two witnesses, the bottle of chloral hydrate sleeping drops had been found in Lily's cosmetic case. Charlie Kenton testified to seeing Lily in Pentwater's bed, and Freddy confirmed that he was not with Lily every minute on the foggy morning of the shoot. One of the loaders at the hunt also recalled seeing Lily Marlowe striding through the woods, gun in hand, shortly after the fatal shot was fired. And she had come from the direction where Pentwater lay dead.

They'd phoned Jack to let him know what had unfolded. Eliza sensed his disappointment about missing all the danger and excitement. He also thought Lily's trial would be a magnet for the press, and her conviction all but certain. Eliza was relieved justice would be done, not so much because of Dwight Pentwater. But poor Madame Evangeline did not deserve to die. Nor did Zoltan Batur deserve to spend another day in jail, awaiting trial for a crime he did not commit. A grudging Brakefield finally agreed with Colin and released Batur.

Clara rubbed her hands along her arms. "Even though the day is sunny, it seems like November is already here. I feel the chill through my tweeds."

Richard hugged her to him. "I'll keep you warm, my darling."

While Higgins seemed scornful of the giddy newlyweds' exchange, Eliza noticed that Colin watched the young couple with interest. Maybe he was thinking the same thing, that he might say that to her one day. However, she was in no hurry to wed. Freddy's unexpected betrayal had left her cautious about romance. A man needed to win her complete trust before she allowed him into her life; even a man with wavy brown hair, a mischievous smile, and a dark-eyed gaze that often made her blush.

"Eliza, would you prefer if I rode with you?" Colin asked, clearly hopeful.

"Hold on," Higgins protested. "I've waited weeks to enjoy my motorcar. If you think I'm riding back to London inside one of the oversized touring cars that Scotland Yard sent while you and Eliza go flying over the roads—"

"Don't worry," Eliza interrupted. "I promised I'd chauffeur you back to London today, and I shall. Although I plan to drive Colin some day soon."

Higgins grinned. "She'll probably drive you quite mad, too."

Colin's eyebrows lifted, as if anticipating the experience. Eliza felt a rush of pleasure, and not just at the prospect of getting behind the wheel.

"Are you certain everything is fine at Wimpole Street?" Richard asked.

"Mrs. Pearce rang me up yesterday," Higgins told him. "The repairs on the kitchen have been completed. In fact, the entire staff has already returned."

"Colonel Pickering is back home, too." Eliza beamed at the prospect. "I can't wait to see his face when we arrive home."

"And you have all your luggage?" Clara looked at the two touring cars, both piled high with suitcases and trunks. Two footmen, one of them Charlie, had loaded the vehicles.

The butler, who had overseen the process, cleared his throat. "Everything has been brought down, my lady."

"Thank you, Baxter," Clara said.

Colin raised an eyebrow at Eliza. "I didn't think it possible for one woman to have so many clothes. Are there any dresses left at Whiteleys and Selfridges?"

Eliza couldn't help but feel pride at the remark. A year ago, she had owned little more than one skirt, a shawl, and two blouses. "I do have a lovely wardrobe."

Shaking his head in amusement, Colin signaled the drivers of the vehicles sent from the Yard. The men began to crank the motors. Colin busied himself with Higgins's roadster, turning on the ignition and then cranking it a half dozen times.

Clara ran down the steps to hug Eliza once again. "I will miss you. And I hope you don't think all my house parties will be like this one."

"I hope not," Higgins said as he got into the passenger seat. "Although I will admit that I was never bored."

"It's a shame about the dead bodies," Eliza said, "but the county will be talking about the fox hunt for years. After all, how many times does an aeroplane buzz right over the riders?"

"We had to cancel the hunt ball because of all the police swarming about." Clara bit her lip. "And no one caught the fox."

"Instead, we caught a famous cinema actress who murdered two people. And at your very first house party, too." Eliza winked at her. "Let the other local squires top that!"

Clara smiled. "What will I do without you?"

"Enjoy time alone with Richard," Eliza said. "Especially since the count and countess have gone back to Austria."

The two young women exchanged happy looks. The von Weisingers left yesterday in high dudgeon. The count paid scant attention to Lily's arrest. All that mattered was that he had seen Eliza wearing the cross of Charlemagne at the hunt. He'd demanded she sell it to him—and at the price he set. Arrogant behavior even for him. When Count Rudolf learned the cross had been given to the police, he flew into what Higgins termed a Teutonic tantrum.

"I told Richard that we'd best not see his sister or her husband for several years," Clara sniffed. "They behaved badly the entire house party. Rudolf was quite beastly about the cross, carrying on about how it was meant to belong to him and the Kaiser."

"If you ask me, he's a little cracked," Eliza said. "At least the countess convinced him to leave. I think she's happy the cross is no longer up for sale."

"I still don't understand all the fuss about a plain gold cross, even if there is some silly legend that goes along with it."

Eliza sighed. "I guess the legend's not silly to those who believe in it."

One such believer stormed out of the house at that moment. Sir Anthony paused on the front steps and glowered at the assembled group. "The servants have brought our bags down to the foyer," he informed the butler. "And my chauffeur is bringing the Rolls around."

Baxter nodded. "Charlie and Albert will see to it." The two footmen hurried into the house. Charlie threw Eliza a quick smile as he went past.

"Leaving already?" Richard asked. "We'd hoped you might stay for luncheon."

"Due to an overzealous police investigation, my wife and I have already stayed far longer than we intended." Sir Anthony directed his resentful answer to Colin Ramsey.

"I feel the same." He put on his Trilby hat.

Eliza thought it gave Colin a jaunty air. "We do, too."

"We'll see you back in London," Higgins told the detective and slipped on his goggles. "Assuming Eliza ever stops chattering."

When Sir Anthony's Rolls drove up behind the other vehicles, Colin climbed into one of the touring cars. "Be careful, Eliza!" he yelled as he drove past. "Don't go too fast!"

"I shall miss you and the Professor. Philippe, too," Clara added. "I was sorry to see him and Nathalie fly away."

"I miss that aeroplane of his." Higgins said. "I'd give serious thought to buying one if I owned as much property as Richard. A one-seater, of course."

"Don't even blooming think about it." Eliza shot him a warning look.

Richard glanced back at the manor house. Sir Anthony had been joined by Annabel, who looked most regal this morning in a gold wool walking suit. "Hurry with your goodbyes to Eliza. If we ignore Sir Anthony and his wife, my mother is sure to hear about it."

"He's right," Eliza said. "We must leave or we'll run out of petrol."

"I was about to remind you," Higgins grumbled.

Clara gave her another quick hug. "Freddy feels awful about everything that happened."

"I know he does. And I've accepted his apology." Eliza frowned. "But things can never be the same between us."

"I thought so." She grabbed Eliza's hands. "But we shall remain friends."

"Forever." Eliza nodded at the Dennison couple, who had now been joined by Richard. "But you still have guests to attend to."

"And another house party to preside over in a week." Clara took a deep breath. "At least this guest list is filled with Richard's friends from university, which means it should be fun. As long as none of them are bent on murder."

Sir Anthony raised his arm. "Professor Higgins, I spoke to Chief Constable Brakefield this morning. He said the police have returned the cross to you. Since it was in the roadster when you purchased it, that legally makes it your property."

"Get in," Higgins hissed at Eliza.

She hurried to the other side of the roadster. Sir Anthony reached the car before she slipped on her goggles. "See here, Higgins, you have no need of the cross," he said.

"Sorry, I cannot hear you over the motor." Higgins gestured at his ears.

"I wish to buy the cross," Sir Anthony said in a louder voice. "Name your price. But I expect it to be within reason. After all, I do not want it for myself."

"I am not selling the cross," Higgins told him. "To anyone."

Sir Anthony leaned against the roadster, now trembling slightly from the motor. His extravagant moustache seemed to tremble as well, but from emotion. "Then be a patriot and give the cross of Charlemagne to me. I'll hand it over to Prime Minister Asquith. Or His Majesty."

"Blimey," Eliza muttered as she donned her wide motoring hat and veil.

"Again, I am not selling the cross. Nor am I giving it to you or King George." Higgins voice turned angry. "Haven't enough people died over the legend of the cross? Someone needs to behave rationally in this matter."

"Rationally? How can you speak of rational behavior when the fate of the world hangs in the balance?"

Eliza noticed that the Ashmores and Annabel appeared nervous about the turn in the conversation. She also noticed none of them chose to be part of it.

"We are heading to war," Sir Anthony went on. "A war certain to drag all of Europe into it. A decent Englishman should want to make sure his country came out victorious. Unless you fancy being dictated to by the Kaiser!"

"Let's go, Eliza," Higgins instructed, but she fumbled with the clutch.

Sir Anthony gripped the sides of the motorcar. "Whoever possesses the cross holds the key to victory. But it is of no use in the hands of an ordinary citizen. It must be held by someone in power. A general, a king, a government minister. Don't you understand?"

"I understand fanaticism when I see it. And folly." Higgins gave a wave as Eliza stepped on the accelerator.

For a horrified moment, Eliza feared Sir Anthony planned to either jump on the running board and ride along, or pull Higgins from his seat. Luckily, the older man did nothing but shake a fist at them as they drove away.

Eliza steered the roadster, which handled quite nicely. "Since Sir Anthony mentioned it, what will you do with the cross?"

"I'm giving it to Dwight Pentwater's widow."

Startled, she almost drove into a privet hedge. "What?"

"It seemed the right thing to do," Higgins said. "After all, when I bought Pentwater's roadster, I had no idea it also contained the cross. What use is it to me? I sent her a letter a few days ago, explaining how I acquired the cross and the legend that surrounds it. If she wants it, I shall mail it to her, But only after I make certain it will not be needed at Miss Marlowe's trial."

Eliza thought about this as she made a left turn onto the road. "If she believes in legends, she might end up giving it to someone in the American government."

"Perhaps. Colin did further research on the Pentwaters. Mrs. Pentwater's brother served in the administration of President Taft. And she's third cousin to the former president, Theodore Roosevelt. If any of them are looking for a magical road to victory. . ." He laughed.

Eliza wasn't as doubtful of legends as Higgins. "If she takes the cross, you may have handed over a big advantage to the United States. They could become the next great power."

"Hah! Before Americans become a world power, they first need to learn how to speak English properly. That won't be for another century at least. I think the cross of Charlemagne is safe in their hands." Higgins sat forward, watching how she handled the clutch. "And I think I'm safe in your hands as well. You seem most confident behind the wheel."

"I am. Especially since I'm no longer worried the car may explode like that motorcar did at the wedding." Eliza put thoughts of that disaster behind her and smiled at the long empty road ahead. "I wonder if we can catch up to the Scotland Yard touring cars. They can't possibly go too fast with all our luggage piled inside."

He and Eliza exchanged excited looks. "Shall we try?" he asked.

She pressed down on the accelerator in response. "Colin won't be pleased."

"Only because he won't be able to catch us." Higgins clapped his hands at the prospect.

"Well, you'd best sit back. I'm going to see just how fast we can go."

"Not too reckless, Eliza," he cautioned. "I don't want to break my other arm."

"Oh, I'll get us safely back to London." Eliza felt as confident behind the wheel as she did on her mare during the fox hunt. "I just need as little traffic as possible."

"Don't forget the most important thing," Higgins added.

"Which is?"

He chuckled. "A little bit of luck."

AUTHORS' NOTE

*F*or centuries, certain objects have been endowed not only with special significance, but with mystical powers. One notable example is the Holy Grail, sought by everyone from the Knights of the Round Table to Monty Python. The Spear of Destiny or Holy Lance is another, with versions (whether authentic or not) kept in Rome under St. Peter's Basilica and in Vienna at the Hofburg. At the heart of *Raiders of the Lost Ark* is the ancient Hebrews' Ark of the Covenant. And the famous ring in J.R.R. Tolkien's trilogy was based on the story of the Ring of Gyges, first told by Plato.

IN *WITH A LITTLE BIT OF BLOOD*, WE WANTED TO INCLUDE A legendary object in the mystery. We almost chose the Spear, which is mentioned in our book. However, we ultimately decided to create our own legendary treasure known as the Cross of Charlemagne. No doubt the great Frankish king owned several crosses. One of them may even have possessed mythical powers. Who can say? After all, myths have to start somewhere. Often they begin in the far reaches of history. But sometimes, two novelists simply dream up the whole thing.

ABOUT THE AUTHOR

D.E. Ireland is the pseudonym of long time friends and award-winning authors, Meg Mims and Sharon Pisacreta. After enjoying separate writing careers in romantic suspense and westerns, they decided to collaborate on a mystery series based on George Bernard Shaw's play *Pygmalion*, which inspired the musical *My Fair Lady*. Since the 2014 debut of the series, The Eliza Doolittle & Henry Higgins Mysteries have been nominated for two Agatha Awards as Best Historical of the Year.

Both authors have also recently published cozy mysteries for Kensington under their respective new pen names: Sharon Farrow and Meg Macy. Sharon's Berry Basket series debuted in 2016, and Meg's Shamelessly Adorable Teddy Bear series was released in 2017. The two Michigan authors have patient husbands, brilliant daughters, and share a love of tea, books, and history. Follow D.E. Ireland, Meg Macy, and Sharon Farrow on Facebook, Twitter, and Amazon.

Made in United States
North Haven, CT
05 May 2023

36272589R00193